Alexx Andria is a *USA*  author who writes about but a soft, warm heart de dirty romance, with lots o sizzling scenes in the bed they happen to end up) and a guaranteed HEA.

Taryn Leigh Taylor likes dinosaurs, bridges and space—both personal and the final frontier variety. She shamelessly indulges in clichés, most notably her Starbucks addiction: grande six-pump, whole milk, no water, chai tea latte—aka 'the usual'—her shoe hoard (*I can stop any time I... Ooh! These are pretty!*) and her penchant for falling in lust with fictional men with great abs. She also really loves books, which was what sent her down the crazy path of writing in the first place. Want to be virtual friends? Check out tarynleightaylor.com, Facebook.com/tarynltaylor1 and Twitter, @tarynltaylor.

If you liked *Beddable Billionaire* and
Forbidden Pleasure, why not try

Close to the Edge by Zara Cox
Getting Lucky by Avril Tremayne

Discover more at millsandboon.co.uk

BEDDABLE BILLIONAIRE

ALEXX ANDRIA

FORBIDDEN PLEASURE

TARYN LEIGH TAYLOR

MILLS & BOON

First Published in Great Britain 2018
by Mills & Boon, an imprint of HarperCollins*Publishers*
1 London Bridge Street, London, SE1 9GF

Beddable Billionaire © 2018 Kimberly Sheetz

Forbidden Pleasure © 2018 Taryn Leigh Taylor

ISBN: 978-0-263-26650-4

MIX
Paper from
responsible sources
FSC
www.fsc.org
FSC C007454

This book is produced from independently certified FSC™ paper
to ensure responsible forest management.
For more information visit www.harpercollins.co.uk/green.

Printed and bound in Spain
by CPI, Barcelona

BEDDABLE BILLIONAIRE

ALEXX ANDRIA

MILLS & BOON

CHAPTER ONE

Lauren

"AND I WANT YOU, Lauren, to cover the story."

"Excuse me, I'm sorry, what?" I paused my notes to meet my editor's stare, stifling the groan that wanted to pop from my mouth. Truthfully, I was only half listening during this morning's staff meeting, but what little I'd heard wasn't exactly flipping my interest switch.

"'Hottest Bachelor in Town.' I want you to write it," Patrice answered, tapping her manicured finger against the slick tabletop. "Pay attention, please."

I didn't say the actual word, but my expression clearly said *blech*, and Patrice Winneham, executive editor of *Luxe* magazine, wasn't known for her willingness to hear objections. "Problem?" she asked with a layer of frost blanketing her tone.

The last thing I wanted to write was some frivolous article on New York's most eligible and, more important, rich bachelors, but I needed my job. "No problem," I lied through my teeth. By now it should've become second nature, but it still curdled my guts to pretend to care about stories that held no bearing on actual life.

Like the world needed another spread on complete and utter nonsense. The longer I worked for *Luxe*, the more I was certain I would be required to turn in my feminist card because of crap assignments like this.

Who knew the going rate for a piece of your soul is the bargain-basement price of rent on a shitty apartment in Brooklyn. From my peripheral I caught our newest and youngest staffer nearly wetting herself to land this gig, and I readily threw her a bone.

"Actually, I really think Daphne would kill a story like that," I suggested, casting a helpful look down the boardroom table toward the young redhead. Daphne was practically nodding her head off in eager agreement, salivating at the prospect. I smiled. "She's got that young voice that I think would really sell the piece far better than me."

Also, because the idea of pandering to an overprivileged prick is about as appealing as jamming a pen in my eye. But I couldn't exactly say that without risking my job, and as shitty as the job was, it paid the bills— granted, *barely*—but still, they were paid.

"Yes, and she's also gullible," Patrice replied without apology, continuing with a briefly held smile, "and would likely end up falling in love with the man before the interview was finished. That's a headache I don't need. No, you'll do the interview. End of story." Patrice added with a warning glower, "And wear something nice. You're representing *Luxe*."

I ignored Patrice's not-so-subtle dig. Fashion wasn't

my God, and I didn't worship at the altar of haute couture. I'd wear what I pleased. "Fit before fashion" was my mantra, and I didn't feel the least bit sorry for the women who chose to trudge around the city in high heels who, by the end of the day, were rubbing the agony from their barking dogs.

Nope, I sailed right past them in my sensible flats, happy as a clam and stealing their cab because I could run faster.

I caught Daphne's crestfallen expression. Poor girl, I could only imagine how her dreams of working at a high-end magazine like *Luxe* were nothing like the reality.

I remembered being that idealistic newbie.

Now I was the jaded staffer who ran on a steady diet of cynicism and sarcasm, with the occasional sprinkling of "WTF?" thrown in for flavor.

Patrice, satisfied that her word was law, moved on with a smug smile. "We have managed to snag one of the sexiest bachelors yet from a distinguished family, old-world money, if you can imagine such a thing anymore. A real *Italian stallion*, if you will, and having this hottie on the cover is going to snag eyeballs, but I need someone experienced to handle the copy."

Irritated and bored but having at least the sense to put on a good face, I forced a smile to ask, "And the name of this sexy and single vagina hound?"

"Wait for it…" Patrice paused for dramatic effect before gushing, "Nico Donato of Donato Inc. His family hails from Italy, starting with a humble yet wildly successful winery in Tuscany. Isn't that dreamy? Does anything else scream *romance* more than the Italian countryside?"

I wouldn't know, I wanted to quip. It'd been a long time since I'd experienced anything resembling romance after my ex ran off when I was five months pregnant—six years ago.

It was safe to say the most romance I'd had in my life consisted of furtive moments spent hiding in the closet with my Magic Wand.

Was it TMI if I admitted I'd already burned through three of those hardy vibrators? I rubbed at the phantom scorch mark left over from my last vibrator when it rudely caught fire in my hand.

So, yeah, romance? Not even sure I would recognize it if it bit me in the ass, but that was okay because men were a complication I didn't need in my life. I was perfectly happy with the way things were, and I didn't need wine and roses from some man to feel complete.

Did I miss an actual warm body to cuddle with on cold nights? Yeah, but then, I could always get a dog or a cat and achieve the same effect, which I'd been seriously considering.

"Wow, I've seen pictures of Nico Donato, and he's definitely a hottie," Daphne gushed, her eyes alight with envy. "I can't imagine a woman alive who would turn him down if he asked."

I tried not to roll my eyes. Continuing my Golden Globe–worthy performance, I nodded like a good staffer and agreed with Patrice because I needed my job. "Sounds fantastic," I murmured, trying not to gag.

Daphne sighed, and I could practically see the cartoon hearts and rainbows floating around her head. Good grief, Patrice was probably right. Sending someone like Daphne to interview this *Italian stallion* would be like sending a lamb to slaughter. Daphne was probably still in that stage of her life when her bra and panties matched.

I was sporting underwear with a hole in it, and my bra was three years old.

Any seduction attempt for my benefit would end in laughter. Mine and his.

Don't get me wrong, I'm not ugly and I do *probably* (maybe) own a matching bra and panty set, but let's face it, fancy panties are uncomfortable, and these days, comfort was king.

#singlemom.

#allmymoneygoestomykid.

#myvibratordoesntjudge.

Patrice was talking again. "I don't know how this man has managed to remain single, but after this issue comes out…we might be able to do a follow-up for the engagement because someone is going to snag him up, I can guarantee it."

"Maybe he's an asshole?" I suggested, and the table erupted with nervous laughter, except Patrice, who frowned. I shrugged, just pointing out what everyone else was thinking but was too afraid to voice. "I mean, that seems like the obvious answer, right? Good-looking, rich but maybe his personality is rotten. There isn't enough money in the world to compensate for a shitty attitude."

"I'm sure he's a lovely human being," Patrice said

pointedly. "And it'll be your job to make sure that comes across."

"And what if, just clarifying, he *isn't* a lovely human being?"

Patrice tapped her Montblanc pen on the polished table surface, the chipped ice in her blue eyes growing colder. "I'm sure he is," she finally answered. "And you'll do a fine job. I look forward to reading your copy."

More anxious laughter floated around the conference table. Why was I poking the bear in the designer suit? *I don't know.* Maybe I was PMSing. Maybe I was tired of writing stupid, fluff articles that did nothing but perpetuate the stereotype that all women cared about were hot men with big cocks.

Or I was PMSing.

Honestly, it could go either way.

It was now or never if I wanted to throw something serious into the ring. I stilled the sudden bouncing of my knee beneath the table and pushed forward with my own idea for the magazine.

"I was thinking we could do an article on Associate Justice Elena Kagan, maybe focus on how women still have to fight for positions historically held by men?"

The silence was not only deafening, but the disdain was actually painful.

Patrice sniffed with distaste. "This is *Luxe*, not *The Legal Review*. No one wants to read about a dusty old woman in a black robe unless she's wearing Donna Karan on the bench."

Daphne tittered and I wanted to shake some sense

into the young twit, but Patrice was right. *Luxe* wasn't going to be breaking ground in the advancement of women's rights anytime soon. *Luxe* was all about designer shoes, perpetuating the harmful stereotypes that fostered unattainable body goals and kept women bitching and fighting among themselves.

God, maybe I was beginning to hate *Luxe*, or maybe I was just becoming a bitter bitch because I hadn't gotten laid in forever. Seeing as that wasn't likely to change anytime soon, I had to suck it up, smile and agree to interview Mr. Big Cock or else I could lose my ability to pay rent.

"I'll make the arrangements," I said, privately scribbling, *Sacrifice dignity and interview man-slut*. "Have you already set up the photographer?"

"All done. Jacques will be shooting the spread. We're thinking… Hamptons…beach time…crisp whites and blues."

"It'll make for good pictures," I agreed but inside I was rolling my eyes. *Like that idea hasn't been done a million times before.* "Everyone loves a hot guy on the beach," I said, parroting what I knew Patrice wanted to hear.

"That they do." Patrice nodded in wholehearted agreement as if she were relieved I'd finally agreed to pull my head from my ass. "And it's easy to sell advertising for beach-themed spreads. Anyway, you all have your assignments. Go on, go forth, *amaze* me."

As I left the conference room, Daphne attached herself to my hip, saying, "Have you seen Nico's picture?

He's gorgeous. Blue eyes to die for, a body made for sin, and he's so sweet. A real charmer."

"How do you know he's sweet?" I countered, wryly amused and vastly curious. "Have you met?"

"Oh, no," Daphne admitted but added quickly, "just look at that face…he seems so sweet. You can tell from the eyes. His eyes tell a story."

"I'm sure they tell some sort of story," I agreed, resisting the urge to roll my eyes so hard they bounced from my skull. Perhaps I should burst her bubble and tell her the story of my *sweet* ex. The one who bailed on me and our son when he realized being a parent was going to be a full-time job that would likely cut into his playtime? I swallowed the urge because I wasn't into wasting energy, and I doubted Daphne would see anything but my being a salty bitch—especially if she found out who my ex was.

Instead, I said, "Sounds like trouble to me, but I'd be happy to be wrong. It's not likely, but it would be a nice surprise."

"You seriously don't want this assignment?" Daphne said, flabbergasted that I would turn my nose up at the opportunity to fawn over some rich guy. "I mean, Nico Donato is mega rich. I'm talking obscenely rich. Like golden toilets, I-wipe-my-ass-with-hundred-dollar-bills *Dubai rich.*"

I smirked. "That rich, huh? Sounds like a delight." Although, why would anyone want to be that rich? Seemed like a lot of headaches. I'd rather be comfortable, not obscenely wealthy. Apparently, I was in the minority, considering present company. "Personally,

I prefer actual toilet paper, but the good stuff, not the tissue paper that shreds the minute you slide it across your ass."

"Are you seriously talking about toilet paper?" Daphne stepped in front of me just as I headed for the break room to grab my yogurt. "Take me with you," she pleaded. "Please? He's the man of my dreams. I'd kill to meet him. What if he's my soul mate?"

"And that's exactly why I won't let you tag along," I said, maneuvering around her. "Trust me, I'm doing you a favor. Men like Donato are narcissists and they spread heartbreak like disease. I'll bet if I did a little digging I'd find scores of women who were used and tossed aside by this rich prick. Just because he's got a nice face—"

Daphne injected, "And body."

I exhaled in irritation as I continued. "Yes, *and* body, doesn't mean he's not the devil." I retrieved my yogurt, adding for Daphne's sake, "You're young. When you get a little more seasoning, you'll figure out that *Dubai-rich* guys are usually the ones you want to steer clear from."

"You're not that much older than me," Daphne pointed out with a frown. "Why do you act like you're an old lady?"

Are we close to the same age? Impossible. Most days I felt a hundred.

"Because I don't think I was ever your age," I answered, popping the spoon in my mouth. "But if you must know, I've been burned before by a sweet talker, and experience breeds wisdom, you know?"

"So, because you got your heart broken you're never going to let anyone else in?"

Ick. When did this conversation turn into a Dr. Phil session? "As much as I adore this little tête-à-tête, I have work to do so…"

Daphne pouted but didn't continue to dog me to my desk (thank God), and I was able to eat my yogurt in relative peace while I did some poking around on the net about Donato.

My Google-fu was pretty decent, and with a few clicks I had pictures and background information on the youngest Donato.

Okay, so he was handsome, I'd give him that.

Yeah, those blue eyes were panty-droppers, and that body looked fairly chiseled from clay.

And Nico was *Dubai rich*, as Daphne liked to call it.

But I couldn't find any information on anything useful or worthwhile that he might've been associated with.

No philanthropy.

No peace work.

No good deeds on record.

However, I did find some paparazzi photos of Nico doing body shots off the belly of a hot-bodied coed during spring break at Lake Havasu.

Yep. I took another bite. *Total douchebag.* Life was so unfair. How did guys like Nico always get ahead when hardworking people, like myself, had to struggle and scrape for every dime?

I wallowed in a moment of self-pity before sighing and printing out the relevant information I would need for my fluff article.

"I love my job," I murmured to myself. "I love my job." To ground my motivation more firmly, I glanced at the picture of my son on my desk. Grady's gap-toothed smile was all the motivation I needed to shut my mouth, put my head down and get the job done.

Houston Beaumont was a useless human being, but our son was the light of my life and I couldn't regret deciding to cancel the adoption paperwork.

Grady wasn't planned—hell, my relationship, if you can call it that, with Houston hadn't been planned either—but I'd do anything for that cute little dirty-blond imp who called me Mama.

And I thanked my lucky stars every day that Houston hadn't tried to sue for custody. He'd been more than happy to forget all about me and his son.

I didn't mind being a single mom if it meant knowing that Grady didn't have to be shuttled between two different worlds—mine and his father's.

Drawing a deep breath, I nodded to myself, girding my loins, so to speak, so I could swallow my dignity without choking.

I could do this. No sweat.

At least one thing was for certain—there was no way Donato was going to charm the pants off me—a fact he would discover right away if he was dumb enough to try.

CHAPTER TWO

Nico

"Nice to meet you, Mr. Donato. Lauren Hughes, *Luxe* magazine."

The tall brunette thrust her hand toward me as if she were a man—strong, no-nonsense, obligatory—her deep brown eyes the only feature worth noting if I were to go off first impressions.

The handshake lasted all of two seconds, no lingering, and then she was sitting primly at the farthest point on the sofa in my living room, recorder in hand, expression blandly expectant, as if preparing to mentally vacate as soon as I started talking.

"Pleasure to meet you, Miss Hughes," I said, my gaze quickly taking in the shape-swallowing shift dress that completely obscured her figure and the functional flats that finished off the wretched ensemble. I think my maid dressed better than this woman. "I hope the traffic wasn't too heavy."

"Dealing with traffic is just one of those things you get used to when you live in New York," she said with a brief smile. The look in her eyes told me she wasn't one for small talk, which suited me fine because I hated it, too—but I was definitely not quite sure what to make of this stiff-as-a-board reporter.

Definitely not what I was expecting, and I was fucking disappointed. Where was the hot chick in the curve-hugging pencil skirt, glasses sitting demurely on the bridge of her nose, hair upswept in a delicate yet artfully messy bun? *Not sitting on my sofa, that's for sure.*

"Have you always been a New Yorker?" she asked with a direct stare. No makeup that I could tell. Not even a hint of mascara to brighten up her eyes. A pity. Those dark eyes with a little assistance might even be pretty. "My editor tells me that your family is from Italy, originally."

"Yes, so the legend says," I answered, trying for a little wry humor. When she didn't so much as offer a polite chuckle, I cleared my throat and followed with, "Tuscany, actually, but we've been in New York for two generations now. Our Italian roots are fairly weak at this point. All I inherited from my Italian ancestors is a love of fine women, wine and pasta."

"Ah."

"Your skin tone is beautiful. Are you Latina?" Was she Latina? Or perhaps Native American? Maybe even Creole?

"A hodgepodge of nationalities," she answered, adjusting herself on the sofa. "Just lucked out in the skin department, I guess. So, tell me, how does it feel to be named one of New York's most eligible bachelors?"

"Well, you know the saying, the only thing worse

than being talked about is not being talked about," I said with a wink. "But it should be interesting to see what crawls out of the woodwork once the magazine hits the stands. I'm always down for an adventure."

"If you're not interested in finding love, you could've turned down the interview," she said, again with that brief smile that I was beginning to suspect was patronizing. "I'm sure we could've found someone who was more aligned with the purpose of the spread."

"Who said I'm not looking for love?"

"Well, I mean, it was kind of implied by your earlier statement. To call the women who might be interested as things that 'crawl out of the woodwork' sounds insulting, don't you think?"

Annoyance threatened to color my tone as I admitted, "That was a poor choice of words. Maybe I'm more embarrassed by the attention than I like to let on. The truth is, I've never considered myself interesting enough for an entire magazine spread, and I'm not quite sure how I was selected."

False humility was always good for a few grace points, but I think Lauren saw right through my attempt, which, in itself, threw off my game.

Hell, everything about this woman threw me.

I'd thought *Luxe* might've sent one of their show ponies to interview me. Maybe an intern with a tight body, perky tits and an ass that would put a gymnast to shame; or, a more sophisticated staffer with legs for days and long blond hair, perfect for a man's fist to wrap around to guide a hot mouth onto a ready cock.

I bit back my growing disappointment. No nubile intern; no savvy staffer. *Luxe* had sent *her*.

The dour killjoy.

Was that a coffee stain on her dress?

And that austere bun squatting on top of her head was tight enough to give her a poor man's face-lift.

"So…you work at Luxe?" I asked, sinking into the sofa, regarding her curiously. Perhaps she was a freelance writer…

"Three years now," Lauren answered with a short smile before moving on. "I can appreciate how busy you are, so thank you for agreeing to this interview. My editor, Patrice, was excited to have one of the hottest bachelors in the city as the center feature."

Funny how her words said one thing but her tone said something completely different. This was starting off as the weirdest interview I'd ever granted. Didn't she realize I was a catch? That there were scores of women who wanted to be on this sofa with me? *Beneath me, specifically.* Frankly, on a hotness scale of one to ten, she was reaching for a four; *she* ought to be the one *excited* to be interviewing me.

But she didn't look tickled or impressed. Or even happy to be there. Was that a tick of boredom in those chocolate eyes?

My male pride demanded a better response. I couldn't have a four turning her nose up at me. Maybe I just needed to warm her up.

"Tell me about yourself," I suggested with a charming smile, the one that never failed to soften even the most rigid of women. "Do you enjoy working for *Luxe*?"

"Not here to interview me," she said with a wag of her finger like a schoolmarm. "We're here to talk about you."

"I like to get to know the people who are interviewing me," I returned, lobbing the ball back into her court, which she let drop with an unsatisfying *splat* when she remained silent, her fake, professional smile firmly in place. "Nothing? Hmm…have we met before?" I asked, half wondering if I'd slept with her at some point and forgotten to call her afterward. I mean, I couldn't see myself purposefully sleeping with a four, but if vodka was involved…anything was possible.

"Not likely," Lauren answered, puzzled by my question, and frankly, I was a little relieved until she said, "I doubt we run in the same circles," and it was that tiny undercurrent of condescension that narrowed my gaze.

"It just seems that maybe we've met before and perhaps I made a bad impression…"

"Not at all," she assured me, but her gaze remained unimpressed and flatly disinterested with anything that came out of my mouth, as if she were doing penance for a crime in a past life. Did I smell or something? I shifted against the unfamiliar sense of disdain emanating from the woman. "So, just tell me what you'd like the people to know about Nico Donato," she suggested as if being helpful. "Charities you support, hobbies, what you do to make the world a better place?"

Suddenly, everything clicked. I saw her game now. It all made sense. The frumpy clothes, the sour attitude, the barely concealed contempt…and now the leading question that she was fairly certain she knew the answer to…all meant to paint me into a corner of her choosing.

Lauren Hughes wasn't here to give me a fair shake; she was here to judge me. Time to make things interesting. If she thought she had me figured out, I'd give her something meaty to chew on. I grinned, sharing, "Actually, I don't mean to brag but last week, I paid all the alcohol tabs at Buxom. Probably spent close to ten grand on that bill, but I was happy to do it. That's just me…always giving."

"Buxom…the strip club?" she repeated, her expression screwing into a frown.

"It's more of a gentleman's club, but yeah, I suppose you could call it a strip club, but you know, those girls work so hard. It's really a misunderstood profession. I'm sure at least one of those ladies is working to put herself through law school, and how can you not support higher education, right?"

"Very generous of you," Lauren returned drily, her lips pursing a little before saying, "It must be very nice to be able to fund other people's vices."

"Vice is fun, you should try it sometime."

"Thanks but I think I'm good."

"Oh, come now, surely there's something taboo that flips your switch."

"Sorry, pretty boring."

That I can believe. But for the sake of argument, I said, "Indulge me," my interest in the interview taking a hard left in a different direction. I wanted to see how ruffled I could make Little Miss Sourpuss's feathers. "Perhaps…you enjoy a little spanking now and then?

A little 'tie me up, tie me down' action behind closed doors?"

A flush climbed her throat to stain her cheeks as she shut me down. "Not really," she answered, gesturing with professional courtesy to the recorder in her hand even as I sensed I'd gotten under her skin. "Shall we return to the interview, please?"

"Oh? Isn't that what we were doing?"

"I can't put in the article that you frequent Buxom. It's not the most savory bit of information for an article trying to make you sound like a catch."

"I am a catch."

She shrugged as if to say, *we can agree to disagree*, but suggested, "Let's get back to basics. I have some tried-and-true questions that usually lead to good, safe answers. Shall we?"

Sounds boring as hell. "Lead on."

"Puppies or kittens?"

"Neither. They both shed, vomit and shit all over the place." I gestured to my penthouse suite. "Clearly, I value a clean space in which to entertain."

"Hmm...do you like any sort of pet?"

I considered her question, but I really couldn't think of anything. Living things were too much work. Unfortunately, I learned that the hard way when I was seven. *RIP, poor Bubbles the goldfish.* "No, not really."

"Nothing?" she pressed, as incredulous as if I'd admitted I enjoy tripping old people in my spare time. "Not even a hamster or a rabbit?"

I smiled, wondering how far I could push Miss Hughes's boundaries. I wasn't above playing dirty either—because dirty was fun. I drew a breath as if in thought, then said, "I do enjoy games."

"Oh? Like board games? Clue, Monopoly, that sort of thing?" she asked, cocking her head with curiosity. "Or like card games?"

"Have you ever heard of pony play?"

Her expression screwed into a cute mask of confusion. "Pony play? Like polo or something?"

I chuckled, enjoying this way more than I should, but I was hungry for that sudden blush that would follow my explanation. For a brief—and I'm talking nanosecond brief—moment, when the high color brightened her cheeks, she was almost pretty.

And I was curious just how far I could push.

I started to explain, using my hands for illustration. "Imagine a beautiful mane attached to a short, notched column and then imagine that column going straight up a lovely ass, held in place by the cheeks, then you fit your sweet horsey with a halter and a bit and if you're lucky, you get to ride her all night."

She gasped in shock, thrown off her game. Flustered, she shut off her recorder, shooting me a dark, exasperated look, but those cheeks were so hot I could fry an egg.

And holy fuck, miracle of miracles, she'd just rocketed past a level four and hit a solid seven.

"Mr. Donato…that…that…that's *disgusting*."

I laughed. "Don't knock it till you try it."

"And inappropriate. Like, *really* inappropriate for the purposes of this interview. I can't go writing that you like to stick things up women's asses and ride them like horses. I mean, c'mon!"

I pretended to be perplexed. "I thought you wanted something authentic. This is the real me. I believe my potential mate should share my open-minded views on sex. Otherwise we're not going to make it. I'd rather be honest and up-front from the start, don't you think? Imagine all the pain and heartache we'd both suffer if I wasn't honest and then when we discover we're incompatible sexually, it's nothing but tears and accusations. I've seen it too many times. Honesty is the best policy when it comes to sex. If you haven't learned that yet, you will."

I'd caught her neatly with seemingly earnest logic, and there wasn't much she could say to refute my point.

Lauren pursed her lips as if holding back what she really wanted to say. *Go ahead girl, let loose. Tell me what a perverted dick I am.* I wanted to push all her buttons. "Mr. Donato—"

"Please call me Nico. *Mr. Donato* is so formal and boring. Besides, when I hear Mr. Donato, I immediately look for my oldest brother, Luca, or my father—both are giant killjoys, if you know what I mean, and I'm nothing like either of them." I settled my gaze on her with intrigue and fluttered my fingers suggestively as I followed with, "Tell me, what taboo sexual act gets you all revved up? Surely, there's something that gets the home fires burning…"

But instead of taking the bait, she narrowed her gaze and shut me down with a hard "May I speak frankly?"

This ought to be interesting. I gestured with magnanimous flourish. "Please do."

"I know you have a reputation for being a playboy—"

"I have a reputation?" I repeated, pretending to be concerned. "Tell me…are they talking about my cock? Pardon my bluntness, but if they are saying it's anything less than a full eight inches, they are lying through their damn teeth."

Lauren ignored my provocative statement and pushed forward, saying, "Your reputation as a Lothario precedes you, Mr. Donato," deliberately using my formal title rather than my name. "But I'm here to interview you as an eligible bachelor—an interview you agreed to, if I may remind you, so if you wouldn't mind at least pretending to take this seriously, we can finish with the interview and I'll be on my way. How does that sound?"

Now it was my turn to be annoyed. What would it take to knock loose the stick wedged up her ass? Even as she was determined to keep me at arm's length and locked out, the subtle widening of her eyes gave away more than she knew—and that fired up my need for more.

"How about dinner, tonight?" I proposed, imagining what she might look like if her hair wasn't pulled to the back of her skull like a nun's visiting the pope.

"No, thank you," she answered, pursing her lips with irritation. "The interview, please."

Such a dogged sense of duty. I released a sigh and leaned back, motioning for her to continue. "Fine. I'll answer your questions but only if you'll answer mine."

"That's not how this works." Exasperation colored

her voice but not to the level I imagined she was feeling. If I were a betting man, I'd say Lauren Hughes wanted to hog-tie me, land a swift kick to my nuts and stuff my silk tie down my throat.

Not the usual response I received from women.

And, fuck me, I liked it.

The game we were playing had just leveled up.

CHAPTER THREE

Lauren

I PINNED NICO with a pointed gaze, my patience at its thinnest, realizing that my instincts were correct and that this interview was a waste of my time. Patrice could find a different person to dance in circles with this egomaniac. "I'm not here to play games. If you'd like to reschedule for when you're feeling less like an immature jerk, please let me know." I rose and shouldered my purse, ready to leave.

"Hold up," Nico said, managing to hustle fast enough to catch me before I walked out the door. "I'm sorry. What can I say? I'm an immature jerk at times. Would you believe you make me nervous? Can we start over?"

I make *him* nervous? I wasn't sure I bought that line, but there was something vaguely earnest about his statement that made me pause. If I could salvage this interview, it would work in my favor, but there was something about Nico that set my teeth on edge. Still, my life would be ten times easier if I could manage to get this story filed, and I couldn't do that without his interview. I blew out a short breath before relenting with a wary, "You promise to behave?"

His blue eyes sparkled with mischief, but he managed a very solemn "Scout's honor"—which was laughable in itself but at least he'd tried to apologize, right? I supposed I could give him another chance.

"I sincerely doubt you've ever been a Scout in your life," I murmured, settling on the sofa again; but when he joined me on the same sofa, I narrowed my gaze, suspicious all over again. "Wouldn't you be more comfortable over there?" I motioned to his previous seat.

"Actually," he said with mild embarrassment, "I have a hard time hearing in my left ear—sailing accident when I was a kid—so in all seriousness, if we're going to do this, I need to sit a bit more closely."

I felt a bit sheepish as my mouth shaped an embarrassed moue and nodded. "Okay, then." Nico waited patiently while I fished my recorder from my purse, ready to start again. "Describe your perfect date," I proposed, thrusting the recorder toward Nico with an expectant expression.

He didn't hesitate. "Sex. Dirty, sexy, sweaty sex."

Oh, good grief. Was it too much to ask to get a PG-13 answer from the man? "Can you perhaps give me *something* to work with? I can't write that all it takes to make a perfect date in your book is lots of sex."

"Why not? It's the truth," he said, and this time I could tell he was being completely honest. I stiffened against the unwelcome and inappropriate thrill that chased my spine as he added, "It's the best way to get to know someone."

I hesitated, trying to decide which way to proceed. My gut said to pack up and leave, but I was genuinely curious as to why he believed in his answer. *Curiosity killed the cat, remember?* And yet, I challenged for the sake of argument, "Seriously? Pardon me if I call bullshit. Don't you find that just a little shallow?"

"Not at all," he said, enjoying the chance to defend his answer. "What's a date all about? Getting to know someone, right?"

I took the bait and nodded slowly, remaining wary. "Yes, I suppose so."

He smiled, asking, "May I?" reaching for my hand. I hesitated but relented, allowing Nico to grasp my free hand. He flipped my hand, palm-side down, to trace the small veins beneath my skin. I fought to keep the shivers at bay, trying to remain outwardly unaffected, even bored. "Let's say the underside of your palm represents your private self and the top of your hand represents the shield we put up to protect the soft parts of our hand that we only trust with those we know won't hurt us."

"Okay," I said, puzzled, drawing a short breath as my heart rate quickened. "How does that relate to sex on the first date?"

"I challenge you to tell me any other way to truly get to know someone without using sex." He slowly rotated my hand so my palm faced up. "Sex reveals vulnerabilities, our deep truths, and strips away the facades that we readily wear to hide ourselves from the world. In other words, sex removes the shield, leaving us with our soft spots unprotected."

I swallowed as tiny trembles I couldn't contain shook

my body. I pressed my lips together before my tongue
darted to wet my bottom lip. Suddenly, it was very
warm in his apartment, and the air had become charged
with electricity. "I...guess I see your point...but it's a
stretch," I lied, loathe to let him see how his little demonstration had turned up my internal heat.

He laughed, disagreeing. "In truth, Miss Hughes...
sex is the great equalizer, and what better way to de-
termine whether or not you are a match than when you
are in your deepest reality?"

I allowed him to hold my hand a moment longer than
necessary, then quickly withdrew, shaking my head
with a wobbly "Interesting theory but I'm not sure I can
put that in the article. *Luxe* isn't that kind of magazine.
We're more about classy, not trashy."

I was totally lying. Patrice would eat that shit up and
probably highlight the passage in a glitzy pull quote,
but I couldn't bring myself to admit that.

The awful truth was, Nico had somehow turned a
far-fetched explanation into the sexiest demonstration
I'd ever experienced, and I hated the way I felt way too
breathless for my own comfort. I wasn't like Daphne,
easily seduced or beguiled with a few choice words,
but I could still feel the phantom touch of his fingers
tracing my skin.

Nico didn't seem to mind and shrugged. "I'm only
being honest. You asked what my idea of a perfect date
would be, and I answered you."

I rubbed at my hand. "So lie to me," I quipped with
a flustered laugh, realizing my gaffe, then amended
quickly, "I mean, don't lie but maybe use your imagi-

nation. You have to remember that women are going to read this and want to know how they can impress you. This is your chance to put your dreams out there."

"As in my dream woman?" he asked for clarification, shaking his head, as if he knew there was no such thing. Something about that fatalistic opinion struck me as sad, though I wasn't a hopeless romantic by any means. I knew that true love was just a greeting card sentiment, but a part of me wished it were real. Maybe deep down, Nico did, too.

"Sure," I answered, curious as to what he considered the epitome of a female partner.

But Nico didn't seem interested in following that plot thread and detoured neatly as his gaze traveled the angle of my neck as sensuously as if his lips were nibbling a trail. "Were you ever a dancer?" he surprised me by asking.

My cheeks flushed with heat as I admitted, "Uh, yes, when I was younger. A long time ago."

"But you're not anymore."

"No."

"Why'd you give it up?"

Even though my hopeful ballet career died a long time ago, it still hurt to revisit those memories. I should've snapped my mouth shut but I didn't. "I hurt my knee performing a *grand jeté* when I was sixteen. It was never the same afterward and I knew I'd never make it to the New York City Ballet with that kind of injury, so I quit dancing altogether."

"Tragic," he murmured, and I sensed he was being genuine. His expression turned quizzical. "From what I understand, injuries are common for dancers but many heal with the right care and therapy. Why didn't you?"

Nico could never possibly understand how something like that would've been totally outside of my family's capabilities financially. I'd known the minute the muscle had torn that my career was done. "My parents didn't have the money for the intensive care that my injury required to put me back to where I was," I explained, stiffening against the inevitable ache in my heart for what would never be. "I wasn't going to ask my parents to bankrupt themselves so I could continue dancing." The clip in my tone was a warning that he was treading on dangerous ground. I lifted the recorder with a pointed look. "Now, about that dream woman..."

Nico smiled, slow and easy, ignoring my lead. "I've always had a thing for dancers. There's just something about the graceful way they carry themselves that always seems to stick with them, even long after they've stopped dancing."

I couldn't argue. I prided myself on maintaining proper posture, a throwback to my dancing days. An imaginary string pulled taut perpetually suspended my head. I could still hear my dance instructor's voice, *"Backs straight, chins high, dahling!"*

"Do you miss dancing?" he asked, interrupting my short reverie.

I exhaled a long breath. "It was a long time ago."

"That's not an answer," he chided.

"I'm not the one being interviewed."

His gaze inadvertently dipped to my dress, and I could practically feel his judgment, same as when Patrice openly curled her lip at my fashion choices. I lifted my chin and met his gaze squarely, almost daring him to make a comment so I could shoot him down. *I swear, don't people have better things to do than judge what other people are wearing? Is the world really that shallow?* Of course it was… I worked for a fashion magazine and I saw it firsthand.

Nico surprised me when he pulled away, his gaze narrowing as if he'd heard my internal dialogue. "Let's get down to brass tacks. You don't like me very much," he stated matter-of-factly. "Why?"

My cheeks flushed with guilt. I really needed to work on my poker skills if he saw through me so easily. Or maybe I hadn't really tried all that hard to disguise my contempt. Either way, my inability to smother what I was thinking or feeling had just bitten me in the ass—again.

"I like you just fine," I protested, trying for an earnest expression, but I felt as if I probably looked like the Joker with a pasted-on smile so I tried a different tack. "I mean, fine enough to do this interview. I doubt we have enough in common to enjoy a friendship, but other than that… I'm sure you're great."

"You're a terrible liar," he said, enjoying my sudden squirming. "Why don't you like me?"

He wasn't going to stop pressing. I could lay it all on the line and risk everything or I could try to lie through my teeth and maybe flirt a little. The latter made my dignity shrivel like a raisin, so that left me with pure honesty. I shut off the recorder—again. "Not that it matters for the sake of this interview, but maybe, I don't care for your *personality* type."

"Which is?"

I waved away his question. "Are we really doing this? Look, I'm sure there are plenty of women who would give their right foot to date you, I'm just not one of them."

"I didn't ask if you wanted to *date* me, I asked why you didn't *like* me. But since you brought it up, why wouldn't you want to date me?"

I hesitated, wondering how I'd lost control of this interview. I should've realized the Donatos were master manipulators. I should've been more diligent—or walked out when I'd had the chance.

But my chance to right the ship had just sailed.

Nico snorted with derision. "C'mon, you really think I can't smell your condescension from a mile away? Sweetheart, you're going to have to be a better actress than that if you're going to fool anyone into believing that you don't think I'm a big pile of shit." I opened my mouth to protest, but he wasn't finished. "What I don't understand is why *Luxe* would insult my family in such a manner as to send someone who clearly hates me to do this interview. I mean, what the fuck? Was this all a joke or something?"

Just apologize and appease his monster-sized ego. The answer seemed so simple, and yet I couldn't do it. I stiffened, wary. "If you planned on being a dick from the start, why didn't you let me leave?"

He shrugged. "I was curious but now I'm just bored and irritated."

"Why should my opinion matter at all?" I countered, feeling reckless. There was something about Nico that I couldn't quite shake, something that made me want to push when otherwise I might wisely fold.

Or maybe I was just tired of being railroaded for the sake of a paycheck. Patrice had never been my biggest fan, and this colossal train wreck of an interview shouldn't come as too big of a surprise, right?

Would she fire me?

Maybe?

Nico leaned forward, invading my space. "You think I'm another useless trust-fund baby with nothing better to do than spend my money on hookers and blow or at the very least strippers and booze." When I didn't deny it, he barked a laugh at my expense, as if I were an unprepared newb who hadn't done a lick of research. "My family donates gobs of money to various organizations and charities, but it is scattered among the different companies we own. We choose not to advertise our philanthropic endeavors because we believe that's private and we aren't looking for accolades. So we don't talk much about those things, but because we don't advertise, you make an assumption that I'm just another rich playboy who wipes his ass with money."

I had thought all of those things. Had I underestimated him? Was it possible? Right now I felt like an embittered, snarky bitch who hated all men, and it wasn't a nice feeling at all. "I may have misjudged you on first appearances," I admitted in a low tone, "but you haven't done much to disabuse me of my first impression."

"Was I supposed to? Or were you supposed to come here with an open mind?"

I swallowed, squarely put into my place by the most unlikely of people.

"You were rude," he stated flatly.

I chewed the side of my cheek before uttering a reluctant "Yes."

"You admit it?"

I'd have rather swallowed knives but nodded. "I didn't realize I was being so rude. Please let me start over."

"I should probably just ask for another reporter. Might be for the best."

"Please don't."

"I think it would be better for everyone involved."

"I assure you, it's not. Unless you want an idiot writing your article," I ground out. For someone who was supposed to be groveling, I was terrible at it.

"Nobody likes to be judged," he said quietly, and I understood where he was coming from. I suppose not even Nico Donato was free from judgment, though I never imagined that he might care what others thought.

"I'm sorry," I said again, meaning it this time. "I shouldn't have come in with a preconceived idea of who you were." Nico appeared mollified enough to accept my apology. I drew a deep breath and tried a real smile. "Can we start over? Wipe the slate clean? I promise you, even though I might've started with a bad attitude, I'm a pretty good writer. No one else at *Luxe* will do as good a job as me."

Nico regarded me with speculation, his blue eyes

deepening a shade. As much as I wanted to ignore the obvious, Nico Donato was easy on the eyes, and it'd been a long time since I'd allowed a man to enter my thoughts in any sort of sexual way.

Raw energy pulsed between us, parching my throat and leaving me out of sorts. Patching things between us might save my job, but I feared something far more frightening than job hunting in New York with a near-useless degree.

Nico had a thing about him…some kind of sexual voodoo, and I could already feel something happening between us even if it was in fits and starts—but it took only a spark to burn down a forest.

And that was the part that worried me.

CHAPTER FOUR

Nico

"I'M REALLY NOT an asshole," I insisted, but I couldn't quite prevent the tiny half smile curving my mouth. Even I couldn't make that statement with a straight face, but the fact that she handled my curveball without missing a beat was arousing as fuck. I had to know more about this woman—by any means possible. "Okay, how about this… I will answer any question you have for me…over dinner."

"Dinner," she repeated with open suspicion. "Why dinner?"

"Let's be honest…we both bungled this interview. Let's wipe the slate clean and start fresh. I'm willing to believe that we're both reasonable human beings, so why not forget this terrible first impression happened and start over. Preferably over a glass of wine."

Her gaze narrowed, but the tiny smile playing at the corners of her mouth told me she enjoyed negotiating as much as I did. *Oh, the things people reveal without realizing it.* "Dinner, no wine. Purely business. No funny business," she countered, her gaze glittering as she tacked on, "at a well-lit restaurant."

I shook my head. "Here."

"I'd rather a restaurant."

I knew if I pushed, she'd push back. She wasn't the kind of woman who was easily impressed or intimidated, so I had to try something else. "May I be completely honest?" I asked. She nodded slowly, curious. "It may come as a surprise, but I love to cook. It's the one thing that I wasn't given simply because of who I am. I've earned my skills through plenty of trial and error. If I'm going to have a shot of changing your perception of me, cooking you a meal is the best way I know how."

Her stunned silence was more telling than she knew. What she couldn't know was that I was being completely honest. I felt most comfortable in the kitchen, and I took great pride in knowing that every skill I had with food was 100 percent legit. Of course, I withheld the mention that I'd discovered long ago that women found men who can cook irresistible. I couldn't count how many panties had dropped over a seemingly innocent homemade dish of *risotto alla Milanese* paired with a perfectly roasted leg of lamb.

After a long, contemplative pause, Lauren nodded, accepting my proposal. "You have yourself a clean slate, Mr. Donato. I'll see you tonight. Seven o'clock," she said, rising as she thrust her hand toward me to seal the deal. I chuckled and accepted the handshake when I really wanted to brush my lips across that pale, soft skin to watch the goose bumps cause an all-out riot. I wanted to know what stole Lauren's breath and caused those beautiful dark eyes to darken further—and I definitely wanted to know what she was hiding beneath that ugly dress. However, I played the part of the gentleman, opening her door and watching her leave without a further suggestive remark or inappropriate suggestion.

Pretty proud of myself, actually. I rarely denied myself whatever pleasure caught my eye, but I suspected Lauren was a diamond hidden inside that crusty coal and I was more interested in discovering how to reveal what I was truly interested in.

The question was, what about Lauren turned my clock? Hell, I hadn't a clue. Generally speaking, I preferred women to be soft and malleable, maybe even a little on the vapid side. But then, I wasn't accustomed to women actively pushing me away. Usually it was the other way around. Most times I had to shake the women off with a stick.

Got quite annoying, actually.

But not Lauren.

Her employment with *Luxe* came to mind, as she clearly didn't fit the blueprint for the self-indulgent magazine.

Hence, the plot thickens, eh?

Everything about the woman intrigued me, and for fuck's sake, I was bored enough to dig into the mystery.

CHAPTER FIVE

Lauren

I COULDN'T EXPLAIN what had happened between Nico and me. I'm not entirely sure how he'd managed to turn the tables so neatly, but I had to give the man props for style and finesse.

For all his talk about wanting a fresh start to make a better impression, I wasn't buying into his story, but there was something about Nico that made me want to play the game.

Was this how it started? There was a saying, "bad judgment made for good stories," and it certainly applied to my current situation. I should've shut him down, told Patrice that Donato wasn't a good fit for the center feature and moved on. But somewhere between being completely annoyed and defensive to the point where he actually had me anticipating a countermove, my interest level had changed.

I had no doubt he was playing a game with me, but I wasn't without my own skills. If he thought he could charm the pants off me with an impressive culinary show, he was headed for an aching case of blue balls, but I wasn't above enjoying a fine home-cooked meal on someone else's dime and effort.

My ex had come from a wealthy family, and Houston had pulled out all the stops to impress me. Unfortunately, it'd worked on a naive girl, but I wasn't that girl anymore. Getting knocked up and abandoned did a lot to make a girl grow up.

When I'd met Houston, I'd been just out of college, and much more trusting.

Now I was fairly certain everyone had an agenda.

Except my sweet son.

Oh, crud. Speaking of, I'd have to find a babysitter for Grady tonight. I didn't want to call my mom because she'd ask questions, but the last time I left Grady with my best friend, Ronnie, he'd gotten Grady hooked on *Drag Race*. It'd taken weeks to convince Grady that a feather boa was *not* an acceptable choice for kindergarten attire. I mean, don't get me wrong, I loved that Grady was exposed to different lifestyles and completely open to alternative ways to be a human being. But I had a hard enough time as it was with the school administrator each time Grady said or did something that shocked the pants off his teacher.

I called my younger sister, Claire, hoping that she was available. Voice mail.

I chewed my bottom lip, vacillating between calling my mom and calling Ronnie.

I went with Ronnie.

"Hey, babe, you available to watch Grady tonight for me?" I asked, hailing a cab.

"Oh, honey child, why do you do this to me? You know I would die to watch the little man, but I totally have plans already. Unless you don't mind if I take him with me," he answered with a dubious tone that immediately set off alarm bells.

"Where are you going?" I asked, wary. "No drag shows."

"Oh, poo. Well, if you're going to be like that, then no, I already have plans."

I laughed, shaking my head. "You know you can't take Grady to a drag show. Most are held at a bar."

"Don't be ridiculous. This is a private show, and mostly kid-friendly. I think."

Yeah, I wasn't about to take the chance. "Not this time," I said, chuckling. It wasn't that I didn't trust Grady to be safe with Ronnie, but sometimes my friend didn't think about how impressionable a six-year-old was, and learning how to effectively tuck a penis wasn't a skill set I needed my son to pick up anytime soon. "No worries. Enjoy your show," I said and clicked off.

That left my mom.

Ugh. My mom and I were often on opposite sides of everything. For example, my mom thought I ought to be going after Grady's dad for child support even though I'd explained that it was better for Grady and me if Houston wasn't involved. I wasn't about to poke the sleeping bear. Houston was content to pretend that he didn't have a son, and I was totally fine with that. But my mom saw only the potential dollar signs floating out the window.

"He needs to take responsibility for his son," she'd

said during one of the many pointless arguments on the subject. "He has enough money—he needs to pay up."

"I don't want Houston around Grady," I'd replied, hoping the conversation was finished. "We're better off. Houston isn't exactly ready to be a father."

"You should've thought of that before getting knocked up," Ellen Hughes disparaged with a cool look. "If your father were alive today…well, let's just say he'd be having words with that young man."

I winced, hating when she brought up the subject of my dad. "Leave Dad out of this," I warned. "The man has earned his rest after being married to you for thirty years." It was harsh, but things tended to slip out when I argued with my mother.

"Lauren Elizabeth Hughes, you watch your mouth. I didn't raise you to be disrespectful." My mother's mouth pinched as she added disapprovingly, "A boy needs his father."

"No, he doesn't if that father is a useless playboy who cares more about partying than raising a child," I returned sharply, giving my mother "the look" as I finished putting away Grady's toys. My mother took the hint and gathered her things to leave. "Do you need me to call a cab?" I asked helpfully, but my mom was already out the door.

So, yeah, I wasn't super excited to have her babysit.

I could always bring Grady with me.

The thought popped into my head almost as a joke, but then I realized maybe that was an excellent idea.

I doubted Nico would try anything inappropriate with a six-year-old boy in attendance.

Maybe I was risking my mom card for using my kid as a shield, but the idea had merit. The more I thought about it, the more I realized it was a viable solution to a sticky issue.

With Grady there, I could keep the conversation on point and I could also use Grady as a legitimate reason to leave on time.

I'd get my interview and escape with my integrity.

Problem solved.

CHAPTER SIX

Nico

IN PREPARATION FOR TONIGHT, I had the best mood music set, soft lighting and a menu course that never failed to impress.

My buddies never failed to give me shit about my enjoyment of cooking, but I took pride in my work.

I believed men should be able to do two things well: cook and fuck.

And I excelled at both.

My doorbell went off, and I smiled at her punctuality.

I strode to the door with a wide smile, ready to go another round with Miss Hughes, but when I opened the door I stopped short, my smile freezing in place as confusion rapidly set in.

"Hello, my name is Grady." A small boy with glasses perched on his button nose thrust his little hand up at me. I faltered, inelegantly surprised by the unexpected plus-one, but Lauren filled in the blanks quickly—and, if I wasn't mistaken, I caught a spark of mischief in her dark eyes.

"Single mom, no babysitter so that means it's take-your-kid-to-work night. I hope you don't mind." She smiled broadly as if she knew throwing a kid in the mix had just crumpled all of my elaborate plans. Just then, a sexy song came on the playlist and I felt as exposed as if she'd caught me with my pants down.

Hot damn, she'd just taken things to the next level.

But I was nothing if not quick on my feet and recovered with a smile. "No worries, nice to meet you, little man," I said. I shook the boy's hand, impressed with his solid handshake. "Come in. You're in luck that I didn't plan for the lobster soufflé. I thought I might go with something a little less stuffy for our interview. I hope you like spaghetti."

Grady answered first, piping in, "I love *pasketti*. It's my favorite, but are you going to make garlic bread, too?"

Precocious little kid. I liked him already. "Of course," I answered. "Have you ever known a self-respecting Italian to serve a meal without bread?"

"Good man," Grady said, nodding with approval as he made his way into my living room, taking in the surroundings. "My mom says that you're a rich man with poor morals, but how good are you in the kitchen?"

Lauren gasped, embarrassed by her son's honesty. "Grady! Oh my goodness, I'm so sorry," she exclaimed, sending Grady a look that said, *cool it, kid*, but a smile pulled at my mouth. If I had a quarter for every time I'd embarrassed my mother by what'd popped from my mouth…well, I'd be even richer than I already was. "I don't know what's come over him. We have this problem at school, too. We can't always say what we want to say whenever we think it. Isn't that right, Grady? Please apologize."

"Not necessary," I assured her, grinning more widely. Yeah, I definitely liked the kid, especially when I knew now that I could probably get whatever information I needed out of the loose-lipped terrorist. "That's the thing about kids and drunks—they're always honest." I winked at Grady, then gestured for him to follow me into the kitchen. "But to answer your question, I kick ass when I'm cooking. The bigger question, little man, is what are *you* going to do to make yourself useful?"

My brow arched with mock sternness, but he wasn't intimidated in the least, which I found another point in his favor.

"I can do whatever you can do," he boasted without a hint of bashfulness but added when Lauren laughed a little nervously, "Except work the oven. Mama says I'm too young, even though I watched a YouTube video on how to work the burners and that worked out pretty good."

"What did the world do before YouTube?" I asked, only half joking because I was fairly certain YouTube was going to make college courses obsolete at some point. "But your mom is probably right about the oven. Best leave that to the adults or at least someone tall enough to ride the big-kid rides at Disneyland."

"Grady, I'm sure Nico is kidding about having you help."

"I'm absolutely not kidding. You're going to work,

too," I told her, earning a wary smile. "The best way to get to know someone is in the kitchen."

"Then you're gonna find out real fast that my mom doesn't make very good food," Grady confided, then cast his mother an apologetic look. "But you try real hard, and that's what counts."

I laughed. "Can I rent this kid for parties? He's a riot."

Lauren blushed and rubbed her hands together as she surveyed the layout of ingredients I had spread around. "Yeah, I wish I could say he was lying, but he's right. I'm all thumbs in the kitchen."

I smiled, noting that she'd changed into something far less reminiscent of a flour sack—jeans and a simple T-shirt—and unlike the ugly dress, the jeans molded perfectly to her hips and ass, blasting away the impression that she'd been hiding a less-than-stellar figure.

Hell, if I was being honest, Lauren had the kind of banging curves that always managed to turn my head. I was a sucker for wide hips, a fat ass and a small waist—and Lauren had it all. I took a brief second to whisper for her ears only, "How did you manage to hide that beautiful ass beneath that ugly dress? The jeans are a big improvement." Before she could gasp, I pulled away and continued in a normal tone, "Lucky for you, most of the dinner is already prepared and your parts are easy."

"Mama, maybe Nico can teach you a few things, too?"

Oh, little man, I'd love to teach your mama a thing or two. The thought raced across my mind, but I kept the comment behind my teeth, choosing to indulge the kid with a smile. "Sure, if your mama is open to learning, that is…"

Lauren caught the double entendre but instead of shooting me down with a look, she blushed a little, which only made me wish I could sample those pouty lips and grip a handful of that amazing ass.

Forget everything I'd said earlier about Lauren not being my type. Clearly, I was being fed bad intel because honest and true, if she'd walked in wearing what she was wearing right now, I would've changed my tactics immediately and the day would've ended with her in my bed.

Now I had to go a different route to get what I wanted.

But an easy victory was a boring one.

I pulled a chair over for Grady to stand on so he was level with the counter. "All right, little chef, you're on butter duty. I've made a garlic spread already, and it's your job to cover this freshly baked French bread with the spread so I can put it in the oven to cook. Can you handle it? I mean, it's an important job, so don't blow smoke up my behind if you're not up to the task."

Grady giggled and rolled his eyes as if I were an idiot and accepted the duty by grabbing the spreading spatula. I received an assured "I got this," and he went to work carefully spreading the garlic butter. I turned to Lauren with a cocked brow. "Now, as for you…can you manage chopping up the veggies for the salad without losing a finger?"

Lauren answered around a smile that stubbornly wouldn't stop forming. "Yes, I can handle the salad prep. I'm not a complete idiot in the kitchen."

"I don't know, junior here didn't exactly give you a glowing recommendation, and he knows you best," I said, winking at my pint-size partner in crime. The happy grin I earned twisted something unfamiliar for a brief moment, but I recovered in a blink to tease, "I'm no vampire, I don't want blood on the arugula."

Lauren laughed and shook her head, grabbing the cutting board and the assorted vegetables. "Just do your thing and I'll do mine."

"Excellent," I said, throwing some fresh basil in the sauce I'd already started the moment Lauren had left earlier that day. "The upside to being two generations removed from my Italy roots is that I was raised on solid, authentic Italian cooking and I know the difference between good parmigiana and crap."

"Do you mind if I set the recorder so we can do the interview at the same time?" Lauren asked, already reaching for her device. I shrugged as if I didn't care, but I didn't want her so focused on the interview that she completely missed all the subtle cues I was sending her way.

"Mama is a good writer. What do you do?" Grady asked. "Mama said you're just rich, but don't you have to do something to get rich?"

"Starting with the hardball questions, all right, all right," I said with an appreciative whistle. "Okay, so yeah, your mama is right, my family is wealthy, and because of that, I have a trust fund that enables me to pretty much do whatever I want—such as learn how to perfect the ultimate spaghetti dinner to impress difficult reporters."

Lauren blushed and bit her lip, no doubt to keep from skewering me in front of her kid, but I liked the way things were going thus far. In fact, the only thing that would improve the night was a glass of wine, a detail I planned to handle right now.

"My mama is hard to impress," Grady warned, finishing his butter duty. "Uncle Ronnie says it's 'cuz she's been too long without a man, but I think he's wrong 'cuz Mama has me and I'm the man of the house. I can take care of Mama just fine."

At that, I burst out laughing as Lauren's cheeks burned a brilliant shade of magenta. She fairly choked on the words, "Grady, let's go wash your hands. You're all buttery, sweetheart," before shooting me a pointed look when I struggled to contain my laughter.

"First door on your right," I managed, gesturing to the hallway, still smiling at the intel dropped from precious little Grady's gob. *So, Mama Hughes is on a bit of a dry spell, huh?* It didn't surprise me that Lauren wasn't a casual dater, especially with a kid like Grady on her heels. He probably kept her on her toes and served as an efficient cock-blocker.

I poured two glasses of 2009 Chateau Lafite Rothschild, a complex Bordeaux of red blends from Pauillac, Bordeaux, France, but I was at a loss as to what to serve Grady. I wasn't exactly equipped with juice boxes for the preschool set.

When Lauren and Grady returned, I handed Lauren her glass above her mild protests, and turned to Grady. "Here's the deal. I have water, cranberry juice and root beer. What's your poison?"

"Cranberry, please."

Odd choice for a kid but I'd oblige. "One cranberry, coming up."

Lauren explained, "Grady has a weakened kidney. It's nothing serious, but the doctor put him on cranberry juice since he was about three years old, so he developed a taste for it."

Kidney issue? I slid the short glass over to Grady. "So, it's nothing serious? What happened?"

"Mama." Grady looked at Lauren, and I understood that whatever ailed the kid embarrassed him so I dropped it.

"I'm starved," I announced, moving to the bubbling pot of pasta. I removed the pot and drained and dropped the pasta into the awaiting sauce so it could absorb some of the sauce's flavor. "In Italy, this is called *pasta saltata in padella*," I explained when I caught both Grady and Lauren watching with interest.

"Well, it smells good," Lauren admitted. "Did you learn how to make pasta from your mother?"

"Actually, a combination of my mother and the family cook, Greta. My brothers were always expected to trail after our father because of the family business, but that left me to do as I pleased. I happened to enjoy eating good food, so I naturally ended up learning how to cook for myself."

"Which no doubt has made you plenty of points with the ladies," Lauren said drily, and I didn't deny it. "Should I put that in the article, that you'll cook if she cleans?"

"Sounds like an equitable arrangement," I said,

though in my head I answered a bit differently. I cook, she sucks my cock and I leave the cleanup for the maid in the morning. Not to be left out, my shaft hardened as if it were part of the main course.

Turning quickly, I took a minute on the pretense of checking the pasta, but I simply didn't want to face Lauren with a giant, inappropriate boner with her kid sitting right there.

C'mon, think of basketball, the World Series, ugh, Brussels sprouts, anything...

It was probably only seconds but it felt like a lifetime before I could reasonably present myself without sending Lauren packing with her kid under her arm to escape the rich pervert who seemed to be turned on by a terrific bowl of pasta.

Of course, that wasn't the reason, but I doubted she'd appreciate if I admitted I sprung a monster erection at the thought of her sucking my cock here in my kitchen.

"Who's hungry?" I asked, carrying the bowl to the table where I already had place settings set. Then I realized I needed another for Grady. Without missing a beat, I grabbed a plate, utensils and a linen napkin and handed them to Grady, instructing him to set his place. To Lauren, I said, "Mind if you grab the wine?"

"I probably shouldn't have any more wine," she said but grabbed the wine for me. "I still have work to finish tonight."

"Wine makes Mama sleepy," Grady chimed in, settling into the chair as if it were the most normal thing in the world to eat with a stranger. "And she has to tuck me in or else I can't sleep right."

"Is there anything this kid doesn't know?" I teased, serving up a plate for Lauren while she dished her son. "I mean, the intel I could get…it's hard not to wonder."

She graced me with a short look and reminded Grady to put his napkin in his lap before returning to her own plate with an appreciative inhale. "Well, it certainly smells incredible. Let's see if you overhyped your skills or you were uncharacteristically humble."

"Proceed. I await your opinion." I laughed and waited for her first bite.

She took an exploratory bite and closed her eyes with involuntary pleasure. "Oh, God, I can't believe I'm going to say this but…you were a bit modest in your own skills. This is the best thing I've ever had in my mouth."

SPROING!

Thank God I was seated with a napkin covering my lap. The thought of Lauren's mouth…it was too much to handle. I covered my discomfort with a wide grin. "Is that so?" I turned to Grady. "Okay, little man…what do you say? Is your mom pulling my leg or does my spaghetti truly knock your socks off?"

Grady held up his finger in a "just a minute" motion, then twirled his fork for a mouthful. After an exploratory bite, his eyes brightened and he nodded vigorously. *"Deeeee-licious!"*

Was it weird that Grady's praise made me squirm a little with pride?

I didn't know this kid. I barely knew his mother.

But everything I knew so far, I was kinda into.

A little voice warned that I was messing with things that were out of my depth.

But that was part of the allure.

Hell, I never said I was a saint and I never pretended to be. I looked to Lauren with a smile, wineglass in hand.

"Shall we start the interview?"

CHAPTER SEVEN

Lauren

As much as I wanted to find fault with Nico's culinary skills, I couldn't. He made a mean dish of pasta, and that wine pairing was divine. After listening to how Nico prepared his sauce, simmering it for hours after I left, I was embarrassed to admit that spaghetti in my house came from a jar.

"You're very proud of your heritage," I said after Nico shared some of his family's history. "How did your family go from a wine-making operation to the global empire that Donato Inc. is today?"

"Is that part of the article?" he asked, smiling above the rim of his glass, those dazzling eyes something of rare beauty. Or maybe that was the wine talking. No, I could admit he had gorgeous eyes without wanting to sleep with him. He refilled both our glasses, and even though I knew I shouldn't, I didn't stop him. Grady, having finished and becoming bored with grown-up talk, had gleefully taken up Nico's offer to level up his gamer tag on his gaming system. It would've been mean to refuse Nico's offer, but I wished I still had Grady for a buffer. "To be honest, the business side of my family's operation has never interested me. I was never in line for a serious position—my father has his heir and a spare, which makes me the spare 'spare'—so I don't really care how our family rose to the place where we are now. I reap the benefit, and that's all that matters."

"You don't mind that your father doesn't think of you in the same way as your brothers?"

"If you're asking if I have daddy issues, the answer is emphatically no. Why would I want the stress of running the empire on my shoulders? I'd much rather spend my time pursuing happy things. If you met my brothers, you'd see what I mean. It's a blessing, in my opinion, that I'm not on my father's radar."

"But that just seems wrong. A father is supposed to love his children equally." I didn't want to feel bad for Nico, but a part of me did. "I mean, what kind of relationship do you have with your father?"

Nico chuckled but I sensed I'd hit a chord. He shifted as he explained, "My father is an old-world misogynist with whom I have nothing in common, so it's safe to say I don't have much of a relationship with the old fart and I'm not missing out on anything."

"That's sad. You missed out on what it's like to have a great father. Mine died when I was fifteen, but he was my world and we were very close. Losing him still hurts to this day."

"Well, I guess I can't miss what I never had."

A true statement, but Nico's flippant shrug was incongruent with the sudden shuttering of his gaze to focus on the wine left in his glass. "Are you close with your brothers?" I asked.

"Do you have any siblings?" he countered.

"A younger sister, Claire. She's in her last year at NYU."

"And are you close?"

"Yeah, I like to think so, but the age gap makes things a little difficult at times. I mean, she's still in that college frame of mind, and I've moved on from that stage."

"Because you have a kid."

"Not only because of that but I suppose it was a big motivating factor in my need to grow up."

"So…single mom…there's a story there…" he fished, but I wasn't about to share that particular story, so I shut him down.

I placed my empty wineglass on the table and turned off my recorder. "I should probably get going. It's getting late."

Nico made a show of checking his watch and disagreed. "It's barely ten o'clock. The clubs are just starting to open. This is when the night begins."

"Not when you have a sleepy six-year-old," I said, rising. "I've already stayed way longer than I'd planned." That was an embarrassing understatement. I wasn't even sure if I had enough information for my article in spite of spending hours in Nico's company. "But I didn't count on you being a master chef and surprisingly consummate host," I admitted sheepishly.

Nico laughed, amused by my admission. A dimple in his right cheek flashed, and I felt my knees tremble suspiciously. It'd been a long time since I'd felt anything remotely resembling attraction, since Houston made his grand exit, and I didn't particularly appreciate the familiar tingle now.

Yes, definitely time to go.

I walked into the living room to gather Grady and found him sacked out. Mom guilt set in hard. I bit my lip, chagrined. "Damn it," I murmured, "he's already asleep."

"It's the pasta. Best sleeping aid in the world," Nico boasted, nodding as if he'd accomplished some great feat as to put a six-year-old to sleep.

"I hate to burst your bubble, but Grady's internal clock put him to sleep, not your pasta. My son has never had a problem dropping off, no matter where he is. I should've known better and left earlier."

"It's not the end of the world," Nico said. "Just stay."

I balked. "Excuse me?"

"Calm down, Mama Bear. I have a spare bedroom. The sheets are clean and the pillows like clouds. I don't mind if you and Grady take the spare."

"Yes, but I mind," I told him, unable to believe he would think I would stay the night with him, separate bedroom or not. The fact that my mind went somewhere it shouldn't sharpened my tone. "It's not appropriate."

But he didn't seem to notice and chided playfully, "I don't get many opportunities to play the gentleman. You would rob me of the chance to play the hero?"

My cheeks flushed as butterflies erupted in my stomach. Maybe it was the wine, but he just got ten times hotter—which really should've been a crime.

"It's just not... I mean, what would people say? I have a reputation to protect. Not to mention if my editor found out...it would be all bad."

Nico still didn't see the problem. "We're adults. We're allowed to make our own choices."

"Clearly," I said with a hint of exasperation. "Which is why we both should know better."

"It's not as if I'm asking you to share *my* bed," he said, sending an illicit shiver down my backside. "Now, *that* might be construed as...inappropriate."

"Y-yes, completely inappropriate," I agreed, bobbing my head vigorously, though my stomach muscles had just tightened at the idea. "I wouldn't even consider it." What a total lie. *I'd just considered it.* Maybe for a microsecond, but it still counted.

"Neither would I."

And yet, his gaze was saying something else entirely. His gaze, if my senses weren't malfunctioning, was saying, if given half the chance, he'd fuck me raw.

My stomach tightened again. I didn't like this feeling. Everything was tingling and aware—including my lady parts, which I would've much preferred to remain silent and dead when around Nico Donato. Except, as fantasy material went... Nico was pretty hot. I wasn't above using him for mental purposes later...but to be honest, I was tired of getting myself off by myself. Just for the sake of argument, Nico might be the perfect way to scratch that itch without fear of anything turning serious, which I didn't need or want.

In that case, it wouldn't be *me* becoming a notch on *his* bedpost, but rather, the other way around. The idea had merit. Or I'd had too much wine. It could go either way.

However, for tonight, home was where I'd sleep.

"Your offer is very generous but I can't," I said firmly. "There's no way I could explain to Grady why we spent the night at a stranger's house without uncomfortable questions. You might've already noticed, he's very smart."

"A point in his favor," Nico said. "Most kids are irritating. Yours is surprisingly entertaining."

I chuckled ruefully. "Well, he has his moments, but you can imagine what kind of questions his head might conjure if we stayed."

"Fair enough but you will let me call for a car."

"I can call an Uber," I protested, but Nico wouldn't budge. There was something oddly protective about his determination to ensure our safety that plucked at my primitive female brain. I withheld a sigh of longing, wishing for a brief moment that I didn't suffer from the knowledge that all men were pigs and had ulterior motives.

Because if I *didn't* suffer that knowledge I might even enjoy an evening tangled up with Nico, skin on skin, covered in sex sweat and moaning loud enough to cause the neighbors to complain.

I rubbed my suddenly damp palms, needing to get away from Nico. Maybe Uncle Ronnie was right—it'd been too long since I'd been with a man—because I was actually starting to fantasize about banging boots with Nico Donato, a man I held zero respect for and would never trust.

But I bet the sex would be fantastic.

Of course it would be!

Watching Nico do his thing in the kitchen had been sexy as hell. A man who had the patience to simmer a sauce all day had the wherewithal to pleasure a woman with just as much attention to detail.

God, it'd been so long since I'd had sex with another human being.

On the tail of that mournful thought, Nico returned, saying, "The car is coming. He should be here in a few minutes."

"Oh! Yes, th-thank you," I said, stumbling on my words, sounding to my own ears like an idiot. I shouldered my purse and started to reach for Grady, but Nico wasn't having it and instead hoisted my boy up like he weighed nothing. Grady, adorable in sleep, his lips pursed, simply lay against Nico's shoulder as if it were natural to do so. "You don't have to do that, I can carry him," I said, troubled by how much I liked the sight of Nico holding Grady. What the hell had Nico put in that spaghetti sauce? I was clearly losing my mind.

"Nonsense," Nico said, going to the door. "Like I'm going to send you and the boy down to the car by yourselves. The city at night is no place for a mom and her son to be alone. I'll feel better knowing you made it safely to the car."

Again with the tingling. Were my ovaries doing the polka? "That's very nice of you," I said, my tongue sticking to the roof of my mouth. Maybe I'd had too much wine. I wasn't thinking clearly. But I couldn't quite help but wonder if maybe I'd misjudged Nico earlier. He'd been nothing but an entertaining and gracious host tonight. Aside from the one comment, he'd been on his best behavior.

And I hadn't hated the fact that he'd noticed my ass.

I purposefully downplayed my looks and figure because I didn't want to deal with the complications of entanglements, but I'd forgotten how good it felt to be noticed by the opposite sex.

To see that banked hunger in a man's eyes.

To know that they were interested.

But I didn't want Nico to be interested in me.

At least, the logical part of my brain didn't want that.

The decidedly female part of my brain was cooing and purring and practically begging to thrust my ass in his face.

Had I mentioned that it'd been a long time since I'd had sex? That drought was making me pretty damn thirsty right now, and Nico was starting to look like a mountain spring of cool, fresh water.

We got to the bottom floor of the building, and true to his word, a shiny black town car idled softly, waiting for us.

"Do you have a car on retainer?" I joked as Nico gently put Grady into the vehicle and strapped him into the seat belt. He closed the door gently, standing between the car and me.

"It's a perk," he answered with a cheeky grin that sent my stomach flip-flopping. I'd grown up in the city, and having a car of any sort was a luxury most people couldn't afford, except for special occasions.

"Well…um, thank you for a surprisingly lovely evening," I said, thrusting my hand toward him for a benign handshake, but Nico just stared at me with amusement as if we both knew a handshake wasn't going to happen. Instead, he accepted my hand gently and pressed a soft kiss on the top, his lips lingering long enough to create havoc with my nerve endings. The gesture was both gentlemanlike and erotic. My breath was suspiciously breathy as I said, "Th-that wasn't necessary…"

"But I disagree," he said, his gaze finding mine. Those eyes were killers. I could only imagine how many women had fallen to their doom in their blue depths— and gladly so. "What if I said, I want to see you again?"

"I'd say that's probably a bad idea," I answered, but my belly trembled. "It would be unprofessional."

"And why is that?"

"Because it is."

"So this is it?" he asked. I jerked a nod, shivering but not because of the cold. His subtle smile was my undoing. "Well, then, if this is to be it…" and then he moved in, slowly enough that I had plenty of time to stop him, but I didn't. I tilted my chin and his lips were on mine. Electric heat zapped between us, binding us. Curse it all, I opened my mouth a little more, inviting his tongue to dance with mine. He obliged with a sexy growl that I felt to my toes. The sidewalk seemed to slant beneath my feet, and I clung to Nico, losing all sense of reason for a blinding moment. It was all sorts of wrong, but I wasn't going to see him again and it'd been so long since I'd felt a man's touch that I might've succumbed to the advances of the FedEx driver if he'd given me clear enough signals.

At least, I clung to that justification so I didn't chew myself to pieces over indulging in this single moment with Nico.

Our breath mingled as our tongues twisted, the heat building between us enough to melt snow. My clothes scratched against my skin, an irritant. It was a blessing that Nico hadn't tried to kiss me in his apartment because I might've stayed—with him, in his bed—and it probably would've been the best sex of my life.

How did I know that? Well, because *oh, God, help me*, he was an amazing kisser and I could only imagine what he could do when given free rein.

Orgasms for days.

Yep. That was what Nico would deliver. I knew it. My certainty was bone-deep.

Argh, don't think of bone.

Time to stop. Time to be responsible.

Goddamn morals and ethics—why couldn't I just be like the rest of the women who would gladly throw their panties at his feet for a single glance from him.

Because I wasn't.

And because of that—I broke the kiss.

Reluctantly. Oh, yes, very reluctantly, but I broke it nonetheless.

"Good night, Nico," I managed as I slid out of his grasp and ducked into the awaiting car as if the devil himself were leering at my soul.

I didn't breathe until we were far enough away that I couldn't still see his silhouette watching us leave.

Then, and only then, did I draw a shaky breath, my

fingers lightly touching where Nico's lips had been,
closing my eyes to savor the lingering pleasure of being
touched by a skillful lover…if only for a heartbeat.

CHAPTER EIGHT

Nico

I WATCHED THE car until it was out of sight.

The night had turned out like nothing I'd planned.

Never had a night bombed so bad and yet been so wonderful at the same time.

I had a raging boner—and no one to ease the pain of my erection—and yet, I couldn't stop smiling.

So, Lauren was a single mom with a fantastic ass. Never would've called that one.

Her kid was pretty chill. I didn't usually dig kids, but Grady was entertaining and smart. Kinda reminded me of myself at that age, so of course, I thought the kid was brilliant.

Under most circumstances I avoided single moms. I didn't have the patience to deal with the drama, and truthfully, I'd never met a single mother I'd felt worth the hassle to try to figure it out.

Until Lauren.

Yeah, Grady was a great kid. The little monster was different, precocious and very protective of his mom, and yet he'd spilled valuable intel with impunity. But the kid had definitely cock-blocked me, a fact his mother had counted on.

Lauren's crafty intelligence turned me on in a way I hadn't felt in a long time.

And that kiss.

Definitely worth exploring in the future.

Except, I knew the only reason Lauren allowed the kiss was because she felt safe in the knowledge that we wouldn't see each other again.

I chuckled as I returned to my apartment. *Naive woman.* Now that I'd had a taste, I wanted more. Who took one tiny bite of New York–style cheesecake and then pushed away the plate with a satisfied "I'm good"?

Exactly. No one.

And Lauren was my New York–style cheesecake. On the surface, plain and unadorned with flash and extraneous details, but once a bite crossed your lips, you realized, nothing else was necessary. In fact, to add more would be to take away from the robust flavor of the dessert's complexity.

Lauren was smooth and rich—decadent and forbidden.

How could I not want more?

As if punctuating the thought, my erection wouldn't subside. I flopped onto the sofa as I jerked my jeans down around my hips. I palmed my cock, groaning as I closed my eyes, envisioning Lauren's sweet lips closing over the head, her teeth grazing ever so lightly as I fed my cock down her throat.

My imagination was a poor substitute for the real deal, but I'd have to make do.

I pictured Lauren between my legs, my hands threading through her thick, dark hair as her mouth slid up and down my shaft, her slender fingers gently cupping my balls as she worked my cock.

I pumped faster, hungry for the friction. In my imagination, Lauren met my gaze while her mouth worked me. I nearly lost it at the thought. I groaned more loudly as I fucked my own hand harder. My heart rate quickened as the tingling started in my balls, rattling the cages and shaking the foundation.

"Jesus, Lauren." I moaned as my orgasm hit with a ferocity I was unprepared for. I came hard, spilling everywhere as I continued to pump against my palm, gasping as my release stole my breath and left me wheezing from the sheer force.

It was several minutes before I could think again, my heart still thundering.

I rolled to the side, grimacing at the mess I'd made. I jerked my shirt off and used it to clean up, tossing it to the floor for the maid to deal with later.

A sigh escaped my parted lips and I rose slowly from the sofa, no longer suffering an erection, but the release had been only partially satisfying.

I wanted the real deal.

What did Lauren sound like when she came? Was she loud or breathy? What did she taste like? Was she sweet or musky? I liked both but I wanted to know Lauren's essence, the unique taste of her as she came, preferably when she gushed into my mouth.

Before the kiss, Lauren might've been able to play off that she wasn't interested, but that woman had set my ass on fire with her response.

She was a powder keg of need and want—and I was just the man to give her what she craved.

But she wasn't going to just give in. Lauren was too stubborn for such an easy win.

No, this situation required finesse and a certain level of clever manipulation behind the scenes to make things happen.

As I noodled the situation, my wandering gaze settled on a gilded invitation I'd tossed to the coffee table. I was expected to make an appearance, smile, nod and wave, to represent Donato Inc. Seeing as I wasn't actually needed on the business front, my brothers often threw me the public appearances.

But I needed a date.

Usually, I selected one of my regular fuck buddies, someone who understood I wasn't interested in dating, just a hot body on my arm, and an even hotter time in bed afterward. No expectations, no entanglements: a good time for everyone involved.

I wanted Lauren to be my plus-one.

Of course, she'd decline—spouting something to the effect that being my date would be inappropriate—but what if I made it impossible for her to turn me down?

A cunning smile curved my lips. All it would take would be a little nudge here, a little encouragement there and I could get Patrice, Lauren's editor, to make it happen.

But I couldn't make it look obvious or else Lauren would sniff out my hand.

Subtlety was the key.

Times were hard in publishing these days. The right dollar amount in the advertising department might grease the wheels well enough. *Luxe* could always use a high-rolling client within their pages.

Donato Inc. owned several boutique wineries— my father collected wineries like some might collect stamps—and it just so happened that one of the wineries was debuting a new tasting room in Manhattan. I could run a series of ads for the tasting room, which would be a legitimate but quite pricey expense on the guise of promoting our little boutique winery.

The acquisition of a high-end client would tickle the advertising execs, and Patrice would bend to whatever I asked.

Including strong-arming her reluctant reporter to be my date for the event.

Yes, the more I gave it thought, the more the idea had merit.

I would place the appropriate calls tomorrow.

Inordinately pleased with myself, I retired to my bed to dream of all the dirty, delicious and downright damnable things I wanted to do to the delectable Miss Hughes, the hottest MILF I'd ever met.

CHAPTER NINE

Lauren

WHAT?" I ASKED, not quite sure I'd heard Patrice correctly. "I'm going where?"

But Patrice was already anticipating my refusal and frowned in my direction over the horn-rimmed glasses she insisted were the height of fashion but in my opinion only made her look like an owl.

"I don't know why you insist on being so damn difficult. It's not often that the hottest bachelor in town is willing to have you as his date at a very high-end, high-profile event."

My head was spinning. Nico wanted me to go where? "Don't you think that's a little unprofessional? The article hasn't even run yet. I shouldn't be seen out and about chumming it up with the man we're trying to tell the world is available."

"I didn't say to *date* him," Patrice said as if I were being deliberately ignorant. "And on the contrary, being seen out and about with Donato is excellent publicity for *Luxe*. You can subtly drop some hints about the upcoming feature, create some buzz."

"Did Nico put you up to this?" I asked flatly. Patrice answered with an unamused stare. I shifted, defending myself. "It just seems odd that he would pick me to go as his date. I barely know him. Surely he has other women he could invite."

"Nico has nothing to do with this. I put this in motion, not Nico," she said sharply. "I caught wind of the event, found out that Nico would be there and asked Nico if he wouldn't mind squiring you about for the sake of the upcoming article. He was a perfect gentleman about it, and I appreciated his willingness to be a good sport."

In spite of Patrice's answer, I smelled a rat. I couldn't exactly tell Patrice about the red-hot kiss Nico and I had shared a few days ago at his apartment without looking like a complete hypocrite, but there was no way in hell Patrice just casually discovered that Nico needed a date for the event.

No, this had Nico's hands all over it.

I made a show of checking my calendar. "As much as I would love to go and talk up *Luxe*, I'm busy that night."

"Busy how?" Patrice asked, her brow climbing with disbelief.

I tried not to take offense, but Patrice's constant disdain for my social life—however dull it was—got old. "I have a date," I lied.

"Yes, I know...with Nico Donato," Patrice replied, daring me to say otherwise.

"No, I mean, an actual date with a man. I mean, of course it's a man, but someone I might actually have a connection with. We've been talking for a few weeks and we've finally found time in our busy schedules to meet up. He's an engineer," I finished with a smile, seeming enamored with my fake date. I tacked on brightly, "Oh! And we have reservations at Tochi's, and you know how hard it is to get a reservation at that place. I couldn't possibly cancel on such late notice."

Patrice's mouth pursed with displeasure. "This looks very bad for *Luxe*."

I wanted to quip, *I didn't realize* Luxe *had entered the escort business*, but wisely didn't. Instead, I suggested, "Send Daphne. She'd love to spend an evening with Mr. Donato, and I'm sure it would be good for her to network for new story leads. Those dinners are terribly boring unless you know who to talk to. Daphne could use the practice."

"If I wanted Daphne, I would've given her the assignment."

I was on dangerous ground with Patrice, but she couldn't actually make me go as Nico's date, could she? I mean, surely that was breaking a few HR rules.

I held my breath as I awaited her decision. Just when I thought I was going to lose and she was going to force me to cancel my fake date, she relented with a sour look. "Well, I guess all I can say is enjoy your date. I'm sure Daphne will have a lovely time," she said, dismissing me.

Phew. Dodged a bullet. I didn't trust myself around Nico after that kiss. It was too good and I was still thinking about it way too much. That damn kiss had ignited some questionable ideas that were getting harder to dismiss—I didn't need anything to pitch fuel on the fire.

However, if I were being honest, it pinched a little at the thought of Daphne landing in Nico's arms, and that was precisely why it was the right decision to avoid him.

The man could probably convince a nun to toss her habit with one flick of that tongue, but I wasn't about to lose my fucking mind over one kiss.

But would it be so terrible to have some fun? I used to know how to have a good time, but I seemed to have forgotten the basics.

Kissing was fun; sex was better.

Just playing devil's advocate for a second…how bad would it be to have a little fun with Nico—assuming neither of us was looking for anything real or permanent?

Unlike my sister, Claire, I didn't believe in soul mates and happily-ever-after.

You know what I believed in? Hot tea with honey on cold mornings, freedom of the press and the satisfaction found in paying my own bills.

The rest was hogwash.

Maybe at one time I believed in that happily-ever-after stuff, but life had disabused me of that silliness.

I found satisfaction and fulfillment in a job well done. And as I put the finishing touches on my article on Donato, I knew I'd hit the mark. As I'd told Nico, no matter my personal feelings, I could deliver a well-written article on any subject.

I paused to admire my work, pleased with myself. Maybe Nico wasn't quite the narcissistic man-child with Peter Pan syndrome I'd initially thought, but like I'd said to Grady, Nico didn't actually do anything to earn his millions; he was a trust-fund baby, and I had a hard time respecting someone who did nothing to support themselves.

My dad had been a hard worker, and I expected nothing less from other men.

So how'd I fall in love with Houston, another trust-fund kid? Chalk it up to being young and dumb, I supposed.

Not anymore. I took pride in my ability to weed out the undesirable disguised as handsome, worldly men.

I exhaled a little too heavily even as I was mentally patting myself on the back.

Made for lonely nights, that was for sure.

The city was filled with undesirables, as evidenced by my empty social calendar.

Out of my peripheral, Daphne made her way over to me, her eyes sparkling and practically bubbling with excitement. "You are never going to believe who I'm going to accompany to the Griffin Center dinner." Daphne didn't wait for an answer before she gushed, "Nico Donato!"

I smiled, trying for some mentorly advice. "Remember, this is a business function, so don't let him put the moves on you. You're representing *Luxe*. Take this opportunity to glean some fresh story leads. If you listen carefully enough once the champagne starts flowing, you'll be surprised how easy it is to pick up leads."

But Daphne wasn't interested in career advice. "Okay, what do you think his favorite color is? I mean, black is always classy but a little funeral-ish, you know? How about a lemony yellow? I could totally rock a yellow dress, right?"

"Are you listening to me? This is not a date, and you'd do well to remember that fact. Nico is not going to fall head over heels in love with you. Likely, he'll be super charming, throw around some useless facts about the wine and then try to kiss you. Just remember...you are one of many."

Daphne made a sour face. "You are such a wet blanket. Haven't you ever just wanted to have a good time? You are the oldest young person I've ever met."

I balked. "I have plenty of fun. Loads of it, actually. I mean, crazy, wild fun, even. I just know when to do it appropriately." *Gahh, I sound like an old lady.*

"That right there means you don't have the slightest idea how to have fun."

I forced a laugh, but her comment was starting to poke at a nerve I'd never realized was tender. Was that how the office viewed me? The fuddy-duddy? Embarrassment caused me to blurt, "I'll have you know, I have a date the night of the event."

Oh, good grief, why was I pushing that ridiculous lie?

"You have a date? Like an actual date?" Daphne asked, incredulous.

The fact that Daphne found my claim hard to believe was telling. Yep, I was the office matron. "Yes, and we're going to Tochi's for dinner." I was going to hell for lying so blatantly, but I was already committed. If I wasn't careful I'd end up scrounging in the restaurant's back alley in the hopes of finding a tossed receipt that I could claim as my own for proof I'd been there. "I'm super excited. He's an engineer."

"What's his name?"

I faltered. "Um, George."

"George what?"

"George the engineer."

"What's his last name?" Daphne asked stubbornly.

"That's personal."

"I think you're bluffing."

I forced a laugh. "And why would I do that?"

"I don't know, but I'm pretty good at sniffing out bullshit, and something stinks."

"Well, I have no reason to lie." *My ego disagrees.* "Anyway, have fun, and please remember, you're representing *Luxe*." I paused, then suggested with only a dash of petty cattiness, "Wear the yellow," because unlike Daphne's inflated opinion of herself, she absolutely could not pull off a lemon yellow dress; it would make her look like a washed-out heroin addict.

And I was glad.

"Thanks," Daphne said happily, forgetting about her bullshit meter. "Have fun on your date."

The smile I'd held for Daphne's benefit dropped like a ton of bricks as soon as she was gone.

Daphne was a pretty girl. Nico liked pretty girls.

And I didn't care in the least.

Right?

Absolutely. In fact, I was totally looking forward to

spending the evening cuddled up with my son, eating popcorn and watching *Transformers* (for the hundredth time). Maybe I'd splurge and order a pizza.

And maybe I'd wash it all down with a bottle of wine.

Yep, I sighed. Sounded like a solid plan.

A familiar—but solid—plan.

CHAPTER TEN

Nico

PATRICE WAS BLATHERING.

"Daphne is a great girl. I think you'll really enjoy her company. She's young and vibrant and so excited to spend an evening with you as your guest at the Griffin dinner event. Such an honor, really. Have I mentioned how excited we are at *Luxe* to feature you in our double issue? It's such a coup."

Who the hell was Daphne? No, strike that, I didn't give two shits about Daphne because she wasn't Lauren. I'd come down to the *Luxe* offices to confirm all the details, and this wasn't what I'd had in mind. I cut through Patrice's bullshit, kiss-ass routine like a hot knife through butter. "I thought we'd discussed you were sending Miss Hughes," I reminded Patrice with a subtle frown. "I have an excellent rapport with Lauren, and I was looking forward to spending the evening with *her*."

"Yes, well, unfortunately, she had a date already scheduled, and believe you me, if you knew how much that girl needs to loosen up, you'd understand why I couldn't make her cancel."

I looked at Patrice sharply. "She had a date?"

"Yes, some engineer. Said they got reservations at Tochi's. Lucky girl, right? I've heard the reservations are a bear to obtain for anyone who isn't royalty or a Donato," she said with a patronizing wink.

I didn't like the idea of Lauren dating anyone, and the fact that I didn't like it gave me pause. Should I care if Lauren was dating? She was nothing to me except an intriguing side note. Except, it bothered me. *A lot.* "Well, good for her," I murmured, seemingly in support but inside I was ordering a hit on the mystery man who wasn't me. "Although, to be honest, Tochi's is a little overrated for my tastes. To each his own, I suppose. The chef is an insufferable prick."

My thoughts churned even as I kept my expression neutral. Who was this asshole wooing Lauren? And what made him better than me? She was more than willing to turn me down—me, a Donato—and yet, she'd cut out to eat some mediocre Japanese food with some stranger?

I needed to know more about this engineer.

"Did she happen to mention a name?"

Patrice stared at me blankly. "A name? Who?"

"The name of Lauren's *engineer*," I answered, my patience thinning. "Surely, she must've mentioned a name."

Patrice appeared confused by my interest. "Not really. Lauren and I aren't exactly close. She's an excellent reporter but a bit of a cold fish. Why?"

Lauren was anything but cold. I knew that firsthand. One just needed to know how to turn up the heat. And now I was irritated as fuck.

"I hate to be a stickler for details, but our understanding was that *Lauren* would accompany me to the event and *Luxe* would reap the benefit of a new advertising client with deep pockets. By my estimation, you haven't held up your end of the bargain."

Patrice tittered nervously. "I couldn't exactly *force* her to attend the event with you without violating laws. This isn't medieval London. Surely, you can understand that. I did the best that I could."

But I wasn't feeling generous. "Obviously, your best wasn't good enough."

An uncomfortable moment passed between us. Patrice realized I wasn't kidding and paled, defending herself. "Mr. Donato, I *assure* you, I did my utmost to accommodate you in your request, but going beyond that would open *Luxe* up to a lawsuit."

I didn't care. I was too miffed about Lauren going out on a date with someone other than myself. But I supposed Patrice had a small point. I forced a smile. "Of course. I'm not accustomed to having people fail me. Forgive my manners. However, as much as it saddens me, I have to rescind my offer of patronage. If I were to forgive this incident, I believe it would set a precedent, which I feel would directly affect my family's interests. Good day, Ms. Winneham."

I started for the door, but Patrice was on my heel. "Forgive me, Mr. Donato, I had no idea how strongly you felt about Lauren. Give me another opportunity to rectify the situation."

"And how do you propose to do that?" I asked, mildly curious. "You've already claimed that you couldn't possibly put *Luxe* in a dangerous legal position, which I can understand, but I don't see what else can be done to repair our business relationship."

But Patrice had painted herself in a corner. There was little she could do to salvage my business. "We could feature you again," she suggested lamely, twisting her hands in desperation. Was I a bastard for putting the squeeze on the woman? Perhaps, but I'd already pictured the evening Lauren and I were going to have, and now it was ruined, which didn't put me in a forgiving frame of mind.

I exhaled with boredom. "I think once is plenty."

"Lauren is a very talented writer...maybe she could...write your memoirs!"

"I didn't realize *Luxe* was in the ghostwriting business," I said with derision.

"We're not," Patrice hastened to add, "but as a freelancer in a noncompeting venture... I'm sure *Luxe* would have no objections."

I opened my mouth to shoot holes into Patrice's offer but stopped short. Doing an autobiography would require hours of time spent together as she learned all about my life. I had zero interest in publishing a book, but if it meant having Lauren around on the pretense of doing the job, I was willing to play the part. But I knew Lauren would likely turn down the offer on principle alone, no matter how much I offered to pay for her services. "Your idea has merit," I admitted, though I would need to make some tweaks. The only way Lauren would take the job was if she were desperate. As if her very livelihood depended on it.

Which meant I'd have to play a little dirty.

Dirtier than usual.

"I want you to fire Lauren."

Patrice gasped, her eyes widening. "Excuse me?"

"Fire her."

"I can't do that!"

"Sure you can. Aren't you the executive editor? Or is there someone else I should speak with?"

"She's done nothing wrong, and she has a child, for Christ's sake."

I smiled. "That's not your problem, is it?"

Patrice's lip trembled as she pleaded, "Mr. Donato… please, let's talk about this."

"There's nothing to talk about. I want her fired."

"I can't fire her without cause."

"Of course you can. New York is an at-will state. You can fire her for wearing purple or chewing her food strangely. Honestly, you don't need a reason as long as the action isn't discriminatory. Blame it on budget cuts," I suggested, gesturing with a flippant motion. "But I want her done with *Luxe* by this afternoon. Are we clear?" I rose, straightening my cuffs with a bright smile to add, "Oh, and if you mention this conversation to anyone, I'll ruin you. Is that understood?"

Patrice blinked back tears but nodded. "Why are you doing this?"

I laughed. "Because I think I like her," I answered,

already moving on to plan B. "Oh, and please let Daphne down gently. I won't be needing her services."

I left Patrice's office, pleased with the sudden reversal of fortune. Sometimes you had to find the silver lining.

Patrice would fire Lauren and I would hire her, turning into her knight in shining armor when she needed one the most.

Take that, Mr. Engineer. I win.

CHAPTER ELEVEN

Lauren

"I'M F-FIRED?" I stammered, tears burning my eyeballs. "What do you mean? I don't understand…was there a problem with the article? I can make changes. Seriously, Patrice…what's going on?"

Patrice was distant as she answered, choosing to avoid eye contact. "It's not my call. Budget cuts. The directive came from above. I'm sorry. We can offer a small severance package and I would be happy to provide you with references, but I need you out of your desk by this afternoon."

Was I in a nightmare? My lips were dry and my throat parched. I might even need to puke. "Patrice… please. I need this job. I've been good to *Luxe*. I don't understand."

"It comes down to dollars and cents. Basic economics. You know that the world of publishing is going through hard times, and we've been asked to make cuts. Daphne makes less than you. Therefore, losing you is the better economic decision. I'm sorry."

Patrice looked as if she also wanted to vomit, but I was too devastated to feel sympathy. I gulped down the lump in my throat and focused on the financial side of the sordid business of getting canned for the greater good. "What is my severance?" I asked.

Patrice scribbled a number on a piece of paper and slid it over to me. I gasped, definitely about to throw up. "I can't even pay one month's rent with that, Patrice. This is New York, not Kansas. Come on, you know this is bullshit."

At that Patrice cut me a short look. "I advise that you move quickly. Security will be here soon to escort you from the building, and we don't want to make a scene."

This was really happening. Patrice wasn't backing down. A terrible thought came to me, and I had nothing to lose at this point so I voiced it. "Did Nico have anything to do with this?"

"Get over yourself, Lauren," she snapped. "Not everything is some kind of conspiracy theory. It's about the budget. I'm sorry."

Ashamed, I nodded and wiped at the tears leaking down my cheek. "I'll get my things."

Patrice nodded stiffly and returned to her computer, seemingly absorbed with important *Luxe* business while my world just fell apart.

I caught Daphne's stunned expression and I knew bad news traveled fast in a small office. I lifted my chin and ignored everyone as I quietly and efficiently packed my things in a small file box, my vision blurred through a sheen of tears.

What was I going to do?

The severance was a joke. What about health care? I needed to carry benefits for Grady. I couldn't take the chance that he might relapse and need to be in the hospital. The bills would bankrupt me without health insurance.

I left *Luxe* without looking back. I took the subway instead of hailing a cab because it was cheaper and I would need every dime just to make it to the end of the month.

If push came to shove, I could probably move back in with my mom, but I was loath to do that. The woman would drive me insane within a week.

But if I couldn't pay rent...

Okay, stop freaking out. You're talented, you will find another job. I just needed to brush up my résumé and start sending out the feelers. I used to freelance. Maybe I could email a few of my old clients and see if they needed any piecework.

Or maybe I could just crawl into bed, pull the covers over my head and stay there for the rest of my life.

But what about Grady? My little sunshine. My pride stung, but maybe it was time to hit Houston up for child support. Even a little bit would help. But what if he wanted joint custody in exchange for support? I know I'd sound like a bitch if I just said, "No, I don't want you to have anything to do with my son, but if you could cut a check once a month and stay the hell away, that would be great." But damn, I wish I had that option.

I really didn't want Houston around Grady, for any reason. I didn't want Grady to turn out anything like his father, and I felt sick thinking of Houston's influence on my son. Maybe people could change, but Houston obviously hadn't changed enough to reach out in all these years.

Nico popped into mind, but I rejected anything associated with Donato as quickly as it formed.

I would save myself. I didn't need anyone else to come along and play the hero.

It was easy enough to say the words, hard as hell to stop the fear from curdling my guts.

The clock was ticking against me. I didn't have the luxury of picking and choosing; I needed a replacement job now.

New York landlords weren't known for their sympathy. If I couldn't pay, I'd get tossed out. Kid or not.

I was still stunned by the events of the day. This morning I had a job; by afternoon, I didn't.

And Patrice had never once mentioned that budget cuts may be imminent. I mean, I know the executive editor wasn't going to discuss company financials, but no matter how hard the execs tried to keep a lid on those things, inevitably, information leaked.

But nothing, not a peep had trickled down. It was as if Patrice had just woken up that morning and decided to ruin my life because I chose not to go with Nico to that stupid dinner.

Right about now I wished I'd just girded my loins and suffered through the damn event. Maybe Patrice was right and it wouldn't have mattered, but my gut couldn't quite quit the suspicion that somehow, Nico was involved.

Maybe I was being suspicious and overly harsh, especially given that Nico had been a perfect gentleman, but there were too many pieces that simply didn't fit the puzzle.

I wiped at the sweat on my brow, my pitiful box of belongings between my feet on the subway. I caught a few knowing glances, but no one engaged or asked questions. Too many people knew the walk of shame when it came to losing their jobs.

Times were hard for everyone.

Except Donato.

Yeah, it was fucking roses for the trust-fund boy.

God, I was turning into a bitter bitch.

Better to focus on the real issue—getting a new job.

I couldn't spend energy on conspiracy theories (as Patrice called them) because I needed to rebound. *Fast*.

If push came to shove, I could waitress. I held a master's degree in journalism, but waiting tables might be where I ended up.

Money well spent. I should've gone into finance. Except I hated math, and being surrounded by numbers all day made me want to jump from a window.

So, that brought me back to waitressing. Or stripping.

Fuck me. I buried my head in my hands and ugly cried.

CHAPTER TWELVE

Nico

PATIENCE WAS A virtue I didn't have, but I managed to wait three days before putting my plan into action.

I knew Lauren was probably heading into the panic zone by now, which would make the conditions perfect for my offer. I felt a little guilty for causing that panic, but I'd be remedying it soon.

It was distressingly easy to find her address—even if I hadn't had every resource available to me, a crazed lunatic could've found her address without breaking a sweat. I walked up to the older brownstone.

The neighborhood was on the decline but at one time might've been quite adorable. The buildings were in need of repair, but lazy landlords with nothing but greed on their minds had taken a toll. I hated to see formerly grand architecture disintegrate, but there were more instances of this kind of urban decay than could be fixed by one family, even one as wealthy as mine.

I pushed the buzzer and waited.

"Hello?" Lauren sounded from the intercom. "Can I help you?"

"It's me, Nico. May I come in?"

A long pause followed before Lauren said, "I don't think that's a good idea."

I cut to the chase. "I know about your circumstances. I've come to offer you a job. Are you interested?"

"How do you know about my circumstances?" she asked, suspicion in her tone. I had to tread cautiously. Lauren was smart. I had one chance to make this work.

"Look, I'm not having this conversation on the street. If you've had better offers, then I'll go, but I thought you might be at least open to hearing me out."

There was a long enough pause that I thought perhaps she was ignoring me, but finally the buzzer sounded and the interior door popped open.

I barely kept the triumph from my expression as I entered the building.

The brownstone had been converted to a duplex, and Lauren's apartment was the downstairs unit. The place wasn't awful, but I didn't like the idea of Lauren and Grady living there alone. Evidence of poor management was everywhere. The weather stripping on the interior door was rotting, which meant during the winter, the cold air probably whistled through the open crack and it wouldn't take much to kick open the street-side door if someone were of a mind to gain entry.

Muted sounds of another family living in the upstairs unit filtered down, and I shifted against the discomfort of knowing that Lauren and Grady lived in such close quarters with strangers.

I was seized by the irrational urge to tell Lauren to pack her shit—she was moving—but I knew that idea was bound to blow up like the Fourth of July when I tired of her company.

Her door opened and my heart stuttered with uncharacteristic excitement. "Nico? What's this about?" she asked, her gaze wary. Her hair was pulled back in a loose braid that draped over her shoulder. She was wearing black yoga pants with an iconic rock T-shirt. And it was the sexiest thing I'd ever seen on a woman.

That ass… I bit back a tortured groan.

"May I come in, please?" I asked. Just then Grady popped his head around his mom's thigh and grinned broadly, prompting a smile on my part, too. "Hey there, little man. Have you been taking good care of your mama?"

"Of course. Except, we're probably gonna be 'victed soon 'cause Mama can't pay Mr. Tubbins."

Lauren's cheeks flared and she practically wilted with shame and embarrassment at her son's loose lips. She threw her hands up and walked away, gesturing for me to come in as she flopped onto the sofa with a defeated expression. My conscience pinched knowing I'd put her in this position, but once she accepted my offer, all would be well—better, in fact, because I would pay her far more than that magazine ever had.

So, in a way, I was a hero. Kinda like a secret Santa.

I closed the door and took a moment to survey her small apartment. No screens on the windows. Anyone could climb the fire escape and slip into her apartment during the hot, humid summer. The aged kitchen made my eyes bleed. The carpet, worn and mashed and probably crawling with bacteria... *Good God, this is like living in communist Russia.*

I gestured to the paperwork strewn everywhere with an arched brow. "Hurricane or art project?" I asked.

"I've been going through my portfolio, looking for the best articles to include in my job proposals. I submit electronically but I tend to think better when I have something in my hands, so I've always had paper copies of my work. But it seems no one is hiring right now. I've sent out countless résumés and offers for spec work, but I haven't had one nibble. Patrice promised me she'd give me a good reference but... I haven't had a single callback."

"I already know you're a good writer and I don't need references. I want to hire you."

"How do you know I'm a good writer?" she asked.

"Patrice let me read the copy you wrote for the feature. Very good," I lied smoothly. "Impressive. And she was the one who recommended you for the job. Seems she felt bad about having to let you go."

Lauren's surprise was colored by a touch of confusion, but she accepted my answer, immediately curious. "What do you want to hire me to do?" Before I could answer, she turned to Grady, saying, "Why don't you go watch TV in your room while I talk with Mr. Donato? We have some adult stuff to work out."

Grady rolled his eyes. "Like I don't know what adult stuff means. You can kiss him and I won't care, Mama. Like Uncle Ronnie says—"

"Grady! I'm not kissing Mr. Donato," Lauren cut

in with a nervous laugh before Grady could spill more "Uncle Ronnie" gems. "We just have business to discuss and it's going to be very boring."

Grady didn't buy it, but he had enough respect for his mother to stop arguing. He disappeared into his room, but he left the door open. The more I knew about this kid, the more I liked. I didn't even try to hide my grin. "He's pretty smart."

"Too smart sometimes," Lauren grumbled, shooting me a warning look. "What kind of job are you offering?"

Instead of answering right away, I gestured to the windows. "Does your landlord know that this is a safety hazard?"

"I rarely open them, and Grady knows to stay away when they are."

"Doesn't matter. It's a landlord's responsibility to ensure that all safety laws are being upheld on his property. The weather stripping is rotten and you have cockroaches." I'd seen one on the stairs as I passed. "My guess is that if the housing authority came to inspect this property, the list of violations would be epic."

"Did you come to criticize my home or offer me a job?" she asked with a subtle scowl.

The longer I stood in this place, the surer I was I didn't want Lauren and her son living there, but one problem at a time. "I was impressed with your professionalism," I said. "I know I didn't make it easy for you, and yet, you handled yourself well. A pet project that I've been sitting on for a while returned with a vengeance, and I knew I'd finally found the person I wanted to work with."

"What project?"

"My autobiography."

She barked a short laugh. "You haven't lived long enough to be interesting enough to warrant a book about your life."

I cut her a pointed look. "You have a funny way of putting your best foot forward for a job interview."

"Is that what this is?" she asked. "Because even if you were serious... I don't think I would take the job."

"And why is that?"

"Because in all fairness, I don't know that I'm the right person for the job. I'm a journalist, not a ghost-writer. I mean, you should go with someone with more experience. If I were a different sort of person I would take your money without thinking twice, even though I've never ghostwritten anything in my life, but I'm not that kind of person."

I wasn't going to budge. "I admire your talent and I want to hire you."

"I'm flattered but... I don't know...what if you end up hating what I write?"

"Then I'll fire you and hire someone else," I said with a shrug.

She barked a laugh. "It's that easy, huh? Just throwing money around?"

"Pretty much."

Her gaze narrowed. "Let's just say for a nanosecond that I was considering your offer...what would working for you entail and what would the compensation be?"

"I would offer a lump sum for your services."

"And those services would be…"

"Ghostwriting my autobiography."

"And that's it?"

I gave her a stern look. "I would require your full attention. It would likely entail odd hours and numerous revisions. If I'm going to do this, I want it done a particular way."

"And what is the point of this autobiography?" she asked, curious.

"So the world can know my journey."

"Does the world care?"

I laughed in spite of the insult. "I'd like to think so, but either way, as long as you're being paid, what does it matter?"

Lauren conceded my point, but she wasn't exactly sold. God, I loved how smart she was. "I don't know, Nico. I mean, I'm not entirely sure it's a good idea if we work together."

"Why not?"

A small nervous laugh escaped as she glanced at Grady's door and said, "Well, because…you know… we kissed."

"And?" I pretended ignorance. "I've kissed many people."

Her laughter faded and she glared, lowering her voice. "Yes, I'm sure you have, which is precisely why I don't want to join your roster."

"I can separate business from pleasure."

"You didn't before."

"That was *your* business, not mine," I said quietly.

"Now the shoe is on the other foot. I am hiring you for your brain, not your body."

Her cheeks flared with heat, and she crossed her arms across her chest, lifting her chin to say, "Good, because I'm more than just a body. I do have a brain. And I like to use it."

"That's what I just said."

She faltered in adorable silence. I enjoyed how I kept her out of balance. Lauren never knew what to think around me because I kept her guessing. Made the game so much more fun.

"You haven't mentioned my flat fee," Lauren said, ending the whispering and drawing the conversation back to finances. "I'd need to know if it's going to be worth my time."

I chuckled at the absurdity of her statement. "I think fifty thousand is a fair amount," I said, taking immense joy in the way her eyes widened and her jaw dropped. I pretended to think she was offended. "Was that a low-ball offer? I'm prepared to go to seventy-five, but that's my ceiling."

"Seventy-five thousand dollars? Are you insane?" She gasped, paling and sputtering. "Jesus, Nico. That's ridiculous! I could never accept that kind of money for such a small project."

"Ah, that's where you're wrong. It won't be small. I want you fully compensated so I'll feel justified in monopolizing your time. By the end of our agreement, you might feel seventy-five was a bargain."

She swallowed, still reeling. "Are you sure? Still... seems exorbitant."

I glanced around with open disdain. "If it means you could move out of this dump, it would be worth it," I returned to Lauren. "Did the magazine pay so little that this was your only option?"

"New York is expensive," Lauren said in her defense. "And I happen to like it here."

"I hate it," a little-boy voice floated from the recesses of the bedroom. Of course, the little imp had been listening. It's what I would've done, too. Grady appeared, crossing his arms across his chest in an identical gesture of his mother's, determined to be part of this negotiation. "One time I squished a bug when I got up to pee in the middle of the night. I'm scarred for life."

"That was pretty gross," Lauren admitted. "But struggle builds character."

"I have enough character," Grady retorted and I laughed. Grady brightened, saying, "Are you gonna be Mama's new boss? Can we go back to your place for more *sketti*? Do you know how to make lasagna?"

A kid after my own heart. "Are you kidding? Lasagna is my specialty. I'm even better at lasagna than I am at spaghetti."

Grady grinned, turning to Lauren with a plaintive expression. "Please say yes, Mama. I'm hungry."

"It's not fair to tag-team me," she muttered, shooting me a murderous glance that I found sexy as hell. I was close to victory; I could nearly taste the triumph. To Grady she said, "Sweetheart, while Mr. Donato's offer is certainly intriguing, I have to weigh the options."

But Grady, bless his blunt heart, seemed confused. "You said we are broke. Nico is saying he'll give you money to work for him. I don't understand…seems an easy decision to me."

"I agree, Grady." I bent to agree with the boy. "But it's ultimately up to your mom."

"M-ommmmmm," Grady whined, even stamping his foot a little. "You're being *obstenacious*."

"That's not a word," Lauren corrected him. "You're trying to say either obstinate or ostentatious, neither of which apply. Sorry, future wordsmith. Better luck next time."

"Actually I have to disagree with you," I told Lauren. "I definitely feel you're being obstinate. What good reason do you have to turn down my offer aside from your pride? Seems kinda immature when the stakes are so high."

"I have to do what's best for me and Grady," Lauren started, but I wasn't going to let her wiggle out of this one.

"And providing for yourself and your son seems a solid decision, while turning your nose up at a lucrative offer out of some misplaced pride is just shortsighted, wouldn't you agree?"

She laughed. "I see what you're doing. On the surface, you're using logic to prove your point, but you and I both know that there's more to your offer, and it's an insult to pretend otherwise."

The subtle twinkle in her eye gave her away; she was enjoying the game.

I smiled, slow and sure. "The ball is in your court. Do you want the job or not?"

A pregnant pause stretched between us as Lauren

considered my offer. "Fine," she finally said, but before I could crow, she tacked on, "but there's going to be nothing but professional behavior between us, got it?"

"Of course," I agreed with a solicitous nod that reeked of total bullshit and she knew it, but this was half the fun, this subtle undercurrent of tension that coursed between us. I couldn't wait to put her in my bed. I rubbed my hands together, pleased with my victory and practically clicking my heels together. "Pack your bags. You and Grady are leaving this dump. Until we can find you more suitable housing, you and the boy can stay with me."

"Yay!" Grady jumped up and down, shaking his little butt in a makeshift boogie with such spirit, his glasses nearly bounced from his nose.

"Whoa!" Lauren rushed to put the kibosh on Grady's celebration. She looked to me as if I'd just suggested we go jump from an airplane without parachutes. "Are you insane? We can't just move in with you."

"Okay, I get it. It's unorthodox but I'm about to drop a significant investment in your services. I don't trust that this place is safe. If something happens to you, I'm out a lot of money. Think of it this way… I'm ensuring the job gets done."

"Yeah, Mama, it's just *ecobomics*," Grady added helpfully, and I wanted to high-five him.

Lauren bit back a grin at her son's attempt but said, "I don't live in the ghetto, and you're being a snob. This place is very cute, and I like it."

I tried not to roll my eyes and instead turned to Grady. "How about lasagna tonight?" Grady nodded vigorously. "Then we better find a way to convince your mama to stop wasting time and get to packing."

"I'm going with Nico!" Grady shouted, burning out of the living room to his bedroom to pack.

I smiled at Lauren. "I think working together is going to be loads of fun. Don't you?"

"I think you might be the devil." But her smile said the opposite.

"I might be," I agreed, then gestured before checking my watch. "Go pack. The car will be here shortly, and if I'm going to start the pasta, I need to get going quickly."

She shook her head, snickering. I could tell she thought I was biting off more than I could chew. Maybe I was—I'd never lived with a single mom and her kid, but I was eager to give it a shot. Seriously, I hadn't looked forward to anything this much since…hell, I couldn't even remember.

Lauren walked backward slowly, pinning me with her gaze, saying, "You're going to regret this," but I got the impression that was the part she was looking forward to, and that turned me on like you wouldn't believe.

I fully planned to have Lauren eating out of my hand, sucking my cock and falling in love with me before she even realized how it'd happened.

God, I love the game!

CHAPTER THIRTEEN

Lauren

THE HUM IN my body corresponded with the ridiculous curve of my lips that I couldn't ignore as I packed.

Was this really happening?

I grinned as I bypassed my everyday, functional underwear and deliberately grabbed my pretty, rarely worn and uncomfortable panties that I always avoided in favor of comfort.

Yep, I thought as I stuffed the panties into my suitcase, this was totally happening.

Okay, so time to get real. Nico was hot. Nico wanted to have sex with me. Forget all that bullshit he tried to feed me about this "being business." I could see in his eyes that he wanted me.

Felt good to be wanted.

The thing about single motherhood, sometimes you forgot that you were sexy at one time.

But when Nico looked at me—I remembered.

A shiver danced down my skin.

And I missed that feeling.

So yeah, I was packing my suitcase to go work for Nico. I could pretend to hold the line and say I wasn't going to sleep with him because I had more integrity than that, but let's get real, I was only human—and I missed sex.

And I'm not talking about *good* sex, I meant sex, period. At this point, I might settle for a quick grope and poke, but I knew in my gut that Nico would make a night out of whatever sexual circus he had planned in his head.

My toes curled at the thought.

The other part of this equation was the reality I didn't have time to wait out this hiring freeze. Publishing was in a total state of ever-tightening budgets, and it was going to take more time than I had to find a new job.

And fifty thousand dollars—I still couldn't quite believe that offer was real—would allow me to find a quality job rather than a hurried one.

But I would make it clear that Grady wasn't part of the negotiation. I didn't need Nico messing with his head. As far as Grady was concerned, Mama was just doing a job and that's all he needed to know—even though Grady had been suspiciously happy to toss me into Nico's lap. I would've thought Grady might be more resistant to the idea of another man coming into my life.

Go figure.

Finished, I went to Grady's room to find him sitting on his overstuffed suitcase in order to zip it.

"What did you pack?" I asked, laughing. "Let me take a look." My eyes widened as I saw the contents of every drawer and an assortment of toys jammed in the suitcase. I looked at Grady, shaking my head. "Honey, we're not staying forever. I don't think you need all of this."

"Nico said to pack everything that mattered to me," Grady said, lifting his chin. "He also said we're not coming back to this dump."

Of course Nico said that to my impressionable son. First order of business…set Nico straight on the boundaries. However, I needed to get Grady to understand, too. "There's nothing wrong with our little apartment. We've made a lot of great memories here," I said, pulling things to prioritize spring clothing so the suitcase could close. "Think of this as a vacation. It's nice to visit someplace fun and different, but all things—even fun things—come to an end and then we return home."

Nico appeared in the doorjamb and said, "Don't worry, little man. I'll work on your mom. In the meantime, let's shake a leg. This place gives me hives."

"It would do you some good to live like a normal person," I said to Nico, thrusting Grady's luggage at him. "Make yourself useful and carry this, please."

Nico grunted at the impact but chuckled at my ire. "So sassy," he murmured, amused. He grasped Grady's hand and said, "The car is here. Let's get you loaded in while your mama finishes up her own packing."

Protests died on my lips when I saw how Grady gripped Nico's hand with total trust, as if they weren't practically strangers. How did Nico have this hold on my kid? I was baffled at how easily the man had Grady twisted around his finger. It also worried me. I wasn't going to let my son fall in love with Nico only to have

Nico disappear when it no longer amused him to play house.

Sex was one thing; messing with my kid's head was another thing entirely.

A few moments later Nico returned just as I was locking the apartment. He relieved me of my luggage, his smile bright and engaging, but I stopped him with a warning. "Don't you dare break my son's heart, do you hear me?" I said, my tone low. "He's just a little boy. He won't understand when you lose interest and ditch him. Whatever this arrangement means in your head, just know that Grady is off-limits."

"You worry too much. I'd never hurt a kid."

Even if he believed that, I didn't think he understood how his actions could affect a vulnerable six-year-old. "For whatever reasons, Grady seems to like you. Don't make me regret taking this deal. If you break my son's heart, no amount of money will make his pain worth it."

"Down, Mama Bear," he said, that dimple popping as he grinned. "C'mon, the car is waiting."

The Donato name on my résumé could put me in front of the right people. He had a spacious two-bedroom apartment (it was bigger than some houses in the city) and it was, admittedly, in a nicer stretch of the city than my own apartment.

I was going to treat this unorthodox situation as a working vacation with superfancy amenities—and possibly fringe benefits.

"This is going to be fun," Nico said, handing the luggage to the driver. "I've never had roommates before."

I resisted the urge to roll my eyes. "Famous last

words," I retorted as I stepped inside the car to join Grady.

Nico joined us seconds later. From the outside looking in, we appeared a family. I tried not to give the pinch that followed much thought. I'd long given up the idea that I might find someone to fill in the role of daddy and husband. I prided myself on being self-sufficient, and to this point, I had been.

But I wasn't going to lie...a part of me wished life had dealt me a different hand. I hadn't realized what a douche nozzle Houston was until it'd been too late.

I wouldn't make the same mistake twice.

And, to date, I hadn't.

But then, I hadn't actually *dated* either. The idea of allowing someone into my life for anything more than superficial gave me anxiety. Breakups were messy, and I couldn't take the chance that Grady might get hurt in the crossfire.

The easiest solution was to avoid dating.

Which meant no sex.

No companionship.

No one to snuggle with and watch corny television shows.

At this point, I feared my vagina might have cobwebs.

And to add a little more anxiety to the mix, I recently read an article that said without regular sex, a woman's vaginal walls atrophied! I might have an old-lady vag by now!

I searched but the article didn't state how quickly

this process happened. Hopefully, the process hadn't already begun for me.

I snuck a quick look Nico's way, my breath catching. Damn, the man was hot. I'm talking hotter than a New York sidewalk in July. Throwing pride and whatnot aside, I couldn't imagine a better candidate for the job of reintroducing me to orgasms without the aid of a vibrator than Nico Donato.

The question was…should I make the first move or wait and see what Nico put into play first?

Maybe I'd have to play it by ear.

CHAPTER FOURTEEN

Nico

I COULDN'T BELIEVE my good fortune. I truly didn't believe that Lauren would cave so easily. I thought for sure I was going to have to add a little more spice to the pot, but Lauren was a terrible negotiator and I'd gotten off easy.

Fifty thousand was chump change. I could spend that in a weekend with the right motivation.

It felt good to spend it on Lauren knowing that she needed it so desperately. I'd never played the hero before, and it was almost addictive.

Generally speaking, I steered clear of women in financial straits because, well, they became needy and clingy within a heartbeat, and that irritated the fuck out of me.

But Lauren didn't act like a desperate woman. She acted like a boss with her own agenda, and that fired me up. We were two predators circling each other, looking for the weak spot. Except she had a banging body and when I was around her, I sprang boners at the most in-opportune moments.

Which only made our exchanges even more enter-taining.

Ha! I know, crazy.

"Mama made me put back some of my toys," Grady said, looking to me.

"No worries. I can replace whatever you left behind," I assured him, already planning in my head an epic shopping spree at whatever toy store the kid wanted.

"That's not necessary," Lauren said, shooting down my offer. "He doesn't need any new toys. He brought plenty. Trust me, you'll thank me the first time you see his toys strewn about like a hurricane has come through your apartment. Or the first time you step on a Lego with bare feet."

"I have a maid. I doubt it'll bother me."

"You have a maid?" Grady said, impressed. "That's so cool! Does she clean whatever you tell her to?"

"Grady," Lauren admonished, but I enjoyed the boy's enthusiasm. Still, Lauren was quick to say, "I'm sure Mr. Donato cleans up after himself. Just because he has a housekeeper doesn't mean he's a slob."

Her pointed look punctuated her statement, and I actually felt a twinge of embarrassment. I couldn't say that I gave the housekeeper much thought beyond that she came each day to clean up after me.

"Stop calling me Mr. Donato," I said. "I told you it makes me feel like an old man. Besides, now that we're going to live together—"

"This is temporary," she cut in with a firm reminder

above Grady's head for emphasis. "*Temporary*. Like a working vacation for us."

"Of course," I conceded but added, "but until you guys go home, I would appreciate it if you'd stop calling me Mr. Donato. Gives me diarrhea." I faked a shudder. "And makes me feel old."

"Fair enough," Lauren said, surprising me with her agreement. "While we're staying with you…we'll call you Nico."

Grady was watching us go back and forth, his eyes bright. I wondered what was going through his head, though. It also made me wonder why his father wasn't around. Lauren had deemed that information off-limits, but I wanted to solve the mystery. Why wasn't the father part of Grady's life? Was he a deadbeat dad? A criminal? I wasn't exactly of the opinion that boys needed their fathers, if those fathers were assholes. Lauren had done a pretty good job with the boy to this point, so I wasn't about to spout off something ridiculous.

Not to mention, I doubted saying something like that would make points.

And seeing as all this elaborate scheming had one goal—getting Lauren into bed—I wasn't going to waste time on things that created obstacles.

"I'd like to draw up a contract to detail my responsibilities and your expectations as well as the monetary compensation," Lauren said.

I nodded. "Of course. I can have the appropriate contract drawn up by tomorrow."

"Once we've both signed, we can start," she said with

the sharp air of a proper professional. "I would also like to use this project on my résumé."

I shrugged. "Fine." But I didn't want to talk business so quickly. I wanted to get back to the part where Lauren's tongue danced with mine. I was impatient to put circumstances into play, but I had to tread carefully or everything would fall apart, leaving me with an awful case of blue balls—again. I turned to Grady. "Are you in school?"

"Yes, kindergarten," he answered proudly. "I know all my numbers and letters already and I can write my name."

"Excellent. Very important set of skills," I said, earning a small smile from Lauren. "And which school do you attend?"

"Langston Primary."

"Public school," I surmised, looking to Lauren. She answered with a nod. "Is it a good school?"

"It is," Lauren answered, casting me a warning look. I supposed I should back off. I couldn't very well agree to finance Grady's future education when I might lose interest in both of them within a month. Still, I didn't know anything about this Langston Primary, and a child as bright as Grady should have the best. But I had to shelve that thought for now because the car had arrived at my apartment.

I grabbed both suitcases from the trunk while Grady skipped ahead to the doorman. I'd already informed Jepperson that I would be having guests for the next month, so the man was appropriately friendly to the little boy.

"He's nice," Grady said. "He gave me a sucker."

Lauren gasped and relieved Grady of his candy. "You know better than to accept candy from a stranger, Grady!" she said, tossing the candy in the trash can by the elevator. "Honestly, the rules haven't changed just because we're staying somewhere fancier than our place." To me, she said, "Please let your doorman know that he's not to give my son candy."

"He was just being friendly," I said, defending Jepperson. "He's been my doorman for years. I doubt he'd do anything so stupid as to dose my guests."

"When you have kids, you'll understand."

I doubted I'd ever have children so her point was lost on me, but I agreed nonetheless. "I'll let Jepperson know."

"Thank you."

To Grady, I winked privately, earning a grin. My heart gladdened to see the scowl lift from Grady's mug. I was already getting attached to the kid, which probably wasn't a good thing, but I'd worry about the consequences later.

We entered my apartment and I was irritated to see my brother lounging on the sofa, flipping through channels as if he owned the place.

Okay, technically, the apartment was owned by the family trust, but it was still my apartment and I regretted letting him have a key.

"What are you doing here, Dante?" I asked.

But Dante was more interested in my guests, tossing the remote to stare at Lauren and Grady as they stood nearly frozen at the sight of my glowering older brother. "I didn't realize you were having a sleepover," he drawled.

"Well, you didn't ask." To Lauren, I said, "Go ahead and get settled while I talk with my brother."

Lauren hustled Grady into the spare bedroom and closed the door.

Turning to Dante, I didn't hide my irritation. "What the actual fuck are you doing here?"

"I could ask you the same thing."

"I live here."

He gestured toward the spare bedroom, where Lauren and Grady had disappeared. "I'm talking about your guests. Something smells off, even for you, little brother. Whatever you're doing, it better not look bad for the family."

"It has nothing to do with the family and it's none of your business. I'm just helping out a friend."

"A friend? Who is she?" Dante asked.

"What does it matter?"

"Because I don't trust that you're not up to something, and whenever you mess around, it always seems to find its way back home. I won't have you upsetting Mamma with your bullshit. She hasn't been feeling very well."

"What's wrong with Mamma?"

"Nothing serious but Luca's wedding took a lot out of her, and she can't seem to find her energy again."

I was closest to our mother. It bothered me that I hadn't noticed, but then Mamma had a tendency to pretend all was well, even when it wasn't. I think it was a survival method having been married to my father since she was a teen. To say my father was a difficult man was an understatement.

"I'll go see her tomorrow," I said. "Is that what you came to tell me or did you come to lounge on my sofa and eat all my food?"

"No, I was in the neighborhood and I came to confirm that you'll be representing Donato Inc. at the Griffin dinner. You haven't RSVP'd yet and the event is around the corner."

"I'm going," I said, but I didn't want Lauren hearing about the dinner before I could convince her to be my date. "Stop being such a micromanaging asshole. I said I'd go, so I'm going. You don't need to babysit me."

"Stop acting like a child and I'll stop feeling the need to babysit."

Dante always treated me like a kid. It didn't matter that I was a man. All Dante saw was the little brother.

It was annoying as fuck.

"Now, what's the story with your friend?" Dante probed, and I wanted to kick his ass out. "I've never known you to befriend women with kids."

"There's a first time for everything," I quipped, moving to the kitchen, hoping he'd get the hint and leave. "If that's all you needed… I have pasta to make."

"Pasta? What are you making?"

The door opened and Grady burst from the room with Lauren chasing after him. Clearly, he'd had enough of being cloistered, not that I blamed him. "Who are you?" Grady asked without a hint of bashfulness.

Dante drew himself up to tower over the kid, but Grady didn't budge. Lauren nervously thrust her hand toward Dante, introducing herself. "I'm Lauren Hughes. This is my son, Grady. We're guests of your brother's while I write his autobiography."

At that Dante shot me an incredulous look. "Autobiography? What fucking bullshit is this?"

"You said bad words. You're going to need to put two dollars in the swear jar," Grady said with the seriousness of an IRS agent come to perform an audit.

I barked a laugh at Dante's startled expression as I shrugged. "The kid is right. You better watch your mouth or you're going to fund Grady's college tuition."

"Sorry, kid, I'm not accustomed to my brother having anyone under eighteen in his apartment," he said. "But my question stands. Why the hell are you doing an autobiography? You haven't done anything of interest or value in your whole life, unless partying and wasting money are a skill set worth talking about."

"It works for anyone currently in reality television," I answered, my hackles rising. Just because I hadn't been groomed for the family business didn't mean that I was without any skill or talent. It was the same fucking argument with Dante, and it drove me nuts. I purposefully stuffed a preemptive five-dollar bill in a glass and said, "If you're through being an asshole, would you mind getting the hell out? I have plans, and they don't include sparring with you over bullshit family crap."

The tension in the room was uncomfortable. Lauren looked ready to pack Grady up and bail, but she didn't. Dante shot me a look that promised a conversation at a later date but grabbed his keys and headed for the door until Grady stopped him.

"You still owe the swear jar, Mister."

Dante shook his head and looked to me, saying, "Nico can cover my bill. It's about time he paid for someone else's problems instead of the other way around."

And then he slammed out of the apartment.

I met Lauren's questioning gaze, and I was embarrassed that she'd seen Dante tear me down. Lauren had inadvertently poked at a tender nerve the other night when she'd told Grady that I didn't do anything. Dante seemed to go out of his way to make sure I always knew that I was extraneous—useless.

And it never failed to hurt no matter how many times I told myself I loved not having to shoulder any responsibility for the Donato legacy.

Yep. I loved my freedom.

Dante could go fuck himself.

CHAPTER FIFTEEN

Lauren

I WANTED TO ask Nico about his brother, but I could tell from his expression he wasn't in the mood to share— and frankly, it wasn't my business. Whatever struggles created friction in Nico's family were beyond my pay grade, and I didn't want to get involved.

Even though Dante Donato was intimidating, I bristled for Nico.

But what good would come of admitting that I thought Nico's brother was a total ass? Family was still family. At times I thought my sister, Claire, was the spawn of Satan, but I'd fight anyone to the death if they said anything crappy about her. I imagined the same rules applied for Nico. So, it was best to keep quiet.

Dinner, just as before, was fantastic—eating pasta every night was going to destroy my waistline, but it was so hard to turn down good food made by someone else. And Grady, as picky as he was, gobbled up whatever Nico put in front of him. I didn't know if Grady was trying to impress Nico or if he truly just loved the man's cooking, but either way, I was discomfited. I was trying to get out of this situation without permanently damaging my kid, but so far, I wasn't sure if I was succeeding.

Except Grady seemed fine. I'd never seen him clean a plate so quickly—and ask for seconds.

But soon enough it was time to put Grady to bed. After a quick bath and story time, I tucked Grady into the bed and kissed his sweet forehead. Although he was yawning and ready to sleep, I took the opportunity to reiterate how temporary this arrangement was, just to be on the safe side. "Sweetie, I know you love Nico's cooking and Nico has a very nice apartment, but we can't stay forever. He has a life and we have our own life that we will get back to after my job is finished."

"I know, Mama," he said, cracking a yawn. "But I like Nico. He's funny and I like the way he looks at you when you're not looking. It's all warm and fuzzy-like. Kinda how Auntie Claire looks at pumpkin pie with whipped cream at Thanksgiving."

I smothered a laugh. "Auntie Claire does love her pumpkin pie, doesn't she?" Grady nodded, tucking his hand under his chin. I smoothed the hair from his eyes. "But as pumpkin-pie awesome as Nico may seem… I don't want you to get your hopes up for nothing."

"Okay, Mama," Grady said, his eyes fluttering shut. "Night. Nico says tomorrow we're going sailing and I need my rest."

Sailing? What the hell? I pressed another kiss to my son's head and closed the door behind me.

I found Nico on the sofa, a glass of wine in hand and

a glass waiting for me on the coffee table. "What's this about sailing?" I asked with a frown. "Grady said you told him we were going sailing tomorrow."

"I did."

"He has school."

"What's one day of missed kindergarten?" he said, waving away my objections. "Come, sit. Try the wine. It's from a boutique winery my family owns, and it's quite good."

I bristled a little that Nico hadn't asked me first, but there was no way Grady was skipping school. I'd make that clear in the morning, but for now, I accepted the wine. "You have to be careful around Grady. I don't want him hurt."

"I understand."

He was being truthful, even if he didn't realize how easily a kid's heart could get trampled. I sipped my wine, nodding with approval. "It's good," I murmured.

Nico surprised me by asking, "You haven't dated since Grady was born?"

I bit my lip, embarrassed to admit, "No."

"And by that I assume, that means…"

My cheeks heated. "You assume correctly. I haven't had sex in six years."

"Good God, woman, that can't be healthy," Nico said, only half joking.

"According to an article I read in *Women's Health*, it's not. Apparently, vaginal atrophy is a thing I need to start worrying about, on top of everything else that sits on my shoulders."

"To be honest, if I were a woman, that would scare

the hell out of me. I mean, vaginal atrophy, that sounds awful."

"Yes," I agreed, still embarrassed but somehow finding the humor, "it is awful and sad."

"Let me get this straight…you don't get laid because…you think it will affect Grady somehow?"

"It sounds weird when you put it that way. What I mean is, *personally*, I don't like one-night stands, so in order to have sex, I have to have feelings for the guy, and you can't develop feelings unless you spend time together. Babysitters cost money and I'm a single mom on a budget, so that means, by way of simple process of elimination, I don't get sex."

"That's the saddest story I've ever heard."

I barked a short laugh. "Yeah? You should see my checkbook. That story will make you weep." I amended my statement with, "I mean, before I accepted your offer."

"Let me make you an entirely separate proposal, no money involved," he said, surprising me. When I frowned in confusion, he said, "Look, I truly like you. Your kid is fantastic, and I don't say that about most kids. I understand your reasons for staying away from random hookups—in this day and age, it's probably not a good idea for a single mom anyway—but at this rate you're going to be a spinster by the time you get some action, and that just kills me."

"Oh, does it?" I said wryly, sipping my wine. "Please continue."

"You're a vibrant and fucking sexy-as-hell woman. No need to mince words. I'm just throwing it out there.

It's a tragedy to let the prime years of your life slip away because you're too afraid to grab on to some pleasure for yourself. You're a great mom—I can see that plain as day—but you were a woman before you became a mom, right?"

"Well, yeah," I said, shaking my head. "But I was a lot of things before I became a mom. Not everything can be reclaimed from your youth."

"Your sex life can be," he returned simply. "Hear me out…we're not trying to catch feelings, that's when things go sidewise and kids get hurt. Whether we're fucking or not… I still want to be your friend. I mean, like I said, you're a pretty cool person and I want to get to know you better. And not just in the bedroom."

I tried not to smile above the rim of my glass. *And it starts…* "Don't you think that might compromise our working relationship?" I asked. "What if we aren't compatible in the bedroom? We'd have to still work together long enough to finish the job I was hired to do."

He waved away my concern with annoyance. "Forget about the money. I'll have it wired to your account tomorrow, and whether things go sour or the job falls apart, you'll still get paid. You can rest easy on that part."

I gulped the final swallow of wine, silently amazed at how flippantly he threw hundred-dollar bills around like confetti on New Year's Eve. "You're saying you'd pay me before the work was done?"

He shrugged. "I trust you."

I released a shaky breath. "But why? You barely know me."

"I have a good sense about people."

"Yeah? And what do you sense about me?"

He gently took my empty wineglass and set it next to his before coming closer to peer into my eyes. "You really want to know what I thought when I first saw you?"

"Aside from my ugly dress," I reminded him, trying to hold on to some kind of levity to prevent any actual sincerity on his part to touch me.

Nico smiled, but his gaze was burning into mine. "I saw a woman I knew I had no business thinking about in any sort of way."

"And why is that?" I asked, barely able to manage the words with Nico's lips so close to mine.

"Because you were a woman too good for someone like me," he admitted before closing over my mouth, stopping whatever protests may have arisen, the tease of his tongue reminding me how much I'd missed being in the arms of a man, how desperate I was for physical contact of an adult sort.

And Nico was a master with that mouth of his. I had no excuse. I knew I was playing with fire, but somehow the burn felt so good. The warmth of his masculine scent filled my senses, intoxicating me in the most addictive way.

He slowly pulled me closer and I went willingly, the press of his hands against my back a welcome pressure. I missed the confidence of a good lover, the feel of a man's hands firmly guiding me.

Nico instinctively knew when to push and when to let me lead, creating a dance that built an ever-increasing tempo.

"You're the most incredible woman I've ever met," Nico admitted, his voice a soft caress against my nerves. "I've been all around the world and never had the privilege of having someone like you in my arms."

How could I not melt? But if we were going to do this, I needed boundaries of some sort. "You have to promise to be discreet for Grady's sake," I said, breathless. "Promise?"

"Baby, I'll promise you the fucking moon, if that's what you want," Nico growled, his eyes burning with the same hunger as his arms tightened around me.

"I don't want the moon…just your promise that we'll keep this on the DL. I can't have Grady hurt."

"Deal," he said, sealing his mouth to mine with an urgency that I mirrored.

Holy fuck. This is really happening.

He led me to his bedroom. And once the door was closed, I couldn't get my clothes off fast enough.

For the record, I'm not sure who seduced whom first.

Maybe it was a draw.

CHAPTER SIXTEEN

Nico

I KNEW I should've been crowing with victory, but somehow Lauren's sudden change of heart made things ten times more real—the stakes so much higher.

My hands trembled as I unhooked her bra, my nerves drawn tighter than a virgin's on prom night.

I wanted everything to be perfect. I wanted to leave her breathless and moaning and wondering how the hell she'd ever survived without my cock inside her.

The pressure to perform was creating all sorts of havoc on my Johnson.

I sucked in a wild breath as her breasts came into view. "Perfection," I murmured, the word slipping from my mouth without thought.

Lauren blushed, vulnerable, and I knew she felt self-conscious about the faint, silvery lines caused by her pregnancy, but all I saw was beauty. My throat closed as I reached for her, pulling her close. I wanted to taste every inch of her body, to show her with my touch that I thought she was the sexiest female I'd ever laid eyes on, but my hands were shaking like an addict needing a fix and I was the one embarrassed.

"Have you changed your mind?" Lauren asked, anxious.

"God no," I answered, adding, "I'm fucking nervous as hell, though."

"You? Nervous?" Lauren repeated, confused. "Why?"

I couldn't give her a coherent answer without screwing up the moment. To admit that I was scared of underwhelming her, knowing I'd have one shot to make it right, was messing with my mojo. Instead, I scooped her into my arms, shocking her with the sudden motion. She instinctively wrapped her arms around my neck. "Less talk, more action," I said with a grin. When in doubt, let muscle memory take over.

I laid her on the bed and immediately climbed her body, her taut, dusky nipples begging for my mouth. An urgent need to know her taste, her unique flavor, egged me on, and I obliged my desire without hesitation.

She gasped as my mouth closed over her tightened bud. Lauren arched as I suckled, my hand sliding down her trembling belly to find her neatly groomed pussy. God, I wanted to bury my face between those dewed lips. I was like a kid in a candy store, eager to taste everything I could stuff in my mouth.

I slid my finger between her folds, gently probing to find her G-spot with my middle finger. I listened to her subtle cues to zero in on the exact spot that made her shake and quiver, then I slid down to that sweet pussy and dived in.

Spreading her long legs, I lost myself between her slit, seeking and destroying her swollen clit, sucking and teasing until she was gasping and biting her lip to keep from crying out. Somehow, knowing she couldn't let loose because of Grady sleeping in the other room made the entire situation hotter. I wanted her to lose control, to thrash as if a demon were being unleashed inside her. I slowed, only to start again, pushing her harder, deeper into that pleasure abyss of total meltdown. Her thighs quivered as the rapid rise and fall of her chest gave away her nearing release. I pushed her harder, needing to feel her come beneath my tongue, needing to hear those unbridled cries as she crashed.

And God, I wasn't disappointed.

Lauren came with the sweetest cry as she gushed against my mouth. I lapped at her, enjoying every drop, relieved that I could make her come that hard.

"Nico," she whispered when she could speak, her voice raspy as her head lolled on the pillow. "Holy fuck…"

I grinned, rising to seal my mouth to hers again, wanting her to taste herself on my lips. Some women shied away from their own scent but not Lauren. The beautiful heathen kissed me hard, our tongues twinning against one another like drunken snakes in a ritual dance of courtship. My cock hardened to the point of stone; any harder and the skin would've split.

I couldn't wait any longer. I made quick work of sheathing my cock in a condom and then breached her slick folds, splitting her apart with a guttural moan of pure pleasure.

Liquid heat closed around my shaft, and I lost the ability to think for a moment, so lost in the incredible sensation of being inside Lauren.

It was as if she were made for me. I'd fucked a lot of women, but they all faded from memory as soon as I was skin to skin with her.

I was too lost to realize how worrisome that should've been.

All that mattered was this moment.

I lifted her legs onto my shoulders and drove deep, grinding against her G-spot with unerring accuracy. I wanted to hear her come again and again. I didn't think there would ever be a time when I tired of that sound. Her lovely legs, strong and sleek, were up around my ears as I bent her in half, drilling her with my entire length, fucking her so deep that my balls slapped against that plump ass. *Jesus, has sex ever been this good with anyone else?* I didn't have the mental brainpower to do more than focus on building the heat between us. I needed her release so I could claim my own, but I was already losing the battle. My ability to control the need to come was becoming shaky at best.

"L-Lauren," I choked out, my balls tightening as everything began to clench in preparation for launch. "Holy fuck… I can't stop…"

But Lauren was right there with me. Stiffening, she cried out, almost sobbing as she came again, and I groaned as I came harder than ever before, jetting over and over until I was left with absolutely nothing in my body. Everything pulsed wildly as pleasure blotted out rational thought and I floated in a pool of total bliss.

Somehow I had the wherewithal to roll away and toss the used condom into the bedside trash before collapsing beside her, my breath harsh, my heart thundering.

We remained side by side, struggling to catch our breath. I didn't want to talk. Talking would only shed light on something that I didn't want to see clearly. I wanted to curl my arms around her, drawing her against my front, and fall asleep.

Holy Jesus, I wanted to…*cuddle*?

But Lauren did us both a solid and climbed from the bed, scooping up her discarded clothing with a gleefully whispered "Thank you, I needed that," before slipping from my bedroom, leaving me alone.

Which should've been ideal.

How many times had I wished the women I'd brought home would take themselves away so I didn't have to lie there, uncomfortable and wishing I had the entire bed to myself?

Lauren had done that. *Wham, bam, thank you, dude*, and she was gone.

I drew the blankets up around me, feeling ridiculously vulnerable. I wanted to march into the spare bedroom, scoop her up and return her to my bed.

Which, of course, would blow out of the water our agreement to keep things discreet and on the DL.

I wasn't accustomed to taking the needs and wishes of other people into account.

Couldn't say I liked it either.

For Grady's sake, I would adhere to Lauren's wishes.

Getting her into bed had been the deceptively easy part, I realized. Hiding the fact that I wanted to keep her there was going to be the hardest thing I'd ever done.

CHAPTER SEVENTEEN

Lauren

"MAMA, YOU'RE HUMMING," Grady remarked as I rummaged around the kitchen, looking for something to make for breakfast. I whirled around, a guilty smile forming as I tried to tamp it down. "I bet you had a good sleep. Nico's bed is really comfy."

"Yes, it was very nice," I agreed, unable to keep the blush from heating my cheeks. Thank God, Grady was too young to catch those subtle cues, but I needed to cool it with the humming. Every muscle in my body was deliciously sore, reminding me of the workout Nico had given me, and I couldn't stop smiling. I'd managed a quick shower before Grady woke up, needing the private time to put my head on straight, but I was still turned around and twisted up inside in the most wonderful way.

As if hearing my internal dialogue, Nico appeared, adorably rumpled from sleep and sexy as ever. *Did the man ever have an off day?* Didn't seem fair to the rest of the mere mortals in the world.

To Nico, I said, "Good morning," and returned to seeking out cereal or something, but in truth, I was trying not to appear as if anything had changed between us.

But something had changed.

I couldn't deny it. My body was in tune with his in a way that I'd never imagined possible.

Don't get me wrong, I'd enjoyed good sex before, but what'd happened between Nico and I had been beyond good—it'd been...life-altering.

So, pretending it hadn't happened...well, that was easier said than done, but I had to find a way because I wasn't about to let Grady think that Nico was going to be a permanent part of our life.

He squinted against the morning sunlight and rasped, "Are you looking for anything in particular?"

"Breakfast cereal?"

"I don't eat cereal."

"That would explain why I can't find any. No worries, I'll just make toast with peanut butter for Grady, then."

"Do you like that?" Nico asked Grady before reaching for the coffeepot to start brewing.

"It's okay," Grady admitted. "I like pancakes better."

Nico looked to me with a grin. "Then he should have pancakes."

I graced Nico with an indulgent look but said, "We don't have time to make pancakes. Grady has school this morning."

Grady immediately started protesting, "But Nico said we were going sailing today!"

"Well, Nico probably didn't realize that you had school. You can go sailing another time," I said, but I hated the crestfallen expression on my little son's face. How could spending the morning learning the ABCs possibly compare with the open ocean, especially given Grady was already way ahead of his classmates and was most times bored in class. But I had to adhere to structure, so I held the course. "Come on, let's get dressed while your bread is toasting. We have to leave a little earlier to make it on time."

Apparently, Nico was also destroyed by Grady's sad expression and said, "How about a compromise? We sail after school? We can still get in a few hours of quality time on the ocean in the afternoon."

Grady brightened with hope. "Really?"

"Of course. To be honest, I'm usually never awake this early so I often sail in the afternoon."

"Do you have your own sailboat?" Grady asked, his eyes shining.

"I do and it's been too long since I've taken her out. She deserves a little time away from the dock. So here's the deal, you go to school, your mom and I will do a little work, and then afterward, we'll pick you up and hit the water. Deal?"

"That's a deal and a half!" Grady hit an exuberant high five with Nico, and my heart stuttered. I wasn't sure if I was comfortable with how easily Nico had my kid wrapped so tightly around his finger, but I loved seeing Grady so happy. To be honest, most days Grady was such a serious soul, it felt good to see him act his age.

Grady scrambled to the bedroom to dress, and I

turned to Nico to whisper, "Careful making promises to a six-year-old. They have a memory like an elephant and they will not let you forget."

But instead of heeding my warning, Nico said, "Good. We all need an accountability partner from time to time," and I was both awed and fearful of what was happening.

"We are truly going to work, right?" I asked him before Grady returned.

"Sure," he answered, but the glint in his eye made me shiver. "But I didn't say how I was going to work you."

My breath hitched in my throat. I should've shut him down, reminded him that I was here to do a job and that had to be the priority, but my body was still tingling with the aftereffects of what he'd done to me, and I wanted more.

Heaven help me, I wanted more.

I swallowed and dragged my gaze away from the hunger in his, nearly jumping when the toast popped from the toaster. Nico chuckled, knowing where my head was at, but he did me the courtesy of remaining silent as he poured two cups of coffee and slid mine over to me wordlessly. I spread a generous helping of peanut butter on the toast and grabbed a short glass of milk before I could risk meeting Nico's gaze again.

"Thank you," I murmured, lifting the coffee mug, my thoughts stubbornly returning to the memory of last night. Grady returned, looking like a million bucks, if a million bucks wore its shirt inside out and both shoes on the wrong feet. "Baby." I chuckled, going to help him straighten himself out. "One of these days you're going to have to learn your right from your left shoe."

"But they look the same to me," Grady complained with a frown.

Nico chuckled and grabbed a permanent marker from a drawer. "C'mere, little man," he said, helping Grady onto the counter. Then he drew an R and an L on each respective shoe in an inconspicuous spot so it wasn't completely obvious. "There. Now you can just look for the R and L. Easy-peasy."

"Awesome! Mama never lets me draw on my shoes!"

I laughed, sobering slightly to say, "And I still don't, but we can let this one slide. Okay, now you have zero excuses. Eat your toast. We need to leave in about five minutes, and you still need to brush your teeth and wash the sleep from your eyes."

"Aw, Mama, you're always trying to make me fancy. I'm not trying to find a girlfriend yet, you know."

Nico guffawed at that and I chuckled, too. "Well, maybe I just don't want your poor teacher to catch a whiff of your dragon breath and faint."

Grady giggled but said, "Mrs. Tipper is the one with dragon breath. I think she brushes her teeth with dirt."

"Grady Erickson Hughes, you take that back," I admonished. "We don't talk about our teachers like that. Or anyone for that matter."

"Okay, Mama," Grady said but grinned when Nico gave him a conspiratorial wink. Good Lord, Nico was like a kid himself. Grady finished and headed for the bathroom, giving me a minute to scold Nico, but Nico had other plans.

"You—"

His mouth sealed against mine for a stolen kiss, and

my knees threatened to buckle. Everything we'd done together last night came roaring back in full detail, and it took everything I had not to moan like a porn star on cue.

But before I embarrassed myself, Nico released me and I spun out of his arms just in time for Grady to appear, face scrubbed, teeth brushed and ready to slay the dragons of kindergarten.

I may always question my judgment when it came to dating Houston, but we'd made a beautiful child together, and for that, I couldn't spare a moment of regret.

"Let's do this," I said, reaching for his hand.

"The car is downstairs waiting," Nico said, sinking into the sofa with his coffee in hand, a delicious grin on his sexy mug. "I can't wait to get to work when you return."

And by *work* I was fairly certain he meant something else entirely.

Funny thing, I was totally okay with that.

For now.

CHAPTER EIGHTEEN

Nico

MY BODY VIBRATED with anxious energy as I jumped into the shower, dressed and awaited Lauren's return. Last night had been an anomaly, and I was eager to see if it'd simply been the thrill of victory or something else entirely that caused me to react like an alien had taken over my brain.

I wasn't a cuddler by nature. I preferred my space. In fact, I was always the one biting my tongue in half after a hookup so I didn't ruin my chances of seeing the woman again by saying something rude such as, "That was great. The car is waiting downstairs to take you home."

But I hadn't wanted Lauren to leave. I'd wanted her right by my side. I wanted to feel my cock nestled against her backside, my arm wrapped tightly around her midsection.

But I hadn't been relieved at all. I'd been miffed.

Which was why I had to see if my reaction was a one-time event or something else. I needed firmer footing beneath me because right now, I felt as if the world had just tipped over and I was left standing on my head.

The door opened and Lauren returned. I could sense her nervousness, as well. The best way to handle a situation like this was to simply rip the bandage in one fell swoop. Without giving her a chance to think, I met her at the door and kissed her hard, demanding every ounce of her attention, every breath in her body.

Instant arousal burned through me, incinerating all the rational thought and careful planning in my head. All I knew was I needed to be inside Lauren again, and I wasn't about to wait.

However, Lauren was the one who managed to hold on to her senses long enough to gasp, "Wait!" pushing her hand against my chest, wrenching her mouth away.

I blinked away the haze of sexual fog to stare quizzically. "What's wrong?"

"I don't know…this feels…it's too intense. This can't be normal."

I couldn't agree more, which was why I needed to figure out why. I reached for the buttons on her blouse and began plucking them open. "Define normal," I suggested with silky intention, biting my lip on a groan as her breasts came into view. "Has anyone ever told you you have gorgeous tits?"

Lauren blushed, her breath catching. "Not lately."

"Well, they are." I pushed the halves of her open blouse from her shoulders and filled my hands with her full breasts. "A perfect handful—" adding with a look "—and a delicious mouthful." To demonstrate, I sucked a sweet, soft nipple into my mouth and suckled gently.

"Nico," she gasped, the sound like music to me. I spent a little time on her other nipple, and after, I wasted no time in shucking my jeans to stand naked and ready. Lauren sank to her knees in front of me to nuzzle my cock, her reaction twisting me in knots with instant arousal.

"I love the smell of a man's body," she murmured, cupping my balls with tender care before bringing the head of my cock straight to her mouth. I fed my shaft down her throat, and she willingly took every inch, teasing me with her tongue and adding a zing of danger with the graze of her teeth. Her hands worked in tandem with her mouth, sliding up and down my shaft as she worked the head with her mouth. Before long, my legs were shaking and sweat beaded my brow as I got ready to blow.

"I'm going to come," I said from between gritted teeth, trying to hold back, but Lauren didn't back away. She wanted me to come in her mouth. That was the final straw. I broke loose, coming with a shout, my knees nearly buckling and sending me sprawling to the sofa. With a final swipe of her tongue against the ultrasensitive head, she grinned up at me as I rested against the wall, breathing hard.

Lauren rose, went to the kitchen and grabbed a bottled water from the fridge. Then she drank deep before sinking down onto the sofa. I joined her and she offered me a drink, which I gladly slugged down. "Give me a minute," I promised, my throat still dry from breathing so heavily. "Girl, you've got some skills on lock."

Lauren laughed, taking the compliment for what it

was—genuine—and actually reached for her notebook.
"I thought we'd go over some notes, maybe come up
with a framework for your autobiography so we can
figure out how to structure the book."

Was she really talking about business? *Oh, hell no.* I
tugged the notebook from her fingers, ignoring her mild
protest, and tossed it before reaching for her pants and
yanking them free from her body. Lauren laughed as I
parted her legs to feast on her lovely pussy. "We have
to do some work," she said, trying to close her legs, but
I wasn't having it. I hadn't had my breakfast yet.

"Oh, I told you I planned to work you," I said, grinning. "By the time I'm finished with your body, you're
going to have to walk bowlegged to the kitchen to make
me a sandwich."

Lauren pealed with laughter until I buried my face
between her slick folds, eager to reacquaint myself with
the unique taste of her sweet pussy. I was a quick study.
Within moments I had her dialed in. I knew just where
to push, press, lick and suck to have her twisting and
arching against my mouth, keening a cry so hoarse that
I was sure my neighbors were going to lodge a noise
complaint.

And I loved it.

Free to cut loose, Lauren did exactly that—the sound
of her coming was the most erotic thing I'd ever encountered, and I wanted to bottle it up in my imagination so
I could listen to it whenever I needed to stroke myself.

She shuddered and bucked, but I held her in place,
locking her hips with my arms so I could tease and
torture that swollen little nub. Ringing Lauren's bell

had just catapulted to my No. 1 favorite pastime, and I
never wanted to stop.

But after her third orgasm, Lauren weakly pushed
at me, begging me to let her breathe. "Please, Nico…
no more… *Ohhhhh, God!*" Another orgasm rattled her
bones and she went limp, whimpering as the pleasure
buffeted her on its way out.

I turned her loose and swiveled her around so that
her ass was bent over the sofa, her face turned sideways
as she gasped for air. I ripped a condom open, tossed
the packaging and quickly sheathed so I could drill her
as hard as ever.

Her groan as I slowly entered her from behind was
like gasoline on a fire. I pushed myself deep, going to
the hilt, until I was buried inside her, her pussy clenching around me in slick, hot, welcome.

"Fuck, Lauren," I gasped. Now it was my turn to lose
it. My eyes rolled back as I pumped against her, trying
for finesse, but I was desperate to plant myself inside
her. My hips worked furiously as I pounded against
the soft give of her ass, and it didn't take long before I
was coming, too.

I spent myself inside her until I was bone-dry. I
slowly pulled out, careful to keep the condom from
spilling, and tossed it before dropping to the floor, exhausted.

Lauren rolled to the floor to land beside me, her
head rolling to the cushion. There was something so
incredibly beautiful about her when she looked rode
hard. Her hair was wild and her cheeks flushed. She

wasn't wearing a stitch of makeup, and I'd never seen a woman more stunning.

"Why are you staring?" she asked, a rueful smile following as she tried to fix her hair. "I know I probably look like a crazy person."

"You look amazing," I said, reaching to pull her to me as I brushed a tender kiss across her lips. After the kiss, we simply held each other's stare, unsure of what was happening between us, both of us a little afraid to draw attention to it. "Are you hungry?" I asked, breaking the moment and climbing to my feet. "I was just kidding about the sandwich. I'll make us something."

Lauren reached for her panties and retrieved her blouse from the foyer, dressing quickly, much to my disappointment. I would've rather Lauren stayed naked. Easy access and an awesome view, if you asked me.

For myself, I remained naked.

"Ham and turkey panini?" I suggested, already moving to grab the fixings.

"Sounds good."

I made quick work of the panini and returned with the sandwiches.

"Are you going to get dressed?" she asked, accepting her plate, trying not to stare at my cock. "I mean… it might be a good idea."

"I like being naked."

She laughed. "I bet you do."

"Don't you?"

"I have a six-year-old son. Being naked isn't an option."

I shrugged. "He's not here now. Go ahead, be free, go naked."

Lauren laughed, her eyes sparkling. "But if I'm naked I have a feeling we won't get much work done, and we only have so much time before we have to pick up Grady and go sailing as you promised."

"Good point," I admitted, reaching for my pants. As much as I wanted to fuck Lauren at least a few more times, I wasn't going to disappoint Grady by being late.

Dressed and enjoying our sandwiches, I couldn't help but wonder what the story behind Grady's father was. Lauren didn't like to talk about it, but my curiosity didn't much care about boundaries.

"Is Grady's dad dead?" I asked bluntly. "Is that why you don't like to talk about him?"

"He's not dead," Lauren answered. "Though that might make things easier. At least if he were dead, I wouldn't have to explain to Grady that his father had abandoned him without a second look."

"He knows about Grady?"

"Of course he does."

"Does he pay child support?"

Lauren looked at me sharply. "No, and I prefer it that way. If I don't chase after him for support, he's happy to leave us alone. Trust me, Grady is better off without his dad around."

"Who the hell is this guy?"

Lauren ignored my question, drawing attention to her sandwich. "This is pretty good. If the billionaire, independently wealthy gig doesn't pan out, you can always become a chef or at the very least a line cook."

"You deflect so quickly when you don't want to talk

about a subject," I observed, amused. "So what happened between you and your baby daddy?"

"Please don't call him that," Lauren said, grimacing. "It was a humiliating time in my life and I just don't like to talk about it. Besides, Grady and I are a team, we don't need anyone else."

"Everyone needs someone," I reminded her softly, but she just shook her head, disagreeing.

"Nope. My son and I are a duo. We don't need a third wheel."

"How does Grady feel about that?"

Lauren shrugged, picking at her crust. "He hasn't said it bothers him. I assume because it's all he's ever known that he's fine with it."

"Kids are perceptive."

"Yes they are, and Grady can see how good things are, so why throw a wrench into things, you know?" She paused, adding with mild annoyance, "What does it matter to you? Are you trying to play matchmaker or something? Because I'm not interested in being with Grady's father under any circumstances."

"Is he that bad?" I asked, curious.

"He's not bad, he's just…very selfish. Trust me, Grady is better off without an influence like that."

Now I needed a name. I didn't understand how a man could walk away from his kid. Even though I wasn't hoping for a baby mama to show up out of the blue, I would certainly make an effort to be part of the child's life if one did. Besides, my mother would kill me if she found out she had a grandchild out there whom I'd abandoned.

My brother Luca and his new wife, Katherine, were about to add a new generation of Donatos to the mix with the birth of their first child in a month or two, and my mother was practically wetting herself with happiness at the prospect of becoming a *nonna*.

"What's his name?" I pressed, but Lauren wasn't interested in sharing and got up to put her plate away. I rose to follow her. "Is it a secret? Is that why you don't want to tell me?"

She glared. "It's not a secret, it's private." But then she exhaled loudly before adding with chagrin, "And there's a good chance you know him."

CHAPTER NINETEEN

Lauren

I HADN'T PLANNED to admit to Nico that there was a good possibility he knew Houston. The information just kinda fell from my mouth in an embarrassing word vomit.

"Now I have to know," he said. "Out with it. Who is this asshole who may or may not be within my circle?"

I sighed, unable to believe I'd been so careless. "Honestly, I don't want to tell you. We've spent the last six years living peacefully without his influence, and I don't need anyone to rock the boat."

"You don't think at some point this mystery man might decide he wants to be a father and sue for custody?"

I lifted my chin. "There's literally no reason why Grady's father would want to suddenly become involved in his son's life. He doesn't even know him. It would be a disaster and it would completely throw Grady's life out of whack. Trust me, it is better for everyone involved for his father to remain absent."

But Nico wasn't satisfied. He was like a dog with a bone. I never should've said anything. I sincerely regretted opening my mouth. "I've seen your shitty apartment. The man should at least be paying child support."

I hated this argument—it was the same argument my mom threw at me—and just as I said to her, I said to Nico, "It's none of your business. Back off."

Nico seemed to understand that he'd overstepped but nonetheless tried a different tack. "I know you don't want to hear this, but at some point Grady is going to want to know his father. It might be later when he's a teenager, but it will happen at some point. How are you prepared to deal with it?"

Like that wasn't one of my deepest fears already, but I couldn't live in fear of a moment that may or may not happen. "I guess I'll cross that bridge when I come to it. Right now Grady is six years old and completely happy with just him and me."

"And I'm not advocating that you suddenly invite this man into Grady's life, whoever this asshole is. I'm just pointing out that you're walking a tightrope and at some point someone might shake the line."

As much as I wanted to end the conversation and erase it from Nico's memory, I could sense that Nico wasn't going to let it go. If Nico truly wanted to find out who Grady's father was, he could easily do so with minimal effort because all he had to do was throw money at the mystery.

In an effort to avoid Nico poking around and inadvertently messing with the beehive, I decided to come clean, but not without scowling for putting his nose where it didn't belong.

"I'll tell you, but you have to promise me that you will not say anything to him or in any way encourage him to be a part of Grady's life, no matter how you feel about the subject. Do I have your word?"

"Of course."

I didn't know how strong or good Nico's word was, so I'd have to trust him. I drew a deep breath before sharing, "Grady's father is Houston Beaumont."

As expected, Nico's expression was one of shock. I knew they probably ran in the same circles. Houston was a rich asshole, too.

"I've never heard anything about Houston having a kid," he said. "That son of a bitch. What a dick."

I released a breath of relief. A part of me had been afraid that Nico might take Houston's side. A "bros before hoes" kind of thing, but Nico wasn't walking that road in this instance.

"So you and Houston were a thing?" he asked, obviously trying to picture that and failing. I didn't blame Nico; Houston and I had been an odd couple.

"Briefly," I admitted. "I'd thought I was in love with him, but he bailed when I was four months pregnant. He begged me not to say anything about the baby, which is why nobody in his circle knows about it. At first I thought he didn't want me to say anything because he wanted to make a grand announcement, but then I realized he didn't want anyone to know because he'd never had any plans of being a father. Once I realized that,

I didn't want anything to do with him. I was going to raise my baby by myself, and I did."

"Houston comes from a very rich family," Nico said. "He might've been willing to simply pay child support and not have anything to do with the kid."

"That's a gamble I wasn't willing to take. You have to understand that once I saw Houston's true colors I didn't want him having a hand in raising my child. I felt stupid enough as it was that I'd been conned and knocked up by the man. I wasn't about to subject a newborn baby to his bullshit. Besides, Houston would've wanted to see his kid if he was paying money. Houston is very much possession-driven. He would've looked at Grady as nothing more than a possession, and frankly, there's no amount of money in this world that could make that okay with me. So Houston can go fuck himself."

I hadn't meant to reveal so much, but there was something about Nico that unhinged my jaw and the words simply fell out. Maybe it was something I'd needed to say for a long time and I'd finally found an ear willing to listen. Anytime the subject of Houston came up with my mom, she was a broken record. "Go after him for the money." It was the same thing over and over and over again, and I just didn't want to hear it anymore.

But Nico seemed to understand that Houston wasn't a great person to have coparenting a child.

Oddly, his support meant something to me. "How well do you know Houston?" I asked, curious.

"Well enough. We went to school together. He's an asshole but in certain circumstances fun to have around.

However, I wouldn't consider him an actual friend by any means."

"Well, like I said, I've been lucky to this point in that Houston has had zero interest in having anything to do with us. I haven't pressed for child support, and he's been happy to forget that we exist. We don't travel in the same circles, and it's not likely that Houston is going to run into Grady anytime soon or vice versa."

"That's true enough. Have you ever considered asking Houston if he would terminate his parental rights and just be done with it? That way the threat of him popping in whenever he feels like it is removed."

Actually, I had thought of that option. But at the time I couldn't afford an attorney to draw the paperwork, and again, there was always the risk that poking at the issue might ignite some weird need to press the other direction. "I couldn't fathom the risk of losing Grady. If we went to court for custody, the odds were stacked against me. Even though I'm his mother, the judge could've taken one look at Houston's wealth and my meager means and given custody to the father. Houston would've pawned off Grady to some nanny—one he probably would've been screwing—and Grady would've been shuffled off into the background. I wasn't about to take that chance."

"Fair enough. But you have the money now. Payment was wired to your bank this morning. If you want to check your bank balance, you can. You have more than enough to hire a good attorney if you ever wanted to press Houston to terminate his rights."

My breath caught. I'd forgotten about the payment.

I didn't want to rush to my phone to check my bank balance but… I looked at Nico, biting my lip with indecision. "Are you sure, I'd really like to check to see if it's really there."

He chuckled and gestured for me to go ahead. I picked up the phone and checked my bank balance. I nearly choked on my own tongue when I saw how many zeros were in my bank account. I looked at him, still stunned. "I can't believe you actually paid me that much money. It's too much. I feel like I'm taking advantage."

"The fact that you're worried tells me that you wouldn't know how to take advantage of someone if you tried. It's not in your nature. People who take advantage of others don't think twice about it. And honestly, you're worth it."

I couldn't help but warm under his praise. I didn't even care if he meant it was for my writing skills or the fact that we clicked together really well in bed. All that mattered was everything that I'd ever worried about financially was over. I could pay off all my debt—which included two student loans—as well as put money aside for a nest egg. One of the worst things I suffered was the knowledge that I never had enough money left over after each pay period to put aside for a rainy day fund, something my dad had drilled into me since I was twelve. But I'd just made a year's salary for a month's work, and as long as I found a permanent job after, I could.

My eyes brimming with tears, I turned to Nico. "Thank you. You have no idea how money like that has the ability to change someone's life."

Nico shifted with discomfort. "Don't be getting all sappy on me. It's nothing."

"But it is something to me. I understand that you were raised with wealth and this is probably pennies to you, but to me it's everything. And I'm going to work my ass off to prove to you that it was money well spent."

He surprised me with a quick but gentle kiss. "Baby, whatever happens from this point forward I already feel that it was money well spent. I meant what I said when I told you I liked you and Grady. You're both cool people, and in my life finding genuine people is difficult at best. If this helps you work out the kinks in your life, I'm happy to do so."

I couldn't stop the tears this time. I'd sorely misjudged Nico in so many ways. I was ashamed of my judgment and how I'd been such a bitch when we first met. But I could change that. I would absolutely do my best to write his autobiography and do him justice. I didn't know what his beef was with his brother, but I sensed that no one truly saw Nico for who he was.

And I would do my best to draw an accurate portrait with my words.

Sensing the moment was becoming too deep, Nico wiped my tears and helped me to stand. "I say we rinse off, fuck in the shower, rinse off again and then go get Grady to go sailing. Are you down?"

I nodded. "I'm so down."

"All right, then," he said, sealing his mouth to mine for another lingering kiss. "Let's do this. We're on a time crunch."

CHAPTER TWENTY

Nico

FROM THE OUTSIDE looking in, my sailboat wasn't the fanciest, but that's what I liked about the Celestial 48. I'd bought it used and then spent a year overhauling it, customizing the interior with rich teak and shiny chrome fixtures. The *Nauti Kitty* was my sweet mistress that I didn't spend nearly enough time with, and yet she still purred like a kitten whenever I took her out.

"Whoa!" Grady exclaimed as I helped him and his mom onto the deck. "This is awesome! You own this boat?"

"Down to every bolt and barnacle," I answered with a grin, loving how Grady's eyes sparkled with excitement. I'd forgotten how exhilarating it could be to enjoy something through someone else's eyes. My friends always mocked my little boat, saying I was the only billionaire who preferred to slum it when I could afford a luxury yacht ten times over, but there was something about this boat that I'd been drawn to.

Granted, the purchase had been on a whim. A

drunken whim, at that, but I hadn't regretted my decision, not even when I'd sobered up and seen how much work it needed.

"When I bought her, she'd been in sorry shape, but fixing her up has been more fun than I ever imagined it would be. Gave me the opportunity to make her mine."

Lauren agreed with Grady and was similarly awed. "I think she's gorgeous."

My smile deepened. Somehow Lauren's praise meant so much more than anyone else's. "Let me give you a tour before we hit the open water," I said, motioning for them to follow me below deck. The accommodations were cozy, but then, I wasn't accustomed to bringing too many people here. Grady wandered from the galley to the head to the two staterooms, poking his head in each to give a nod of approval after his inspection.

"I like it," he announced. "I think I could live here."

Lauren laughed. "I'm not living on a boat," she said, letting him down gently. "But it is very pretty."

"That she is," I agreed. I pulled a life jacket from a small supply closet and buckled Grady in. "Here's the deal, little man. Anyone under the age of thirteen has to wear one of these if they're going to be above deck. No exceptions, got it?"

Grady nodded solemnly. "Yes, sir."

I chucked his chin playfully. "That's 'Yes, Captain,' sailor. Got it?"

Grady grinned and giggled. "Yes, Captain!"

"Excellent." To Lauren, I said, "If you'd like to wear a life vest, you're welcome to, I have all sizes available right here. It's up to you."

"Are you a good driver or...um, sailor?"

I laughed. "I haven't capsized yet so I take that as a good sign."

Lauren grabbed a vest. "Just in case."

I chuckled and we climbed back to the top, where Lauren and Grady settled into the bench seats, soaking up the sun, while I got the *Nauti Kitty* ready for launch.

The day was gorgeous, perfect for sailing. The wind picked up nicely, and by the time we'd maneuvered out of the dock and hit the open waters, we were on wind power alone and clipping along at a nice leisurely pace.

Because he was interested, I gave Grady a quick lesson on nautical terms.

I felt rather than saw Lauren's attention on Grady and me. I cast her a quick look, and she smiled with a subtle blush at being caught. There was something happening between us that felt different from anything I'd ever experienced.

I didn't know what it was—but it scared me as much as it was exhilarating. I'd been hoping for a new adventure, something to break up the monotony that'd become my life, but I realized as I ruffled Grady's sandy-blond hair that I may have bitten off more than I'd planned.

My thoughts were consumed with Lauren and Grady at all times. I wanted to curl up with Lauren and explore each other's bodies as much as I wanted to show Grady the wonders of the world just waiting to be discovered if one had the resources to make it happen.

"Have you ever been outside of New York?" I asked Grady.

He looked to Lauren. "Have I, Mama?"

She shook her head. "Traveling takes time and money, sweetheart. Good thing for us, there are lots of awesome things to see and do in New York City."

I smiled but the world was so much bigger than one state could possibly hope to provide. "The resource part shouldn't be too much of an obstacle now," I said to Lauren with a wink, but she just laughed. "You ought to take a trip to Europe. My family is from Tuscany. Italy is a place everyone should see at least once."

"Well, after I pay off my student loans and put money away for savings, there won't be a lot left over to traipse around the world, but maybe someday."

I frowned. "Do you need more money?"

"No, not at all. I'm completely satisfied with the amount agreed upon," she said, shaking her head. "I just have different priorities, and running off to Italy isn't one of them, unfortunately."

I wanted Lauren and Grady to see where my roots came from, but I supposed that wasn't my place to insist. Hell, I'd even pay for the entire trip, but again, I was wandering into territory that was strewn with tacks and broken glass—and best avoided.

I set the course and Grady helped me steer while Lauren went down to the galley to fix some sandwiches.

"Did your dad teach you to sail?" Grady asked, his little body in front of mine while we cruised along.

I chuckled. "Nope. My dad didn't have time for sailing. I had a lot of time to fill in my childhood, so I found ways to keep myself occupied. I'd always been fascinated by sailboats, so when the opportunity arose, I snagged it. The old man I bought the *Nauti Kitty* from taught me to sail. He was a crusty old fart, but he knew his stuff. Best damn teacher ever." I paused for a moment, before adding, "Unfortunately, he died a year after I bought the boat."

"Why?"

Liver failure. The man had been a raging alcoholic, but I softened the truth by answering, "He got sick and it was more than his old body could handle."

"That's a bummer."

"Agreed."

"The *Nauti Kitty* was a good buy," Grady said with firm approval. "As Mama would say, it was a bargain!"

I laughed. "How do you know? I might've overpaid. My friends say I should've got it for free and then given it a good burial at sea."

"That's dumb. This boat is fab."

"Fab?"

"That's what Uncle Ronnie says when he likes something."

I nodded. "I agree. The *Nauti Kitty* is fab."

We cruised along in amiable silence until Grady said, "Do you like my mama? 'Cuz I think she likes you."

My tongue felt glued to my palate. I had to tread cautiously. I didn't want Grady getting hurt by anything I might inadvertently set in motion, but I wasn't being dishonest when I answered, "Hell yes. She's pretty cool. Kinda cute, too, but don't let her know that. I wouldn't want her to get a big head or else she won't fit in the narrow corridors below deck."

Grady giggled and I warmed at the sweet sound. "She likes you a lot."

"Yeah? And how do you know?" I asked, curious.

"Because she looks at you funny."

"Ah, the telltale funny look. Maybe she thinks I smell?"

"Not that kind of funny look," Grady said, laughing as he twisted to illustrate, "this kind of funny look."

I guffawed at the googly eyes Grady was making on his mom's behalf. "Boy, I must be blind because I've never seen that particular look on your mama's face."

I'd seen her eyes roll up into her skull as I made her come and I'd seen her eyes squeeze shut with total pleasure as I bent her in half, but I'd never seen those googly eyes.

Grady nodded with the confidence of a six-year-old who already knew his letters and how to write his name, saying, "Yep. She does," and who was I to argue?

"I'll bet it's fun just being you and your mom all the time," I said, fishing for a little intel. "No one to share your mom with or tag-team for extra TV privileges, right?"

Grady shrugged. "I guess."

"You guess?"

"Well, most times. I like when we have movie night. She makes kettle corn and orders pizza. She even lets me drink soda on those special nights, but I overheard Auntie Claire tell Mama that if she doesn't get a man soon her *angina* was going to fall off."

I nearly fell over from laughing so hard. "Her angina? Sounds serious," I said when I managed to catch my breath.

"I know! I don't know what that is, but I don't want

my mama to lose anything just because my real dad is a jerk face and doesn't want to be with her and me. Can you help my mama find a boyfriend so that doesn't happen?"

The earnest request was so sweet that I almost readily applied for the job until I caught my mouth before making an ass of myself. I wasn't boyfriend material. I was a commitment-phobe with an insatiable appetite for the new and undiscovered. I would only break this little family into pieces, but I didn't want Grady worrying about his mom's parts so I said, "Don't worry about your mom. She's one tough cookie and I don't think she's in danger of anything falling off, okay?"

Grady seemed relieved and I resisted the urge to kiss the crown of his head. He was such a great kid. How could Houston not want to be a part of his son's life? I couldn't possibly picture Lauren and Houston together—and I didn't want to—but Houston never should've abandoned his son just because things didn't work out between him and Lauren.

Lauren called out from below deck, saying the sandwiches were ready. I lowered the sails, dropped the anchor so we could enjoy lunch on the calm waters and headed below deck with Grady.

Just as we slid into the bench-style seats at the small table, Grady assured his mom, "You don't have to worry, Mama. Nico says your *angina* is going to be just fine even if you don't get a boyfriend," and I wanted to slide under the table and die.

Right after I quit laughing.

CHAPTER TWENTY-ONE

Lauren

I WAS MORTIFIED to my toes, but Nico's laugh was infectious, especially when Grady was beaming at me as if he'd single-handedly solved all my problems.

"You two seem to be partners in crime," I said, shooting Nico a look as I shook my head. I knew I should've put a stop to whatever was happening between Nico and Grady, but sue me, was it wrong to let my kid enjoy some traditional male energy? I mean, I loved Ronnie from his glittery fingernails to his diva updo, but sometimes I wondered if Grady needed a break from the things Uncle Ronnie accidentally let slip.

Like learning how Uncle Ronnie's boy parts never showed through the shiny, skintight dress that he wore for his act.

But Grady sure seemed to like Nico. Perhaps more than was healthy. I'd always assumed that because he never talked about not having a dad around that he really didn't notice or care.

Maybe I'd been naive to think his silence meant he

was unobservant. Honestly, I should've known better—
Grady noticed *everything*.

Finished with lunch, we headed back up top and
while Grady helped Nico take the helm, I stretched out
on the comfy bench seats, content to let the wind ruffle
my hair and the sun warm my face.

The ocean was calm and the winds light. It was a
perfect day in so many ways.

A subtle pulling in my chest reminded me that Grady
wasn't the only one who needed to remember that this
was all temporary. Nico wasn't looking to sign on for
the long haul, and I didn't want Nico in that capacity
either.

I smiled ruefully to myself at my own meandering
thoughts. Nico, as a father? He was like a giant kid
himself. My gaze drifted to Nico and Grady, and that
subtle pull deepened to something far stronger. Nico
was really good with Grady and Grady thought Nico
was the cat's meow.

As if hearing my thoughts, Nico swiveled his gaze
toward mine, that sexy smile sending ripples of excitement in its wake. *Hot potato, he's delicious.* I bit back a
shy smile, afraid he might be about to read my thoughts
with a single shot of that hot stare.

But Nico just grinned, his dimple flashing, and returned to teaching Grady the ropes about sailing when
it was likely Grady would never have the opportunity
to sail on a boat like this again as it wasn't exactly
within my budget.

"So, I have this dinner thing I have to attend," Nico
said, surprising me. "And I'd like you to go with me."

"What kind of dinner thing?" I asked, curious.

He shrugged. "The usual kind—pretentious food and even more pretentious people—but it would make an interesting chapter in my book."

"How so?"

"Well, seeing as my brothers, Luca and Dante, handle the actual business operations, usually I get thrown the appearances when a Donato is required for networking."

"You're the face of the Donato company?" Lauren asked.

"Well, to a point."

I laughed but shook my head. "I wouldn't know what to wear or how to act. I'm not sure I would be your best choice for a date."

"And what if you're the only choice I want?" he said, stunning me with his counter.

All jokes aside, Nico was serious. He wanted me to be his date? "What if I get in the way of your networking?" I asked, and by networking, I meant something else entirely.

Nico didn't pretend to miss my meaning. "As I said, I only want you."

Stop it, I wanted to growl, because my heart was fluttering dangerously like that of a lovesick idiot and I didn't need the heartache of rejection or betrayal later down the road when everything went sour or when Nico decided he was finished with whatever game he was playing. "I don't have anything to wear," I said, hoping my excuse ended his interest, but I should've known better.

"Tell me your favorite color and I'll have ten dresses delivered for you to consider."

Grady piped up. "Mama's favorite color is vanilla, like the ice cream." *The little coconspirator.*

"Thank you, little man," Nico said, smiling down at Grady in a way that made my heartbeat quicken. "Vanilla it is."

And just like that, in Nico's mind it was settled—I was going to be his plus-one.

I should've protested more vehemently, putting my foot down, but a part of me didn't want to. I was intrigued by the idea of attending a dinner on Nico's arm, not as the reporter skimming the edges of the room, watching body language and keeping an ear open for possible juicy news I could spin into a story.

I was going as his ghostwriter, and based on what he'd just said, his date. Maybe this once, I'd just enjoy the moment. It wasn't often that a billionaire wanted to treat you to a night out dressed to the nines.

"Fine," I said, closing my eyes to simply enjoy what was left of the day. I didn't want to think anymore, or worry, or wonder.

The sun started to dip low in the sky, and Nico turned the boat around to head back to the harbor. There was enough of a bite in the air that Grady and I headed below deck to wrap up in a blanket.

As I snuggled my sweet boy, loving how his hair smelled of ocean air and happiness, I kissed the top of his head, privately smiling to myself. "Did you have fun today?" I asked.

"The best, Mama," Grady answered, and I could hear

the smile in his tone. "Nico says we can take the boat out whenever we want as long as the weather is good."

I bit my lip, tempted to gently correct Grady but decided to leave it alone. No sense in ruining a great day with reality. "It sounded like Nico was teaching you all about sailing. I never knew you were into sailboats that much."

"I love sailboats, Mama, but it's not like one would fit in our yucky apartment so I didn't say anything."

"Our apartment is not yucky," I admonished while rocking him gently. "We love our apartment. It's our home."

"It smells and there're bugs," Grady said. "Can we move? Nico says we should, and I think he's right."

"Well, Nico has his opinion but we have to get back to our life at some point, and I'm sure Nico will be ready to have his spare bedroom back."

"Nico doesn't care. He said if I wanted I could decorate the room any way I like. He said he has an interior decorator who could do whatever I want within a day."

"That's silly," I said, troubled by Nico's promises. "There's no point in redecorating a room that we're only going to be in temporarily."

Grady shrugged. "Nico says it's no big deal. He'll just change it back when we leave."

I supposed that was true. Nico was fairly nonchalant about throwing money around, but I didn't think it was healthy for Grady to assume that money grew on Donato trees.

"How about this…when we get back home, we'll give your room a makeover. Fresh coat of paint, any color you like, and we'll work together on a theme. It'll be a fun project for us."

"Can Nico help?"

Okay, this was going too far. Grady was obviously too enamored with Nico for my comfort. I gently turned Grady to face me. "Honey, I know Nico is lots of fun and he's been super nice to us, but as soon as I finish the job our lives will return to normal, and normal doesn't include Nico."

Grady's expression darkened as his little face screwed into a frown. "I don't want to go back to life without Nico."

"Well, I can't do anything about that," I said frankly. "Nico isn't part of our family."

"He could be."

Frustrated by my inability to communicate to Grady what I was trying to say, I just exhaled and let it go. "We'll talk about it later. You're tired and getting grouchy. You need dinner, a bath and then bed. It's been a busy day."

Grady folded his arms across his chest, still scowling. "I'm not tired. You're just changing the subject. Auntie Claire says that's called *defecting*."

Oh, Auntie Claire. I am going to duct tape your mouth shut one of these days. I cleared my throat and tried to smile as I corrected Grady. "Actually, the word you're looking for is *deflecting*, and I'm not doing that, I'm simply stating facts. Besides, that conversation was over."

"But I still want to talk about it."

"Sorry. I'm pulling rank. Conversation over."

I thought Grady might argue some more, but he seemed to get the hint that I wasn't going to budge.

It was dark by the time we were back to the apartment, and in spite of his protests, Grady was asleep against Nico's shoulder. Thankfully, I'd foreseen this problem and had Grady eat on the boat while we made it back to the dock, but I wouldn't be able to give him a bath as I'd hoped.

I went to take my son from Nico's arms, but he waved me away and took Grady to the bedroom himself. He laid Grady gently on the bed and, after removing his shoes, tucked him into bed.

Fully clothed.

"He needs pajamas," I told Nico, shaking my head with a small smile at how clueless Nico truly was around kids, but it was cute how he'd tried. I made quick work of getting Grady into pajamas and within minutes he was snuggled deep into the blankets, dead to the world.

I found Nico in the kitchen throwing together a small cheese and cracker platter to share with a bottle of wine he had decanted.

I was hungry but I knew the wine would just knock me out. "I'm exhausted," I admitted, selecting a wedge of cheese and a cracker to munch. "I think I'll just shower and head to bed. Thanks for the awesome day."

But Nico wasn't going to let me slink off, and I think a part of me knew that. He grasped my hand and pulled me to him. "I've waited all day to taste those lips again and I'm not going to bed without it."

I sank against him, his lips finding mine. There was

something so perfect about the way we fit together—as if I were coming home after a long journey—and I was just as eager to sink into the familiar.

"How about I draw a bath for the two of us?" he suggested. "I'll wash your back, you wash mine?"

His suggestion was cute, but I already knew that if our naked bodies were in close proximity, we were having sex at some point and I was so tired I could barely keep my eyes open.

Although a bath sounded fantastic, I thought we both could use some distance. I needed to remind myself that Nico wasn't part of my future and it was foolhardy to pretend otherwise, especially when Grady was already too attached.

"Tempting," I said, pulling away. "But I think I'll just go to bed."

Nico frowned but nodded. I could tell he had more he wanted to say, but he didn't and I was grateful. I didn't have the energy to explain what was going through my head, especially when I sensed that Nico wasn't going to see things my way.

I closed the bedroom door softly behind me and exhaled a long breath. Even though fatigue dragged on my bones, a sense of emptiness went deeper. Nico and I had had sex this morning, but my body ached to feel him inside me, even if it were only a quickie.

See? This is a problem.

When the idea of climbing into bed with Nico and falling asleep in his arms sounded like heaven...yeah, that was a big problem.

Seemed Grady wasn't the only one skipping past

the warning signs, headed straight for the chasm of heartbreak.

Stripping down to a T-shirt, I climbed into bed next to Grady and pressed a soft kiss on his forehead before snuggling down to close my eyes.

Careful, Lauren...you're about to fall—hard.

Or maybe I already had.

CHAPTER TWENTY-TWO

Nico

I WAS NERVOUS.

I adjusted my cuff links for the tenth time in as many minutes. Lauren hadn't come out of the bedroom yet.

Did she hate the dress? I'd personally picked out the style, but what if it wasn't to her liking? I would've rather taken her with me so she could model each selection, but I knew she'd never agree and I wasn't about to risk our date.

Grady was with his grandmother—a decision Lauren agonized over to the point that she almost backed out—and tonight I was going to show Lauren what it was like to be pampered.

If she ever comes out of the bedroom, that is.

My heart leaped into my throat as the door slowly opened and Lauren stepped out tentatively as if she had something to worry about.

I lost my ability to breathe.

"You're fucking stunning," I said, my voice trembling in an unmanly fashion. I cleared my throat and tried again, saying, "Truly stunning."

And that was an understatement. The soft vanilla floor-length gown was a sumptuous complement to her olive skin tone, and her chocolate-brown eyes made me melt a little inside. I hurried to unclasp the jewelry box in my shaking hands to reveal the glittering diamond necklace I'd procured from the family jeweler, holding my breath as Lauren gasped with wonder.

"Are you kidding me? Are those real?"

"Very. So please don't lose it," I teased as I carefully lifted the necklace to place around her neck and clasped it into place. Her hand fluttered to the brilliant stones, and I saw her fingers tremble slightly. I grazed the tender column of her neck, murmuring, "That necklace could fund a small country, but it looks perfectly at home on you."

Lauren graced me with a shy smile that sent bolts of arousal straight to my cock, and I had to rein in my desire to mess up her hair and makeup by bending her over the kitchen table before we left. "I don't know what to say…this is too much but I'm so flattered. Thank you, Nico."

I swallowed the lump of pride in my throat. If anyone should be flattered, it was me. I was going to be the luckiest son of a bitch in the room with Lauren on my arm. Speaking of, I gallantly extended my arm for her gloved hand to grasp. "Shall we?"

"We shall." She smiled, her brown eyes sparkling.

Tonight I'd called for a limousine rather than the town car because I wanted Lauren to feel like Cinderella and that I was her prince, but I also wanted more privacy than the town car could provide.

Her smile deepened as she saw the awaiting stretch. Jepperson opened the door with a deep bow and an appreciative "Very beautiful," and helped Lauren into the car. I stuffed a hundred-dollar bill into his hand with a grin and he winked. "Y'all have a good time. I won't wait up."

As the door closed behind me, I leaned back to admire the beauty next to me. How could I have ever missed that delicate bone structure, that stubbornly beautiful intellect shining in her eyes? I must've been blind to believe Lauren plain in any way.

Lauren marveled quietly at the luxury, running her fingers lightly down the soft, black leather, smiling with excitement. "I've never ridden in a limo before."

"And? What do you think?"

"It doesn't suck."

I laughed at her dry humor. Then I said, "I have a surprise for you."

Her eyes widened. "A surprise? Oh, Nico, you've already done way too much…"

I chuckled but this surprise was also a selfish one. "These dinners are notoriously dull, but I think I've found a way to liven things up."

She frowned, curious as I fished my surprise from my interior jacket pocket. Lauren inhaled sharply, her hand flying to her mouth in shock as she said, "Is that… a…oh my God, what is that?"

I held in my hand a small, egg-shaped vibrator and the accompanying remote.

"And just what do you plan to do with that?" she asked, amused.

"I plan," I said, leaning forward to brush my lips across her mouth, "to ever so lovingly place this sweet little torture device inside that delicious pussy of yours so that when I feel things are becoming dull, I'll give it a discreet little flick. The fun part will be watching you squirm knowing there's nothing you can do to stop the pleasure."

"You're the devil," she said, but her mouth curved in a delighted smile. I kissed her harder until she was panting and squirming, the heat between us building quickly. My hand found itself up her gown to discover her without panties. She blushed but her brow rose in challenge. A challenge I readily accepted and that made my cock hard. I used her slick wetness to ease the egg past her soft folds and deep inside. I withdrew and slowly licked her wetness from my fingers. She shuddered in response, her gaze as liquid as her slit.

"Shall we test this sucker out?" I asked, grinning though my cock was already threatening to burst through my pants. She nodded and I flicked the remote, giving her a nice zing. She gasped and gripped the armrest, her cheeks flushing prettily. "Very nice," I said with approval. "At least we know it works."

Lauren laughed, the sound like music to me, and I couldn't help but kiss her again. At this rate, I'd never make it through dinner without needing to fuck her senseless, but I'd give it a good college try.

She shocked me by saying in a throaty tone, "Let me suck your cock," and I couldn't get my pants down fast enough. My cock sprang free and she was on it within a heartbeat. I closed my eyes with pleasure as her hot mouth worked my cock and her hands cupped my balls, squeezing gently. I groaned, loving the feel of Lauren's mouth on me, losing myself to the bliss of a killer blow-job. I didn't want to make a mess on her beautiful dress, but when I tried to make her stop before I blew, she just giggled and kept going.

How could I *not* come so hard with a woman who clearly loved sucking cock like Lauren did?

Yeah, exactly.

With a guttural grunt, I found my release. Lauren swallowed every drop until I was left gasping for air and nearly springing from my seat from a single teasing swipe of her tongue across the ultrasensitive pulsing head of my cock.

"I think you might be the devilish one," I said when I could speak again. To that she just laughed, and I gave the remote a flick, sending a pleasurable bolt straight to her tingly bits.

"That's one powerful little egg," she said with a breathy moan that would've made me instantly hard if I hadn't just blown a wad. "Oh, God…that feels good."

Sadly, we'd arrived at our destination and it was time to be adults. I laughed and pocketed the remote in my interior pocket, patting it with a wink. "Just in case things get dull," I promised, but she and I both knew it was going to be a challenge for me to keep my hands off the remote for the entire night because I loved watching her cheeks flush with pleasure.

And the fact that only she and I knew what was happening was an incredible turn-on.

Not that I needed anything else to turn me on when it came to Lauren. Jesus, at this point, I think watching her brush her teeth would probably cause my dick to harden.

The driver opened our door, and once I climbed out, I helped Lauren, her hand slipping into mine as if it were always meant to be there.

Pride warmed my insides as I caught enviable glances from the other guests, everyone's tongues wagging at the mysterious stranger on my arm.

But to be honest, it wouldn't have mattered if only Lauren and I were attending this function and there were no other people to admire what a beauty I'd snagged—I didn't care what anyone else thought.

"With Fort Knox on my chest, you might need to hire more security," Lauren murmured, glancing with obvious nervousness around her.

"You're safe with me," I assured her and she relaxed.

We entered the ballroom filled wall-to-wall with people in designer dresses and tuxedos, and I felt Lauren's nervousness through the thin sheath of her dress. "People are bound to stare. Keep your head high. You're the most beautiful woman in the room."

"How can you say that?" she whispered. "I think I just saw Gwyneth Paltrow in the corner!"

I shrugged. "She pales in comparison to you, and I'm not just saying that. I mean it, Lauren. You are exquisite—and not just because that dress clings to your every curve. It's because you're something these women could never hope to be."

"Yeah? And what's that?" she asked, dubious.

"Genuine."

A smile broke through her nerves. "You're really charming when you put your mind to it," she said, drawing a little bit closer to me. "You ought to write a book on how to charm the pants off women. I'm sure it would be a bestseller."

I chuckled but there was only one woman I wanted naked at the moment, and she was gracing my arm.

I took two flutes of champagne from a passing attendant and handed one to Lauren with a small toast. "To an evening filled with surprises…" Lauren smiled and we clinked glasses softly before sipping and surveying the room. I spied plenty of people I wanted to avoid for various reasons, but mostly I wanted to find an empty room, lift Lauren's skirt around her hips and remind her why we were so good together.

But if I couldn't do that… I supposed I ought to go and network for the sake of Donato Inc. After all, sailboats didn't pay for themselves, and this was how I earned my play money.

CHAPTER TWENTY-THREE

Lauren

I WAS A fairy princess and Nico was my dirty prince.

We floated across the dance floor, laughing and smiling as if we were the only two people in the world until Nico flicked the tiny remote and I nearly stumbled into his arms, clinging to him as my body shuddered with pleasure. I clung to Nico, inhaling sharply as I tried not to moan, and he simply chuckled with wicked delight as I struggled to maintain my composure.

He released the trigger and I nipped at his neck before allowing him to release me. Nico rewarded me with a feral growl that I felt down to my toes.

It was intensely erotic, and I couldn't stop smiling.

We suffered the obligatory small talk when Nico's presence was required, and after we'd circulated the room enough times, we slipped out of the ballroom and down a quiet hallway, surreptitiously trying doors for one that wasn't locked.

Nico found one and we slipped inside, quietly locking the door behind us.

The room, an office with ornate furnishings inlaid with gilt filigree, was entirely too gaudy for my tastes but I hardly cared about our surroundings. There was one reason and one reason only to be locked in a room with Nico in the dark while the rest of the party prattled on about nonsense.

Nico fumbled with his pants and then he shoved my dress up above my waist, pausing a minute to lift me onto the desk. Papers fluttered and pens tumbled to the floor, giving us away, but we didn't care. I spread my legs and he gently fished out the pleasure egg, tucking it away in his jacket pocket—our little secret.

Then he ravished my mouth as if he couldn't get enough. His tongue, his hands, all roving—tasting and touching—committing to memory every nook and cranny, every hill and valley.

We froze as voices sounded in the hallway, but they receded quickly and I smothered a relieved giggle. I couldn't imagine being caught like this would do Nico any favors when he was supposed to be here on an official capacity for his family business.

Impatient to be inside me, Nico pulled me from the desk and flipped me over to bend over the mahogany. The smooth wood beneath my cheek was cool as Nico gripped my hips and guided himself inside, pushing hard until he'd buried his shaft balls-deep. I groaned, losing myself to the pleasure of being taken like this, and wondered how I'd ever get over someone like Nico. How could anyone else possibly compare?

I groaned softly as he drove, sliding in and out with strong, controlled thrusts, building that beautiful tension like a master cellist slowly built to a crescendo. My fingers curled against the wood, my eyelids squeezing shut as I fought to keep the cry behind my teeth, but Nico's name burst from my lips as I came, clenching and squeezing as every muscle contracted and released in perfect concert.

God, he could fuck.

I was dimly aware of Nico finding his own release, grinning with sated pleasure at how sexy he sounded when he came. There was something so primal about the act of climax that aroused me even as I was content to simply try to slow my thundering heart rate.

Nico withdrew and tossed the condom in the waste bin, then helped me from the desk. We dropped into a spacious divan and lay there in the milky dark, completely disheveled but entirely happy.

Moonlight shafted in through the expansive window and the stars punched diamond sparkles in the midnight tapestry. I didn't know whose office this was or how much trouble we'd be in if we were caught; all I knew was I didn't want this moment to end.

It felt like magic.

"You are the most beautiful woman in the world," Nico murmured, idly playing with an errant curl lazily tumbling down my shoulder. "I can't believe I ever thought you were plain."

I blushed at the memory of that first meeting. "I have a confession…"

I heard the smile in his tone as he said, "Yeah? Confess, my darling."

"I purposefully came to the interview wearing the

ugliest dress I had. I knew of your reputation, but more so than that, Patrice had made a snide comment about my wardrobe, which she was doing constantly, and I think I did it out of spite. I know, stupid."

"Do you miss working at *Luxe*?" he asked.

I hesitated, giving the question serious thought. "I miss some of my coworkers, but I don't miss the bullshit. Publishing is a dog-eat-dog world. It's almost inevitable that you're going to get eaten or take a bite out of someone else at some point. I don't miss that part." I twisted around to meet his serious gaze, those eyes doing something dangerous to my insides, but I managed to stay focused. "We really need to do some work on your project. You hired me to do a job. I don't feel right accepting payment for work I haven't done yet. In fact, you should've only paid me half up front and the other half when I delivered."

"Screw the project," Nico said, yawning, and I frowned. *Screw the project?* Nico seemed to sense my sudden disquiet and he clarified, "I mean, screw the project right now. I don't want to talk work. I want to enjoy having the most incredible woman on my arm."

I relented—I mean, how could I not when he said things that made me melt?—saying, "Well, when you put it that way…" I brushed a soft kiss across his lips and he reciprocated. I smiled. "Thanks for tonight. It's been exquisite."

"The pleasure has been mine," he said, and while it could've sounded obligatory or trite under any other circumstances, I sensed that Nico meant every word.

Or maybe that was his gift—he could make a woman believe anything that fell from his lips.

"Nico... I'm curious...have you ever been in an actual relationship?" I asked.

He sighed. "Once, no, twice. Both times ended badly."

I bit my lip. I probably shouldn't have asked, but I needed to know if he was even capable of deep emotion or if I was seeing things that didn't exist when he looked at me.

"Tell me how you and Houston met," Nico said, expertly *defecting* as Grady would say.

"I was in college. We met at a party. We were both drunk. He was supposed to be a good time, not a long time, if you know what I mean. But he made me laugh. I was so stressed with midterms that I needed someone to shake things up, make me smile."

"I've never known Houston to be particularly funny," Nico said with a slight sniff, and I giggled at the obvious pinch of jealousy. "But then, I suppose your brain was starving for entertainment," he teased.

I laughed. "Yes, well, it was a perfect storm of bad judgment, and before I realized in time that it was time to cut my losses, I got pregnant."

"And Houston bailed when you told him?"

"Actually, he stuck around for a month or so but when things started to get real, he slowly stopped calling and coming around. Basically, he ghosted me." I realized something, laughing as I shared, "Come to think of it, I guess technically, we're still dating because we never broke up."

"You're definitely broken up," Nico growled, holding me more tightly. "He's a pussy for skipping out on his responsibility."

I recognized that tone and I tried to keep things light. I rose up and shimmied over his hips to straddle him, my fancy dress pooling around my hips as my hot folds rested on top of his quickly hardening cock.

"I don't want to talk about Houston," I said in a silky tone, sliding my pussy over his groin. "I want round two before we're discovered and thrown out for being disrespectful perverts."

"I've been called a pervert my entire life. I wear that badge with honor," Nico growled with a sexy smile tugging at his lips as he reached between us to push up inside me. I rode him slowly, lifting my hips and grinding, loving the way his hands anchored at my waist to guide and control my movements, his hooded gaze centered on the spot where our parts joined.

My name lingered on his gasped warning, and I smiled with anticipation at how well we meshed together sexually. I wanted to ride him to completion, but that wasn't wise.

I rose up and he pulled out with a small groan of disappointment until I replaced one hot, wet orifice with another. We were out of condoms and I wasn't going to risk pregnancy, but it was no tragedy to have Nico in my mouth. I loved his taste and I adored the taste of myself on his skin as I worked him without mercy.

He came with a loud grunt, filling my mouth, and I quickly swallowed, sucking every last drop down my throat, loving how easily I could turn this charming playboy into putty in my hands…er…mouth.

Finished, I wiped my mouth and smiled, though I realized, too late, Nico was going to be a hard habit to break. I helped Nico to his feet and he pulled his pants up and buckled them with an adorable grin that was both sexy and boyish, and I wanted to do even more wicked things together.

Hell, I'd be willing to do just about anything with Nico. Even butt stuff. And that was saying a lot because I'd tried anal sex once and swore to never do it again.

"Why did your relationships end?" I asked, unable to let it go. I needed to know if Nico was simply incapable of deep emotion with another human being. Why? Because a part of me was starting to hope that he felt the same way as me and that, maybe, *just maybe*, we might have something worth exploring.

But if I were spinning my wheels in mud, I needed to stop right now and save myself from drowning.

CHAPTER TWENTY-FOUR

Nico

I SENSED THE energy in the room change between us. Even though Lauren was trying to seem nonchalant about her probing question, I could sense that it was anything but lighthearted.

I knew I ought to play it off with some sort of teasing answer and distract her with something else—my mouth on hers, perhaps—but something compelled me to be honest.

Which, in my experience, was never a good thing.

"I...uh, well, I was an idiot."

"Most men are idiots," Lauren teased and I didn't disagree, but I think I excelled in making the worst possible decision in any given situation. She cocked her head with interest as she asked, "What did you do?"

I hesitated, torn between tossing a joke or going for the bald truth. I opted for truth even though I wouldn't come out looking so hot. "I cheated. Both times. It was hurtful and wrong, and I didn't have a solid good reason for what I'd done to either of them. Both were great women who didn't deserve how I hurt them."

A long pause stretched between us. I knew how most women felt about "cheaters," and I didn't blame them. Hell, my brother's wife, Katherine, threatened to bail on a marriage contract that'd been in play since she was sixteen because she'd thought Luca had cheated on her.

It all came out in the wash that he hadn't—Luca wasn't that kind of guy to begin with and he'd been head over heels in love with Katherine since forever—but the hell she'd put him through to get to the aisle wasn't for the faint of heart.

Let me just say, there was a hostel and a soup kitchen involved.

"Were you sorry?" Lauren asked quietly, breaking into my thoughts. I didn't want her to think being genuinely contrite made any difference in the hurt I'd caused, but yeah, of course I'd been sorry.

"People caught red-handed doing something wrong are usually very sorry. Doesn't change what I did. Twice. Seems I have a thing about *not* learning from my past mistakes." I shrugged into my tuxedo jacket. "The thing is, I have this aversion to commitment, it seems. Just when things are going great, I have to go and do something awful to ruin it all. It's my MO, which is why I don't get into relationships anymore. Best to stay single. That way no one gets hurt."

Even though it was dark, I could sense Lauren's disquiet at my admission. I smothered the urge to smooth over my admission with a lie to preserve the sweetness between us, but I couldn't sully the first real thing I'd allowed myself to feel in years by being disingenuous.

"People make mistakes and they change and grow," Lauren said. "Or they don't and they keep making the same mistakes, but either way, it's their choice one way or another."

"Which is why you don't date anymore either because of Houston."

"I don't date because I have a sensitive six-year-old who is more important to me than the inconvenience of suffering a few nights of loneliness."

"Lauren, I was honest with you, do me the courtesy of being the same," I said, not letting her skate past without at least owning her actions, as well. "You're afraid of being hurt." Her silence confirmed my assumption and prompted me to admit, "Well, I am, too. I'm afraid of hurting another good woman."

A woman like you.

I didn't like how the mood had changed. The night, to this point, had been the most fantastic on record, and I hated how such serious talk had put a blemish on an otherwise perfect evening. I gathered Lauren in my arms, and she went willingly. I inhaled the sweet scent of her perfume and skin and committed it to memory. I knew this feeling and I knew to run from it before everything soured like milk left out in the hot sun.

Eventually, every relationship I was in curdled.

I wouldn't do that to Lauren and Grady.

Which meant I needed to either cut ties now and risk hurt feelings or finish my so-called project and end things on a professional note as agreed upon.

My inclination was to cut ties, but that would save only my feelings. Spending more time with Lauren and Grady, even under the guise of the project, would only prolong the inevitable and suck all of us deeper into quicksand.

I should've never interfered with Lauren's life. If I hadn't barreled my way into her life, she would've been happy to go along as she always had, meting out a meager lifestyle on her paltry salary, but strong in her heart.

Now I was the thorn, burrowed deep, unwittingly killing her.

"We'll get started on the project tomorrow. Seriously."

She brightened, happy to be working again. "Awesome. I promise you won't regret hiring me. I can't wait to write your story. I'm going to make the world see the real you. *Including* your brothers."

Her genuine enthusiasm only made me feel wretched. The project had been a sham and my actions underhanded, but I had to see it through, even if I just stuck the finished manuscript in a box and lit it on fire. Dante was right; no one wanted to read about my life, what little I'd done with it.

But for now, I'd play the game for Lauren's sake because she deserved far better than having me crash into her life and ruin it.

I grasped her hand and asked with a rueful grin, "Shall we make our escape?" She nodded with a tremulous smile, and we slipped from the room to the exit where the car awaited.

CHAPTER TWENTY-FIVE

Lauren

NICO HAD ADMITTED the very thing I'd suspected all along—he was averse to commitment, which meant he wasn't the right fit for Grady and me.

His admission should've snapped me out of whatever spell Nico had been weaving around me, but it only served to make me want to cry. There was a side of him that was so incredibly sweet and generous, but maybe I was just falling for the charm and not the real Nico.

Who was the real Nico? I didn't know.

For that matter, I didn't know anything about him aside from that we were fantastic in bed together and my son thought he was better than sliced bread with peanut butter.

I didn't know his friends—aside from Houston, if Nico could call him that.

I didn't know his family—aside from that one awkward encounter with his brother Dante.

I didn't even know his favorite color.

Basically, I knew nothing because he never planned to make me a permanent part of his life.

To be fair, I'd known this from the start and supported it, but now the knowledge hurt.

Since it was late, I'd prearranged for Grady to stay the night with my mom, which meant I was free to sleep with Nico for the entire night if I chose.

But did I want to do that?

Probably not a good idea.

We arrived at the apartment—his place already felt like home—and just as I was about to turn toward the spare bedroom, Nico caught my hand and shook his head, that one wordless motion telling me everything I needed to know.

No words. No more conversation. Just our bodies doing what our bodies did best.

I closed my eyes as he undressed me with all the tender attention of a man who hadn't been with me only an hour prior, and I allowed the pleasure to roll over me as his tongue slipped between my folds to lick and suck until I broke out in a sweat and came hard.

Shuddering as the pleasure went bone-deep, I sighed as the last wave crashed over me, settling against Nico's naked body, limp and content.

And that was how I fell asleep.

The following morning I awoke before Nico. I rolled to my side and propped my head with my hand, smiling as he slept. He was the most beautiful man I'd ever seen. Truly. Almost too pretty. Between that wash of dark hair and those classic cheekbones, not to mention

that killer body, he could give a Calvin Klein underwear model a run.

But from what I knew of the Donato men, they were
all handsome. I could easily see how women wobbled
to their knees whenever one was around.

All signs pointed toward walking away, cutting my
losses, but when I looked at him, my heart did funny
things and my lips wanted to smile, if only to give shape
to the feeling in my soul.

As much as I liked to think I'd been in love with
Houston…what I felt for Nico was nothing like how I'd
felt about Houston.

This felt deeper, more stable and yet wildly intoxicating.

The way Nico was with Grady—there was no faking
that emotion. He might be able to fool me, but whatever was happening between him and my son was 100
percent real.

And it was the same for Grady.

Damn it—I knew I shouldn't have let Grady get attached, but how could I not when Grady had been so
happy?

Nico's eyes opened slowly and he graced me with a
sleepy smile as he reached for me. "Stalker," he murmured. "Did you take pictures while I was sleeping,
too?"

"Only a few for blackmail purposes later," I answered, giggling as he burrowed his face against the
crook of my neck. "You should be worried. I caught
you drooling."

"Ah, truly damaging, indeed." He kissed the back of

my neck, sending goose bumps rioting down my skin. "And what other trouble have you been up to while I slept? Does it include breakfast?"

I laughed. "Yes, I made a full-course meal while you drooled. Are you nuts? Eat a bowl of cereal."

"Damn, the honeymoon is over," he drawled, and I laughed harder until his hand started to travel down my belly, then my breath caught and I bit my lip, anticipating his touch. "I can't seem to get enough of you," he admitted, his fingers lightly skimming the soft skin of my folds. "Are you a witch or something? I think you've dosed me with Love Potion No. 9."

I stilled, turning to him. "I might ask the same of you," I countered, dancing around the highly charged word floating between us. I'd fallen for him. I'd done the very thing I'd sworn I wouldn't. But how did Nico feel about me?

Was love even an option?

His brow lifted even as his fingers continued to lightly strum the sensitive skin. "There's definitely some voodoo going on," he said. "I think the only answer is to constantly fuck each other's brains out in order for the magic to wear off."

I laughed but I stilled his hand. "I'm not sure that will work. I think it would only make things worse."

"Well, it's worth a try," he said, rolling on top of me, and as much as I craved the pressure of his body pressing down on mine, I shook my head. He frowned. "Are you okay? What's wrong?"

"I can't think when you're on top of me and your

cock is nudging between my thighs," I admitted, encouraging him to roll off, but he didn't see the appeal.

"Morning sex is good for clearing the mind," he said, but when he saw I wasn't kidding, he rolled off with a sigh. "I guess you could blow me and that would be okay."

I snorted and climbed from the bed, wrapping a silk robe around me. "We have work to do. I'm going to shower, eat some breakfast and then go get Grady. In the meantime, I suggest you do the same. I want to get some notes down while Grady is at school. I think I could have a rough draft of notes compiled within a week if we buckle down. Sound good?"

Nico looked bored with that plan, but he didn't protest any further. "Yes, Mistress Hughes," he said, making a whip-cracking motion and sound. "Whatever you desire."

I laughed. "I desire a cup of coffee and a jelly doughnut. Can you make that happen?"

"Coffee, yes. Doughnut, no."

I winked. "Get moving, lazy bones," I said, and left him there on the bed with a raging boner.

CHAPTER TWENTY-SIX

Nico

IN HINDSIGHT IT was always easier to see when you should have taken a left instead of a right, but that was the beauty of hindsight—clarity.

I knew Lauren wanted to get started as soon as she returned, but I needed some advice and maybe an ass-kicking. I texted Lauren to let her know I had errands to run and I wouldn't be back to the apartment until later that afternoon, and then I headed to my brother Luca's house.

One of the concessions Katherine had insisted upon in order to marry my brother was that they would not live in the Donato mansion, even though it was big enough to house a football team comfortably. I didn't blame her—my mother ruled the mansion with an iron fist and it was her way or the highway. Not to mention it was just way too big. It was like living in a cavernous museum with a full-time staff and a controlling drill sergeant for a roommate.

Luca and Katherine had purchased a modest home

near enough to our parents' place but far enough to create some distance when they needed space.

Katherine opened the door, her distended belly coming into view before she did. "You look ready to pop," I joked, but my observation wasn't appreciated and she responded with a scowl. *Note to self: pregnant women lose their sense of humor along with their waistline.* Of course, then I wondered how Lauren had weathered pregnancy and I had to school my thoughts away from that topic altogether because, oddly, my cock started to tingle at the thought of Lauren's body swelling with a kid. Notably, *my* kid, and that was a problem.

Katherine gestured toward Luca's office, stating, "He's in there," before waddling off in the opposite direction, her hand resting on the small of her back as if that would change the fact that she was practically tipping over.

I walked into the office and found my brother behind the desk, looking so much like a younger version of our father, Giovanni. Luca had always been our father's favorite, even though he had a funny way of showing it. Our father had never been the warm and cuddly type. Maybe that was why I had commitment issues. Though, to my knowledge, our father had never cheated on our mother. Giovanni was just an asshole. I honestly couldn't imagine anyone else wanting to sleep with him, because he was just unpleasant most days.

Not that you would know it by our mother. Our mother still thought he was handsome and virile. I suppose that was the way it was supposed to be. No matter what you looked like on the outside, your husband or wife should always have your back. I guess that was one lesson that our parents had succeeded in teaching.

Go, Team Donato.

I sank into the chair across from my brother with a loud sigh.

Luca smiled as he looked up from his computer. "Feeling a bit dramatic? What's the problem today?"

True, to this point my troubles had been small, but the weight of the world was resting on my shoulders, even though I'd pretty much put the weight there myself.

"How's married life? Katherine seems pretty grumpy. Are you already in the doghouse?" I asked, choosing not to jump right into my problem.

But Luca wasn't stupid. "You didn't really come over to talk about my pregnant wife, did you? That's not really your style."

Yeah, he was right. I was stalling. I leaned forward. "Here's the deal, withhold your judgment until I've finished telling my story," I warned. Luca nodded and I pressed forward. "I may have done something really stupid, and I don't know how to get myself out of it without hurting someone that I've come to care about."

That got his attention. "My little brother actually caring for someone? Surely that's a sign of the coming Apocalypse."

Ha, ha. "I'm being serious. I need your advice."

Luca sobered appropriately. "All right, I'm all ears. Lay it on me."

I didn't pull any punches or soften the truth. I told Luca everything from how I'd manipulated the situation to place Lauren in my debt as well as how I'd maneuvered her into my bed. I also admitted that I had feelings for her and for Grady.

Luca steepled his fingers in thought, his brow dipping as a subtle frown formed. He wasn't happy. I braced myself for the lecture I deserved. "Nico, when are you going to learn you have to stop fucking with people's heads?"

"That's just it, Luca. I think I…" The word stuck on my tongue, but I felt it in my heart and I just threw it out there. "Jesus, Luca, I think I love her."

"You *think*? If you have a question at the end of that statement, then you don't actually love her. Love is something that grabs you by the balls and doesn't let go. If you don't feel that emotion in your soul, it's not love and you need to let her go before things go south, fast."

Which was exactly what Dante had said in a different way. But, of course, Dante's biggest fear had been that my dalliances might somehow rebound on the family business.

More miserable than before, I said, "I know I should just let her go, but every time I think about saying the words I can't get them out. I mean, she's so great. Even if you took away all the physical attributes that I'm into, I'd still be over the moon about her. She's smart, talented and fucking funny as hell. And that kid of hers? He's bloody fantastic. I took them sailing the other day and it reminded me why I love sailing. I want to take Grady sailing every day because he loves it. I want to buy him his own damn sailboat. I'm having all sorts of dangerous thoughts, and I can't make them stop. Do you know where they live? In a shitty apartment in

Brooklyn and I want to…hell, I want them to live with me forever. For real, not just temporarily."

Luca pumped his hands with a "Whoa, brother, calm down. You're dealing with emotions that you have no experience with. You can't handle people like Lauren and Grady with inexperienced hands. That kid isn't yours, and I'm not sure you're ready to be a father."

"I'd be a far better father than his actual dad. The loser just abandoned his own kid. What the fuck is that shit?"

"Not your problem," Luca reminded me in a stern tone. Then he added something else, "Think of how our parents would react to your bringing home a single mother with a kid. You know how Mom feels about those things. It's just best to cut ties cleanly and quickly before things get way too messy."

Of course, Luca was right. But it was the absolute last thing that I wanted to do. I wanted to do the opposite of Luca's advice. I wanted to, maybe, marry Lauren, and I said as much. "Yeah, well, what if I'm in love with Lauren and I wanted to marry her? Our parents would just have to deal with it."

Luca shook his head at my defiant statement. "That's your problem, little brother, you're always thinking of yourself and not how your actions affect others. Do you really think Lauren wants to be part of this family? Katherine's known us her entire life and she nearly couldn't marry me because of everything it entailed. What makes you think Lauren is going to want to jump into the chaos that is the Donato family?"

All valid points.

I didn't care.

"You'd like her."

Luca sighed, shaking his head. "Why'd you come over here to ask for advice you weren't going to take?"

"I think I love her. No, I do love her," I asserted, feeling stronger every second the more I allowed myself to say the words. "I want to marry her."

"You're getting ahead of yourself. You don't even know if she wants to marry you," Luca warned.

"Why wouldn't she?" I countered, feeling smug. If Luca knew how well I made her come, he wouldn't ask that question. If there was one area I felt 100 percent secure, it was in the bedroom. And there was no denying Lauren and I created sparks whenever we were near one another. "Yes, she'll want to marry me."

"Let's just pretend for a second that she's willing to marry you…is she still going to feel that way once she finds out how you manipulated her? In my experience, women tend to take a dim view on that sort of shit."

"I won't tell her and thus she'll never know," I said. "I'm sure there are things you've never told Katherine."

"If you take one bit of advice from me today I hope it's this…don't fucking lie to the woman you profess to love. Lies always manage to rise to the top, like a fucking body in a lake. There's no amount of cement that can keep the truth from popping up."

I shifted with unease. If Lauren found out about my involvement with her getting let go from *Luxe*, she'd never forgive me—that was a fact.

"If she finds out after we're married, she'll forgive

me," I said, but Luca's expression just told me I sounded like an idiot.

Maybe I was, but I had to take that risk. Besides, what were the odds that Lauren would find out, anyway?

I grinned at Luca. "Guess I'd better make a stop at the jewelers. I have a purchase to make."

CHAPTER TWENTY-SEVEN

Lauren

I WASN'T SURPRISED Nico had texted to tell me our plans to work would have to wait for the time being. For someone who had hired me to do a job, he was fairly reluctant to actually sit down and get the project started.

I didn't mind the break, though. I managed to stop by my apartment and water my plants as well as check my mail. After shredding the junk and doing some general cleanup so the place wasn't a wreck when we returned, I grabbed some fresh clothes for both me and Grady and started to head back to Nico's until I decided to detour and pick up takeout from my favorite Americana restaurant.

Chester's was my and Grady's go-to spot for burgers and fries. I ordered and waited, stepping aside with my phone in hand, checking my emails for any word on the countless résumés I'd sent out.

But as I waited, a familiar voice at my back caused me to turn.

Patrice.

I forced a polite smile at the awkward encounter. I hadn't realized Patrice was a fan of burgers—I'd always pictured her as more of a sushi and wheatgrass kind of person—but there she was, standing in all her pinched-expression glory, giving me the most condescending look I'd ever seen.

"How are you?" I asked, making conversation. "How is *Luxe*?"

"I wouldn't know. I was fired."

I tried not to let my jaw drop. "I'm so sorry. What happened?"

"As if you don't know," she returned with a sour expression that confused me. "Your boyfriend's little shenanigans cost me my job." She patted her hair as she drew herself up. "Thankfully, I have plenty of friends in this business and I was able to rebound. Unlike you, I'd dare say. How's the job hunting going?"

I narrowed my gaze. "What are you talking about?"

"After what your boyfriend pulled, you'll be lucky if you can find a job writing ad copy for dog food."

I was starting to fume, but I needed to know what the hell Patrice was talking about before I punched her in the nose. "I have no idea what you're talking about, but if you've been bad-mouthing me to prospective employers, I could sue you for defamation."

"I haven't said anything that wasn't true," Patrice said, undeterred. "And don't act so innocent. I'm sure you were well aware of what that asshole Donato was up to when he forced me to fire you."

The contents of my stomach dropped to my bowels.

"What?" I could barely get the word out, my throat had closed so tightly. "I don't understand."

Patrice stared as if she didn't believe me, but when she realized I was genuinely floored, her expression turned sly and vindictive. "Trying to play the victim? How quaint. Donato came to me, promising advertising dollars for *Luxe* if I convinced you to attend the Griffin dinner with him. I tried, but you had other plans. I never imagined he'd pull his campaign because of something so silly, but he threatened to do just that, saying that if I didn't fire you that he'd pull every cent of a very lucrative deal that I'd already sent to advertising. Against my better judgment... I did it. Well, corporate caught wind of what'd happened and said I'd grossly abused my power and let me go."

I could only stare. I thought I was going to vomit.

Patrice sniffed. "But it seems you landed on your feet. Everyone saw you and Donato cuddled up at the Griffin dinner, looking like two lovesick puppies. *Luxe* got the advertising campaign, but I got the shaft. Seems everyone came out on top but me."

"I didn't have anything to do with Nico's...deception," I said, my eyes blurring. Nico had betrayed me in the worst way. I couldn't quite reconcile the facts when my heart was screaming.

"Well, you can kiss my ass for a good reference because I don't believe you."

I swallowed the lump in my throat. How could I be so stupid as to believe Nico was capable of anything genuine? Anything real?

Oh, God, and I'd exposed Grady to Nico's manipulation, as well. I didn't wait for my food and simply bolted.

Patrice's laughter seemed to follow me, or maybe it was just the voice in my head telling me I should've known better.

Either way, Grady and I weren't going to stay another minute in Nico's place.

In my current state of mind, I was afraid I might murder him.

CHAPTER TWENTY-EIGHT

Nico

EVERYTHING WAS READY. My hands were shaking, but my mind was made up.

"Marry me," I practiced in the mirror several times, thrusting the black jewelry box toward an imaginary and ecstatic Lauren.

"Lauren…will you please marry me?"

"Lauren…make me an honest man…marry me!"

"Will you freaking marry me, please?"

"Grady, can I marry your mom?"

I double-checked that I looked on point. I wanted to look my best for my future wife.

I shivered at the word *wife*. Who would've thought that Nico Donato could be tamed? I chuckled, feeling pretty proud of myself. I was already picturing our wedding. Of course, Grady would be my best man. I couldn't imagine anyone I would want more than Grady standing beside me as I married Lauren.

A contented sigh rattled free, and I checked my watch. Lauren should be here any minute.

As if on cue, the apartment door flew open and Lauren came in, Grady in tow, but she was anything but smiling.

"Grady, pack your things," she said, her tone leaving no room for argument. Grady shot me a sad look that killed me, and I couldn't process what was happening fast enough.

"Whoa, what's going on?" I asked, chasing after Lauren as she started shoving clothes into her suitcase, ignoring me. "Lauren…what's wrong?"

"Mama said you did a bad thing…" Grady answered, sucking in his bottom lip to hide the tremble. "What did you do, Nico?"

A chill settled over me, but my skin felt damp. I swallowed, not quite sure how to answer. Surely she couldn't have found out about *Luxe*…was it possible Luca had sold me out? My world tilted and I searched for words. "Sweetheart—"

She whirled on me, her eyes blazing, "Don't you dare call me sweetheart or any word remotely attached to an endearment, or I swear I will split your skull open with this lamp."

Holy shit, she knew. How? "Let me explain," I said, forgoing any attempt at covering my tracks. It didn't matter how she knew. I had to fix things now or lose everything.

"There is nothing you could possibly say that would forgive what you did to me, Nico. You forced Patrice to fire me? So that you could…make me attend a dinner with you? What the fuck is wrong with you?"

"To be fair, if you hadn't turned Patrice down in the

first place, none of this would've happened." *Ah, shit*. I knew the minute the words fell from my fool mouth they were the wrong thing to say. I stumbled on more words in my rush to pull my foot out of my mouth. "I was wrong to do what I did. All I can say is I'm sorry… I wasn't thinking of how that might end up, but things worked out for the better, right? I mean, there's no way you could've made it working at *Luxe* for much longer. Now you can afford to live somewhere nicer…somewhere—"

"I like where I live," she cut coldly, jerking her suitcase closed and zipping with a savage motion before going to Grady's and doing the same. Grady was crying quietly, and I wanted to die. Hell, how had things gone so sideways in such a short amount of time? "Lose my number," she said in a low tone that seethed with rage. "I fucking hate you."

I wanted to grab her and make her listen, but I knew I didn't have the right to touch her right now; plus, I was a little afraid she might actually make good on her threat and split my head open with the lamp.

"Grady…"

But they were gone, the door slamming behind them. The last image of Grady, tears running down his round cheeks from behind those owlish glasses, breaking my heart in two.

Holy fuck.

My entire world had just collapsed right at the moment I'd discovered what my entire world was made of.

I stared at the closed door, my heart thundering in my chest.

"I want to marry you, Lauren. Jesus… I'm sorry."

The ring box slipped from my fingers to drop to the floor.

What was I going to do?

How did I make this better? Was it even possible? Or had I just lost the one woman who was made just for me over a dumbass move that I'd take back in a heartbeat if I could.

I was out of my depth, but I knew I needed to give Lauren some space, even though every nerve in my body was screaming at me to follow her and drag her back.

She just needed to go home and calm down, breathe and realize that I was sorry, and then she would forgive me and we would get back on track to bliss.

Yeah, solid plan. Except my heart was still skipping beats, my palms were sweaty and I felt like I needed to puke.

God, help me. I really fucked up this time.

CHAPTER TWENTY-NINE

Lauren

FOR THE FIFTH consecutive day, a huge, ostentatious flower arrangement arrived, and for the fifth consecutive time, I dumped it down the trash chute.

Grady, unusually quiet since leaving Nico's apartment, watched as I silently fumed at Nico's dogged refusal to leave us alone.

The calls and texts—I blocked.

The flowers—I trashed.

The voice mail on my home machine—I deleted.

Somehow, he even managed to find my email; I deleted that, too.

I didn't want anything to do with Nico. I was half tempted to donate the money he'd given me for the fake project to charity, but I needed money to live.

So, even though I hated it, I had to keep the cash, and that just pissed me off all over again.

True to Patrice's word, she'd trashed me around town. No one would hire me right now. Not even the small newspaper I'd contacted out of desperation.

At this point I'd happily take writing ad copy for dog food, but not even they were willing to hire me.

If Nico's project had been real I could've used it as a great springboard, but just like everything associated with Nico, it was fake and useless.

Each morning, I cried in the shower so Grady didn't see me break down, but sometimes I couldn't help myself and I found tears running down my cheeks.

Like right now.

"Mama?" Grady's worried voice ate at me. I wiped away the tears and tried to smile for his benefit. He crawled into my lap and I rested my chin on his little head. "Are you going to stay mad at Nico for a long time?"

I cursed his name inside my head, hurting for my son as much as I hurt for myself. "Probably," I answered truthfully.

"What if he said he's sorry?" Grady asked. "You said that saying sorry is the best thing to do when you've done something bad."

"Yes, but it doesn't always work that way with adults," I said, wishing I could erase Nico from Grady's memory. "Nico isn't going to be part of our lives anymore. We need to put him behind us and focus on moving forward."

But Grady wasn't interested in moving forward. "But I miss him."

"Eventually, you'll stop missing him," I assured my little guy, but I wasn't sure if that was true because there was a Nico-sized hole in my heart that I didn't think would ever heal. I wasn't going to pretend that Grady wasn't suffering the same pain. I could only hope that eventually Nico would fade away in both our memories.

Fat chance, but I could hope.

"What did he do?" Grady asked.

"Honey, it's grown-up stuff. I don't want to talk about it right now, okay?" I kissed his forehead and held him tight. "We don't need Nico anyway. We're a team, right?"

Grady nodded, but I felt his sadness weighing me down like a rock in my pocket.

"How about we order pizza and have a movie night?"

But Grady didn't want pizza or popcorn or even soda. He hated our apartment, wanted to go sailing and wanted to see Nico. Nothing I did was going to measure up, and I just had to weather his disappointment. I'd done the cruelest and most careless thing imaginable— I'd given my little son a glimpse of what it might be like to have a father and then I'd taken it all away with little explanation aside from "Nico did a bad thing." It was little wonder Grady was sullen, sad and angry.

And I didn't know what to do to fix things. I had a sinking feeling that only time would make things better, but that didn't do much for either of our broken hearts.

CHAPTER THIRTY

Nico

I'D NEVER EXPERIENCED the awful drag of time until a month had passed since Lauren left and I thought surely it'd been longer than thirty days.

My ragged heart felt as if it'd been chewed and spit out by a rabid dog and then shit on.

Against my better judgment, I agreed to accompany Dante to the club to hit a couple of balls at the driving range. Golf wasn't my usual go-to sport to let off some steam, but seeing as I'd been hibernating in my apartment, existing on takeout and ice cream, I didn't think I'd have the stamina for much else.

I'd even gained a few pounds.

"You need to hit the gym," Dante said with a grimace when I groaned to tie my shoes. "You look like you've gained twenty pounds."

"Fuck off," I muttered, breathing a little heavier as I stood up. "So I've gained a few pounds, big deal. I've been a little messed up."

"Don't be a pussy," Dante said as we walked into

the country club, flashing a cool smile to everyone who made the effort to notice us. "You've been moping around in that apartment so much you've started to grow mold. Pick yourself up, shake it off and move on. Isn't that what you do best?"

Yeah, but I'd never been in love with any of the women I'd moved on from. Not the case with Lauren. I still dreamed about her, fantasized about her and missed her like a fat kid missed cake.

Except, according to Dante, I was becoming the fat kid.

"She won't accept any of my calls," I said, ignoring Dante's look of disgust. "I've had flowers delivered, but she throws them away. How do I know that? I paid the neighbor to tell me if she accepts or tosses them. She tosses them. Right down the garbage chute. I tried leaving a voice mail on her home phone, but she changed her number. Aside from stalking her—"

"Sounds like you're already doing that," Dante cut in drily. "Give it a rest. You sound pathetic."

"I love her," I said simply. "I can't give up."

"She's moved on. You need to, as well."

We got to the range and I started to grab my nine iron when I heard a familiar voice. I turned to see Houston Beaumont laughing it up with his buddies a few lanes down. I looked away, not wanting to see the man because I didn't trust my ability to remain calm when I was already unstable as fuck.

Living on Häagen-Dazs and Chinese food wasn't great for your mental health or your waistline, apparently.

My plan was to ignore him entirely but Houston saw

us and headed over, completely unaware that I wanted to shove my nine iron so far up his ass the hosel of my club used his uvula as my tee.

"Holy crap, it's the Donato boys. I haven't seen you in ages. How the fuck are you?" Houston asked, clapping Dante on the back. "How's business?"

"Business is good," Dante answered, squinting against the sun. Houston had never been one of Dante's favorite people, but now he was Public Enemy No. 1 in my eyes.

Because I was already in a shitastic mood, I decided to poke the bear and see what happened.

"So, you have a kid…" I said, watching his reaction. "Never knew that until recently."

Dante narrowed his gaze and realized quickly enough where I was going with this. He cut his stare to Houston, and we were both suddenly judging him and Houston knew it.

"Uh, well, so she says," Houston tried joking, playing off my question. His buddies shifted nervously. I knew I had to be radiating rage, but I didn't care. I was so pissed off and mad at the world that I'd take the first sorry sap with the misfortune to cross me. It just so happened, fate was smiling at me and threw me a bone by putting Houston Beaumont in my path.

"You're a piece of shit," I said, my voice hard as steel. "Anyone who abandons their kid is an asshole."

"Hey, fuck you, you don't know my life. How the fuck was I even supposed to know if the kid was mine? I've seen pictures. He doesn't look anything like me.

You know how girls like her are…the kid could've been anyone's."

Now he was calling Lauren a whore? I advanced toward Houston, my fists curled. "You're right, the boy doesn't look anything like you—that's a blessing—but I'd advise you to watch your mouth before it overloads your ass. You're five seconds away from getting my fist in it."

Houston scowled and bowed up on me, going toe-to-toe. "You seem to know a lot about business that doesn't concern you, Donato. Why don't you back the fuck up and stick your nose elsewhere."

"Lauren and Grady *are* my business," I growled. "You don't deserve to say their names, much less talk shit about them."

Houston looked to Dante for backup but Dante was enjoying the show, resting his arm on his driver, a cool smile on his face. Like I said, Dante had never been a Houston fan, not enough action to back up his running mouth.

"Yeah? Fuck you, Donato. You want to champion a slut who had the bad luck to get knocked up, go ahead… but step off before I fuck up your world."

That was all the invitation I needed. I reared back and popped Houston in the nose with a savage cross that sent blood spraying from his busted schnoz, and I took immense satisfaction in the gurgling howls as I dragged him up from the ground, my hands curling in his golf polo. "Don't you ever talk about Lauren, think about Lauren or even breathe in her direction, you hear me? Because if you do, I'm going to rearrange your fucking face so bad your own mother wouldn't recognize you. Understand?"

I shoved Houston into the arms of his buddies, and they dragged him off before I thought better of letting him go with only one punch. He'd need surgery to fix that nose if he didn't want to look like a boxer who went one too many rounds in the ring.

I shook my hand, flexing. Dante handed me the cloth used to wipe down the clubs, and I cleaned off the blood from my knuckles. "Feel better?" he asked drily.

"Yeah, a little."

Dante sighed. "You know he's going to sue for assault."

"Let him." I didn't care. Hell, I didn't care about much. "That fucker abandoned Lauren and Grady. He hasn't paid a single penny toward Grady's support and Lauren has shouldered the responsibility all on her own."

"Since when did you become the champion of single mothers?" Dante's brow rose with sardonic amusement, but I didn't dignify the question with an answer. He knew it had everything to do with Lauren, not the fact that she was a single mom. Dante shook his head with mild annoyance. "Either go fix this situation or let it go. You can't go popping people in the face every time someone pushes your buttons about Lauren."

"Haven't you been listening? She won't take my calls, emails or texts. She returns every gift, throws away the flowers. What the hell am I supposed to do? Toss her over my shoulder and drag her to my place?"

Dante exhaled with irritation as if I were being deliberately stupid before saying, "If you want to win her back you have to figure out why she's this upset in the first place. Is it truly because you manipulated her out of a shitty job and paid her an exorbitant fee for a fake project? Something tells me she could get over that. What's really the problem? Dig a little deeper. The answer is staring you in the face."

I scowled at Dante, irritated and frustrated that my brother seemed to know the answer but was making me work for it.

But Dante was right. I didn't think the real issue was the job. Sure, she was pissed as hell, but she'd get over that eventually. An image of Grady's stricken expression, tears tracking down his face, blazed across my brain, and I knew there was only one thing that Lauren would never forgive—someone hurting her son.

And I'd hurt Grady by not being honest. I should've come clean with Lauren about the project and my hand in her lost position. I would've eaten all the crow she demanded, but I know I could've won her back. Grady never would've had to know, and right now, I know Lauren would've been wearing my ring.

Grady would've become my son.

My son.

The words hit me hard. The weight of such responsibility should've crushed me, but it felt amazing. I wanted to be Grady's father.

I wanted to be Lauren's husband.

More than anything.

And I meant all the way—not just because I wanted to marry his mama.

I wanted Grady to be a Donato.

I met my brother's gaze. "I need to talk to a lawyer."

Dante smiled, testing out his driver with a slow swing as he said, "Hope it works out for you, little brother," and I left the range.

I was sending all the wrong gifts, completely missing the one thing Lauren and Grady wanted.

A family.

Well, hot damn, that was what they were going to get.

CHAPTER THIRTY-ONE

Lauren

I WAS JUST settling in for the night. Grady was tucked against my side, the television on, but I wasn't actually watching anything in particular while Grady played a game on his phone.

I knew getting over a broken heart took time, but why did every minute seem more agonizing than the last? Nico had somehow burrowed his way into my heart in record time, and I was both irritated and flabbergasted at how I could love him so deeply when we still barely knew each other.

I never did find out his favorite color.

Or his middle name.

Or what his pet peeves were.

I knew his secret tickle spots and how to make him laugh. I knew that he snored lightly when he was in a deep sleep. I knew that he loved to cook and took pride in his culinary talents.

But all of that was surface stuff.

I hadn't known how cruelly he could twist the knife

in my back or how easily he could ruin lives without forethought.

According to Ronnie, I was being ridiculous.

"Honestly, his methods were unorthodox, but he did you a favor getting you out of *Luxe*. You were in a rut, girlfriend" had been Ronnie's take on the whole sordid mess. Even if I could forgive Nico for manipulating a situation for his own gain, I couldn't forget how crushed Grady had been when everything fell to crap.

Maybe if Nico had been honest…maybe it wouldn't have mattered. Wasting energy on wondering was stupid and an exercise in emotional agony.

I had to move on, not only for my sake but for Grady's.

I withheld a sad sigh, not wanting to worry my little guy. Since moving out of Nico's, he'd been withdrawn and his eyes had lost that sweet spark that'd always melted my heart.

I knew he was brokenhearted, too, and that killed me.

Mom guilt, in all its varying shapes and sizes, was enough to cripple a rhino. I'd give anything to take it all back so my son didn't end up hurt.

I startled at the knock on the door. It was too late for visitors. Suddenly, all the complaints and concerns Nico had expressed about my apartment came flooding to me in a panic. I didn't have anything in the way of a weapon unless you could count my sharp wit. "Grady, go to your room," I told Grady, helping him up. I waited until he was safely in his bedroom before going to the door, grabbing a heavy candelabra to use as a bat if need be. "Who is it?"

A pause long enough to stop my heart and create visions of my own death at the hands of a psycho followed until I heard, "It's me, Nico."

And then my heart rate sped up like I'd just smoked crack. "What do you want?" I asked, my voice catching and betraying my hurt and hope in the same breath. "Go away."

"May I come in? I have something for you."

"There's nothing you have that I want."

"Please."

It was the humble plea that broke me. Nico wasn't blustering or trying to be charming. He was simply asking in the most sincere way possible if he could come in for a moment.

I shouldn't let him in.

I should tell him to get the hell out.

But I didn't—I couldn't.

The truth was, I missed him.

I slowly unlocked the door and stepped away so he could come in. My breath caught. He looked as if he hadn't slept in weeks. His cheeks were puffy and…was that a little belly?

Had he been mainlining jelly doughnuts this whole time? Somehow the fact that our separation had affected him so viscerally made me tremble all the harder because there was no faking his pain.

I closed the door, locking it, but I cast a nervous glance toward Grady's bedroom, afraid of Grady's reaction to Nico's showing up. I was grateful when Grady remained in his bedroom but I knew he wouldn't stay there for long, so I needed Nico to get to the point.

"What do you want?" I asked, folding my arms across my chest.

Nico held a manila envelope in his hand. I caught a subtle shake as he handed me the envelope. "This is for you and Grady."

I frowned, confused. "What is this?"

"Just open it. You'll see."

Was this some sort of gimmick? Another fake project? I sighed and decided to humor him just so he'd leave. I opened the envelope and pulled a sheaf of legal paperwork. I frowned, even more confused when I saw Grady's name on the documents.

"What is this?" I repeated, my palms becoming sweaty. I saw Houston's name, and my vision blurred. This couldn't be what I thought it was. My gaze flew to Nico's, needing confirmation before I started crying. "Nico…what am I looking at?"

"Houston Beaumont has relinquished his parental rights to Grady. You'll never have to worry about him showing up on a whim, using his family money and influence to force visitation. Grady is yours and yours alone."

I'd never dared to dream that Houston would sign away his rights. It was what I'd always wanted but had been too afraid to push out of fear that Houston might retaliate and insist on being a part of Grady's life. I bit my lip, unable to stop the tears. I clutched the paperwork to my chest, unable to form words, so overwhelmed by the treasure in my hand. "How did you do this?"

"I convinced him that it was in his best interest to

leave you and Grady alone. After a short conversation, he agreed."

I shook my head, confused and stunned. "Just like that? A conversation?"

"Well, I punched him in the face first, but after that, he seemed more than willing to walk away."

Nico had punched Houston. *In the face.* I smothered my watery laugh behind my hand. God, how many times had I wished I could do exactly that? But Nico had somehow made the impossible happen. I stared at the paperwork again, afraid I was dreaming or lying in a coma somewhere, hallucinating.

"This is real, right?" I couldn't help myself. "This isn't a joke or some kind of scheme?"

"I wouldn't joke about this. It's one hundred percent legal and binding, so I hope it's what you really want."

"God, yes," I exclaimed, holding the paperwork tightly. *Thank you* seemed so inadequate a statement for what I was feeling in my soul, but I said it anyway. "I'm so incredibly grateful. Thank you." Tears dribbled down my cheeks as I met his gaze, questioning. "But why? Why would you do this for us?"

Nico drew himself up with a deep breath, and I'd never seen him appear so vulnerable or scared. He swallowed, wetting his bottom lip, before answering humbly, "Because I couldn't make Grady *my* son until Houston was out of the picture." I gasped, my breath hitching in my chest as I shook my head, more tears coming. Was he actually asking if… Was this happening? Nico slowly went down on one knee, producing a black jewelry box, and I nearly fainted.

"Marry me, Lauren."

One simple statement held such power and depth—the power to make or break three separate lives.

He opened the box, and the prettiest diamond engagement ring twinkled in the light. "Nico…" I whispered, shaking my head. I couldn't see straight. My nerves were raw. "I… I…"

But then Grady burst from the bedroom, clearly listening to everything we'd been saying, and he was suddenly wrapped around me like a monkey, jabbering, "Say yes, Mama! Say yes! *Pllllease!*"

My heart sang through the sheen of tears that washed away the pain of the last wretched month, but I couldn't get my mouth to work. My throat had closed, and each time I tried to open my mouth, all I could do was gape like a fish and cry.

"Is that a yes?" Nico asked, peering up at me, his blue eyes worried.

I bobbed my head in a desperate motion, saying yes with my heart. Nico jumped up and placed the ring on my finger, still shaking, then sealed his mouth to mine, his joy and relief an echo of my own. I tasted his tears and mine. Forehead to forehead, he murmured with the utmost sincerity, "Thank God. I can't live without you, Lauren. I'm a lost soul and a pitiful bastard without you in my life." He drew a shuddering breath as he vowed fervently, "I promise to work every day to be the man you and Grady deserve."

I wanted to shout to the rooftops that he already was. Still clutching the paperwork to my chest, I watched as Nico then dropped down to Grady's level and said with the seriousness the occasion warranted, "Will you be my son, Grady Hughes? Will you do me the honor of becoming Grady Donato?"

Grady's little eyes welled with tears but he nodded vigorously in answer, and Nico folded him in his arms as if he'd always belonged there.

I couldn't love Nico more than I did in this moment. Everything else faded until it was only the three of us who existed in this world.

I knew he wasn't perfect, that he'd made mistakes and would likely make more, but Nico loved us with a pure heart, and for that, I loved him all the more.

And in the warm space of that love, I forgave him for all the stupid crap he'd done before this moment.

Nico rose, hoisting Grady up with him, pulling me in for a deep kiss. In his kiss, I tasted love, commitment, laughter and joy—and I knew I'd finally found what I never knew I'd been searching for.

Nico was my soul mate, my touchstone, the future father to all my children and the man I couldn't wait to start a life with.

Even if I still didn't know his favorite color.

* * * * *

FORBIDDEN PLEASURE

TARYN LEIGH TAYLOR

MILLS & BOON

For Xtal—I can't thank you enough for everything you do, most notably putting up with me during the writing process. No jokes this time, just the stone-cold truth.

And for Jo—Thanks for making this period of great transition so easy and seamless. It's been a pleasure working with you. (Except on the nights our teams face off against each other and I'm forced to despise you on principle. But all the rest of the time it's been great!)

CHAPTER ONE

EMMA MATHISON WAS ready to get wild.

She reached up and undid the top button of her blouse.

Well, at least as wild as she could get for someone who was still in the office at eight o'clock on a Friday night.

At some point during the last three years, it had become the status quo—dinner at her desk, working until eight or nine, home to bed, and returning bright and early in the morning to do it all again. Emma couldn't remember the last time she'd had plans. With a sigh, she leaned forward over the sink, inspecting herself in the harsh fluorescent lighting.

She barely recognized the professional-looking woman in the mirror. Blond chignon, subdued makeup, conservative blouse. The result of years spent focused everywhere but on herself—fighting to keep it together both financially and emotionally as Alzheimer's stripped her beautiful, vivacious, hard-working mother of her memories, her personality and finally her life.

Emma touched her thumb to the simple silver band she wore on the middle finger of her right hand. Ana

Petrović-Mathison's most prized possession—her wedding ring. The loss was still a gut punch, but she made herself breathe through it. Her mother had worn it as a tribute to a life well-lived. Emma wore it now as a warning that life was short.

Fourteen-hour workdays that barely made a dent in the pile of medical bills. A roster of acquaintances on Facebook, but no real friends. A tiny apartment where no one waited to welcome her home. It scared Emma, the realization that if she suffered the same fate as her mother, if Alzheimer's came for her one day, she had no memories to lose.

But there was still time to change that, to reclaim the woman she'd been before hospitals and hopelessness and grief had worn her down to a meek, biddable shell of her former self.

Starting now.

She tugged the bobby pins from her hair, shaking it out so it fell in loose waves down her back. Dropping the pins into her secondhand Michael Kors tote, she pulled out a tube of red lipstick. It had been an impulse purchase, the opposite of the pinks and nudes she usually opted for, but like the sexy lingerie hiding beneath her staid blouse and demure pencil skirt, it had been carefully chosen to keep her courage up.

And yeah, she thought, painting her lips ruby red before tucking the lipstick away, maybe the bathroom at Whitfield Industries was not the most auspicious place to launch her emancipation, but if she'd learned one thing over the last three years, it was that life wasn't perfect.

If you waited for the stars to align, you missed out.

To that end, she readjusted her boobs to get every dollar's worth of "lift and separate" out of her extravagantly priced bra and gave herself a final once-over.

With a deep breath, Emma stared at the daring, crimson-lipped woman reflecting back at her. The one who was about to go and seduce her boss.

"Time to make some memories," she told her reflection.

She undid two more buttons on her blouse, grabbed her bag from the edge of the sink and then strode across the tiled floor with visions of the kick-ass, take-no-prisoners life she planned to live from here on out.

Despite her bathroom bravado, her pace slowed the closer she got to her target. Ignoring the sudden rush of nerves, Emma lifted her chin. "Do not chicken out now." She said the words aloud, half admonishment, half plea. Then, with a deep, steadying breath, she forced herself to turn the corner and the object of all her lusty fantasies came into view.

Max Whitfield.

It was often said that the CEO of Whitfield Industries was as handsome as he was controlled. Mostly, Emma had taught herself to ignore it, to focus on work. But tonight, standing outside the glass wall of his office for the last time, she let herself notice everything about him.

He was tirelessly poring over the files on his desk. His charcoal-gray jacket hung on the back of his chair, and his shirtsleeves were rolled up his tanned forearms. He'd loosened his red silk tie enough to pop the top button of his collar. Behind him, the lights of Los Angeles twinkled like fallen stars, but he kept his head down and his back to the million-dollar view. His modern, masculine office was lit only by his desk lamp and his computer screen, his preferred lighting scheme once the sun had set.

Max had always reminded her of a panther—beautiful and predatory and not to be underestimated. It wasn't just his ebony hair and amber eyes, but the way he moved, lithe and graceful. Purposeful. No wasted movement. The constant threat of danger, even in repose.

He was the kind of man who made a woman wonder—when she unwrapped him, would she find that slick, urbane control went all the way to the core, or did it hide something more dangerous, something desperate to be unleashed?

In her fantasies, she vacillated between the two extremes—sometimes imagining him as a fiery, insatiable lover, sometimes ice-cold and bossy, controlled throughout.

And tonight, she intended to find out which version of Max was real.

She set her tote on his admin assistant's desk—Sherri had left over an hour ago—and pulled out her employment contract. *Here goes nothing.* Squaring her shoulders, she stepped forward.

Max looked up sharply when she knocked, but the tightness in his jaw faded when he recognized her, and he motioned for her to enter. With a glance at his watch, he added, "I didn't realize it was so late. What can I do for you, Emma?"

She covered her disappointment at his lack of reaction to her new look with a smile she hoped was more come-hither than professional.

His desk wasn't ornate—the clean, simple lines of black onyx had always struck Emma as sleek and powerful, like the man who sat behind it. On a usual day, this would be the point where he launched into a rapid-fire series of orders, but tonight he said nothing, regarding her with the infamous poker face that Emma knew hid all manner of secrets.

She was careful not to let her hands shake as she set the contract on top of the files in front of him.

He ignored it, didn't even glance down. Just stared at her from across the expanse of his desk, hypnotic golden eyes boring into hers with the intensity she'd come to associate with him. Max Whitfield didn't do anything halfway.

"You didn't sign it."

It wasn't a question.

She didn't ask how he knew.

Max hadn't taken his family's scandal-ridden company from the brink of bankruptcy to a tech juggernaut within the span of five years by not knowing how to read people.

Only then did she realize she'd given herself away and was absently twisting the plain silver band on her middle finger. She dropped her hands and lifted her chin.

"So you're really going through with this?"

"If by *this*, you mean quitting, then yes. I'm really

going through with this." Emma pushed a small metal statue of a horse's head with a mane of flames out of the way so she could perch a hip on the corner of his desk before she crossed her left leg over her right. It was a bold move, not one she'd ever made before, but this was a now-or-never situation—and she was Team Now, all the way. At least until he cocked an eyebrow at the liberty she'd just taken.

Her heart thudded in slow, thick beats as he trailed his imperious gaze down her body and let it linger for a moment too long on her knee, making her excruciatingly aware of how far her dress had slid up her thigh when she'd sat.

God, if having his eyes on her could make her feel this good, she couldn't wait to get his hands on her.

She waited patiently until he'd looked his fill and flicked his attention back to her face.

The raw power of him made Emma's skin hum with potential, but she faced down the electricity's source. Max didn't respect cowards. He lived in a world of high-stakes negotiations where death was preferable to shows of weakness.

"I don't know what more I can say."

"That's easy," Max countered, leaning back in his chair. "Say you'll stay."

The statement hung between them, suspended in air so thick it brushed against her skin and left goose bumps in its wake. They'd always had chemistry. Since the first time they'd laid eyes on one another. And with the same sardonic expression on his face as he wore now, he'd given her the research and development job she'd so brazenly demanded. In the space of a handshake, the sexual awareness bubbling between them had been leashed, muzzled and banished by unspoken agreement to the dungeon of professionalism.

But ever since she'd handed in her notice three weeks ago, and he'd countered with the very generous terms outlined in the unsigned contract she'd just placed on his desk, the sensual beast had awoken, prowling in the shadows, growing bolder, encroaching more often and more forcefully as their time together drew to an end. And tonight, she was going to let it loose.

Emma didn't move. And this time she would not speak first.

There was a note of respect in his voice when he conceded. "What will it take?"

"I'm sorry?"

"How much? Name your price."

It was as close to begging as she'd ever heard him get. She didn't like the answering flutter in her chest that made her want to stay. Max had a way of taking control, and she couldn't afford to let him. Not tonight.

"This isn't a negotiation. I don't have a price."

Max steepled his fingers, looking like every titan of industry in every anti-capitalist movie ever made. "*Everyone* has a price."

Her answering laugh was tinged with scorn. "Really, Max? Resorting to tired clichés already? I'd always credited you with more stamina than that."

The slow grin that dawned across his handsome features stirred something deep and primal in her belly, a silent refutation of her verbal jab that let her know that he could more than provide *whatever* she needed for as long as she needed it. It was a rare smile for him, not the feral one he used for business, but the charming one that slipped out sometimes when he was genuinely amused.

"What can I say? I have a deep appreciation for the classics." Max dropped his hands, then sat forward in his chair. "Now, get off my desk. You don't work here anymore."

Emma had already followed the command before she realized she'd done it. *Dammit.* No retreat, she reminded herself, straightening the seams of her black pencil skirt, wishing the slit was a little more daring, achingly aware of the garters beneath. Ignoring the implied dismissal, she crossed her arms over her chest, taking care to enhance her cleavage as she did so. "You're right. So maybe you should pour me a drink. We can toast the end of our working relationship."

Oh God. Had she just said that?

He raised a contemplative eyebrow.

It was hard to breathe.

Without a word, he stood in that dangerously graceful way he had and walked over to the sideboard near the window. Her heart gave a funny little lurch at the realization it was the last time she was going to see him.

She allowed her gaze to linger a moment, to fix the height and breadth of him in her mind. The quiet authority of him as, with quick, efficient movements, Max pulled the stopper from the crystal decanter and poured a drink.

Then he poured another, which caused a completely

different kind of lurch, this one much, much lower than her heart.

This was going to happen.

Emma's palms prickled as he grabbed both glasses and joined her in front of his desk. The fact that he stood about a foot closer than he'd ever stood before was not lost on her. She accepted the drink he held out to her, her skin slick against the expensive crystal.

Max regarded her for a moment, his expression un-readable, before he raised his glass. "To whatever comes next."

His voice was deep, rich and more intoxicating than the premium liquor he'd handed her.

She clinked her glass to his and joined him in a sip of his preferred single malt Scotch.

The liquid was smooth and strong as it slipped over her tongue.

"Tell me it's not Kearney."

"What?"

"Tell me you're not leaving to work for that son of a bitch."

Emma was oddly touched by the surly order that na-mechecked his most hated rival, the CEO of Cybercore. In Max-speak, that might be as close as she would ever get to "It's been nice working with you." Not that she was fishing for compliments.

"Why would you think that?" she asked, taking an-other sip.

"Because business is war. You have to take what you want. And Liam Kearney has a long history of taking what's mine."

Emma choked on her mouthful of Scotch.

Surely he hadn't meant...

She glanced up at his stern, handsome face, but his eyes were shuttered, focused on the liquid swirling in the glass thanks to a practiced flick of his wrist, like he was lost in an unpleasant memory.

Her voice was soft when she finally spoke, and despite her better judgment, held the reverence of a vow. "I'm not going to work for that son of a bitch."

Emma was vindicated by the twitch of his lips that betrayed, if not outright relief, at least mild amusement, though she wasn't sure if it was at the solemnness of her response or at himself for stooping to ask the question. "Drink your Scotch, Emma."

It sounded almost like a warning. She stared at the contents of her glass. "We've never had a drink together before." The words were unnecessary, obvious, but she couldn't stop them anymore than she could stop her gaze from lifting to his.

If she hadn't spent the last three years working with him, day in and day out, she might have missed the tick in his jaw, the subtle darkening of his eyes.

"You've never not worked for me before," he countered, raising the glass to his lips.

Heat flared in her belly, incinerating the oxygen and making it hard to breathe. Her skin buzzed at the change in the atmosphere.

She fortified herself with another sip of the amber liquid that was as heady and intoxicating as the look in his eyes. Warmth tingled through her.

"And that…changes things?" she asked, testing the waters.

Max tossed back the rest of his drink and set the heavy crystal on his desk with undue precision. She felt him breathe, as though he'd stolen all the air from around her for a moment, before it came back in a rush.

"Change is inevitable."

The urge to give into the pull of him, the magnetism, was overwhelming.

Before she could talk herself out of it, Emma stepped closer, raised up on her tiptoes, leveraging every inch from the platforms of her discount Louboutins.

Their breath mingled as she brushed her lips softly against his.

The sweet shock of what she'd done made her knees weak, and she steadied herself with her right palm against his chest. The hard muscle leaped beneath her fingers, like he was bracing himself for whatever came next. Emboldened by his reaction and warmed by the afterburn of the best Scotch the world had to offer, Emma leaned closer and pressed her mouth to his again, lingering this time to sample the delicious heat flickering between them.

She kept her eyes closed as she settled back into her black heels, cementing the feel of his lips beneath hers, the tingle of contact racing through her veins, even as she pulled her hand back from his chest. When she opened her eyes, he was staring down at her, controlled and handsome as ever, his face devoid of any particular expression. The way he looked at the negotiation table.

She let herself smile anyway. "I've wanted to do that

for a long time. You're right. Taking what you want is incredibly…satisfying."

He stepped even closer, and Emma's head swam from his proximity as she lifted her chin to maintain eye contact.

"Are you?" The question, delivered without emotion, caught her off guard.

"Am I what?"

"Are you satisfied? Because I'm not."

She didn't even realize that she was still holding the highball glass in her left hand until he tugged it from her numb fingers and set it on the edge of his desk. The muted thud barely registered on her consciousness as something wicked sparked in the amber gaze that held her rapt. "What's happening right now has always been…"

She didn't blink, didn't breathe, didn't move.

Time slipped by to the heavy thud of her pulse and her mind spun, desperate to fill in the blank.

Inappropriate?

Illogical?

Insane?

Max slid his hands in his pockets, the outward picture of relaxed male elegance, but when he spoke, his tone was low and rough.

"Inevitable."

CHAPTER TWO

INEVITABLE.

The word reverberated through her entire body, confirmation that Max wanted her.

She wanted him, too. All of him. All of this.

He was standing there, his eyes lit with challenge, hers for the taking. And all she had to do was reach out.

With trembling fingers, Emma grasped his tie, tugging until she'd released the silk from its Windsor knot. For the first time since this had started, she broke eye contact, dropping her gaze to the tanned column of his throat as she unfastened the first button.

Her fingers grew defter as she worked her way down the placket of his shirt, eyes hungrily following the swath of skin left in the wake of the gaping fabric—his collarbones, the smattering of dark hair across his broad chest, the ridged perfection of his abs and the intriguing trail of hair that narrowed before it disappeared behind the square buckle of his black belt.

She tugged his shirttails free from the waistband of his pants, then dropped her hands to her sides, beholding the perfection of him. Of the moment. This was it, she realized. Her first memory. And she didn't want to forget a single detail.

Max pulled his right hand from his pocket and reached toward her. With a deftness that she found intensely erotic, he traced his finger along her skin, from her exposed collarbone down to her cleavage, the light touch singing her nerve endings.

Her whole world narrowed to the sweet friction of skin on skin and her breasts swelled against the confines of the black lace cups of her bra. She gasped at the instantaneous reaction and something wicked kindled in her belly as he began a methodical assault on her buttons, popping them open one by one until he'd reached the waistband of her skirt. He regarded his handiwork for a moment, the thin band of skin revealed by her open shirt, before unpocketing his other hand. Her breath caught in her chest as he grabbed the edges of her blouse, spreading them apart so she was exposed from neck to navel.

Max grasped her hips, then pulled her to him. The air temperature spiked from tropical to volcanic as her breasts made contact with his chest, heat rolling off him in waves. *So damn hot.* Her nipples puckered painfully against the scratchy black lace, and she sucked air into her lungs on a gasp. He smelled like sex and man and hard liquor, and the heady combination had her halfway to wherever he wanted to take her.

As if he could sense it, Max's fingers flexed against her hips before his big hands traced the side seams of her skirt. His leisurely exploration made her restless, antsy, but before she could do something about it, Max fisted the material and began the trip back up her thighs, bringing her skirt along for the ride, higher, higher, and Emma thought she might die from the slow, sweet torture of anticipation.

Cool air swirled around her legs, wringing a moan from her. *Oh God, just a little more.*

It took a second before she realized his hands had stopped moving, that he'd taken a step back. Her eyes fluttered open and she was startled by the hungry look on his face. Emma followed his gaze, realizing he'd revealed the black garter belt that held up her nude stockings.

His face was dark and his voice was rough. "You're full of surprises tonight, Ms. Mathison."

She swayed toward him as heat pooled between her legs. He always called her Emma, but this fit the fantasy that was playing out right now, and it was so perfect, so deliciously naughty, that she thought she might come.

"Yes, sir."

His head jerked up at that, eyes flaring with an emotion that Emma couldn't identify, but whatever it was, it was the first time she'd ever seen him lose that steely edge of control that was part of his legend. The jolt of it was like a lightning bolt to her core.

Whatever silly game they'd been playing was over.

In one fluid motion, he hiked her skirt up over her hips, then backed her up against his desk. The hard edge of it dug into her thighs.

Emma's teeth scored her bottom lip in anticipation, and his deep chuckle ignited something warm and twisty in her gut. "Not yet," he told her, but the promise of *soon* echoed in the timber of his voice. She sucked in a breath as his fingers traced the black elastic of her garters down to the clasp.

"These are so fucking sexy."

He was pretty fucking sexy himself, she decided as he traced the lacy edge of her stockings from front to back before his big hands gripped her thighs and boosted her onto the smooth onyx surface. It was cool against her bare skin, but her shiver had more to do with the man in front of her filling up the space between her parted knees.

She'd always known Max Whitfield was a force to be reckoned with when he had a goal within his sights, but now that she was the goal, the true depth of his focus was staggering. When he looked at her, the world narrowed to the heat in his eyes and the pounding of her pulse.

He leaned close, planting a hand on the desk on either side of her hips. Eagerness fizzed in her chest and time slowed as he wet his lips. She braced herself for impact, but it was futile. There was no preparing for Max.

He pounced like the predator she'd likened him to, devouring her mouth with such singular determination that she had to grab his shoulders to keep from falling back. Finally having her hands on him was a revelation. He was hard muscle and leashed power and it felt so damn good to touch him. To taste him.

He kissed like a man who knew what he wanted, teasing her until she welcomed the invasion of his tongue, then retreating only to start the entire process over, lowering her back onto the desk until she was almost horizontal.

Emma was so focused on his kiss that she didn't realize he'd shifted his position until his hand slipped between her legs. The brush of his thumb against the wet lace of her underwear was like the zap of a live wire, sizzling through her, and Max swore into her mouth when her hips bucked at the intimate touch.

He pulled back so quickly every part of her cried out at the loss of his touch.

She levered herself up onto her elbows.

Please. More, she wanted to say, but when she looked up at him, he was breathing hard, staring at her with such speculative intensity that she couldn't form words.

He just stood there, raking his eyes down her body. There was something so deliciously raw about being sprawled back on her elbows on his desk, her blouse spread open, her skirt pushed up around her waist, her knees spread apart and her fancy underwear on display for him.

"Don't move."

The order made her breath come faster, and she obeyed as he rounded the desk.

She spared a moment to be thankful that she'd let the saleswoman talk her into the garter belt when she'd splurged on the sexy undies, but then Max stepped back into view, his eyes full of promise and a condom packet in his hand, and suddenly she cared less about what was under her clothes and more about what was under his.

Her eyes widened as he unbuckled his belt.

Undid his pants.

Pulled himself free of his underwear.

Oh God. Yes, please.

The sight of his hand on his cock made her wet. He was so starkly beautiful, hard and masculine, and her body was vibrating for him. She pushed herself up to a sitting position as he sheathed himself with the condom, desperate to be closer to him.

His eyes cut to hers, pinning her to the spot. "I thought I told you not to move."

Emma burst into flames. She must have. Spontaneous combustion was the only explanation for the wave of heat that washed over her.

Then he grabbed her by the backs of her knees and jerked her hips to the edge of the desk, and she went molten.

Emma couldn't get enough of him. He'd been a fantasy for so long, but the reality of him surpassed everything she'd ever known. The perfect mix of heat and ice.

She wrapped her legs around his waist, slipped her hands under his shirt so she could feel the smooth expanse of his skin and let Max do what he did best: take control.

Fuck.

Things were under control until the goddamn garters. Until she called him sir. Now the woman in his arms wasn't a pleasant diversion but an all-consuming need.

Max prided himself on being disciplined, but Emma was undoing him with nothing more than a garter belt and eyes so expressive that he could read her soul. Right now, though, it was her body that had his attention.

Her high heels digging into the backs of his legs, her hands kneading his shoulders. A scrap of black lace was all that stood between him and the kind of physical gratification that drowned out all the issues that were pounding like a nail gun in his brain—lawsuits and tech glitches and launches and the bullshit that came with righting a sinking tech company. He wanted to bury himself in her and forget the rest.

Max ran his knuckles up the inside of her thigh, stopping short of those pretty, lacy panties that had him riding the edge of anticipation.

He was so fucking turned on, galvanized by the erotic turn the evening had taken. Despite the overwhelming ache in his balls, the desperation in his muscles, he held back. Stayed perfectly, agonizingly still. Just for a minute. Just to be sure he was in control of himself. Just until she was frustrated enough that her eyes flicked from dazed pleasure to "is this happening, or what?"

Only then did he give her what they both wanted.

In one fluid movement, he slipped her underwear aside and thrust deep, his thumb riding her clit. She moaned, raking his skin with her nails, and everything faded into pure, raw sensation. The slick, scorching friction of their joining was all exactly what he needed right now. Her breath was hot on his neck. She smelled like booze and sex, and he was ravenous for her.

Max removed his hand from between them, bracing it on the desk so he could tip her back farther. She tightened her legs around him as he sped his hips, short-stroking until she was wild beneath him. She was close. Restless and panting, clutching him to her, her lace-covered breasts scraped against his sensitized chest, driving him mad.

And Max was so goddamn ready to feel her come apart in his arms.

He shoved the fingers of his free hand into her hair, cradling her head as he laid her back, kissing her hard. He reached down, hooking his right elbow under her knee, and braced his forearm on the desk, opening her. The change in angle made her gasp, allowed him to pull out almost completely before pumping into her with slow, deep thrusts designed to push her over the edge.

"Come for me, Emma," he ordered, or maybe he begged. It didn't matter, not when he was drunk on her whiskey-flavored tongue and the pressure of her impending climax as her muscles drew tight with anticipation. *Fuck yes.* "Just like that. I want to feel you squeezing my cock."

She cried out as his words pushed her over the edge and with a groaning curse, Max gave into instinct, his chest crushing her breasts as he buried himself deep and took what he'd wanted since she'd sat on his desk, all womanly curves and dawning confidence. Pleasure exploded through his veins and he came fast and hard, his hips jerking with the aftershocks of the powerful orgasm.

It took a moment to steady his breath in the aftermath, and another moment after that before he stood, freeing her leg and helping her up to a sitting position.

She didn't look at him, and Max didn't like that it bothered him.

Frowning, he watched Emma stand, turning modestly as she adjusted things, tugged her skirt back into place, dealt with the buttons on her blouse.

Max disposed of the condom and fastened his pants but didn't bother rebuttoning his shirt or grabbing his tie from the floor beside his desk. Instead, he kept a wary eye on her body language, preparing himself for whatever awaited him when she turned around.

His decisions tonight had been deliberate—he didn't do anything without considering all the implications. But the passion that had flared between them had been…unexpected. And technically, she'd quit before anything had happened. They were both adults. The rationalization did nothing to stem his sudden unease. For the first time that evening, he wondered if he'd been right to take things as far as he had. Was she thinking the same thing?

He was expecting recriminations in those expressive blue eyes, or worse, hero worship. But when she finally turned to face him, what he saw almost dropped him to his knees. With sex-tousled hair, a misbuttoned blouse and her skirt slightly askew, Emma Mathison looked radiant and satisfied and deliciously well-fucked.

"Thanks for everything, Max." The words were husky and low, and he felt them in his groin, even before she added, "It's been a pleasure."

With her head high, her shoulders squared and a Mona Lisa smile tilting the corner of her kiss-stung lips, she walked out of his office, grabbed her purse from Sherri's desk on her way to the elevator. And she didn't look back once.

Double fuck.

Max reached for her unfinished Scotch, then downed it in one swallow.

It had been a very, very long time since he'd underestimated someone.

CHAPTER THREE

FOCUS AND DECISIVE ACTION…that was the difference between losing and winning, the difference between winning and winning big. Timing was everything. It was
a lesson Max Whitfield knew better than most. He had
no time for visits from the ghost-of-sexual-encounters-
past.

So why the hell was he sitting there, half-hard, remembering things best forgotten?

Remembering her.

That mouth. So prim, even when it was painted scar-
let.

Fuck, the things he'd wanted her to do with that
mouth. Down on her knees, calling him sir with a
wicked gleam in her blue eyes.

Now he couldn't look at his desk without remembering the press of the black garter belt against the pale
skin of her thighs, without hearing the gasps that escaped her lips, as though she was surprised by the heat
between them. He wasn't surprised. Hell, he was consumed, and he'd barely gotten his hands on her.

He exhaled at his lapse in judgment.

Taking her on his desk has been a mistake.

"Am I boring you, Whitfield?"

Max's gaze snapped to the man in the chair across from him.

Wes Brennan. Founder and CEO of Soteria Security. World-class asshole.

A brilliant asshole, obviously, but an asshole just the same.

"Not at all. I believe you were telling me about the massive breach in security you failed to prevent."

Max took an inordinate amount of pleasure at the flat, cold look that invaded Brennan's eyes.

"That spyware was caught in less than twelve hours. That's worth every zero you pay Soteria." Brennan always distanced himself from the company.

"It had goddamn better be. I want this handled."

If this got out, it would ruin him. Whitfield Industries was on the brink of reinvention. Five years after Max had ousted his corrupt father and begun to erase the era of scandal and questionable morals that had dogged the company during Charles Whitfield's reign, he was on the verge of reestablishing his grandfather's company as a leader in the world of financial services. He couldn't afford any screwups, and he certainly couldn't afford any bad press.

"Handling things is what Soteria does," Brennan assured him, like Max had insulted his honor or something.

Not that he gave a shit. The only thing Max could afford to care about right now was results.

A flash of movement in his peripheral vision tugged Max's attention to the glass door with his name on it.

"What's so important that you need me here on a Saturday afternoon?" Vivienne Grant breezed into his office, her red skirt suit almost as impeccable as her confidence.

Max allowed himself a glance at Brennan and was vindicated by the momentary crack in the man's cool facade before it was swallowed up behind bored hostility. The stiff formality that invaded the room whenever Vivienne and Brennan were present was unmistakable. He didn't know what had gone on between his chief counsel and the cybersecurity specialist, and as long as it didn't affect his business, he didn't particularly give a damn. Still, he allowed himself a moment to revel in Brennan's discomfort.

"I believe the two of you are acquainted?"

His unnecessary introduction put a hitch in Vivienne's self-assured stride, but she recovered nicely, bestowing a coolly regal nod at the other occupant of the room as she took a seat in the chair farthest from him. "Wes."

"Vivienne."

Max ignored the chill in the room. "Excellent. Now that we're all here, let's discuss our next steps."

"As I was saying, the security breach is internal. I don't think—"

Vivienne's head snapped up at Brennan's words, her eyes locking with Max's. "What *internal breach*? Do you have a suspect in mind? What the hell is going on?"

Max leaned back in his chair, forcing the relaxed

pose, even though every nerve in his body was coiled tight. "We're waiting for answers."

"I might have a couple."

The voice at the door stole the attention in the room.

Jesse Hastings was Soteria Security's second in command. More personable than his business partner, Hastings was the de facto face of the company and his geniality was responsible for scoring the majority of Soteria's clients. But he really shone when you put him behind the keyboard, so when he'd insisted on helping Brennan handle this clusterfuck personally, Max had agreed. With any luck, having both of Soteria's big dogs on the case would see it resolved quickly and quietly.

"I'm just not sure you're going to like them," Hastings continued, leaning a broad shoulder against the doorjamb. "Are we waiting for Kaylee?"

The reference to his absent PR director soured his mood further. She hadn't picked up her fucking phone. If his little sister wasn't so damn good at her job, he'd have fired her when he'd purged the company of the bulk of his father's hires. "She'll be briefed first thing Monday morning. What have you got?"

"It's definitely a contained breach, but whoever's behind this is good. The information's been fragmented and rerouted through hell and back. It's going to take a while to piece together what's been leaked. But I can tell you that all the activity is localized to one computer."

Hastings raised his eyebrows, waiting until he received Max's nod to continue.

"Emma Mathison's."

Max was careful to keep his expression neutral, but his hand clenched involuntarily. Vivienne and Hastings didn't notice, but Max's jaw tightened when Brennan's eyebrow lifted with cool interest.

Smug prick.

Vivienne's face was pale when she turned back to Max. "You really think Emma sold you out? That seems…out of character. I mean, has she been acting strangely?"

Besides quitting while she lounged on his desk?

Besides her secret, self-satisfied smiles?

Besides fucking him into oblivion in thigh-highs and garters on his goddamn desk?

"She didn't sign her contract extension."

Hastings frowned at that.

"Did she say why?" Vivienne asked. "Was it something to do with her mother? She was in the hospital a while ago. Emma didn't say much about it, but she seemed worried."

His lead counsel had the kind of mind that liked to connect all the dots, but Max didn't have time for conjecture right now. He needed facts. "While I'm touched by your concern for Emma's family's well-being, let's try to stick to the salient points."

"Well, I'm not sure you're going to like those either," Jesse countered, his expression marred with concern. He walked toward them.

"I ran a couple of checks," he explained, unbuttoning his suit jacket as he took the empty seat between Vivienne and Wes. "There's a ten-thousand-dollar deposit in her primary bank account, and one Emma Marija Mathison is booked on a plane that's leaving the country on Monday."

Max's jaw tensed. "Where?"

Jesse raked a hand through his hair, and Max could tell by the stalling maneuver that he was *not* going to like the answer.

"Croatia."

Son of a bitch. No US extradition laws in Croatia.

"Do we think she acted alone?" Vivienne was still looking for the next dot.

"The spyware is no joke," Hastings told her. "I'm going to need some time to figure out what she got and who she got it to." He glanced at Brennan. "If Wes hadn't tweaked our monitoring program, we might not have caught this at all."

Vivienne exhaled, then uncrossed and recrossed her legs. "So we've got nothing right now except that the spyware was on her computer? Any surveillance footage?"

Jesse shook his head. "Scrambled. I'll work as fast as I can to figure out what she got, but the encryption is top-notch. It's going to take more time than we have. Her flight leaves Monday morning, and we can't afford to let her leave the country, that's for damn sure."

"I can file charges," Vivienne said. "Something to stall her, but I'll need—"

Max cut her off. "No charges."

Two sets of eyes snapped toward him with surprise. Brennan remained annoyingly apathetic and glanced at his watch.

"We're two weeks out from the launch of a crypto currency payment system that will change the way America does business." Max leaned back in his chair. "Now is not the time to ring the alarms."

Vivienne frowned, as she tucked her hair behind her left ear. She darted a glance at the security guys, though Max got the impression it was more directed at Brennan than Hastings. "A massive internal security breach happens on Emma's computer, and you're just going to let her get away with it?"

Max narrowed his eyes at the accusation, and Vivienne took a deep breath, dropping her gaze, chastened at the realization that she'd pushed him too far. Brennan's shoulders stiffened, but he was smart enough to keep his mouth shut.

Incidents involving Emma Mathison had commanded his full attention twice in as many days. And while he'd infinitely preferred last night's naked encounter over this afternoon's occurrence, letting this trend continue on any level was not acceptable.

"I want answers on Monday morning," he snapped at Brennan, waiting for the man's curt nod before skipping past Hastings, straight to Vivienne. "You're working alone on this. Wait for my instructions, and don't bring anyone else into the loop. No associates, no paralegals, no one."

"Understood."

"What about Emma? The plane ticket?" Hastings asked. "Did you want me to—"

"I want you to do your job," Max said coolly, vindicated when Hastings paled at the reprimand. Max turned his attention to the sheaf of papers on the corner of his desk. "I'll take care of Emma."

CHAPTER FOUR

MAX BANGED ON the door with more force than he'd intended.

He'd been offended by the shabby Villa Apartments that were listed as Emma's home address on her employment record. Now that he was inside the ancient building, his opinion sank even lower.

He paid her well. Better than well. There was no reason she should be living in this shithole. Which, Max realized, lent credence to Jesse Hastings's insinuations of guilt.

Despite regular paychecks from him, she obviously needed money for something, and desperation led people to do uncharacteristic things. His chest tightened at the realization that Emma Mathison wasn't finished surprising him.

Life would have been much easier if he'd kept his hands off her in the first place. He'd managed it for the last three years. Which meant fuck all, since it had taken less than five minutes after she'd resigned before he'd dragged her into his arms. It had seemed a smart play at the time.

Well, perhaps smart was overstating it, but it was low risk.

She'd quit, so she wasn't technically an employee.

This SecurePay launch had him working every waking hour. He barely had time to shower some days, let alone maintain any sort of relationship with a woman, no matter how casual. Not that what had happened between him and Emma had anything to do with a relationship. It was more like an experiment. A curiosity that needed sating.

Confirmation that their chemistry was as combustible as he'd always expected it would be. And now he was paying for that lapse in judgment.

Max heard shuffling behind the inconsequential piece of wood that was acting as a barrier between her and the outside world, but he didn't understand how something that barely blocked sound was supposed to keep her safe from intruders. Especially since the peephole was nothing more than a quarter-sized hole covered in ratty duct tape. Which was practically inviting thieves inside in this neighborhood. His left hand tightened on the sheaf of papers he held.

His musings were cut short by the slide of a chain, followed by the snick of a lock disengaging. The door swung open and there she was.

Last night's seductress was gone. In her place was a fresh-faced ingenue with impossibly wide eyes who looked like she'd stepped out of a laughably wholesome 1960s film.

His gaze slid the length of her body, from the top of her shiny blond ponytail, past her fuzzy white sweater, barely-there jean shorts and down the length of her legs until he reached the tips of her toes, painted bubble-gum pink. Max's thoughts, however, were anything but virtuous.

Every part of him that she'd touched the night before flared with heat, begging for an encore. He still wanted her. Despite everything he'd found out today. Despite the mounting evidence against her. The heat stirring in his veins iced over at the reminder, and he braced his shoulders against the onslaught of lust. He would not underestimate her again.

"Max?"

Surprised. A little breathless. But no fear. No guilt.

"What are you doing here?"

He ignored the question, shifting his focus over Emma's left shoulder at the bare, scarred walls of the old apartment. A couple of cardboard boxes were stacked in the middle of the mostly empty room. "If you needed a raise this badly, you should have told me."

Her forehead creased with puzzlement. "What? Oh." Her laugh was tinged with embarrassment. "It's a rental," she explained, moving out of his way as he stepped past her, onto the threadbare brown carpet. "I never spent much time here anyway."

Max thought back to the long hours she'd put in at the office. He'd always respected her work ethic. He gestured to the boxes. "Going somewhere?"

She nodded, closing the shoddy excuse for a door, but even as he searched her face for guile, there was none.

"On vacation, actually. Thought I'd see how the other half lives." Her smile faded at his lack of reaction, and he watched in fascination as her body language grew wary, matching his mood. She'd always been good at reading a room.

"I'm sorry. Where are my manners? Can I get you something to drink?" she asked, heading toward the outdated kitchenette.

Max foiled her attempted retreat by following her, but he stopped at the nearest side of the counter, allowing her to take cover on the far side of it. "Turns out you're going to have to reschedule that vacation. Something's come up." He tossed her contract extension on the counter between them. It landed with a heavy thud. "Sign this."

That got her attention. She stiffened, a slight frown marring her forehead as she recognized the document. "What is this?"

"Exactly what you think it is," he confirmed.

"I have a flight to Dubrovnik booked for Monday."

"Postpone it."

"I can't afford—" She stopped herself. Took a deep breath. Then restarted, the way she sometimes did in their project meetings when one of the board members wasn't taking her ideas seriously. It was the most herself Emma had been since she'd opened the door to him. Well, the most like the Emma he'd thought she was. Ever since Friday night, he wasn't sure he knew her at all.

"I am not postponing anything. I've sold almost everything I own to pay for this trip—my furniture, my clothes, my car. The lease on this place is up on Tuesday, my plane ticket is nonrefundable. I'm going to Croatia on Monday, and you have no say in the matter."

"Unfortunately, that's no longer the case. This morning, Soteria Security discovered a spyware program running on your computer."

She froze at the implicit accusation.

"It was loaded manually and discovered the day after your contract expired. The day after you formally rejected a generous extension of employment. The shallowest of security checks shows that you received an anomalous lump-sum payment of ten thousand dollars and used it to buy an open-ended plane ticket to a country with no extradition policy."

She paled with each charge, bracing her hands on the counter like she might faint. Or throw up. And despite himself, he wanted to believe in her innocence.

"Do you understand how this looks?"

"What exactly are you accusing me of?" Her voice was small, but she was heartbreakingly brave as she met his eyes.

Why he felt like he'd fallen from grace right then did not bear contemplating.

Max tipped his chin at the contract. "I'm merely offering you a way out of this. Until this security breach is resolved to my satisfaction, you will resume your role as chief analyst of research and development. We will erase everything that happened since you walked into my office and quit."

She flinched at that, and though he hadn't been referring to their hot and sweaty desk-fuck, he didn't correct her misunderstanding. It was best for everyone if they went back to their normal working relationship.

"Report to Vivienne Grant's office when you arrive on Monday morning. She can draw up an amendment to ensure you're reimbursed for the wasted plane ticket. And you can let her know if there are any further concerns we've failed to address here today. Now, sign the contract."

"Why are you doing this?"

He would not be swayed by the wounded look in her eyes. He made sure his shrug was dismissive. "It's nothing personal, Emma. It's—"

"Business?" she scoffed, her magnificent eyes glinting sharply, like daggers. "Spare me the trite maxims. Just take your bullshit contract and go."

Max took the centering breath of a sniper setting up a kill shot. "I have millions of dollars and the future of my company invested in the launch of SecurePay. The timing on this is crucial. If the media finds out we've been hacked, the project is dead in the water." Even the prospect of failure, after everything he'd sacrificed over the last five years to bring SecurePay to market, was like a hot poker to his ribs. It was enough to crack his usual icy veneer. "So until this situation has been neutralized and contained, I will do whatever it takes to ensure this launch goes off without a hitch. And that doesn't include key members of my team fleeing the country in the wake of a goddamn internal security breach!"

Her lips trembled, but she lifted her chin in a magnificent show of bravado. "I don't work for you anymore,

TARYN LEIGH TAYLOR   265

Mr. Whitfield." His name sounded toxic on her lips. "Keep your money. I don't want it. I'm leaving Monday morning, and there's nothing you can do about it."

Max respected the rally, the way her dawning anger brought a flush to her cheeks and put the spark back in her eyes.

It was too little, too late, but she didn't seem to realize that yet. He felt honor bound to make his imminent victory clear. He didn't want any misunderstandings between them.

"People who've been accused of corporate espionage usually have a hard time boarding commercial flights. Or so I've heard."

Her mouth fell open at the threat. "You wouldn't."

He kept his gaze level, implacable, until she realized the truth. That he could. And he would. It was best that she understood that from the get-go.

"You bastard."

Max accepted the epithet with a tip of his chin as he pulled a pen from his inside breast pocket and held it out to her. "Sign the contract, Emma."

She shot him a mutinous glare as she snatched the pen from his fingers, and his respect notched up again for her ability to know when she was beat. She slashed her signature across the page in black ink and shoved the contract and the pen in his direction.

Despite the heat of the movement, her eyes were ice-cold when they met his. "Get out."

Always gracious in victory, Max returned the pen to the inside pocket of his suit jacket, then picked up the papers and left.

CHAPTER FIVE

IF MAX WANTED a war, she'd give him one.

Emma's jaw was locked for battle as she strode out of Vivienne Grant's office and headed straight for the elevator. She managed a distracted smile of thanks at the man who held the door open, so she could shepherd herself and the suitcase of all her worldly possessions inside. It was born out of instinctual courtesy, not sincerity, though. Right now, smiling was the last thing she wanted to do.

Her simmering rage was evident in the jab of her thumb against the button that would take her to the top floor, where that pompous, dictatorial, gorgeous asshole she worked for was probably sitting in his swanky office, plotting new ways to infuriate her. She readjusted the straps of her leather tote against her shoulder as the silver door slid shut.

To add to her sour mood, the elevator stopped to acquire and drop off passengers on each of the four floors between Legal and her destination, dragging out the inevitable.

Emma straightened the placket of her black silk

blouse and plucked a piece of fuzz off her pencil skirt. Her sex clothes, as she'd ignominiously dubbed them.

She wasn't kidding when she'd told Max she'd purged her closet of office-appropriate attire. And that morning, when she'd been getting dressed while cursing his name, she'd liked the idea of taunting him with the outfit. It was the reason she hadn't pinned the slit in her skirt closed…or worn a bra. Small acts of rebellion designed to put him on notice. He might have forced her to come back, but he wasn't getting the mild-mannered, desperate-to-please employee she'd once been.

Now that her meeting with his bulldog of a lawyer was over, though, Emma realized the joke was on her. She might not have signed the farcical document that had been presented that morning, but she had signed the contract Max had tossed on her kitchen counter Saturday night. And Emma got the impression that Vivienne had taken an almost sadistic pleasure in laying out the terms that she'd so rashly agreed to with that hastily scrawled signature.

Emma strode out of the elevator before the door was fully open, her heels clicking against the marble tiles as she headed for her desk. Maybe one of her coworkers would loan her a damn sweater before she had to meet with—

"Emma."

Speak of the devil…

Her name sounded like a curse on Max's lips, sharp and angry, and though it jacked up her pulse, she was careful not to show it. She stopped and slid him a disdainful glance, vindicated that his deep voice sounded tight when he added, "May I see you in my office?"

It wasn't really a question, and Emma knew it, so she hesitated just long enough to annoy him. Not that she could tell if it worked. He was already back on lock-down, his handsome features an implacable mask. But it didn't matter. She was annoyed enough for the both of them.

"Of course. I'm just going to drop my purse and suit-case off at my desk, and I'll—"

"Now." Steel edged the word, brooking no opposition.

Pasting an amused smile on her lips, she shot Max's fascinated executive assistant an eyeroll. "This one's in a mood," she said, thumbing in Max's direction before stepping past him into the glass-walled office.

"See that we're not disturbed," he told Sherri, closing the door behind them.

Emma plunked herself in the closest of the visitor's chairs, bristling with coiled energy. Max, blasé as ever, took his time as he made his way to the other side of the desk. He sat, and with the push of a hidden button on the underside of the black onyx desktop, the entire expanse of glass between them and the rest of the office frosted for privacy. And then they were all alone, her itching for a fight, him cold and unaffected.

"You wanted me?"

Her double entendre landed like a gauntlet, and the scattered haze of sexual tension that was lingering in the room courtesy of their Friday night tryst coalesced into a lightning bolt of awareness arcing between them.

"What I *want*," he informed her, the bite in his voice frigid against her heated skin, "is to know what the hell you think you're doing?"

So, not completely unaffected after all.

Emma crossed her legs, enjoying the tiny victory, and the slit of her skirt parted to midthigh. Max's sightline dipped to her leg.

"Reporting for duty, *Mr. Whitfield*. As per your orders."

He raked his gaze up her body, pausing meaningfully on the peaked outline of her nipples against the black satin of her blouse, a condition made worse by his attention, before continuing up to her throat, her lips and finally meeting her eyes. Max arched an eyebrow, the gesture thick with innuendo.

"And what *duty* did you think you'd be reporting for, exactly?"

Smug prick.

Her smile was a big 'screw you' drenched in high-fructose corn syrup. "Oh, now that I'm back, I'm open to whatever *position* you had in mind. *Sir.*"

The slow, feral grin that slid across his face escalated the sexual arms race they were engaged in. "Don't call me sir unless you mean it, Emma." He leaned back in his chair. "Didn't anyone ever teach you not to make promises you don't intend to keep?"

"Who says I don't intend to keep them?"

"Do you? Is that why you're wearing this delightfully indecent outfit?"

It was Emma's turn to raise an eyebrow. "It's the

same thing I had on Friday night. You didn't seem to have a problem with it then."

He ran his knuckles along his jaw. "As I recall, you were wearing a bra on Friday night. In the future, stick to the dress code."

The warning made her smile. "Here's a fun fact: there's actually no mention of undergarments in the entire policy."

She stood then, walked over to the window to give him a moment to wonder what else she may or may not be wearing, in case he had the inclination to do so. "But feel free to send me home if you feel like I'm not living up to the hallowed reputation of Whitfield Industries."

"I get the impression that you're trying to upset me."

"And why would I do that?" She tried to sound off-hand as he got to his feet and joined her by the window.

"I'm not going to dissolve the contract, Emma." The words were soft. Matter-of-fact. Final. "I have too much at stake. SecurePay is going to launch next week, on time, and you are going to help me make sure it does. You signed the employment contract. If you don't want the perks you were offered this morning to go with it, that's your choice."

"Because it's insulting!" Emma whirled to face him, not in the least surprised to discover Vivienne Grant had called up to let him know how the meeting had gone, but angry nonetheless. "A residence? A driver? A clothing allowance? What your lawyer presented to me this morning was basically a mistress contract, minus the sex in return for your generosity."

His eyes narrowed dangerously at that. "I don't need

to bribe women into my bed. They come when I tell
them to."

The veiled reference to Friday night snapped her
spine straight.

*"Come for me, Emma. Just like that. I want to feel
you squeezing my cock."*

Bastard, she thought, even as heat uncoiled in her
belly.

"You told me why you couldn't work for me. No
house. No transportation. *No clothes.*"

He let the last reason hang meaningfully for a moment, as though he knew her mind would conjure visions of naked skin, shifting muscles, sweaty bodies, her
imaginings made all the more visceral now she knew
how it felt to have Max thrusting inside her.

"I was merely trying to rectify those concerns. That's
how negotiation works." He stepped closer, his nearness muddling her senses. Making her want things she
shouldn't. "In order to reach an accord, sometimes one
party submits to the demands of the other party."

She glared up at him, resenting the innuendo. "What
happened between us wasn't a negotiation. It was a hos-
tile takeover."

"You seemed to enjoy yourself." His voice was pure
sex, and she hated him for it in that moment.

"You know what, Max? Fuck you."

"You already did," he said darkly.

And that, she realized as she turned back to the window, was exactly the problem. He just didn't know how
right he was.

If her time here was just about waiting for him to

discover she wasn't the one who installed the spyware on her computer, she would have gladly stayed while Max's cybersecurity team did whatever they needed to do to prove her innocence.

The problem, however, was that the longer she stuck around waiting to be cleared for the corporate espionage she'd had nothing to do with, the more opportunity they'd have to figure out that she had, in fact, been *espionaging* in what could be construed as a *corporate-esque* manner...

When Max found out she'd been feeding carefully curated bits of information to his own father—a man he openly despised—for the entirety of her tenure at Whitfield Industries, well, it was almost enough to make a girl wish she'd been the one who'd installed the spyware on her computer.

Emma squared her shoulders, crushed the flare of guilt. She'd had her reasons for accepting Charles Whitfield's bargain, and if she had it to do over, she'd make the deal again.

Max was a big boy. With millions of dollars and an army of lawyers. He'd figure a way out of this unscathed. Her fate, on the other hand, wasn't quite so certain. She needed to take care of herself.

To that end, she injected some steel in her spine and her voice as she faced him. "You seemed to enjoy yourself," she taunted, throwing his earlier words back in his face, as though no time had elapsed since he'd spoken.

"You outrageous little—"

His hands manacled her upper arms, hauling her against him as his mouth crashed down on hers.

Emma meant to resist, truly she did, but her lips parted under the siege of angry lust, and when she raised her arms to push him away, they ended up twining around his neck and pulling him closer.

Stupid arms.

Max grabbed her ass and hauled her up his body before executing a quarter turn and shoving her back against the window. They both grunted at the rough pleasure of their bodies colliding. Emma wrapped her legs around his waist, vaguely aware that the ripping sound that accompanied the grind of his hips against hers meant the slit in her skirt was probably up to her navel now, but she was too lost in the taste and feel of Max to care.

A loud beep echoed through the room, intruding before things got really interesting, and he cursed against her mouth, letting her go so fast that she almost stumbled.

The beep sounded again, and Max stalked toward the desk, running his hands through his hair and tugging his tie straight as he reached out and hit a button on his phone, leaving Emma breathless and frustrated, and a little lust-drunk, if she were being honest. With a frown, she glanced down at her skirt.

"What?" he snapped.

The slit wasn't quite to her navel, but the frayed material made her think its fate lay with a trash can, not a seamstress. As it stood, she was going to need a couple of safety pins to finish off the workday without getting charged with indecent exposure.

Sherri's voice flooded the room. "Kaylee's here to

see you. She says it's urgent. And I have Jesse Hastings on the line for your ten o'clock."

"Tell them both to wait. We're almost done here."

He hit the disconnect button and put his hands on his hips, but he didn't say anything.

"So…" Emma glanced over at the opaque glass wall. "What do you suppose Sherri thinks is happening in here right now?"

"I pay her not to speculate." And just like that, Max was all business again. "Who knows that you quit?"

Emma sighed and pushed away from the window, walking toward the front of Max's desk. By the time she'd secured her position at Whitfield Industries, the need for overtime pay and her mother's worsening condition had taken up any time she'd have used to cultivate coworkers into friends. Somehow, it had seemed easier not to bother. "If that's all you're worried about, then we're done here. I didn't tell anyone I was leaving except for you."

"Good. Let's keep it that way. If we're going to catch whoever is behind this, discretion is key."

The words snapped her like a rubber band. "What? I thought I was your suspect."

Max's amber eyes roved her face, looking for something, some answer. It felt…personal. Not like business at all.

She swallowed against the buzz of attraction that charged the air.

After what felt like an eternity, Max turned his attention to the files on his desk. "You've been cleared."

The gruff announcement blindsided her.

"What are you talking about? If you're not investigating me, why did you come to my place with that contract? Why am I here?"

When Max looked at her again, his impassive mask was back in place. "As I said, the SecurePay launch needs to go off without a hitch. And in order to unearth the mole before the release date, we need our traitor to feel confident that we are still unaware of the leak."

Hope crept through her veins. Maybe there was still a chance for her to get out of this mess with minimal damage. To Max. To herself. She just needed to keep a cool head. "So, I'm supposed to jump back into my job like nothing happened this weekend?"

She'd been expecting access restrictions, at the very least.

"Exactly like nothing happened this weekend," he confirmed.

Despite the absolution, something kept her senses on high alert, like her body was reacting to the distant clang of a warning bell that was just beyond her hearing. Something about this didn't feel right.

Emma tempered her frown at this new development and grabbed her bag from the visitor's chair. She hooked it over her forearm, positioning it strategically in front of her ruined skirt so she didn't flash anyone on the way out, pulling her suitcase with her other hand.

She was almost at the door when Max's voice stopped her.

"And Emma?"

She glanced over her shoulder, eyebrows raised in question.

"Wear a fucking bra tomorrow."

He needn't have worried. She wouldn't make that mistake again, but she kept her voice tart when she answered. "I'll wear whatever I want."

Max scrubbed a hand down his face and hit the button that summoned Sherri's voice like a high-tech genie.

"Yes, sir?"

"Tell Kaylee I don't have time to see her right now. And find out who I need to talk to about getting the dress code amended before tomorrow."

"The dress code?"

"That's what I said. Let Hastings know I'll be with him in five minutes."

Emma made sure to flash him a victorious smile as she walked out of his office, but it faded long before she reached her desk. The flare of hope she'd experienced in his office sputtered and died.

The whole point of seducing Max had been that she'd never see him again. And the whole point of quitting her job was to escape the reckoning that seemed almost inevitable now. Whitfield Industries had one of the top cyber security firms in the nation on retainer. It was only a matter of time before Max discovered what she had done.

Max dropped into the chair behind his desk, legs spread wide to accommodate the results of his earlier lack of willpower with Emma. He hit the button beneath his desk that unfrosted the wall of his office with more force than was necessary.

He was drowning in a security breach that could

derail SecurePay, and here he was, acting like a horny teenager with the top suspect, about to conduct a meeting with raging erection.

"What was that all about?"

The sudden intrusion snapped his head up, and Max didn't bother to smooth the annoyance from his features as his unwanted visitor stormed in without knocking. Not that he expected such civilities from her. He might be known for his poker face, but no one taxed it quite as much as his sister.

He shot a raised eyebrow at his assistant through the glass wall, but Sherri just shrugged and turned back to her computer. Nobody stopped Kaylee when she put her mind to something. Except for their mother. Sylvia Whitfield alone held the key to deflating his impetuous little sister.

"I don't have time for this right now. I'm late for a conference call."

"Then maybe next time you have a massive security leak, you'll remember to invite your head of PR to the meeting everyone else was at. That way you won't have to make time in your busy schedule for impromptu meetings like this one."

Max settled back in his chair, accepting the inevitable.

"Jesse Hastings had some talking points delivered in case any of this gets leaked and we need to clean it up." She tossed the file in her hand onto the desk. "Why is this the first I'm hearing of it?"

"Because the first *I* heard about it was Saturday morning, and as you know, reaching my head of PR before noon on a Saturday is impossible. And since it seems that whatever it is that keeps you out until all hours on Friday nights continues to be more important than your job, I took care of things myself."

Kaylee's frown pissed him off. He wouldn't have to lecture her all the time if she'd just put some goddamn effort into doing her part to help drag Whitfield Industries into the twenty-first century.

"Just because some of us have lives," she mumbled, reminding him of her sullen younger self.

He shifted uncomfortably in his chair. Apparently teenage regression was rampant today.

"Some of us," Max countered, his voice deadly calm, "are working our asses off to make a future for this company."

Instead of a retort, Kaylee gave a heavy sigh. "Believe it or not, I didn't come here to fight with you." She dropped into one of the chairs that faced Max's desk. "So, level with me. How bad is this?"

Max raked a hand through his hair. "As bad as it gets, considering we're launching in a week. If this gets out, it will tank consumer confidence. And considering how brazen and sophisticated this one is…"

"You don't think the attack is over," Kaylee finished.

Max kept his face carefully expressionless, despite his growing ire. He had the best security firm in the business working for him, and still they were floundering for answers. But Kaylee didn't need to worry about that. He'd deal with it. "Brennan and Hastings are doing everything they can to keep you from having to use that spin degree of yours. Still, it never hurts to be prepared."

Kaylee nodded. "I agree. So don't cut me out again." She might have the power to drive him crazy, but his little sister was smart and capable. He would never have kept her on after he'd ousted their father if she couldn't hack the job. But he wasn't about to let her get the last word, either.

"Answer your phone and I won't have to. Now, get out."

Max hit the intercom button before Kaylee could argue. "Sherri, patch Hastings through."

The phone beeped a second later, and he ignored Kaylee's glare as he brought the receiver to his ear. "Hastings, Max Whitfield here. I apologize for the delay. What have you got for me?"

Max grabbed the file from his desk and held it out to her. Kaylee rolled her eyes as she snatched it from his fingers, but she got up and left.

"No problem." Hastings voice was as good-natured as ever, despite the wait. "I know this is a busy time for you. Are we good to implement?"

"Yes. I told Emma she was cleared." The lie was still bitter on Max's tongue. "Against my better judgment, so you'd better be right about this."

On the other end of the phone line, Jesse Hastings sounded much less conflicted about the situation. "Well, we're about to find out. I'm monitoring her computer remotely. I've got two camera angles on her workstation, and I can hear everything she says while she's at her desk. With any luck, she'll try to get a hold of her coconspirator, even if it's just to say that she's back in position. That should give a direction to follow at the very least."

Max thought it was a waste of time. Emma had worked for him for three years. She was a smart and methodical employee, with an incredible attention for detail. If she was the guilty party, she'd installed the spyware on her computer and walked away from Whitfield Industries with every intention of never returning, and he sincerely doubted she had any business left to attend to.

There was a reason she'd almost gotten away with it—she'd struck quickly and decisively. She certainly wasn't going to pick up where she left off when only a fool wouldn't suspect her entire workstation was bugged and monitored after what had happened. And Emma Mathison was a lot of things, but a fool was not one of them.

That being said, Max wasn't a fool, either.

And he would protect SecurePay at any cost. He'd fought for five years to bring a viable universal digital crypto currency to the market, and thanks to tireless work from his team, he was going to beat Liam Kearney's competing product to market. Whitfield Industries was poised to make the threat of credit card fraud virtually nonexistent.

Max's jaw flexed at the prospect. The cost had been steep—his father despised Max for cutting him out of the business for the blackmail scheme his dad had implemented to lock down the software on which SecurePay was built. The extortion had ultimately led

to the death of his tech mentor, John Beckett, a man
Max had both liked and respected, which in turn had
destroyed his friendship with John's son, Aidan, who
blamed the Whitfields for the accident that had stolen
John before his time.

Casualties that haunted him, even this close to the
brink of success.

Max had put SecurePay above everything in his life,
and if it failed…well, it couldn't. It was as simple as that.

No matter what his gut told him, he couldn't allow
himself to trust Emma. Or let his body's craving for hers
cloud the situation. Right now, all roads pointed to her
guilt, and he would not let himself forget that she was
here against her will because he'd threatened her with
corporate espionage charges.

The thought made him ill. He'd spent the last five
years trying to absolve himself of his father's tainted
legacy, and now he was following in the bastard's foot-
steps. Blackmailing people to do his bidding. But there
was no help for that now. He was committed to SecurePay, and he would uncover the mole in his company, no matter what it took.

CHAPTER SIX

AT PRECISELY FIVE O'CLOCK, Emma shut off her computer and gathered her things.

She'd never realized just how decadent it was, leaving work at a sane hour, though some of the mutinous joy in it was stolen by the fact that Max wasn't in his office to witness her unprecedented on-time departure.

She had to make do with Sherri's surprised, "See you tomorrow," when Emma had wished her goodnight and headed for the elevator.

The lobby was buzzing with people as she headed for the front door, her suitcase wheels bumping over the tiled floor, and she spared a moment to imagine exactly where they were going. What their lives were like. The things they'd experienced while she'd spent the last three years high in a tower, working herself to exhaustion. It had started as a way to afford the growing care requirements for her mother's worsening condition and ended as a way to distract herself from the pain of losing her mom.

And all that time, the world kept turning. People, these people, scurrying off to happy hours and dinners, rushing home to spend time with their families. Simple pleasures she'd forgotten existed.

Emma pushed through the glass door and stepped into the evening sunshine. She had no such plans. No one to meet for dinner and drinks. No one to rush home to. No home at all, she realized suddenly.

Shit.

She'd meant to look into a hotel today, but she'd been so furious after meeting with Vivienne, and then Max, and finding pins for her skirt...

A sudden prickle at the back of her neck alerted her to the presence of the tall, handsome man leaning casually against the gleaming black town car parked at the curb. He was scrolling through his phone, but as though he was privy to the same zing of awareness, he looked up, zeroing in on her before she could avert her eyes, pretend she hadn't noticed him there. Waiting. For her?

Emma hated that her skin came alive in his presence.

Max pushed away from the vehicle, tucking his smartphone in the interior breast pocket of his suit before he pulled open the door. "Get in."

She stopped in front of him. "You could try asking."

"Get in the car, Emma."

She readjusted her purse on her shoulder, so she could cross her arms.

"Please," he added tersely.

"No."

His hand tightened on the top of the door, whitening his knuckles. "Do we have a problem here?"

"You mean besides the fact that you're being a dictator...heavy on the *dick*?"

To her surprise, the churlish insult drew a flicker of a smile from him.

"You're different than you were before I had you on my desk."

His blunt musings made her frown.

"I think you mean before *I* had *you* on your desk. If you'll recall, I made the first move."

Max gave an indifferent shrug. "If you say so."

Let it go, she counselled herself. *He's just baiting you.* "I mean, I kissed you." She tried to sound nonchalant about it. "That's clearly a move. No one would classify that as *not* a move."

He tipped his head, and the arrogance of it made her bristle.

"What? What's…" Emma mimicked his action, doing her best to imbue it with the right amount of condescension.

"If that's how you want to remember it," he clarified, so supremely blasé that it sparked something in her belly.

A need to prove herself. A need to make him admit that he'd felt something shift that night, a night that had required all her courage. She needed to know that her emancipation had registered. That she'd made him want, made him burn. That she hadn't been the only one lost to the maelstrom of sensations.

She dropped her arms, stepped closer. Only a few feet of sidewalk separated them now. "That's not just how I *remember* it, that's how it happened."

"Oh really?" Max let go of the door, cut the gap between them with a step of his own. The noise of traffic and passersby receded, replaced with the throb of her pulse, the rumble of his voice resonating in her chest.

"I *dared* you to kiss me. And despite a million reservations, you did. I like that I make you lose control."

The egotistical, patronizing, inconveniently true statement stiffened her spine. Emma's scoff was forced, born of pride and fear. "You wish."

The grin that tilted his lips was positively predatory. "Shall I prove it?"

Her body begged her to let him. Something dangerous and fizzy was working its way through her bloodstream as she swayed closer to him, desperate for a taste of the magic that seemed to spark whenever they were together. They'd unleashed something dangerous that night in his office, something Emma didn't know how to control.

Max's breathing shallowed, and his hooded gaze flicked to her mouth. He talked a good game, but he wasn't immune to what was happening between them. He might be better than her at hiding it, but the magnetism between them was not one-sided.

The blare of a horn broke the spell before their lips touched, and she jerked back from him.

He sighed. Pushed the door open wider with one hand and grabbed her suitcase with the other. "Will you get in the car now?"

Emma relented, too off-balance to do anything else. She slid into the sumptuous black leather interior, and he shut the door behind her. A muted thud behind her meant her suitcase was now being held captive in the trunk. She twisted the ring on her middle finger as she waited for Max to crawl into the back seat beside her.

The car slid away from the curb as soon as he'd pulled the door closed behind him.

"I think we need to establish some rules for our working relationship, going forward."

"Let me guess. Rule number one: wear a fucking bra?" she inquired sweetly.

The slightest frown marred his brow. "We have to keep things professional in the office. And stop being so insubordinate."

"Then stop being an asshole."

"I can see these rules are going to be difficult for you," he said drily.

"Hey, technically, I didn't break that one. We're not in the office anymore."

"You're right." Just like that, the banked fire in his eyes blazed to life, and he turned a little, angling his upper body toward her. "Come here."

The timber of his voice sent a shiver of anticipation through her.

"Don't talk to me like that." The warning was more breathless then she'd have liked.

"Like what?"

"Stay. Sit. Come. You're always ordering me around like I'm some Labrador retriever, desperate for you to pet me."

He reached up, brushed a finger along the edge of her jaw, and her breath stuttered in her lungs.

"*Are* you desperate for me to pet you?"

Oh, God, yes.

"I like it when you come, Emma."

Her heart lurched with the need to be closer, to test how near she could get before the burning consumed her.

Then her hand was on his shoulder, and his hand was on her waist, and despite the confines of the car, he was pulling her close as she levered up so that she was straddling him, her knees digging into the cushy leather seat on either side of his hips.

"I've been hard since you walked out of my office this morning," he confessed, dragging his lips against the hollow of her throat, "wondering what you've got on underneath this skirt."

Emma buried her fingers in his dark hair, hands clenching as she tried to keep her wits, tried not to drown in him. "I think you're supposed to seek medical attention when that problem persists for more than four hours."

The joke faded to a breathless rasp as he swiped his tongue against her collarbone.

"I don't need a doctor." His fingers dug into her hips. "I just need to get my hands on you so I can stop wondering exactly how many dress code infractions you're committing."

Max tried to pull her more fully against him, but her skirt held her hostage.

"I'm stuck," she whispered, looking down at the straining safety pins and gaping material along her thigh that prevented her from widening her stance.

He grabbed the hem of her skirt and ripped the slit back open, scattering the pins and freeing her.

They both groaned as she spread her knees, settling into his lap. He set his hands on her legs, tucking his fingers just beneath the edge of her skirt.

Emma's breath caught as he stared into her eyes, his palms slowly moving up her thighs, beneath her skirt, searching for answers.

Without conscious volition, their breaths had synced up, short pants of need that had her fingers clenching in his hair. She bit her lip, unable to look away from his eyes, searching hers so intensely as his hands trekked upwards, smoothing along the outside of her thighs, curving around her bare ass. He sucked in a breath, his fingers moving inexorably upward until his fingers finally encountered the lacy waistband of her thong.

"Disappointed?"

"Not even close," he assured her, tracing the band from back to front before he stroked a finger right down her center, pressing the wet lace of her panties against her core.

She gasped as sparks unfurled through her body, her hips canting forward in the search for more pressure.

He obliged her, breaching the flimsy barrier of her underwear and sliding two fingers deep inside her without further preliminaries.

She bit her lip to keep herself from crying out, because she had no idea if the glass partition between them and the front seat was soundproof, but after a few more strokes of his fingers, she stopped caring.

"You're so fucking wet," he rasped, dropping his forehead against her collarbone as he thrust inside her again and again, setting up a rhythm that had her mus-

cles clenching in a desperate attempt to quell the need
building deep inside her.

Just when she wasn't sure she could endure another
second of the sharp-edged pleasure, he twisted his
wrist, pressing his thumb against her clit in a circular
motion that sent her spiraling over the edge.

She collapsed against him, her face tucked into the
crook of his neck as she tried to catch her breath, savoring the aftershocks rippling through her body.

Finally, she found the strength to pull back, pausing
just long enough to press a quick, hard kiss to his mouth
before she slid off his lap and onto the seat beside him.

"Oh, man," she breathed, and he shot her a wicked
grin, made even sexier because his hair was mussed,
and his tie was askew. He looked disreputable. Not like
the unflappable CEO of Whitfield Industries she was
used to.

He leaned close, and she tilted her chin up, but he bypassed her mouth, his breath tickling the shell of her ear.

"You're going to want to pull your skirt down before
Sully opens the door."

It took a moment for the import of his words to register. Along with the fact that the car was at a complete
standstill. They'd arrived.

"Oh, shit."

Emma had barely gotten her skirt over her hips when
the door flew open, but Max, adaptable as always, was
already filling up the doorway with his broad shoulders
as he got out, giving her a few precious seconds to finish restoring some semblance of order to her skirt. He
stood there, blocking her from view as he exchanged

pleasantries with his driver, and she used the reprieve
to position her tote bag as a modesty shield before he
turned and helped her out of the car.

CHAPTER SEVEN

EMMA'S EYES WIDENED as she joined Max on the sidewalk in front of the lavish entrance of the infamous Berkshire Suites. She'd heard of the luxury hotel, of course, but the reality of it was something else entirely. Television footage and photographs had not prepared her for the grandiosity of it all. "There's more to see inside. Shall we?"

The words were a murmur, delivered softly in her ear, sending an avalanche of shivers down her spine and snapping her out of her open-mouthed stupor.

She turned to tell him that no, in fact, they *shan't* do a damn thing and how dare he bring her to a hotel to finish what they'd started in the car, a move that was not only presumptuous, but insulting, too.

Then Max placed a hand at the small of her back, and the possessively intimate touch hit her like the voltage from a cattle prod. She was already up the wide stone steps, clearing the glass doors that had been swept out of their path by liveried doormen, and being dazzled by her first view of the lobby before she had the chance to say anything.

Elegant, but not subtle, the place practically oozed money, and lots of it. It was opulence manifest—dark wood, rich brocade, intricate tilework, glittering chandeliers and vases spilling with fresh flowers. It was like something out of a movie. Who lived like this?

"Mr. Whitfield. Welcome back."

Emma shot the man beside her a sidelong glance. Well, she should have seen that one coming.

Max turned toward the distinguished, middle-aged man who strode toward them and shook his hand.

"We had the liberty of having a new key made up."

Max tucked the swipe card in his pocket.

"Thank you, Gerald. May I present Emma Mathison?"

She shouldn't like this, she told herself. The casual gallantry, the coupledom of it all.

"Welcome, Ms. Mathison," the man said with a polite nod. "If the two of you will follow me, it would be my pleasure to show you upstairs.

Everyone's eyes were on them as they headed for the elevator, and Emma double-checked that her leather tote was still covering the giant tear in her skirt.

Not that anyone was looking at her.

It was funny, she'd seen the phenomenon before, around the office. The way Max drew attention when he walked into a room. She'd always thought it was because he was the boss, but it seemed his magnetism extended into the real world, too.

Well, if you considered this playground of the rich and famous *real*, she supposed.

Max guided her into the elevator and left his hand

resting against the dip of her spine. She was starting to get used to the steady hum of connection that it caused.

"Would you prefer they take the next car, sir?" Gerald asked as two older ladies approached.

"Not necessary," Max assured him.

Gerald held the door open for the women, one tall and regal, her gray-streaked hair, one short and pleasant-looking, her white hair cut in a stylish bob.

"Mrs. Fernandez. Mrs. Tuttle. I hope you ladies enjoyed your afternoon of shopping."

"We did. Thank you, Gerald," one of the women replied as they boarded the elevator, but Emma didn't see who it was, because under the guise of making room for the new passengers, Max's fingers had trekked over to her hip and tugged her in front of him.

"Your purchases were delivered earlier," the concierge informed them as the door slid closed, "and I took the liberty of having them brought up to your rooms."

Max stepped closer. Except for the light touch of his hand, he wasn't touching her, but he might as well have been. He was like a wall of heat behind her, and her skin tingled with the knowledge that if she leaned back a scant inch or two, she'd have all that delicious muscle pressed against her from shoulder to knee.

As if he'd read her mind, his grip tightened on her waist.

The shorter lady, closest to Emma, shot her a conspiratorial wink. "If only our husbands were as attentive as Gerald here."

Emma forced herself to concentrate, to smile at the quip, even as Max's thumb stroked a lazy back-and-forth along the top of her skirt, igniting everything that had been on simmer since they'd gotten out of the car. Since he'd given her a blinding orgasm with the same fingers that were digging into her hip.

"Also, Mr. Fernandez called to say that he and Mr. Tuttle will be later than expected, so your dinner reservation has been moved to seven o'clock."

The ladies shook their heads in unison, but they looked more amused than exasperated.

"After forty-three years of marriage, I guess that shouldn't come as a surprise," the taller woman said. "At least one of us has found a man with the good manners to be home on time for dinner. I hope this means he's taking good care of you and not leaving you alone in the city while he works all hours."

To Emma's surprise, Max's voice rumbled near her ear. "I'm definitely not leaving her alone, ma'am."

"That's excellent. Just what I hoped to hear."

Emma didn't like the way her heart bumped against her ribs at Max's kindness, indulging in small talk she would have expected him to find annoying.

She leaned back ever so slightly, giving into the heat of his body, needed the contact.

"What a lovely couple you two make."

Emma started, pulling away from Max. "Oh, we're not…"

"Thank you, ladies." Max cut in, drawing her back against him. "And I'm sure the business at hand must be very important if it's keeping your husbands away from such beautiful dinner companions."

The shorter lady tittered at the compliment. "Well,

aren't you a charming young man? Handsome, too." She turned her attention to Emma. "This one's a keeper," she stage-whispered as the elevator doors slid open.

"Nice meeting you. Enjoy your dinner," Emma managed weakly. The words came out too breathy.

"Oh, we will," the taller woman assured her as she and her friend stepped out of the elevator. "Just not quite as much as you will," she added, her eyes flicking to Max as the doors slid closed behind them.

They arrived at the penthouse two floors later.

"Will you require anything else this evening, Mr. Whitfield?" Gerald asked.

"I think we can take it from here."

"Of course, sir. Have a lovely night, Ms. Mathison."

Emma returned the nod, her knees a little shaky as she and Max stepped out of the elevator and headed toward the only door on the left-hand side of the hallway. They walked quickly, eagerly, and close enough that their arms and hands brushed inadvertently along the way, keeping her body tuned up for the main event.

Somewhere between getting out of the car and the elevator ride that had been a master class in foreplay, Emma found she couldn't summon her earlier outrage at Max's presumptuousness, because now, a hotel seemed the perfect place to finish what they'd started in the back seat, and she couldn't wait to get her hands on him again.

What was happening to her?

It was like she'd opened Pandora's box to find it contained nothing but lust and now she couldn't remember what it was like *not* to want him.

Emma turned toward him as they arrived at the door, leaning against the wall and watching him as he retrieved the keycard from his pocket.

The lady in the elevator was wrong. Max wasn't charming—that was far too bland a description for his ability to read a room, to adapt to the situation at hand. Charismatic was a more appropriate adjective, she decided. Handsome, though, was right on the money.

The dangerous kind of handsome that grabbed her by the hormones and stoked something wild in her. She licked her lips and his eyes darkened as he stepped close. Emma lifted her chin automatically, but he bypassed her lips, and his breath ruffled the hair tucked behind her ear.

"You're leaning on the keypad." His voice was so low and sexy that it took her a second to parse the quotidian words. But before she could frown at him, he slipped his hand between her and the wall and the resulting arch of her back brought her breasts into contact with his chest. The door clicked as the locking mechanism released. With a grin, he grabbed the knob with his other hand, pushing it open.

"After you," he insisted, and in retribution, she made sure to press against him as much as possible as she slipped through the doorway and into the room, reveling in his groan.

In a feat of magic, or more likely the quest for a better tip, her suitcase was already inside, looking dingy and cheap against the gleaming wooden floor.

"Wow."

It was a beautiful suite, with a top-of-the-line kitchenette to the right and a sunken living room to the left, complete with modern white-leather furniture and floor-to-ceiling windows that looked out across Los Angeles, shown off to glorious advantage in the evening light.

The snick of the door closing sounded a moment before his deep voice.

"Glad you approve."

Max stepped close behind her, stealing her attention from the killer view. Her head lolled to the side, giving his lips easy access to her neck, and he pressed a kiss there as he slid his left hand around her waist and pulled her back against his hard body.

The sensuous spell he'd woven in the elevator rushed through her with a vengeance.

Her bag slipped from her fingers, landing on the floor with a thud, and her breath came out in a rush as Max traced his finger down her right arm, from shoulder to wrist, before pressing something against her palm and curling her fingers around it.

His lips brushed her ear.

"Charge whatever you need to the room."

And then his body was gone, leaving her needy and confused and having no trouble summoning the outrage that she'd been unable to find out in the hallway.

She spun around, holding up the keycard in her hand.

"That's it?" she asked, incredulous as Max opened the door. "You're going?"

His gaze dipped to the rip in her skirt, which was now well past midthigh and working its way toward indecent. All it would take was one good tug and it would probably fall right off...

"I saw your face when we pulled up to the hotel," he said, lifting his eyes to hers. "I know why you think I brought you here, and I know how you felt about it. So yes. I'm leaving."

He stepped into the hallway.

"But if you decide you want...*anything*, my room's just on the other side of the hall."

Then he strode away, leaving the door to click shut behind him. Her body cried out at the loss.

With a frustrated sigh, she grabbed her bag off the floor and set it on the marble countertop.

Stupid body.

CHAPTER EIGHT

MAX PULLED OFF his jacket as the door to his suite closed behind him and draped the expensive fabric over the back of the couch. He needed a drink.

This thing with Emma was messing with his head. He unbuttoned his cuffs, rolling his sleeve up his right forearm, before following suit with the left.

He couldn't keep his hands off her, and when she wasn't around, he couldn't keep his mind off her. The near constant case of blue balls was distracting as hell, especially now, when he should be laser-focused on SecurePay, on bringing down whoever was trying to screw him over. And he definitely shouldn't keep ignoring the fact that it might be her.

He was just about to head for the fully stocked bar cart that sat in the far corner of the sunken living room and pour himself a glass of whatever bottle he picked up first, but a knock at his door stole his attention.

Emma.

The drink could wait.

He wet his lips. Walked to the door. Pulled it out of his way and braced a shoulder against the jamb.

"Why are you here?"

He cocked an eyebrow at her question.

"I mean, I know why you brought me here. Well, I thought I did, anyway. But why do you have a room?"

"I live here."

That surprised her. He could tell by her quick frown, the way she opened her mouth to say something, but shut it without a word, before opening it again.

"You live in a hotel?"

"I rent this floor." He shrugged. "It's close to the office."

Not that he needed to justify himself.

Emma looked down at the hallway carpet beneath her feet, then up at him. She was beautiful, and he had the urge to reach out and tuck her golden curls behind her ear, but she beat him to it.

"So, you didn't bring me to a hotel to fuck," she said, her voice soft, and the curse word on angelic lips made his cock swell.

She stepped closer. He breathed her in, and she smelled like the ocean and sun-warmed skin. Clean. Fresh. A little bit sweet.

"You brought me back to your place…"

An alluring gleam lit her blue eyes and she clasped her hands behind her back.

Max pushed the door open in wordless invitation. Lust licked at his belly as she ducked under his arm.

"…to fuck," she finished, now that she was inside.

He turned to face her.

"And that changes things?" he asked, reaching up to

pull his tie off. It hit the floor with a whisper of sound, but his senses were so keyed up that it seemed louder.

She nodded, and he popped the button on his collar.

"It does, actually. You don't strike me like a man who brings a lot of women home." Emma reached for the top button of her shirt.

"And just what kind of man do I strike you as?"

"Discerning. Brilliant. Jaded." She undid another with each word. "Strong. Sexy. Good with your hands." He followed her lead until they were both out of buttons.

"But not one who gets laid often?"

He walked toward her as she tugged off her shirt, abandoning it on the floor.

No fucking bra. He didn't know what his problem was earlier, because right now it seemed an inspired sartorial choice.

Her breasts were plump and perfect, and he backed her up against the counter of the breakfast nook, not stopping until he could feel her taut nipples against his chest.

"I think you do all right for yourself."

He slid his hands up her torso before lifting her onto the marble surface.

"Just not here."

He ignored the accuracy of her assessment, let her push his shirt off his shoulders, down his arms, and when it dropped to the tile, Max's hands settled on her knees as he stepped between them, nuzzling her ear. "I've been dying to touch you."

She ran her palms over his shoulders and across his back. "All we've done lately is touch."

"Not enough. Not like I wanted to." He slid his hands up her thighs. The tear in her skirt went higher than he'd realized, and he had the sudden urge to finish what he'd started.

"Those were just appetizers," he told her, pressing a kiss to the curve of her jaw. "A quick and dirty fuck on my desk." He nipped her earlobe. "A cursory grope against the window." He dragged his tongue up her neck. "And a frantic hand job in the back of a car."

She made a sound of protest when he pulled back, but her eyes followed his movement as he grabbed either side of the frayed black material in his hands.

"I didn't get to undress you." With a sharp yank, what was left of her skirt came apart, leaving her in nothing but her teal panties.

Still too many clothes.

"I didn't get to run my hands over your body."

He skimmed his fingers across her clavicle, down the slope of her breast before palming it, giving her the pressure she craved, if her groan was anything to go by.

"And I didn't get to taste you." He kissed her shoulder as he ran his thumb back and forth over her nipple, once, twice, and she gasped at the contact.

"Do you like that?"

Her answer was no more than a whimper as he lowered his head and drew her into his mouth. Emma arched under the suction as he worked the pink bud with his tongue, and she had to grab him to keep her balance, her fingernails scoring his shoulders. He lavished the other breast with the same attention, made her squirm under the onslaught until he had to come up for air.

"Tell me what else you want," he ordered.

Her eyes were drowsy with pleasure when they met his, and her smile was sinfully naughty. "How about I show you instead?"

She planted a hand on his chest and pushed him back a foot so she could hop down from the counter.

Emma grabbed his hand, and he followed as she tugged him across the suite, down the steps to the sunken living room, stopping in front of the floor-to-ceiling windows overlooking downtown LA. The sky was turning pink and yellow as sunset approached.

"I don't think you'll be needing these anymore," she mused playfully, unbuckling his belt and unzipping his pants. He rasped out a breath as she sent them sliding down his thighs.

Then she was on her knees in front of him, pulling off his shoes, his socks, shoving his pants out of the way before divesting him of his boxer-briefs, leaving him naked. Exposed. So goddamn ready for her.

He was *this close* to losing all semblance of self-restraint. The air vibrated with desire. Desperation. Sex.

Max's knees almost buckled at the first swipe of her tongue, and his breath escaped in a hiss as pleasure seared his every nerve ending. He reached out, bracing a hand against the window to steady himself.

He wanted to hold her there, fuck her mouth until he couldn't think anymore, just feel.

He didn't, though, because he was too close to the edge. He didn't trust himself to control whatever she'd let loose. Not when she was making him crazy, and he couldn't get enough of her mouth.

He looked down at Emma, one hand gripping his thigh, the other at the base of his shaft, his cock disappearing between her lips. She was so fucking gorgeous.

Then, as though she could feel his gaze, she looked up at him and his hips jerked with need. It wasn't just her mouth he couldn't get enough of, it was all of her.

This woman.

If he were being honest with himself, he'd been attracted to her since the day they'd met. But it had always been in that detached way that came from knowing that it would never become anything. And once something was off the table, Max put it to the back of his mind.

But now...

"Jesus, Emma." He raked his fingers through her hair. "That's so fucking good."

She accepted the compliment by sucking him deep, driving him closer and closer to climax. His hand in her hair tightened to a fist. He didn't want to come. Not yet. Not until he was inside her.

"You have to stop."

She did, and he dropped to his knees in front of her, kissing the questioning look off her face.

"I'm not done with you yet," he assured her, before he grabbed his pants and removed the condom from his wallet.

She bit her lip as he sheathed himself, and then he was pushing her back onto the soft, shaggy area rug beneath them, as she wound herself around him.

It felt so damn good to be in control of something

where the outcome was certain, even if it was just his own orgasm. Well, his and Emma's. She was blowing his mind in all the best ways right now. Making sure she enjoyed herself was the least he could do.

Everything had been so messed up since his little coup d'état, and while ousting his father had been the right business decision, it had led to a world of trouble for Max. This security breach was the latest in a long line of annoyances, crises and calamities that he'd been wrestling under control since he'd put the old man out to pasture.

He'd been going full throttle for five years, trying to whip this project of his into reality. To prove he was right about the direction he was steering Whitfield Industries. It had been his sole focus for so long.

Until Emma Mathison had strode into his office, thrown his offer of employment in his face, and then rocked his world right off its axis.

Just like she was about to again. Because if he'd thought fucking her on his desk had been good, it was nothing compared to having her naked and writhing for him.

"Do you want me inside you?"

The words were rough on his lips, and he watched in fascination as her breath came faster. "Yes."

"Ask me for it."

"I want you to fuck me, sir."

He stared down at the amazing woman beneath him, the one who'd worked almost as many hours as he had over the last three years to make SecurePay a success, and he realized that, while it had been so perfect that night in his office, when they'd been playing their roles, all part of one night of fantasy, that wasn't what he wanted now.

"Say my name." It sounded more like a plea than an order.

"Fuck me, Max."

Oh God. That was it. He was lost. His arousal surged as he pulled her close, shoving her panties down her thighs. He needed to get so goddamn deep that neither of them could breathe.

Finally—*Jesus, finally*—he was right where he wanted to be, driving into her, stifling her moans with his mouth as he kissed her. He loved the way she wriggled beneath him, clasping him to her as she rubbed against him, letting him know that she was as turned on as he was.

This was hot, frantic. It felt so good to have Emma naked and stretched out beneath him.

When he couldn't stave off the inevitable any longer, he braced his forearm on the floor beside her head, and shoved his free hand beneath her hips, changing the angle and sending her to the stars seconds before he joined her there.

CHAPTER NINE

"I'm starving."

Max turned his head on the shaggy, faux-sheepskin rug, looking big and sleepy and smug. "Yeah, okay. But I need a minute."

Emma couldn't help her giggle, which was a little embarrassing, but spread out on the floor next to a man with a body that excelled at being naked, she was too sated to care. This playful side of Max was completely new to her. "I meant for food."

He grunted and slung his forearm across his eyes. "That sounds good, too."

"I'm going to order pizza." She allowed herself a moment to stare at him, all muscles and sinew, like a jungle cat in repose, before she pushed herself up off the floor and walked over to the sofa.

"Make it a large."

With a smile, she crawled onto the couch on her knees, leaning over the arm rest to grab the phone, intimately aware that Max had shifted onto his side, his head propped on his hand, his eyes roaming every inch of her skin.

"Stop looking at me like that." Her voice sounded breathless, as though the flicker of heat in his gaze had used up the oxygen in her lungs.

"Like what?"

"Like you want to eat me."

He lifted an eyebrow in confirmation of her phrasing, and that flicker became a flame.

"I meant that you keep sizing me up." Emma did her best to smother it. "Like a panther looking for its next meal."

Max repositioned himself on the rug, his muscles shifting and bunching with the movement, doing nothing to dispel the metaphor.

"A panther?" he asked, and to her surprise, a hint of smugness laced his deep voice. "I think I like that."

She waved her hand dismissively. "Panther. Weasel. Anteater. Any kind of predator, really."

His chuckle was low, and it prickled over her skin. "Suddenly I'm less flattered."

"I'm sure your ego will recover." He was far too sure of himself for her peace of mind.

"I suspect so. My recovery time is known to be above average."

Self-preservation and non-sexual hunger had her grabbing the receiver and dialing the number she knew by heart so she could order a large Guido's Supreme with extra cheese before he managed to distract her from her task completely.

"They have pizza at the hotel," he advised as she hung up.

The look she shot him as she got to her feet dripped

with reproach. "I'm sorry. This place might do a lot of things well, but there is no way they know anything about pizza."

Emma walked back toward him, caught in his gravitational pull.

"They probably make it all frou-frou, with thin-crust, and caramelized pears and goat cheese or something. I got you a real pizza. A man's pizza."

When she was close enough, he reached up and grabbed her fingers, rolling onto his back and pulling her down on top of him. He captured her mouth in a slow, deep kiss that woke her libido and sent it pacing low in her belly.

"A man's pizza, huh? You think you can handle it?"

"Please." She rolled her eyes as she slid off him so he could sit up. "I handled you, didn't I?"

Oh, Jesus. That smile.

The air left her lungs in a rush. So much for getting Max out of her system. The more she touched him, the more she wanted to touch him.

He stood up and held out a hand for her, which she accepted.

"Maybe you should handle me again," he suggested, pulling her up onto her feet and against his body in one fluid move. Then he leaned in for another decadent kiss. "How long until the pizza gets here?"

"Thirty minutes."

"Just enough time for a shower. C'mon," he said, giving her hand a tug and she realized for the first time that he hadn't let go of it during the kiss. She let him lead her out of the living room, through the hallway and the master suite, and into the bathroom, not stopping until they were standing in the most incredible shower. Sleek tiles, with a giant fixture in the ceiling above them, and several other showerheads at staggered heights.

Max reached around her to turn it on, and warm water rained over them. Emma watched, entranced, as Max tipped his face up, pushed his dark, wet hair back with both hands as water raced along the dips and planes of his body. She was caught in a beautiful storm with a beautiful man, and she didn't want to miss a moment of it.

"Got any shampoo in here?"

He tipped his chin toward a recessed space under one of the showerheads, and she noticed three nozzles.

"The left one," he instructed, and Emma reached in tentatively. It whined out a handful of delicious smelling shampoo.

"Fancy."

As she sudsed up her hair, Max shoved his palm under the nozzle on the far right and began lathering the clear gel across his chest and arms, down his stomach...lower. Body wash never looked so good, and she resented having to close her eyes to rinse her hair.

She didn't want to miss anything about this glimpse into the real Max.

He was always so elusive, and she wanted to know more about the man who ruled over Whitfield Industries. The man who pushed her, and the entire SecurePay team to do the best, be the best, every single day because he wouldn't settle for anything less.

He'd always intrigued her, but after she'd accepted

Charles Whitfield's deal, after she'd realized that she'd been had, she hadn't felt she deserved to know anything personal about Max. She'd never even googled him.

But here, in this alternate universe they'd created, she gave herself permission to indulge her curiosity... just a little.

"Did you grow up around here?"

Max nodded and reached for the shampoo. His forearm slid along her upper arm, and she shivered at the contact, despite the warmth of the water.

"Beverly Hills," he provided, soaping up his hair.

She should have known.

"You?"

"El Segundo." She took a chance on the middle dispenser, glad when a dollop of conditioner appeared in her hand.

"Did you like it there?"

"I have good memories, but it was hard after my dad died. The whole place kind of felt like him, you know? But my mom and I couldn't afford to leave. My parents weren't wealthy people. They worked for wealthy people." She smiled against the sad memories, working the cream rinse through her wet hair. "And now I work for you. I've been a voyeur of the life of rich people my whole life."

She'd meant it as a joke, an escape valve on a conversation too close to her heart, but the evocative nature of her comment reignited the charge in the air. A fact that wasn't lost on Max, judging by the suggestive raise of his brow.

"And? Do you like what you see?"

Hell yes.

He was wet and naked, and shampoo suds were streaming over his wide shoulders, slipping down the length of a body that had gotten her off more in the last two days than she'd managed in the two years prior.

She liked what she saw a *lot*.

Emma licked her lips and his eyes darkened. Her hands had stilled in her hair, and she had to force herself to resume finger-combing conditioner through the strands. "What's not to like?" Even to her own ears, the words sounded breathless, needy. "You fascinate me."

Max shoved his hair back from his forehead again.

"Oh?" He was surprised, and she liked that she could knock him off balance.

"You live in a hotel. You take a car service. You order your meals from room service. What sort of man sets up his entire life as a business trip?"

Max looked more contemplative than put out. "My priority is seeing that Whitfield Industries succeeds. My father did his best to kill it, and now it's my job to resurrect what's left of the business my grandfather built."

"Your job, yes. But your life?"

Now he did frown. "That's a very naive view of the situation."

"Is it? I watched my mother lose everything. She was a bright star, lovely, vivacious, full of life. And I had to stand by and watch her fade. And it didn't happen right away. It didn't happen when she wasn't fit to work anymore."

Emma held her hands under the spray of the closest

showerhead, watching the drops erase the remnants of the conditioner on her palms.

"It happened when she started losing pieces of herself. She didn't remember the song we used to dance to in the kitchen while she cooked. Her eyes stopped lighting up at the mention of my father. She didn't run her fingers over the picture of him she kept beside her bed. And after a while, she looked right through me. Like a stranger."

The memory still squeezed at her heart. She'd never doubted for a second that her mother loved her, but that slow erosion had seemed far worse, far crueler, than losing her all at once.

"And it hurt. It killed me to watch her disappear, even though she was right in front of me. But I realized that, as much as it hurt to watch her lose those memories, that life she led, it was ultimately a gift. Because how awful would it be to not have any memories for Alzheimer's to steal? To not even realize that you were losing someone because nothing about them had changed?

"I want those memories, Max. I don't want my life to be an indistinguishable montage of workdays that mean nothing when I'm looking back at my life."

Max frowned. "You don't like working at Whitfield?"

Emma angled her head so that the water would rinse her hair clean. "It's been incredible. It's pushed me and challenged me. Launching SecurePay will be the culmination of work that I'm incredibly proud of. But I don't want it to be the only thing I ever did in my life. I want to walk the beaches of Dubrovnik and see where my mother grew up. I want to know that I've lived my life."

They stared at one another, water falling like rain around them, in an envelope of silence that she found surprisingly comfortable.

"I never looked at work like that. Leaving a lasting legacy has always been important to me."

She smiled at that. Leave it to this man to have such a succinct, straight-forward explanation for eighty-hour work weeks.

He stepped close, brushed his lips against hers, but when she would have kissed him back, he slid his mouth along her cheek, to her ear.

"Turn around. I think you missed a spot."

She licked water from her lips as she obeyed. God. The things this man did to her with just his voice. Made her want. Made her wet.

He kissed her shoulder as he reached for the nozzle full of body wash. Then he was running soapy palms down her back, palming the globes of her ass.

The delicious pressure over-balanced her, and she braced her hands on the slick tile in front of her.

"The pizza will be here any minute," she reminded him shakily. Reminded herself.

He slid a hand up her torso, brushing his knuckles along the underside of her breast. "I'm hungry now." His tongue on her neck made her breath catch.

"We're never going to hear the doorbell in here. And no matter how good you are, you're never going to be better than Guido's."

"If that's a challenge, I'm up for it." He pressed his hips against her.

She did her best not to moan, flipping around to face him, the tiles chilly against the heat of her back, his body, big and warm and wet in front of her.

"Despite what you might have heard, a woman can't live on salad and sex alone."

"Who said anything about salad?" he asked, capturing her mouth and licking inside in a seductively lazy rhythm that pushed her to the brink of capitulation.

She wrapped her arms around his neck to reciprocate, but as she did, she realized the water had stopped.

"This pizza had better be life-changing," he warned, pulling back after dropping a quick kiss on the tip of her nose.

She followed his magnificent ass out of the shower, accepting the fluffy white towel he handed her. She wrapped it around her body watching as he grabbed one for himself and toweled off, gloriously, unself-consciously naked and semi-hard and in no particular hurry to cover up either fact. Not that she minded.

To be honest, she was a little sad when he finally knotted it around his hips and headed for the bedroom. She used her moment alone to wring the excess water from her hair and exchange her towel for one of the plush hotel robes on the shelf beside the shower. Then she stole his comb from the counter and restored some order to the wet tangle of her hair as she considered the pieces of Max that she'd learned, mentally fitting them into the beautiful, enigmatic puzzle of him.

The doorbell shook her out of her musing.

"Emma! Man pizza is here."

She cleaned the strands of blond hair from his comb and threw them away. It wouldn't do to leave a part of herself here. This was convenient sex and fast food. Nothing more.

"Be right out."

CHAPTER TEN

MAX GLANCED UP from the bar cart as Emma joined him in the living room. She looked fresh and lovely wrapped in the large hotel robe, her wet hair slicked back from her face. She smiled absently at him as she curled into the corner of the couch and flicked open the pizza box he'd left on the coffee table. She grabbed a slice and took a giant bite. He wasn't sure if she knew she'd verbalized her hum of pleasure as she swallowed, but every cell in his body was vibrantly aware. She was so effortlessly sensual, and it grabbed him right in the gut.

Emma chewed thoughtfully as she eyed him from her perch. She trailed her gaze from his face to his shoulders, down his bare chest, then all the way to his feet, before she swallowed.

"Never really took you for a sweatpants kind of guy," she said, drawing her legs up under her and arranging the terry cloth robe to cover them. His eyes lingered for a moment on her bare toes peeping out, before he met her gaze again. "But they're probably made of cashmere or something, huh?"

They were.

"Did you want some wine?" he offered. She nodded as she took another bite of pizza, and he poured two glasses from the bottle he'd uncorked while he was waiting for her to appear.

He joined her on the couch, placing a glass of wine on either side of the square box.

"It's so good," she encouraged, gesturing toward the pizza, her mouth full.

With a smile at her enthusiasm, he grabbed a slice. It smelled fantastic—spicy and savory—and he realized how hungry he was.

The flavor exploded on his tongue in some magic ratio of pizza toppings to grease, and he savored the glimpse of gustatory heaven. Emma hadn't been kidding. It was the best pizza he'd ever tasted.

"The greatest, right?"

"It's good," he said, downplaying the review just to enjoy the look of outrage on her pretty face. "I mean, I don't know if it's *shower-sex good*, but it's solid." He took another bite.

She rolled her eyes. "Now I know you're lying. There's no way this isn't the best thing you've ever had in your mouth."

His grin was involuntary. "You're the best thing I've ever had in my mouth, and I haven't even gotten to taste you like I want to yet."

"Stop sexualizing my pizza," she admonished with a frown, shoving the last of her pizza in her mouth.

Despite the rebuke, he noticed that she started absently spinning the ring on the middle finger of her right hand. It was a habit of hers he'd noticed lately. She tended to play with it when she was uncomfortable. Or deep in thought. He wondered which one it was right now as he finished off his slice.

"What's with the ring?" he asked, grabbing his wine glass.

Emma looked down at her right hand, back up at him. "It's my mom's wedding ring."

Not the answer he'd been expecting.

"I sold most of her stuff, but I couldn't bring myself to part with this."

"Why did you sell her things?" He took a sip of the full-bodied red.

She shrugged her shoulder, and the neck of the bath-robe parted, exposing her collarbone. "Medical bills have a way of multiplying. And they don't stop just be-cause the treatment does." A hint of bitterness coated her grief. She looked small to him right then. Alone.

Max set his wine back on the table.

He was struck with the realization that her mother's death seemed recent enough that the emotion was still perilously close to the surface. Hadn't Vivienne men-tioned something about her mother being in the hospital recently? "When?" The question fell out of his mouth without thinking, and he dreaded the answer.

She bit her lip, like she was as wary about telling him as he was about asking. But she did. "Six months ago."

Well, damn.

"Why didn't you say something?"

It was a stupid question. They'd never talked about this kind of stuff before. Personal stuff. He felt like an asshole, the vague memory of signing off on a week of vacation for her around that time worming its way into his brain. He recalled that he'd resented it. How he'd thought it was bad timing, with the SecurePay launch approaching, and so much to do in the meantime.

"I didn't want to talk about it," she said simply.

He understood that. But he was still an asshole.

He didn't realize he'd reached for her until he felt the softness of her cheek against the back of his knuckles. He tucked her hair behind her ear.

Maybe she wanted to talk about it now.

"What was your mother like?"

The question surprised her, but in a good way, if the widening of her eyes and her lack of hesitation were any indication. "She was wonderful." She said it matter-of-factly, with no hesitation.

Max envied her certainty. It was not something he'd shared in recent memory. Of course, there must have been a time he would have answered similarly, but when he thought of his mother now, she inspired none of the warmth he heard in Emma's voice.

"You must have loved her a lot."

There was a tragic beauty to her smile. "I did. I do. My mother was an amazing baker. She used to let me help make *medenjaci* cookies. They're like Croatian gingerbread, but you make them with honey. And that smell, spicy and warm, that's what love smelled like, you know? They were my dad's favorite. He used to ask her to make them for him instead of a birthday cake, he loved them so much. And after he died, whenever I really missed him, we'd make them together."

Her smile wobbled a little, and Max's chest constricted. He very deliberately grabbed a second slice of pizza, if not quashing the temptation to comfort her, at least making it more difficult for himself.

"They met when my mother and her family came to Los Angeles on holiday, but their rental car broke down. My dad was an apprentice mechanic at the shop they got towed to. They made eyes at each other while the mechanic and her dad fiddled around with the car. They fell madly in love, and before she left a week later, he asked her to marry him."

Max paused with the pizza halfway to his mouth. "And she said yes?" He didn't mean to sound quite so incredulous.

Emma nodded. "She said yes. She was twenty, and he was twenty-two and she gave up everything she knew to stay in America. To be with him."

She stared at the ring on her finger, like she was trying to see her mother in it.

"My mom got a job as a janitor and improved her English by taking night classes. They never had very much, but they were mostly happy. As happy as people can be, I think. But even so, she always seemed a little wistful when she spoke of Croatia, about her childhood in Dubrovnik. Like she had a little bit of homesickness that never went away. I always planned to take her back there one day."

Max swallowed the pizza he'd been chewing. It was difficult to imagine a childhood more different from his own. "It's nice that you want to see where she grew up."

"What's your family like?"

He stiffened at the innocuous question. One that any

person in possession of the most rudimentary social skills might ask. And the last one he wanted to answer. "Nothing like yours, I can tell you that."

The half-eaten slice in his hand was suddenly unappetizing. He set it back in the box.

"My mother is a failed politician whose career went down in a flaming scandal of newspaper headlines when she got caught fucking her handsome young intern, and my father retaliated by fucking a pretty, even-younger stripper."

A strangled-sounding "Oh" was all Emma managed at his blunt summation of the sordid story.

"Obviously, her senatorial bid came to a crashing halt before it even got off the ground. Now the only thing she cares about is propriety, and what other people think of her, and by extension, us."

Max shook his head at the ridiculousness of that particular obsession.

The damage was done. His mother of all people should realize that you couldn't rewrite the past.

If someone betrayed you, if you betrayed someone else, then the only option left was to accept the consequences and move forward as best you could.

Try as she might, and she *did* try, his mother would never escape the scandal.

Just as he would never forgive his father for what he'd done to John Beckett.

And Aidan would never forgive him.

That was how life worked.

"How old were you when it happened?"

"Ten."

He didn't deserve the heart-melting expression she was giving him, or rather, the boy he'd been. As the eldest, he'd had a lot more autonomy than Kaylee. Mostly because he thrived under rules and had always worked hard for the day when he'd be the one setting them for other people.

His sister, on the other hand, was strangled by them. And when her political career gasped out its last breath, Sylvia Whitfield had turned her considerable will to ensuring Kaylee's rebellious streak was extinguished. But try as she might to smother it, it always seemed to flare up again.

It was one of the things about his sister that Max respected the hell out of, even when it was annoying as fuck.

He used to try to help Kaylee. To intervene. Run some interference. Until his father had made it clear he would destroy anything, and anyone, Max cared about. After that, he'd learned to keep his distance.

"Kaylee was only six. And my mother's been ruining my little sister's life ever since."

And judging by the crestfallen look on Emma's face, Sylvia Whitfield had just ruined their night as well.

He took a sip of wine, but it tasted sour in his mouth. This was why he didn't talk about his family. With anyone. It was a guaranteed mood killer, especially for him.

Sex was one thing, but this… Max was a firm believer of keeping his business life and personal life separate. But whatever strange intimacy that had sprung up during their shower conversation seemed not to have dissipated completely, and just like that, he'd crossed yet another line with Emma Mathison.

A line he should have had the brains to stay far away from.

Something shifted in the room, as though he'd abolished the moment of emotional honesty with the sheer force of his will. Emma lowered her feet to the floor. The smile she shot him was reserved.

It was as though they'd both realized they'd stepped into a minefield of feelings, and retreat was their only option.

Which was probably for the best.

"It's getting late," she said.

He nodded at the lie.

"I should probably go. I've got an early morning, and thanks to my boss, I need to make sure I've got a bra to wear. He's a real stickler about the dress code."

Max forced a smile at the joke.

She got up. He did, too, though more out of a sense of propriety than a desire to hasten her departure.

"Mind if I wear this back to my room?"

His brain snapped to attention at that. "You're staying?"

"*Temporarily.* If the offer stands."

He nodded. Followed her to the door of his suite.

"Stay as long as you like."

She turned to face him as she stepped into the hall. "Thanks for the pizza. I guess I'll see you tomorrow."

"Tomorrow," he repeated.

When he shut the door behind her, Max walked back to the living room to grab his wine as he contemplated the relief that washed through him when she'd said she was staying. He had a bad feeling he was in the kind of trouble you didn't know you were in until it was already too late.

CHAPTER ELEVEN

IT WAS TROUBLE all right. The full extent of which finally registered the next morning, when he found himself watching for Emma's arrival.

She'd accepted the hotel room. *Temporarily.* But according to his driver, who'd been sent back to the hotel after dropping Max at work, she hadn't accepted a ride.

Max had spent the last hour surreptitiously surveilling the elevator in between emails and phone calls. Which was how he knew it had slid open at nine sharp, to reveal Emma, looking professional as ever in her white shirt, blue pencil skirt and nude heels. She didn't glance at him as she passed, but it was done deliberately enough that he could tell she'd had to concentrate to pull it off.

The fact that it pleased him let him know he had to euthanize this ridiculous fixation immediately.

With the single-minded focus that he prided himself on, Max immersed himself in his work day. And he succeeded at keeping his mind clear of her, too. Until his four-thirty meeting with Soteria.

He set the report Brennan had just handed him on the corner of his desk as he sat.

"Give it to me straight. What are we dealing with?"

"In my professional opinion, Emma Mathison is not the originator of the hack."

Relief poured through him at the assessment.

"Not only has she got no tech or coding background that would lead me to believe she could write something this sophisticated, she also shut her computer down at eight o'clock that night. Whoever loaded the malware turned her computer back on and overrode her login. It took some time to load and her cell phone was pinging from a tower near her apartment before it should have been, considering she didn't just leave the memory stick in the computer."

No. Max could vouch for the fact that she hadn't returned to her workstation that night.

"So you don't think it's Emma, but you don't know who it is?"

"I've got Jesse digging."

"That's what you've been saying since Saturday. I don't need to tell you that it's not what I wanted to hear."

The tick in Brennan's jaw said he was well aware. "It's not what I wanted to tell you, either. Whoever did this knew what they were up against. It's sophisticated code, sure, but it was deployed in an old-fashioned way. Whoever it was had strong intel about how Whitfield Industries is set up. Us finding the leak so quickly means they lost a lot of time they would have had to siphon info. Jesse's still working on the encryption, so we should have a better idea of what they got in a day or so."

"What does this mean for the launch?"

"That's up to you. The stuff we've found so far is in the report." Brennan gestured at Max's desk. "Honestly, none of it's too damaging, information-wise, but…"

"But it's a PR nightmare if the breach hits the press," Max finished. Just what he didn't need.

Brennan shrugged. "You're going to have to decide if that's a risk you're willing to take, because from what we've uncovered so far, wrecking your brand seems to be more of the focus than stealing your tech."

Max's shoulders were rigid beneath his suit jacket. "Find out who did this. Now."

Brennan gave a curt nod and got to his feet.

Max faked a casualness he didn't feel. Soteira might not have answers yet, but perhaps a certain someone else he had working the case might be having better luck.

The second Brennan had cleared the door to his office, he pulled his secondary phone—the one that was strictly for contacting AJ—out of the hidden safe in the bottom drawer and set it on his desk.

It was a pain in the ass, but when you were working with geniuses, you put up with the quirks. And AJ definitely had her quirks. Four years ago, Soteria had caught her trying to hack into Whitfield Industries, and according to Brennan, she'd almost done it—but had gotten caught in some trap door hidden deep in the code.

He might not be Max's favorite guy on the planet, but Brennan was great at what he did, and not easily impressed. He'd helped Max track her down, and Max had set AJ up as an off-the-books consultant to help test his cyber defenses when the occasion called for it. Or, in moments like this one, to double the mind power trying to help him figure out who the hell was trying to ruin him. And he was eager to hear what his *independent consultant* had managed to unearth. He touched the screen to start a video chat.

Then, against his better judgment, he unfrosted the glass wall. Emma would be leaving soon.

It was, he realized, the first time he'd ever called AJ without having his office in privacy mode. She picked up on the first ring. AJ was always hungry for an assignment, and the more it tested her considerable skills, the better.

It was one of the reasons he let her get away with many of her other transgressions. The screen was filled mostly with her face, dark curly hair around a café-au-lait complexion, but there was enough of her T-shirt visible to prove that she was dressed in her signature all-black.

"What have you got for me?"

"I'm great, Max, thank you for asking. And you?"

He frowned at the implied condemnation and AJ got down to business.

"I don't know how she could possibly have pulled off the hack. There's nothing in her background to hint at the kind of tech genius it would take to get around anything Soteria dreamed up. I mean, not to cast aspersions, but the woman only owns a smartphone and a tablet. You know how I feel about that."

"So she didn't code the program, but that doesn't mean she didn't install it." Max pointed out. "Any luck with the surveillance footage?"

AJ shook her head, then leaned forward so that her face took up more of the screen, obliterating any glimpse of the brick wall behind her. "I ran into the same issue Jesse had. Got nada from the security feed. Lucky for you, this is one of those times when nothing is actually something."

AJ did love a little drama. It was in such direct contrast to her life, holed up in a shitty loft that she didn't know he knew about, that it never ceased to annoy Max. He lifted an unimpressed brow. "Don't stop now. I'm on the edge of my seat."

"Oh sure, play it all casual and urbane, like you don't care. Just makes it all the sweeter when I blow your mind." AJ gave him a smug smile. "I don't think it was wiped, I think the camera was turned off. Trouble is, I can't tell if the shutdown was remote or not. But either way, we're still dealing with a manual load, which means someone was inside your building."

Max swore under his breath. Thanks to the other security precautions, Soteria didn't have anyone watching the camera feeds live. And that meant Emma was still in play as someone who had the means to have installed that spyware.

"Told you so," his hacker gloated, but her face turned suddenly serious. "What's that look, boss? Because if your gut has info that can help me out, you'd better spill."

Considering AJ had already picked up on his preoccupation, Max led her slightly astray and gave her the other most likely suspect in the hack. "Cybercore."

The company name was bitter on his tongue. He tended not to lead investigators down any particular path, preferring that they find it on their own. But he wanted to be sure he'd turned over every rock. Tunnel vision on Emma would do him no good. Not professionally. Or personally, he reminded himself.

"Liam Kearney, huh?" She looked contemplative for a moment. "Yeah. That fits. The douchebag is always gunning for you, and SecurePay is way ahead of his stupid payment chip. He makes spy gear, so corporate espionage seems like a weapon he'd keep in his arsenal. I'll look into him. See if anything pops. And I'm still running the security logs from that day to see if there was any unusual activity or visitors prior to the camera shutdown."

"Good. Let me know if you find anything at all."

"I will. But I still don't know why you want me to. You're paying me an awful lot of money to follow the same path that Soteria's already following. And I know that Wes Brennan's personal attention doesn't come cheap these days."

"I need to be thorough. This breach could sink SecurePay. We're less than one week out from launch. I need this handled quickly and efficiently. You told me you're the best."

AJ lifted her chin. "Well, sure. Because I *am* the best. But double-or-nothing my fee says that Wes told you that *he's* the best."

Max nodded. "He would also point out that he's the one who caught you hacking the system."

"Hey, even a blind squirrel catches a master hacker sometimes. He got lucky. I got better."

"I'm just hoping one of you is right."

AJ frowned at him, but he ignored it. He needed results, not posturing. And he didn't want her to figure out that he'd assigned her a little side job that he hadn't brought up with Soteria. Better to let her think it was a race to the finish. AJ thrived on competition.

"Besides the grievous sin of not owning a proper computer, did anything else ring when you looked into Ms. Mathison?"

The mention of Emma had him glancing toward the elevator.

On screen, AJ shot him a look he couldn't quite decipher. "Oh, it's Ms. Mathison, is it? Okay, boss. If that's the way you wanna play it. Everything checks out in my preliminary run. Dad died years ago in a work accident, mom kicked more recently. Alzheimer's. She was staying at a really swank home that catered to that sort of thing, top of the line medical facility. Looks like your *Ms. Mathison* funneled as much of every paycheck as she could spare into the digs, including her bonus checks, hence the shithole apartment she was renting."

AJ shrugged. "After her mom died, she put together a modest funeral, and tucked half the life insurance payout away, sank the other half into a plane ticket back to her mother's homeland. Itinerary was pretty sparse. She was definitely doing her best to pull off one of those Croatia on ten dollars a day kind of trips. But I'll keep digging."

The object of his…investigation, strode past on her way out. It was precisely five o'clock. This time, instead of ignoring him, she shot him a lingering glance and a flirty finger wave as she boarded the elevator.

"Hello? Earth to Max."

His gaze snapped back to the phone.

AJ's expression was quizzical. "What was that all about?"

"Nothing." He hit the button that frosted his office glass. "Continue."

"Testy today, boss. Might wanna lay off the coffee. That stuff'll kill ya."

"AJ…" He let her name hang there, a warning.

"Fine. But I wish you'd just read the stuff I told you about before outright dismissing the idea that the government might have doctored the caffeine supply. Anyway, like I said, this is all just surface stuff. I'll follow the money and see where it leads."

"You do that. And keep it clean. I don't want Brennan and Hastings knowing that I've got you second-guessing their every move."

She scoffed. "No chance of that. I'm a goddamned ninja."

"And Brennan's a ninja slayer," he goaded, a release-valve on his frustration.

She frowned at the slight. "How many times do I have to tell you? The man knows his code, but now that he's sold out and gone corporate, he's lost his edge. Wes couldn't catch me now if he tried."

"Is that so?"

"My stealth knows no bounds," she assured him.

"In that case, I heard Aidan Beckett is back in town…" It was a long shot that this had anything to do with him, but Max let the implication dangle anyway. Better safe than sorry. As always, AJ's brilliant mind was already strategizing ten steps ahead.

"I'll tug a couple of lines, see if I can find out what brought that on."

"Get in touch if you find anything."

"I always do. So what kind of bonus do I get if I beat the esteemed Wes Brennan and find you your mole first?"

"You get me the info I need before Brennan and before this product launches on Tuesday, I'll see that the compensation matches my gratitude. And I would be very, very grateful."

AJ grinned. "That's what I like to hear. Got my eye on a new leather jacket…one that matches the interior of the new ride I'm gonna buy with your money. It's been a pleasure chatting with you, boss, but I've got to go. I've got a spy to catch."

Max sat back in his chair, contemplating AJ's information. The app was on schedule, so as long as this breach didn't hit the press, they should be good to launch next week. Still, he'd feel better if he had more answers than questions.

He shuffled some papers. Glanced through Brennan's report. Reviewed a couple of proofs the marketing department had sent over. By 5:30 p.m., he gave up and headed home.

Thanks to rush hour, it was just past six when Max arrived back at the hotel. He took the elevator to the penthouse, but instead of heading straight for his room, his gaze snagged on her door. He'd kept thoughts of her at bay for most of the day, but now he realized how close to the surface she'd been. She invaded his mind, his blood, his fantasies. Just like she'd done so often since Friday night.

Emma.

He wanted her with a disturbingly singular focus, and no matter how many times he reminded himself she might be the reason the future of SecurePay hung in the balance, it didn't lessen his desire. Because while there was a possibility she was the instigator of his problems, she was undeniably the only cure.

When she was in his arms, he could breathe. Lose himself. Forget how much was riding on Tuesday's launch and all the bullshit that accompanied it—the security breach, his father's treachery, how much he wished that John Beckett could see SecurePay come to fruition, how much he hoped that Aidan Beckett would appreciate the result of his father's work made manifest.

He approached her door, standing there like an addict, his fist raised to knock, desperate for a hit of her.

Christ, she was dangerous.

It wasn't safe to need someone this much. It couldn't be.

Max jerked his hand back from the door before he made a fool of himself. Instead, he loosened his tie and popped the button on his collar.

He didn't need her. He wanted her.

It was completely different.

And with a deep breath, he was in control of himself again. Just like he needed to be. Max pulled his wallet out as he crossed the hallway to his own room, unlocking it with his key card.

He stepped inside.

Stopped.

The air whooshed from his lungs as the door swung shut behind him.

Emma stood in the sunken living room, her body silhouetted against the window as she stared out at the Los Angeles skyline, twinkling at dusk.

Max's hands fisted. He swallowed, his throat suddenly parched.

Her hair was down, loose waves cascading over her shoulders and back. She was clad in a black bra and panties, the garter belt from Friday night holding up fishnet thigh-highs. She turned her head to the side, allowing him a glimpse of her profile as she lifted the wineglass in her left hand and took a sip.

Blood thundered in his ears when her tongue darted out to erase a drop of wine from her bottom lip. Or to fuck with him. She was too far away to tell.

When she finally turned on those black stilettos that made her legs look a mile long, his cock jerked at the sight of her—so beautiful it fucking hurt, everything about her promising sin or salvation, and in that moment, he didn't give a damn which way it shook out, as long as he got to put his hands on her.

As though in response to his thoughts, a teasing smile tilted her crimson-painted lips.

"Honey, you're home."

CHAPTER TWELVE

ONE DAY. IT HAD been one day since she'd had her hands on him, but it felt like forever. She'd done a little shopping on her lunch break, intending to grab a few more office-appropriate pieces to get her through her indentured work program. But when her thoughts turned to Max, as they so often did, there was a lot less resentment and a lot more sizzle than she'd intended.

How the hell had she managed to keep her hands off him for the last three years?

She'd snagged the fishnets from a rack near the register on a whim, and sweet-talked Gerald into letting her into Max's room by claiming he'd sent her back to grab some important paperwork that he required.

And she'd cursed herself for doing it the entire time.

The plan had been one magical night with Max. She'd only given into the attraction because it was her last day, and she had a plane ticket to the other side of an ocean.

This part—the awkward intrusion of reality—wasn't supposed to have happened.

But it had, and now things were all messed up.

She should be mad at him for the high-handed power move that had kept her trapped in Los Angeles when she should be discovering the charms of Dubrovnik.

She *was* mad at him. But she wanted him, too.

Emma wasn't sure how it had happened, when exactly he'd become a necessity. She craved him, his body, what he made her feel.

He was power incarnate, always in control, and it turned her on and drove her wild, even as it anchored her.

Then last night had happened.

The tender way he'd touched her after asking about her mother—that was some next level shit. The kind that went beyond physical gratification. And that, she could not have.

What the hell had she been thinking?

Telling him those things. Telling him about her mother. And for what? Some deluded attempt to absolve herself for the bad choices she'd made? An effort to make Max understand how hurt and lost and scared she'd been when she'd realized her mother wasn't going to get better, only worse?

To what end?

So he'd forgive her for betraying him? So he'd understand, even a little, why she'd leaked information to Charles?

He wouldn't forgive her. He wouldn't understand.

They were just fucking, she reminded herself crudely. That's all it was, all it could be.

Telling him about her mom, wanting more, that was

just a lapse brought on by a night of great sex and great pizza. It didn't mean anything. She was still in control.

And she was going to prove it right now. Prove to herself that she was in charge. Prove it to him. He could have her body. And she could have his. Nothing more.

She crossed the room, abandoning her wine on the coffee table on her way past.

"Put your hands in your pockets."

"What?"

She stopped directly in front of him.

"I said, 'Put your hands in your pockets.'"

He obeyed, and as a reward, she grabbed him by his black and grey tie, tugging him close and claiming his lips.

God, it felt good to have her mouth on him again, to breathe in his scent—the perfect combination of clean, warm man and dark, spicy cologne.

When he angled his head to take over the kiss, she pulled back.

"Uhn-uh," she chided. "In case I didn't make it clear, I'm in charge here. I'll tell you when you can kiss me. When and where you can touch. And that's strike one."

He quirked a brow at that, but he kept his mouth shut as she started walking backwards to the bedroom, pulling him along by his tie.

Max kept his eyes on hers for the entire journey, stoking the heat licking at her belly. There was something incredibly sensual about ordering a big, beautiful man around while wearing fishnet stockings.

And she was just getting started.

She tugged Max to the side of the bed before dropping his tie.

"Stay," she instructed, and his sexy mouth kicked up at the corner as he watched her take a seat on the edge of the mattress, his hands still in his pockets.

The slow, sensual beat of the song playing on her iPhone made the massive master bedroom feel more intimate. His eyes darted around the room, taking in the candles she'd placed on every flat surface, then the box of condoms on the bedside table, before landing back on her. "I take it this means I'll be playing the role of Labrador Retriever tonight?"

The reference to her admonition in the car yesterday brought an answering smile to her lips as she crossed her legs. "I wouldn't have to resort to this if you weren't so domineering all the time," she teased. "And you know what they say: turnaround is fair play."

He nodded, slow and predatory. "Why don't you turn around and get on your knees and we'll test that theory?"

The rough challenge made everything inside her clench and throb with need. "See? I haven't even gotten you out of your clothes yet, and you're already getting bossy. That's strike two. Now, take off your jacket."

He shrugged out of the immaculately tailored garment, tossing it into her outstretched hand. She closed her fingers around the soft, fine material, warm from his body, carrying with it the scent of his expensive cologne.

He reached for his tie.

"So impatient to get naked for me?"

"You don't want me to?"

Oh, she did. She set his jacket on the bed behind her, pausing as though she was considering the question.

"I'll allow it," she deigned, with her most regal nod, even as her toes curled in her stilettos as those beautiful, capable hands of his made deft work of unknotting the diagonally striped silk.

"Shirt, too," she added, as though it were an afterthought.

Watching Max strip down was a singular pleasure. He undressed like he did everything else—perfectly and precisely. No hesitation, but he didn't rush, either. He worked his way down the front of his shirt before flicking the material off his beautiful shoulders, undoing each of the buttons on his cuffs in turn, so he could pull the shirt off completely. And then he was hers to admire, muscles gleaming in the candlelight.

Lean. Powerful.

"That's enough for now."

She stood up, tugged his shirt and tie from his hand. "Take off your shoes and get on the bed."

Max toed off the gleaming black oxfords and moved the pillow out of the way before he took a seat, with his back against the headboard and his long legs stretched out in front of him.

Emma tossed his clothes on the far side of the bed as she joined him on the mattress. His eyes darkened, dropped to her cleavage while she crawled toward him until her knees were on either side of his thighs.

She leaned forward and pressed a soft kiss to his mouth.

His hands came up immediately, palms spanning the sides of her rib cage, his thumbs skating along the underwire of her bra. It took everything she had to sit back, grab his wrists, halt his lazy exploration of her body. "I told you no touching."

She pushed his hands down to the bed. "You can't help it, can you? Can't stand the loss of control. But that's strike three. And now I have to punish you."

His hands fisted against the mattress, and the bob of his Adam's apple made her want to lick his neck.

She reached for his belt, making quick work of the buckle. The slither of leather on fabric filled the room as she tugged it off him.

Her smile was wicked as she dragged the soft black leather contemplatively across her fingers.

His breathing changed—a series of shallow pants.

"I think maybe I'll tie you up," she mused, as though the idea had only just occurred to her. Emma scraped her fingernail lightly along his skin, from shoulder to biceps to forearm, then lifted his arm until his wrist was in line with his shoulder. "Teach you a lesson."

Emma licked her lips as she pressed the back of his hand against the slatted wood of the headboard, holding it there with her right hand so she could grab the belt from her lap.

His muscles drew tight as she pressed the leather against his wrist. It took her a second to realize the jerk of his body wasn't need, it was retreat.

"Not the belt."

The harshness of his voice took her aback, and she

dropped his wrist and the belt as her gaze snapped to his ashen face. There was a desperation there that scared her.

"Max?" She searched the amber depths of his eyes, trying to understand the sudden shift, but he was looking through her, breathing hard. "What's wrong?"

She cupped his cheek with her palm, angled his head up, looking for connection, trying to get him to see her. "Come back to me, baby."

He closed his eyes and his breath sawed from his lungs.

"Not the fucking belt," he repeated. But when he opened them, his eyes had lost that glassy look. Anger had replaced the fear in his voice.

She shook her head to reassure him, even as she watched him battle for control. She leaned her forehead against his. "I'm not going to hurt you," she whispered, pressing a kiss to his lips. Then another. And another. Until he kissed her back.

CHAPTER THIRTEEN

HAVING HER MOUTH on him helped. Dulled the anxiety that had jacked up his heart rate and made his palms sweat, blindsiding him with its intensity.

"You can't win big if you're soft. That's your problem. You care too much, but you can't help yourself, can you?"

He leaned into the kiss, ignored her "no touching" rule and cradled her face in his hands, shoving his tongue in her mouth with more desperation than finesse in his quest to recapture the hazy spell of lust she'd ensnared him in the moment he'd walked through the door.

"It's your fault I have to punish you. Now, stand still."

He groaned as she leaned into him, understanding his wordless plea and pressing her body against his, her arms around his neck, pulling him close as she kissed him back.

The kiss, her touch, helped calm his heart, until he could hear the music she'd put on and not just the rush of blood in his ears. The air-conditioning cooled the sweat on his skin, making him shiver.

"You'll thank me for this one day. For teaching you a lesson. For making you a man."

She was just going to tie him up. He wanted her to.

And then she'd run that fucking belt over her fingers, pressed it to his wrist and he was back there.

The bite of leather on his skin, the wash of pain along his back, biting his lip so hard to keep from crying out, from making it worse, that he tasted the salt of blood, but not tears. Never tears.

Everything jumbled together, memories and reality colliding, twisting in his gut until he couldn't tell them apart anymore.

"I'm so sorry, Max."

Emma. Emma's voice in his ear, soothing him. Emma's hands in his hair, saving him. Bringing him back.

"This was a bad idea. I never meant to… We can stop, okay? We'll stop."

Unshed tears glistened in her eyes, extinguishing all trace of the feisty seductress who'd broken into his hotel room.

No. Dammit. His father had taken too much from him already. Kaylee. John. Aidan. He wasn't taking this.

Her.

He was in control of his own goddamn life, Max reminded himself, and if he wanted to be tied up by the sexy, beautiful woman straddling his lap, then no one was going to stop him.

"Use the tie. Loose knots." His voice was hoarse.

Her fingers stilled in his hair and she shook her head.

The compassion in her eyes humbled him.

Max reached out, catching the end of his tie between

his index and middle finger, pulling it free from the tangle of his shirt and lifting it between them.

"Do it."

Emma swallowed as her eyes dropped to the black and grey striped silk. Her fingers tightened against the back of his neck. She didn't want to. Probably afraid he'd freak out again.

He wouldn't.

And he needed her help to prove it to himself.

Please.

The blood rushing in his ears was too loud, so he wasn't sure if he'd spoken the word aloud, or just mouthed it.

She lowered her hands from the back of his neck, and he braced for her decision, one of the wooden slats of the headboard digging into his spine.

His breath rushed from his chest when her fingers brushed his, but he didn't look down. He couldn't break this eye contact with her, this lifeline.

She tugged the silk from his grip.

"What did I tell you about being bossy?" Her voice shook a little, but it didn't matter. All that mattered was that she was doing this for him. With him.

Emma set his hand on her thigh, palm up, and he watched as she slipped the skinny end of the tie around his wrist, knotting it so the hole was wide enough for him to pull his hand free. If he wanted to.

Her eyes met his as she pushed his wrist against the headboard again.

Her skin was warm against his.

She waited for his slight nod before she looped the tie through the wood, behind his head.

Emma lifted his other arm and repeated the process with the wide end of the tie around that wrist.

Max focused on taking deep, even breaths.

When she was done, she faced him again.

Instead of asking how he was, or worse, telling him everything was going to be fine, she just reached behind her and unclasped her bra, tossing it aside before she cupped his face and pressed her mouth to his, kissing him so deep that his brain shut off.

Desire unfurled in his belly, until there was no room for panic, not even when he wanted to touch her so badly that he strained against his bonds.

She pulled back, cheeks flushed with arousal, her kiss-swollen lips tilted in a teasing half-smile that made his blood run hot.

"No touching, remember?"

Yes. There was his flirty dominatrix. The one who'd met him in the living room and blown his mind.

"Now, let's get you out of these pants."

She reached between them and the slide of his zipper filled his ears, drowning out the music and the doubt, and he lifted his hips as she tugged his clothes down his body and all the way off.

Then she stood beside the bed and shed the layers of her pretty lingerie, until she was perfectly, gorgeously naked for him.

Crawling her way back up his body, Emma planted a knee on either side of his hips and lowered herself until the wet heat of her was pressed against his growing erection.

He groaned, the tie cutting into his wrists as she undulated her hips, rubbing against him, until she was the only thing filling his brain, until she was everything.

And still it wasn't enough. The ache inside him grew, and as if Emma could sense the slow, sweet friction wasn't enough for him anymore, her movements grew less sinuous and more desperate. He groaned, wanting everything her body was promising him.

She reached between them, and he hissed as her fingers circled his erection, her thumb swiping across the sensitive tip of him. Fire sizzled through his veins as his hips bucked, and it took him a moment to realize she's said something. Max tried to pull himself back to the surface.

"I'm on the pill," she repeated.

He couldn't breathe for a second.

"And I'm clean. And I want to feel you inside me."

His heart thudded against his ribs.

"Me, too. Christ, Emma. I need you so bad."

The exquisiteness of sliding into her with nothing between them, the tight, wet heat of her drawing him deep, the trust of it all, it wrecked him. His body was hard, but something inside him had cracked. He wanted to pull his hands free, to pound into her, to lose himself in the wildness of the act, but even as he wanted to let out the darkness, to rut, fuck, use her, let her use him, it wasn't just that anymore.

They knew too much about each other. He respected her. He liked her. And even as she was pulling him out from beneath the weight of secrets he'd kept for too long, so long that they'd changed him and warped him, he had the distinct impression he was drowning in her.

Because as much as he wanted this to be solely about sex, it was about Emma, too.

Respectful, naughty, flirty, so goddamn sweet—he'd take her any way he could get her.

He didn't deserve this. He didn't deserve to feel better.

But then she reached forward, pressing her palms to his, twining their fingers together as she rode him faster and faster, urging him on, and he couldn't stop himself from taking what she was offering—sex and forgiveness and a way to forget. At least temporarily.

"Oh fuck. Max. Please."

She contracted around him, burying her face against his neck as she cried out, and he tightened his fingers around hers as his climax rolled through him, made all the sweeter by the feel of her, so slick and tight around him as he joined her in ecstasy.

CHAPTER FOURTEEN

PREWORK SEX HAD Max feeling pretty mellow. Maybe a little too mellow, he realized, as he lost track yet again of where they were on the agenda of last-minute details that needed attending to before SecurePay went live on Tuesday.

The first time he'd done it, he'd been reminiscing about waking up with Emma in his arms, her hair tickling his chest and the curve of her ass tucked against his hips. She'd pressed his palm against her breast, and he'd kissed the back of her neck, and they'd rocked together in a slow, easy rhythm that had ended in an incredible orgasm and counted as the best wake-up call of his life.

The second offense had him reliving their back seat make-out session, which had started with her teasing him about how he'd cut himself shaving when she'd appeared wet and naked after her shower and devolved into them rounding the bases with a speed that would have impressed his fourteen-year-old self and disgusted his sixteen-year-old self. It had left Emma delightfully rumpled enough to draw a raised eyebrow from his stoic driver when he'd pulled the door open upon their arrival at work.

This latest transgression had him contemplating the merits of spreading Emma on the boardroom table after this never-ending meeting was over and shoving her skirt up her thighs, so he could finally taste her like he wanted to.

Based on the way she was glaring right now, she might not be completely amenable to the idea.

"That's ridiculous!" she burst out, as though reading his dirty mind. It took him a moment to realize the comment was directed at Jim Dawson, the head of marketing, and his earlier edict on SecurePay's ad campaign.

At least someone was paying attention to the meeting.

"Did you have something to add, Emma?" Max asked drily.

"I… I just…" She took a deep, steadying breath. Touched her mother's wedding ring. "I think that's a mistake."

Max leaned back in his chair at the head of the oval boardroom table, his gaze focused on his lone dissenter. A quick survey of the room showed that he wasn't the only one. Emma angled her chin defiantly.

He gestured for her to proceed.

"This close to launch, it's ridiculous to change the price or the marketing campaign to appeal to a wider audience. All the focus groups show that positioning this as a luxury product and a luxury price point will instill the most confidence in the buyers, even those who can't afford the product."

Jim's scoff set off some whispers around the boardroom table. "And what good are 'buyers' who can't afford your product?"

The challenge made Emma drop her eyes to the table that Max's lascivious imagination had been putting to such good use a moment ago, and for a second, he figured the matter was dropped. Then Emma raised her head, and there was a quiet poise to her that clashed with the sparks in her ocean-blue eyes.

That's my girl.

"All of my research suggests that Whitfield Industries' leadership change is going to affect this launch."

He felt the collective attention of the room on him, trying to gauge his reaction, but Max gave them nothing.

"SecurePay is not only Whitfield Industries' first salvo into the tech world, it's also our inaugural product launch with Max as CEO. It's imperative that we keep it on brand and position ourselves as a leader in the industry. When it comes to security, the data clearly shows that people are more likely to trust luxury products with luxury price tags. They associate the higher price with quality, and with the flood of copycat products that will come, it's important that we cement ourselves in the minds of the consumers as the best. Especially with Cybercore set to release their take on secure payment tech later this year."

Again, all eyes darted toward him at the mention of the rival company belonging to Liam Kearney.

Max nodded. "Agreed. We'll move forward as planned. I'll expect a report at our next meeting. And

I want that glitch with the user interface taken care of. We're launching next week, and everything needs to be perfect. Thank you all for your time."

The sound of shuffling paper filled the room as people gathered their things and pushed back from the boardroom table.

"Emma. May I have a word?"

The sympathetic glances of her coworkers, save Jim, who looked rather smug, were not lost on Max as his employees filed out of the boardroom.

She just sat there, arms crossed over her perfect breasts, waiting until they were alone, and the door had swung fully shut.

"Jim is such an ass!"

"You surprised the hell out of him. Out of all of them. You've never been so vocal with your dissent before."

"Maybe I'm just done biding my time, heading back to my desk to compose carefully worded emails that stroke all of your egos while convincing you that my way is actually better," she taunted sweetly.

Her scenario struck him as familiar, as more than a few instances of her doing exactly that sprang to mind.

Huh. Funny he hadn't noticed that before.

Max nodded. "I'm glad. It's a waste of everyone's time. I much prefer having it brought up in the moment."

Emma gaped at him, searching his face for what? Some hint that he was toying with her? Max wasn't one to play games. Not out of bed, anyway.

"You're serious."

"Why wouldn't I be? I respect your opinion. I wouldn't have hired you otherwise."

She tipped her head, as if still not completely certain he was on the level. "I always got more of a 'what I say goes, so don't question it' vibe from you. Challenging you in front of your team always seemed…imprudent."

"What I say does go. But those orders are based on input from people I consider experts in their respective fields. I'm not here to be right. I'm here to win." He let a beat pass. "Besides, I like it when you get vocal."

Awareness settled in the room, warm and heavy.

"What are you doing?" she asked, though the heightened color in her cheeks told him she already knew.

He pushed his chair back from the table.

"Are you flirting with me, Mr. Whitfield?"

He rubbed his knuckles along his jaw. "The fact that you have to ask hurts my feelings a little."

Emma bit her lip to stop her smile, and his thighs flexed in response.

"I can tell. You seem pretty broken up about it."

"I'd consider letting you make it up to me."

"How generous of you," she teased, not realizing that he was dead serious.

His earlier fantasy of feasting on her right there on the boardroom table flashed through his veins, heating his blood. "It could be."

He liked the way her blue eyes darkened in response to the rough promise in his words. Despite that tell, she tried to keep her voice light. "Although I'm intrigued by the offer, I'm afraid I'm under strict orders to keep things professional at work."

"That's a stupid rule."

She lifted a delicate shoulder. "You made it."

Max frowned at the charge. "When did I say that?"

"The other day. In the car," she added, when he continued to look blankly at her.

Oh, yeah. He had the vague recollection of saying something to that effect. "Right before I shoved my hand up your skirt," he recalled aloud.

Simpler times. Back when he still believed he had a chance in hell of outrunning this thing between them.

"Well, disregard it. It was…short-sighted of me. Especially considering that we've been flirting at work for years."

"What? No, we haven't!" She sounded shocked enough that he almost believed she believed that. *Almost*.

"Emma," he chided, getting to his feet.

"Name one time."

"You mean besides me letting you kiss me in my office?"

It was wrong to bait her, but he loved the way her eyes flashed when she was riled up. She didn't disappoint, either.

"The night you got the preliminary focus group feedback about SecurePay."

He watched the shift in her eyes as she recalled the charged moment they'd shared from across his desk when she'd given him the excellent results of her first weeks' worth of work at Whitfield Industries.

"He smiles," she'd said, almost to herself, and the air had gotten thick with…something. She'd quashed it, resurrecting her all-business facade with impressive speed, and he'd let her, because there was nothing but danger down that path. But he liked knowing she remembered it.

"That time in the elevator," he offered, circling to her side of the table.

That memory made her breath come faster. They'd been heading to the ground floor during a particularly busy afternoon, and as the elevator stopped on floor after floor, picking up more passengers, Emma had been forced to shuffle closer and closer to him as space became more prized.

Before long they'd been relegated to the back corner of the elevator, so close that the backs of their hands were pressed together, sending a jolt of awareness through him. And despite the way she kept her gaze fixed on the head of the person in front of her, he'd known she felt it, too, because even after the bulk of the passengers had exited on the sixth floor and Emma had moved away from him, she hadn't moved quite far enough to break the contact between their fingers. A forbidden touch they'd savored until they reached the lobby.

He tugged on her chair, turning her to face him. "Should I go on?"

"You remember that?" Her words were soft, and she sounded a little off balance.

He leaned forward, bracing a palm on each of the armrests, fascinated by the way the muscles in her throat worked as she swallowed.

"A man doesn't forget getting his hands on a woman like you, no matter how innocuous the touch."

She was heart-stopping when she was turned on,

so pink and pretty. It was evident in the flush of her cheeks, the dance of her fingertips along her clavicle. Every cell in his body responded to the charge in the air.

Her lips parted, drawing him forward like a magnet.

"Are you wearing panties?"

"Of course," she breathed. "It's my understanding they're part of the dress code now. Sir."

The blood rushed to his cock.

"I swear to God, if I didn't have a lunch meeting in six minutes I would hike your skirt up and bend you over the table, so I could—"

Sudden movement caught his eye before he could finish his vow, and he straightened when the door to the conference room opened, ignoring Emma's perplexed look as he erected a wall of professionalism to mask the lust of a moment before.

Then the intruder showed himself, and Max lost his cool altogether.

Rage sucker-punched him in the gut, and in his peripheral vision, Emma shrank back from him, though her chair didn't move. She could probably feel the waves of animosity rolling off him. He had a weird urge to pull her behind him, to shelter her from the toxic presence that had invaded his boardroom.

He didn't, though.

Partly because she'd probably kick him for being over-protective, but mostly because he didn't want to draw any attention to her with a snake in the room. Instead, Max did his best to keep the bastard's attention on him by verbalizing the question that had been bang-

ing around in his brain since he'd recognized the unwelcome visitor. "What the fuck are you doing here?"

The man's oily smile made Max's jaw tighten.

"Now, is that any way to greet your father?"

CHAPTER FIFTEEN

EMMA STIFFENED.

Oh God. Not here.

She didn't need to look over her shoulder to see who was responsible for Max's deadly transformation, but she made herself do it anyway. Because like it or not, this was a nightmare she'd brought on herself.

Like his son, Charles Whitfield knew how to dominate a room. He was still in decent shape, though he'd filled out a little in the middle over the years. His salt-and-pepper hair gave him a distinguished look. She was struck, in that moment, by how similar they were physically. She'd never noticed before, because being around Charles always made her feel queasy, whereas being around Max, well…he made her feel all sorts of things.

Right now, though, all she felt was dread.

She stood, pushing the chair back into place. Emma wasn't sure what she was trying to accomplish with the show of solidarity—if she was offering Max her strength or trying to steal some of his.

Charles's gaze slid over to her, and his smugness made her feel slimy.

Max took a step forward, angling his broad shoulders like he was trying to shelter her from Charles's assessing gaze.

"And I repeat, what the fuck are you doing here?"

"I'm meeting your sister for lunch. And as far as I know, there's no reason I shouldn't be here. It's still a free country. I mean, it's not like I've been charged with a *felony* or anything." The words were a challenge, though Emma couldn't quite figure out for what.

Every muscle in Max's body looked strained.

"Now that I think of it, your sister told me to meet her in the lobby. Perhaps your lovely assistant could walk me down?"

Charles's glance sent shivers up her spine. He was toying with her, letting her know he could blow this up whenever he wanted to. His reptilian smile made her want to vomit.

"Emma is a research analyst, not my assistant," Max ground out.

Her blackmailer stepped forward, extending his hand. "I'm Charles Whitfield. Max's father. How do you do, *Emma*?"

Her stomach churned at the ludicrous pantomime. The lies clashed in her ears as she stepped forward and took Charles's hand in a farce of a handshake. He squeezed too hard, and she recognized in the flash of pain the warning he'd intended.

"She doesn't have any more time to usher you around than I do. She's on a tight deadline with a very important project and—"

"It's fine." She had to force the words out. She didn't

want to be alone with Charles Whitfield for even a second. She never did, and after what had happened between her and Max, the prospect felt a million times worse.

But she recognized in his eyes the threat of disobeying him on this…request. They were the same amber as his son's, but where Max's were fiery, Charles Whitfield's eyes were flat. Malevolent.

Max sent her a sharp glare, but she shook her head, ignoring the impulse to lay a hand on his arm. She didn't want to give Charles any more ammunition. She could already tell that he'd noticed the protective way Max had stepped in front of her.

"It's fine. Go to your meeting. I'll walk Mr. Whitfield down to the lobby."

"Come, come, Emma. No need for such formality. Please, call me Charles."

Max searched her face, but Emma nodded at the implied "are you sure?" and he relented. "Next time you and Kaylee are having lunch, meet her at the restaurant."

"Whatever you say, son. After all, you're the *boss*." Charles sneered the word, then turned and headed into the hallway.

Emma took a step to follow, but was surprised when Max grabbed her elbow, stepped close enough that she could feel his body heat along her left side. He tipped his head down, and his voice was low and steely in her ear.

"Take him straight to the lobby. No detours. I'll have security on stand-by. If Kaylee's not already down there, don't wait with him. Come straight back up. If I don't see you in ten minutes, I'm coming looking for you."

Then the heat of him was gone, and he'd turned his back on her, his cell phone pressed to his ear as he spoke with the head of building security.

It seemed a little excessive. Unless there was a reason that Max feared for her physical safety...

The realization hit hard and fast.

Emma took a bracingly deep breath to steady herself, to keep from vomiting at the abuse Max had suffered at his father's hands. Then she stepped out into the hallway.

"Well, well, well," Charles drawled, reigniting the churning in her stomach. "My little songbird forgot to give me the most important information of all. It seems my son isn't as cold to everyone as he is to me."

"Don't call me that," she hissed, ignoring the reference to whatever he might have witnessed between her and Max in the boardroom. She took off down the hallway, leaving Charles to follow in her wake. He caught up more quickly than she would have liked.

"Such a caustic reception."

"Because you make me sick!" she snapped. She'd thought he was bad enough, taking advantage of her mother's Alzheimer's, but now she could barely stand to look at him.

"Strong words. Do not delude yourself into thinking anything has changed here, Emma. You know what's at stake."

The reminder balled her fists. Emma made herself count through the wave of fury.

"I will admit, I'm surprised to see you. Off to chase your family history across the pond, wasn't it? Imagine my surprise when my good friend Rich Dorchester said you'd shown up, bright and early on Monday morning, just like always."

She whirled around to face him at the mention of one of Whitfield Industries' board members. "You have people spying on me?"

Charles's chuckle grated against her skin.

"Rich isn't a spy. He's a fool who can't hold his liquor, and he's happy to chat when I'm buying. When I asked him how Max was making out without you, he seemed...surprised. After that, I was suddenly *desperate* to eat lunch with my lovely daughter, just to touch base and see how she and her brother are faring. I figured I'd kill two birds, as the saying goes."

That he would mask his odious fact-gathering with parental concern made her stomach churn. Not just because she hated the idea of him running the scam on Kaylee, whom Emma liked very much, but because it was the same way he'd reeled in Emma in the first place. She'd had no reference for a parent who would put money before family. Use his daughter for information. Or take a belt to his son.

Shame swamped her as they passed Max's empty office and stepped into the elevator. She was glad to see there was a delivery guy already inside. It would keep her from having to talk to Charles. She kept her eyes forward, watching as the silver doors slid shut.

The guilt was like acid in her stomach. This was all her fault.

She was in too deep. It had seemed like nothing at the time. Leak some information to Charles. It was never anything top secret, and it was always things that were announced publicly a few days later, and for that, her mother was taken care of. Not just taken care of, she had the best care money could buy. It was a no-brainer.

The first time she'd met Charles Whitfield, she'd thought him charming. He'd seemed so sincere, telling her how worried he was about his arrogant, inexperienced son.

"Brilliant though," he'd told her, his voice gruff with pride. Or so she'd thought.

"Max wants to prove himself, but he's not as good as he thinks he is, and you've got to help him."

Charles shook his head. "I've tried, but what child wants his father to interfere? And really, I'm proud of him. It takes a lot of guts to take the reins from your old man. There's greatness in him. He's just not there yet. Still too worried what everyone thinks, and this project can't afford to have Max splitting his focus.

"He's got a lot of eyes on him, and if he fails... Well, we can't let that happen. It would destroy Whitfield Industries. For good, this time. I made mistakes, Emma. I'm not denying it. But with your help, I can avoid making the biggest one of all. A boy needs his father. Max can't see it now, but he will. And with your help, I can make sure I'm there when he comes around.

"You'll be compensated, of course. I understand your mother is unwell..."

The elevator stopped two floors down, and someone else got on.

She was a fool to have agreed. Max wasn't some addlebrained youth, out to prove to his father who had the bigger balls. He was a force to be reckoned with, dangerously brilliant, a man who took quick, decisive action based on a thorough vetting of the information presented to him.

But thanks to an overseas trip that had kept him out of the office for the first three weeks after he'd hired her, she'd already agreed to her devil's bargain before she'd seen for herself which of the Whitfield men needed the other.

And by the time she'd realized she'd been played, she'd had to keep playing.

"Imagine if I stopped paying the other half of your mother's medical bills..."

And then, when the guilt had become too much, and she'd told him she didn't care if he sicced a horde of creditors on her, he'd changed tactics.

"It would be a shame if there was an elder abuse claim that kept you from visiting your mother."

And still, as her mother's condition had worsened, as her bad days started to outnumber the good, Emma couldn't fully regret her choices. Even with the generous salary and project bonuses that Max doled out, Emma had to live chastely to keep the debtors off her back. Without Charles's Faustian bargain, her mother would never have received the top-notch care she got at her very exclusive assisted living facility—the one that had been completely booked up until Charles Whitfield had pulled some strings.

And he'd been pulling Emma's strings ever since.

Because while her mother was alive, she'd had no choice but to dance to his commands.

When her mother had finally found peace, Emma had thought she was free. But there again, Charles Whitfield had other ideas. He owned her, unless she wanted to destroy Max.

"Imagine if the press found out that my son was engaging in insider trading. I've got plenty of witnesses and a couple patsies all lined up to prove he's guilty, should it come to that."

She'd already deceived the brilliant man who'd become her boss. Ruining him was not an option.

Then her contract had expired.

Finally, the leverage had disappeared. Charles couldn't force his son to extend her contract, and she'd made damn sure that he didn't know that Max had offered her an extension. No one had known. Though it pained her, Emma had had no choice but to give up the job she loved to save the man she respected.

The man who had ignited a passion in her that she hadn't known she was capable of.

The man who had ruined her seamless escape with his high-handed orders that found her still employed.

The man she'd betrayed.

But it wasn't Max's fault. The blame lay squarely on her, though she'd tried to mitigate it as best she could. Emma had vowed to give her puppet master as little information as possible, just enough to sate him, just enough that he didn't take anything out on her mother. And she'd been keeping meticulous records of all their interactions ever since.

The elevator stopped on the eighth floor, both of the buffer occupants exited, leaving her alone with Charles.

"What the hell have you done?" Emma decided to attack first, in the hope she might be able to bully, or at least surprise him into giving up his other spy. With that knowledge, she'd have leverage again. She could help Max rid his company of traitors in one fell swoop. She'd report the perpetrator of the cyber leak, and then Emma would quit for good. And this time, nothing would stop her from boarding that plane to Dubrovnik.

Charles's voice was cutting. "You'll have to be more specific."

"You sent me here to do a job, and now you're completely undermining it! Who else do you have on the inside?"

He turned to face her, and she took an involuntary step back.

"I don't need anyone else, not now that our deal is back in effect."

"It's not. I'm done telling you anything until you tell me who else is working for you."

"That's where you're wrong, Ms. Mathison. Unless you want my son to find out what you've been doing behind his back since he hired you. And after seeing the two of you together, I suspect you don't." He narrowed his eyes at her. "Now, what is all this nonsense about me having another spy? What aren't you telling me?"

Emma shook her head, trying for nonchalance. "There was some sort of incident. Now Max has Soteria installing new security measures, which will make our deal more difficult for me," she lied, both to keep her from having to provide as much information and to figure out if Charles was part of the other leak. "I thought you might be…sourcing your information elsewhere. To someone, who unlike me, was dumb enough to get caught."

"Well, isn't that interesting? My son has enemies. Powerful ones. And if he pulls off this launch, corporate espionage will be par for the course. As I told you, he's not ready for the realities of business."

Emma squeezed her hands into fists, her fingernails cutting into her palms. How she itched to slap that smug grin from Charles Whitfield's face. Luckily, she had no doubts that Max could handle himself, and whatever was thrown at him.

"So you didn't have someone hack…his computer?" she lied at the last second. Testing him with details, but not giving him too much.

"Ms. Mathison, I'm going to teach you the secret of my success, so pay attention. You do not hack a tech company. Especially not one that has hired the likes of Jesse Hastings and Wes Brennan to protect it. Why do you think we communicate by telephone and meet in person? You don't scale guarded walls, you tunnel under them."

The elevator door slid open, and Charles sent her a questioning glance. "Aren't you going to walk me out?"

She didn't want to, but Charles made it clear that her feelings didn't have any bearing, so she stepped out of the elevator and into the lobby.

The older man's smile was venomous. "Smart choice.

I'd hate to have to…*remind* you what I could do if you'd made the wrong decision."

"Dad? I told you I'd meet you in the lobby."

Emma looked up to see Kaylee Whitfield, elegant in a gray suit and pink blouse, her dark hair pulled back in a low bun, striding toward them, a slight frown marring her brow as she took in the strange twosome they made. "Hey, Emma. Do you two know each other?"

Emma forced a smile, but Charles jumped in with the easygoing charm she remembered from their first meeting. "Hello, Princess." He leaned forward, pressing a kiss to Kaylee's cheek. "I got here a bit early. Thought I'd head upstairs and say hi to your brother."

"I'm sure he was thrilled," Kaylee said drily, obviously aware of the animosity between the Whitfield men, though her joking demeanor made Emma wonder if she knew just how deep it truly went.

"He was rushing off to some meeting," Charles offered smoothly, "but Emma here offered to see me out."

Kaylee raised an eyebrow at her father. "Yes, well, you only worked here for thirty-five years. I'm sure you'd never have made it to the lobby on your own."

She shot a conspiratorial smile at Emma, even as the sudden trill of a ringtone had Kaylee pulling her purse off her shoulder. "Honestly, he's been retired for five years now, and every time we get together, all he wants to talk about is what the company's up to," Kaylee said, as she dug through her bag. "But at least he golfs sometimes. Max practically lives here and will definitely die at his desk, which has always struck me as excessive considering he doesn't even draw a salary."

Emma's eyes widened at the information.

"I'm sorry," Kaylee said holding up her cell, "but I have to take this. Thanks for helping my dad find his way out of the elevator, Em." She turned to her father as she swiped at the screen. "The driver's waiting for us. We should go," she told him, bringing the phone to her ear.

"Right behind you, Princess."

Charles turned toward Emma, pulling an envelope from the inside pocket of his suit jacket. "On second thought," he said and, under the guise of grabbing her hands in a farewell gesture, pressed the envelope into her grip, "Perhaps it's best that I remind you what's at stake here." His fingers dug into hers, and she could smell stale coffee on his breath as he leaned close and sneered. "Feel free to keep these. I have copies."

She pulled her hands from his, knuckles white.

"It was lovely to see you, Emma. As always, I look forward to working with you again."

Emma was practically vibrating as Charles sauntered off across the busy lobby. She turned her back on him, stepping into the next available elevator.

Using the couple who was riding up with her as a shield from the elevator camera, she ripped into the packet, and flipped through several photocopies of surveillance photos that Charles had obviously had taken of some of their hand-off meetings. Woodenly, Emma folded them and shoved them back inside the envelope. She might be stuck in this ruse for now, but one thing was certain: she would make that vile man pay for all his sins.

CHAPTER SIXTEEN

MAX WAS WAITING for her when she got off the elevator. Her hand gripped the manila envelope so tightly that her fingers ached, and guilt made her stiffen when he placed a hand on her lower back and escorted her into his office. Emma could feel his eyes on her, surreptitiously searching her profile. She wished she'd taken an extra minute to pull herself together after Charles's departure, to splash her face with cold water, to let some of the adrenaline of the encounter dissipate.

She dropped the offensive envelope onto the visitor chair and forced some oxygen into her lungs as Max rounded his desk to hit the privacy button. Then he was in front of her, pulling her close, and the strength of his arms, the solidness of his chest, helped soothe her jagged nerves.

"I thought you had a lunch meeting."

God, she was glad he was here.

"They'll wait. Are you okay? He didn't...you're okay, right? I shouldn't have left you alone with him."

"I'm fine," she lied, pressing closer, needing his body

heat to dissipate the chill creeping through her veins. "It was him, wasn't it?"

She knew already. But she needed to hear Max say it. She needed the rage to fortify her, so she didn't fall apart right now. "He's the one who hit you."

His muscles drew tight. His breathing was shallow. "He thought I needed to toughen up."

Emma pressed her cheek against the hard wall of his chest. "I hate him for you."

Max's hand came up to stroke her hair and she wrapped her arms around his waist, holding him until the tenseness in his body receded. Until he took a deep, even breath.

"I have to work late. Hastings wants to go over some new security precautions, and I'm booked solid this afternoon, so he's going to swing by tonight. But Sully will drive you whenever you're ready to go."

Emma leaned back, though she didn't let go of him as she lifted her head. He slid his hands up her neck to cradle her face in his palms.

"Before you call me out, that's not an order, it's a request. Tonight, I need to know you made it home safe. Okay? Can you let me have this one?"

Home.

Her throat was tight as she nodded. She hoped it was just unshed tears. "Okay."

Max pressed the softest kiss to her lips, and her eyes fluttered closed, savoring it. Letting herself pretend, just for a moment, that life wasn't so damn complicated.

He sighed when he pulled back. Her arms fell to her sides.

"I need to get to this meeting."

"Yeah. Yes. I have a lot of work to do, too." She forced a smile and made her way to the exit.

"Emma."

Her name on his lips stopped her.

She turned, and her blood iced over as Max joined her by the door, with the manila envelope in his hand.

It was all she could do not to jump back from it. Knock it to the ground. Set it on fire.

"You forgot your stuff," he said, holding it out to her.

Her fingers trembled as she accepted it.

"I'll see you later," he promised, dropping a kiss on her forehead, one final intimacy before he pulled the frosted door of his office open and they reentered the real world.

Max strode toward the elevator. Emma headed for her desk. She hugged the offensive envelope against her chest, the pressure of it over her heart her penance for all the decisions she'd made that led her here. But even through the guilt and shame, she could still feel the press of his lips against her skin.

Emma spent most of the afternoon staring blindly at her computer monitor as she tried, and failed, to make it past the first page of her summary report detailing the results of the latest SecurePay focus group.

As promised, Max's driver was outside waiting for her when she finally gave up and called it a night. On a whim, she asked him to stop at a grocery store before taking her back to the hotel.

The sadness that swamped her as she picked up ingredients and kitchen supplies should have been her first clue that her plan to fill the time until Max got home was not her best. But her sudden need to connect to her mother was undeniable, so she persevered despite her misgivings, and between her memory and a hastily googled recipe, she gathered what she needed.

Seeing Charles today had churned up all the feelings Emma had been pushing down for so long. The way he'd exploited her mother's illness, the abuse he'd heaped on Max, her own powerlessness to go back and rectify either of those injustices, had splintered the wall inside of her—the one that let her pretend that she was okay most of the time.

Without it, all that grief, all the stress of her mother's passing was seeping up through the cracks and pooling too near the surface for Emma's peace of mind. Maybe that was part of the reason she needed this connection with her mother right now so desperately.

Her mother had always been happiest when she was baking, but it didn't take long for Emma to remember that her own fond memories of the kitchen were more about being with her mom than the act itself.

Now, surveying the wreckage of oozing honey, spilled flour and dirty dishes, misshapen cookies baking in the oven behind her, Emma felt stupid for even attempting it. For entertaining fanciful notions of domesticity while she waited for Max to come home. Like some idyllic 1950s propaganda.

Emma resented the tear trickling down her cheek. She was such a mess, wishing for fanciful things that could never be.

This quest to make new memories was ridiculous. That wasn't how life worked. You didn't get to just wipe the slate clean and start over. You didn't get to rewrite history.

No matter how many incredible new experiences she had, it wouldn't change the fact that her mother was gone, and she would never meet Max. The lovely, vivacious Ana Petrović-Mathison she'd grown up with was already too far gone by the time she'd gotten the job at Whitfield Industries to remember Emma's stories about her handsome boss from week to week.

She couldn't just erase the fact that she'd doomed any chance of something real with Max before she'd even gotten the chance to know him. When he found out what she'd done... And the fact that she'd done it for Charles made it so much worse.

The scent of burning cookies startled her out of her dark musings, and in that moment, with smoke seeping from the oven, Emma realized that she'd failed to buy any oven mitts. By the time she'd dashed to the bathroom to grab a towel and proceeded to burn the hell out of it trying to get the cookies out of the oven without her hand meeting the same fate, her attempt at Croatian gingerbread had gone from overdone to unsalvageable.

It was only made worse by the lack of cooling racks—another item that had slipped her mind at the store—so she set the cookie sheet on the stove top with a defeated sigh, letting the bottoms of her *medenjaci* cookies finish blackening without any further attempt to rescue them. She'd just have to wait until they were cool before erasing the evidence of her failure by throwing them in the trash.

Emma wiped the tear tracks from her face and got to work. She disposed of the ruined towel before stacking the dirty bowls and measuring cups in the fancy undermount sink.

That made the kitchen look slightly less like a disaster zone, she decided. Her life, on the other hand…

What did she honestly think was going to happen here? The only reason she was still in LA was because Max was trying to save his company.

He'd blackmailed her.

She'd betrayed him.

They'd had spectacular sex.

That wasn't the start of a relationship. It was a recipe for disaster.

Distracted by her bleak thoughts, Emma grabbed the cookie sheet in her quest to clean up, yelping as it singed her skin. It fell from her hand, tumbling onto the marble floor with a loud, tinny rattle, scattering burned cookie carcasses across the gleaming tiles.

Emma sucked the tip of her stinging thumb into her mouth, so she could soothe it with her tongue while she surveyed the carnage.

Shit.

Shaking her head, she turned back to the sink to run her tender skin under the cold water.

A brusque knock on the door stole her attention a moment later.

"Emma? What's going on in there? Are you okay?"

Max.

Her heart perked up at the realization he was back.
Stupid heart.

"Emma, open up."

"I'm coming." She flipped off the tap, wiping wet fingers on her jeans as she hurried toward the sound of his voice. She fumbled with the code she had to punch into the fancy lock, but it only took her two tries before she got the door open.

He had a hand braced on either side of the jamb, and the concern on his face when he met her gaze tore a little hole in her heart. The kind that let feelings seep out.

"I heard a bang. Are you okay?"

"Yeah, that was…me," she finished lamely, thumbing vaguely behind her.

He let out a breath—relief?—and pushed back from the wall. "What are you doing?"

She moved so he could step inside. "What does it look like?"

He glanced around the disaster zone. "If I knew, I wouldn't waste either of our time asking."

Emma wilted as she closed the door. "I wanted to make the cookies my mom used to make for me. I wanted to have the memory of making cookies, damn it."

"That's very—" he took in the mess she'd made of the kitchen "—domestic of you."

She sent him a flat look and walked back to the scene of her crimes against dessert. "You could help instead of just standing there."

"I don't bake," he said, but he followed her into the kitchen.

"Not even when you were a kid?"

Max shook his head. "My mother was more of a fully catered event kind of a woman."

"Well, my mom was a great cook." She was vaguely aware she'd told him something similar the other night, but she was too busy battling the sudden helplessness trying to take control of her tear ducts to come up with anything else. "Shouldn't this be in my DNA or something? Why am I not better at this?"

He stepped forward, reaching toward her cheek.

Emma parried with a step back, bumping her hip against the counter. "What are you doing?" She didn't want to want his kindness right now. Her bruised heart couldn't stand it.

"You have flour on your cheek. Now, stand still."

His fingers were gentle against her jaw as he swiped his thumb against her cheekbone.

Emma bit her lip. Tears swam in her eyes when she finally lifted them to meet Max's gaze, but she did her best to blink them back.

"Cookie baking is harder than it looks."

"I have no doubt." He looked at her for a long time, eyes boring into hers. As though he was searching for an answer. "Okay," he said finally.

"Okay what?"

"I'll help."

Emma sucked in her breath as his big hands closed around her hips. He lifted her easily onto the counter, stepped between her legs. She would never get used to having him close. To the way her body softened when he was near.

"How is this helping?" she asked as he leaned in, his breath hot against her neck.

"I'm distracting you."

And she'd be damned if it wasn't working. She couldn't help the tiny moan that escaped as he trailed kisses up her neck.

It was erotically reminiscent of the first time Max had touched her, running his hands over her skin while she was balanced on the edge of a flat surface, her legs locked around his hips as he set her body on fire—had that really happened only a few days ago? It felt like a lifetime.

"You're getting flour on your suit," she scolded, even as she pressed her flour-marked T-shirt against his chest and wrapped her arms around his neck. He smelled delicious, clean and masculine and nothing like baking, which was everything she could've asked for just then.

"I have other suits." He slid her hips to the edge of the counter, before lifting her off it completely. "And I was going to take this one off anyway."

CHAPTER SEVENTEEN

EMMA TIGHTENED HER legs around him, and the evidence of his desire sent a spear of longing straight through her. She wanted him, like always, but tonight she needed him, too. Needed what he could give her. Needed how he made her feel.

He walked them to the bedroom, and she gloried in the strength of him beneath her hands, all shifting muscles and leashed power wrapped in a bespoke suit. She was a slave to the thrill she got from touching him, tasting him. She'd thought it was the illicitness, the taboo of bedding her boss, and maybe at the beginning it had been. Or maybe that had never been it at all. Maybe it had always been him.

Brilliant. Gorgeous. A force to be reckoned with.

Max.

She couldn't pinpoint the moment he'd become so important to her. The first time she'd stayed late at the office without an ounce of resentment? The first time she'd earned one of his hard-won nods of approval for her work? The first inadvertent brush of his hand against hers? The first taste of his lips?

Maybe none of those. Maybe all of them.

Max stopped beside the bed, lowering her slowly until her toes touched the ground, allowing them both to savor the sinuous slide of her body against his. A pale imitation of skin on skin, but a delectable tease of what was to come.

With soft kisses and restless hands, they began tugging at each other's clothes, unfastening buttons and undoing zippers. Emma couldn't get enough. Undressing Max was like unwrapping a present. The sight of his body never failed to ratchet up her need. She couldn't help but lean forward and press a kiss to his pec, just above his heart, even as he sent her jeans sliding down her hips.

When they were finally naked, Max pulled her close, walking her backward until the mattress brushed the backs of her thighs. Unlike their previous sexual encounters, there was a gravitas to this one that Emma couldn't deny. There was still the pure, unadulterated want that she was used to whenever she touched him, but this was deeper, somehow, less frenzied. As though their passion had matured into something more potent.

He followed her onto the bed, and he was so beautiful, all hard planes and sinewy muscles, his jungle cat grace in evidence again as he moved over her. Their legs tangled together as he ran a hand along her skin, from her hip, up her side until he palmed her breast.

And suddenly, time slowed down.

Tonight, there were none of the dirty words, no words at all, just the soundtrack of their mingled breaths, of her heart beating steady and true.

Sweet kisses and lingering caresses. A slow worship of each other's bodies.

She twined her fingers in his hair as his mouth paid homage to her breast. Each flick of his tongue against her nipple launching a spear of pleasure straight to her core. She shuddered as he traced her areola with the tip of his tongue, then kissed his way to her other breast to accord it the same decadent treatment.

For the first time in a long time, she felt like herself again. Like a woman who could handle things. The realization surprised her, since not ten minutes ago she'd been on the verge of sobbing, cookies spilled across the floor, failing so spectacularly at her task that she'd been ready to give up.

She wanted to devour him, but when she tried to pull him up so she could get her mouth on his, he shook his head.

"Not yet," he told her, in response to her mewl of frustration when he stayed put. "There's something I've been meaning to do, and I'm not going to let you distract me with that pretty mouth of yours until I'm finished."

He slid a little farther down her body, pressing a promissory kiss just above her belly button, and another beneath it. Emma's muscles tensed with anticipation, her fingers curling preemptively against the mattress.

Max settled himself between her legs, and she had to bend her knees to accommodate the breadth of his shoulders. The low throb of greed drummed at the apex of her thighs. She wanted everything he was poised to give her, and she shifted restlessly beneath him, wishing he'd just get on with it already. Not until she felt his breath against the wet heat of her did she realize that she'd closed her eyes. With conscious effort, she forced them open, and the second she did, he lowered his head and licked straight up the center of her.

Stars exploded through her body and she raked her fingernails against the bedspread as her back arched with the sharpness of her need.

Her muscles grew drowsy with pleasure as he shifted his technique, teasing her with only the tip of his tongue, dragging her to the brink before retreating, only to start the process over again. Driving her wild with the electric touch of his mouth and the delicious scrape of his five o'clock shadow against her inner thighs.

The orgasm building inside her was different from the ones before. This one rolled along her nerve endings, slow but powerful, and just out of reach.

She reached for him, burying her fingers in his wavy black hair, with half a mind to push him away because she wasn't sure she could endure another second on the edge of this precipice, and half a mind to hold him right where he was forever and ever.

Before she could decide, his tongue was replaced with the gentle suction of his lips against her clit as his finger sank deep inside her, and the dual sensation of soft and hard, push and pull, sent her climax rushing through her like waves breaking across her skin, and she gasped as she let herself drown in the sweet perfection of it.

He crawled back up her body, lying on his side next to her. She rolled to face him, and the intensity in his amber gaze made her feel like he'd branded her, claimed her. Made her doubt that anyone else in the world could make her feel like he had.

Emma trembled at the thought.

"I've been dreaming about that since we met." He reached over and pushed a strand of hair off her cheek.

Max Whitfield. Slayer of words. "Liar." Her heart flipped happily as she made the accusation.

"Well, I've been dreaming about it *more* since we met naked."

"I'm happy to make your dream a reality anytime," she teased, pushing up onto her elbow.

She leaned close and breathed in his warmth, nuzzling his jaw, pressing her lips to the pulse at the base of his neck.

It was heaven to have her mouth on his skin, to be able to touch him when she wanted. How she wanted.

Emma caught his bottom lip between her teeth, then kissed him slow, deep, wet. He groaned as he shifted onto his back, and she liked knowing he was as desperate as she was for the culmination of the lust that overtook her whenever he was within arm's reach. She was so turned on, she could barely breathe.

"Jesus, you drive me crazy," he muttered, pulling her on top of him and taking control of the kiss, working her mouth with an expertise that had them both panting and desperate in record time.

With a speed and grace that shouldn't have surprised her, Max rolled her onto her back and pushed inside her.

His chest grazed her nipples with each stroke of his hips, and she marveled at the strength of him, the way the muscles in his shoulders and arms bulged with effort as he held himself over her, staring into her eyes as he plunged deep, driving her closer and closer to the edge.

And just when she couldn't stand it anymore, Max increased the pressure, lowering himself so that their bodies were flush, pushing her into the mattress as he caught her mouth with his. Her body detonated again under the weight of him, sending shockwave after shockwave radiating through her, leaving her helpless to do anything but hold him close as he joined her in ecstasy.

CHAPTER EIGHTEEN

"I CAN FEEL you thinking," he teased, and Emma snuggled more fully against him. He stroked the pad of his thumb against her arm, and it was one of those perfect moments that Emma had been searching for. She was in the middle of a memory right now, and part of her wanted to hold on to it, not blow it up like she was about to do. But the other part of her knew that she might never get this opportunity again, and so she took a chance.

"Can I ask you something?"

He angled his chin down so their eyes met. "Why do I get the feeling you're going to, regardless of my answer?"

Her smile was guilty, and he chuckled, the sound of it reverberating through his chest. He pressed a kiss against her hair. "Go ahead."

"Kaylee said something about you not taking a salary?"

He went eerily still, just for a moment, withdrawing as though what she'd said was an affront. "It's nothing."

It was his this-matter-is-finished tone of voice. She'd

seen him shut down heated boardroom arguments with it several times, but tonight, after what they'd shared, she refused to be intimidated.

"Considering you spend all your time at the office, it doesn't seem like nothing," she ventured. He might not answer, but she needed to try. She'd shared so much of herself with him, all that stuff about her mom, and now she wanted something in return. A little piece of the enigmatic man who gave the appearance of being cold and aloof. Tonight, he'd made her body burn with his sexual prowess and her heart melt with his kindness. She wanted to know him better.

Max exhaled. "It's a token. An empty promise I made to myself."

It was more than she'd expected, so she raked her fingers through the smattering of hair on his chest, stroking them back and forth in a lazy rhythm, hoping the silence might coax something further from him.

"My father took advantage of…someone I brought to his attention. A man I respected and greatly admired. He was a brilliant software developer. My father blackmailed him, swindled his intellectual property from him and held him hostage with legalities, until he was just a wrecked shell of a man. So wrecked that he broke a decade of sobriety and drove his car into a pole."

Her palm stilled over his heart, poor comfort, but she needed to touch him. Needed him to know she was there. He stared at her hand on his skin, his expression both blank and quizzical, as though he wasn't quite in the present, but he didn't understand how he'd gotten there.

"Max," she said softly.

He shook his head, and his eyes cleared. "There's a local charity that takes care of families who've lost someone to drunk driving. They provide them with therapy, financial assistance, whatever they need, regardless of whether their loved one was the victim or the perpetrator."

"And you donate your salary."

His nod was almost imperceptible. Something about the specificity of the charity made her heart pinch. "Did he have children?"

The words were a long time coming, and they held an edge of pain, as evidenced by the tightness in Max's voice. "A son. Aidan."

"You know him?"

"We were friends. Before I took over Whitfield Industries."

Something about the way he said it warned her pursuing it further would be a dead end.

"I'm so sorry." Beneath her fingers, his muscles relaxed a fraction. With relief that she hadn't pressed the issue? "That's an incredible thing you're doing, supporting that charity in his honor."

He shook his head, rejecting the praise. "It isn't. It doesn't change anything. It certainly doesn't fix anything. But I've already benefitted too much from the misfortune of others."

She'd known Max was special. From the moment she'd met him, he'd seemed capable, in control. But until tonight, she hadn't imagined the depth of his strength. The profundity of his character.

"Don't look at me like that."

"Like what?"

"Like I'm a good man. I'm not, Emma. Don't fool yourself. I'm just like my father."

The idea that he thought he was anything like Charles Whitfield leant heat to her voice. "You're nothing like him."

"I'm *exactly* like him. I put business before everything. My father should be rotting in jail for what he did to John Beckett."

He said it so matter-of-factly that it shocked her. No rage. His voice was even and modulated, as though he were giving her the weather report.

"But instead of turning him in, I blackmailed him into retirement, which at the time, struck me as poetic justice. And I told myself I did it so my sister wouldn't have to deal with the fallout of toppling the only parent who ever gave her the time of day. So that my mother wouldn't have to survive another scandal. But the truth is, I did it so there'd still be a business for me to take over when I kicked his ass out. And worst of all, I betrayed my best friend to do it."

Max shrugged at the summation, a momentary flash of something real peeking out from behind the crack in the armor. "Bringing SecurePay to the world, making sure that John's contribution sees the light of day, is one way I atone for what I've done. Letting Aidan hate me for it is the other."

"Have you ever tried to explain what happened?" Emma asked. "I'm sure if Aidan knew why you—"

"I don't do it for forgiveness, Emma. I made my

choice, and I live with it. I don't believe in second chances. Some things can't be fixed."

She felt his retreat, the tightening of his muscles, the emotional distance he was trying to erect between them. Emma knew all too well what it was like to have regrets that ate at you. To face reality when all you wanted to do was curl up in a ball and hide. And part of her wanted to give him the space he obviously needed.

But she didn't. Something in her chest keened at the loss of the honesty of the moment they'd just shared, a moment that transcended all the complications that had happened before it. Right now, they were just two people, not a boss and employee, not the betrayed and the betrayer, just a man and a woman.

And Emma wanted it back, for however briefly it might last.

"Don't leave me yet," she said, not sure if he'd understand what she meant, but desperate to make him. Because she couldn't leave him. Not while he was hurting.

Max had been shouldering too many burdens all by himself for far too long. And while Emma knew he'd reject sympathy, she wanted to give him comfort.

To that end, she tucked closer to his side, wrapping an arm around him in as close an approximation of a hug as she could get from this position, and pressed her lips to his chest, right above his heart.

He went deadly still.

"Emma…" He said her name uncertainly, like he wasn't sure if it was a warning or a plea. She didn't let go, though. She just lay there, hugging him, until the stiffness in his muscles receded. Until she felt his breathing even out beneath her cheek.

Only then did she loosen her grip on him, so she could push up on her elbows and look into his eyes. To see for herself that Max was okay. That he was himself again.

He wasn't. Not exactly. His expression was hard, almost dark, and his gaze searched her face, looking for what, she didn't know.

But when he reached up, the hand that cupped her jaw was gentle. His thumb traced her bottom lip. She sighed at the touch, the soft sound kindling a spark in those enigmatic amber eyes.

And that spark set her body ablaze.

"I can't get enough of you."

His words were gravel. They scraped against her nerve endings, and the sweet thrill of arousal turned insistent. His fingers dug into her hip and he rolled her beneath him, chest heaving as he stared down at her, and what she saw in his face stole her breath.

Before, he'd looked at her with desire, but now he looked at her like he needed her, not just any woman, but *her*.

It was world shaking.

And then he canted his hips and pushed deep, and Emma cried out as she wrapped her arms around him, clinging as tightly as she could, afraid if she didn't, she might be swept away completely.

Emma was too tired to discern more than the vague notion of someone moving around.

She and Max had made love half the night, and she'd slept snuggled against his side. In fact, it was the sudden realization that he wasn't there that woke her in the first place.

"What time is it?" she asked, her voice thick and groggy.

"Too early for you to be up. I was trying not to wake you."

She liked hearing Max's deep baritone in the morning. Knowing he'd spent the night next to her.

"But I told Brennan and Hastings I'd meet them at seven, so I have to leave soon. Sully will come back for you."

She managed a muffled sound of acknowledgment, and reached to steal the other pillow, since Max wasn't using it, but something jabbed her in the forearm. She frowned as she scraped her hair off her face, squinting at the white box. "What's this?"

He glanced over his shoulder as he finished his Windsor knot. "Breakfast."

It was *the* tie, she realized. The one she'd used to bind his wrists the night he'd trusted her with one of his deepest secrets. It looked good on him.

He grabbed his suit jacket from the garment bag on the back of the door and then slid into it. It fit his broad shoulders to perfection.

Who'd have thought it could be so erotic watching a man put clothes *on*?

She pulled the sheet over her breasts, before she sat up against the headboard. "You got breakfast and a suit delivered?"

"That's the point of having money. Getting what you want, when you want it."

She rolled her eyes and grabbed the white bakery box, untying the pretty raffia bow. "I'd be more impressed if your suits weren't right next door. This box is probably full of pillow mints or something," she joked.

Then the white edges of cardboard sprang open, revealing its contents.

Her brow creased as she looked up at the powerful man in the suit that cost more than three-months' rent at her old apartment. "But how?"

"I sent Sully to a little Croatian bakery I found." He slipped his watch onto his left wrist, clasping it with quick, efficient movements.

Her heart lurched against her ribs. And that was before he walked over to the bed, and then pressed a kiss to her forehead as he stole one of the prettily iced *medenjaci* cookies from the box and popped it into his mouth.

He chewed thoughtfully for a moment before swallowing. "These are *really* good." He grabbed two more. "I can see why your dad loved your mom's cookies so much."

The casual mention of her family slayed her.

She didn't like the warmth seeping through her chest. Because this wasn't lust.

It was suspiciously more like another L word.

The scary one.

And if she was in love with Max, that made everything so much worse.

A knock at the hotel room door made him glance

over his shoulder. "That must be housekeeping. I asked them to send someone up to take care of the kitchen."

Max walked over to the dresser to grab his wallet.

"I'll let them in on my way out. See you at work?"

He asked the question like nothing had changed, like her whole world hadn't just slid off its axis.

Emma couldn't make her voice work to lie to him, so she nodded instead.

His answering smile stung like a thousand pin pricks.

She stared after him as he left the room, trying to fix the memory in her brain. In her heart. A perfect moment in time to hold close, to look back on after everything imploded.

Because she had to tell him.

She couldn't keep pretending that she could outrun what she'd done. There was no direction that didn't lead to what was happening right now.

I don't believe in second chances. Some things can't be fixed.

This, she realized, was one of those things. She'd screwed up with Max the minute she'd shaken Charles Whitfield's hand.

Tears slipped down her cheeks at the consequences, and she hugged her knees to her chest.

It took a long time for the tears to stop. Even longer for her to find the strength to crawl out of bed.

Emma retrieved her purse from the decorative chair in the corner, and pushed the bedroom door closed on the sounds of someone doing the dishes.

Max would never forgive her for what she'd done. She'd betrayed him, and he was right: there was no fixing it. But maybe, just maybe, she could give him the second chance he deserved with Aidan. With himself.

Reaching into the zippered pocket in her leather tote, she extracted the burner phone Charles had given her, thumbs flying over the keypad.

The text message read: Grand Park fountain @ noon. She hit Send.

CHAPTER NINETEEN

"I'VE TAKEN ALL your reports into consideration—" along with AJ's, but Max didn't tell that to the men sitting on the other side of his desk "—and I've decided to move forward with releasing SecurePay on Tuesday, as scheduled. I'll expect regular updates in the days leading up to the launch."

Brennan stared at him evenly, saying nothing. Hastings jumped amiably into the silence. "Understood. Gotta keep those shareholders happy. I keep trying to get this guy to take Soteria public—" Jesse thumbed in Brennan's direction "—but he won't bite."

Brennan cut his partner a sidelong glance, and Hastings stopped babbling. "We have people monitoring the security feeds and firewall around the clock, and we'll have updates to you twice daily, starting immediately. If you have any further questions or concerns, feel free to contact either of us, twenty-four-seven."

Max and Brennan stood, and Hastings followed their lead. With a round of handshakes, business was concluded, and Max was on to a second meeting with Vivienne, to fill her in on the morning's results and make sure that there were no outstanding legal hiccups that might throw off the launch.

Then he briefed Kaylee on where things stood so she was prepared and ready for the day they unleashed SecurePay into the world. As he escorted his sister out of his office, he decided to see if Emma felt like joining him for lunch.

He'd been so busy that he hadn't seen her since that morning, when she'd been sitting in bed with sleepy eyes and sex-tousled hair, naked under the sheet clutched to her breasts.

Or better yet, they could skip lunch.

"Sherri, can you get Emma on the phone for me?"

"I haven't seen her today. Jim was looking for her earlier."

Max frowned. That was strange. He pulled his cell phone from his inner breast pocket, but she hadn't texted. He tried calling, and it went straight to voice mail.

Maybe she was sick. He glanced at his watch. He could head over to the hotel and check on her before his afternoon meeting.

"I'll be back at one thirty," he told Sherri, as he headed for the elevator. "If the marketing department drops off those proofs of the new campaign I asked for, just leave them on my desk."

He spent the duration of the descent telling himself that this worry winding though his chest was ridiculous, that she was fine. Sherri might have missed her arrival, her battery could have died, maybe she'd used the contact info he'd forced her to take for his driver, and she was just running an errand…but when he emerged from the building, Sully was parked in his usual spot.

Damn.

Max strode toward his car, but before he reached it, a slight figure bumped into him, surprising him out of his tunnel vision. He steadied himself. "Are you oka…"

The question died on his lips as recognition hit. The black leather jacket, black jeans, black boots and a black sweatshirt with the hood pulled up, despite the California heat. He was familiar with the game. And the player.

"Jesus, AJ. I'd better still have my wallet."

The woman grinned as she turned to face him, holding out the expensive brown leather. "Gotta keep the skills sharp."

He grabbed it back, tucking it away. "I thought I paid you enough to render those skills extinct."

"Sure you do. But if I forget all the moves, what good am I? I mean, if I can't pick your pocket, I can't finesse my way past your firewall, either. It's all about the dance, you know?"

"I don't have time to dance right now. What are you doing here?"

Her brown eyes turned serious, and Max didn't like the resulting clench in his gut.

"I need to talk to you."

Max glanced back at the building that housed Whitfield Industries. She shouldn't have come here. And he certainly couldn't take her inside.

"Come on."

He gave Sully the signal to stand down, and his bodyguard and driver lowered his big frame back into the car. Max hurried AJ to the vehicle and followed her inside.

Sully raised the privacy partition as he pulled away from the curb and just started driving, no explanations required. Max made a mental note to increase Sully's bonus.

"Tell me."

"Hello to you, too," she said with an arched eyebrow, pulling the black hood down to reveal her raven curls.

Max returned the rebuke with an unimpressed look.

"Yeah, yeah. I followed the money."

He frowned. "I thought you already did that. You said she checked out."

AJ looked uncomfortable, fidgeting with the drawstring at her neck. It wasn't like her.

"Not Emma's money. Your dad's."

The announcement cold-cocked him.

"Turns out that the place taking care of her mom wasn't just nice—it was really nice. Even the e-transfers with all the zeroes she sent weren't coming close to taking care of the luxury-sized price tag."

"My father."

AJ nodded. "Emma might not be your bad guy on this hack, but she's up to those pretty blue eyes in something shady."

"And you're sure—"

"They're in cahoots? Colluding? In bed together?"

AJ flinched beneath the weight of his glower.

"Whoa. Bad choice of words, I see. Down boy. That was only meant in the figurative sense. But yeah. I think they're connected. Nobody with your dad's rep fronts several grand a month to a veritable stranger without getting something in return. And I did the math. Until you hired her, there are no links between the two of them, financial or otherwise. Which makes you the common denominator."

Max couldn't help but think back to his father showing up at the office. Charles Whitfield was a charming bastard, brilliant at making people feel comfortable. It was his superpower—make them like him, make them trust him, so they didn't even realize he'd manipulated them until it was too late.

It was how his father had managed to keep Whitfield Industries afloat, even as his stubborn refusal to embrace change had the company falling further and further behind its competitors.

Max had worked his ass off to turn Whitfield Industries back into a financial leader and secure his and Kaylee's birthrights. SecurePay was the crown jewel in his plan, the unmitigated success that would win his board's loyalty once and for all. And convince even those who counted themselves among his father's friends and cronies that Max had what it took to guide the company to greatness, if they were willing to keep up with the times.

And put Charles Whitfield's tainted legacy firmly to rest.

In retrospect, Max realized he should have known something was up. At the time, he hadn't given it a second thought—he'd been too furious that Charles had gained access to his building without him knowing— but his father had never passed up an opportunity to charm a beautiful woman, especially if he could make Max look bad while doing it. Yet that day, his father had blown right past charisma to snake oil salesman... almost like he'd been deliberately trying to make her uncomfortable.

And Emma...

The color had drained from her face when she'd seen Charles. But that had been before she knew what he'd done. Before Max had told her everything.

Betrayal hit hard and fast, a sucker punch to the solar plexus. And if he'd thought it had hurt when he found out what a bastard his father was, if he'd thought pain was his best friend vowing revenge on him, well, those things were nothing compared to this.

"You have proof." It wasn't a question. There was a reason that he'd recruited AJ after Wes had caught her poking around in Whitfield Industries' business. She was one of the best, or she wouldn't be in his car right now.

She tugged an envelope from the pocket of her black jacket.

Max didn't bother to open it, just tucked it in the breast pocket of his suit jacket. The show of trust lit something he couldn't quite name in AJ's brown eyes. "Listen, when I was poking around in your father's finances, there was an echo."

"An echo?"

AJ nodded. "Yeah. Nothing concrete, but something that happens sometimes, when I'm in the zone. I know it sounds a bit woo-woo, but it's like I can sense if I'm following a fresh trail, or if I'm stepping in footprints. And with your father's account, it felt like the latter. Like someone had walked the path before me, you know? I can't explain it any better than that. But I don't think I'm the only one who knows what he did for Emma's mom."

Max tried to absorb the ramifications of that, but he couldn't make sense of it. "I'll keep that in mind. Where can we drop you?"

"Near the park is great. I'll hop out just after the courthouse."

Max rapped on the partition, giving Sully their destination, which was only a block and a half away.

"Before you go…"

"Yeah?"

"Were you planning on giving me my watch back?"

With a long-suffering sigh, she pulled it from her other pocket and handed it back to him. "Fine. I guess I'll just take my bonus in cash. Like usual."

AJ reached for the door handle as the car rolled to a stop, but she hesitated. Looked back at him. Her sudden somberness made the back of his neck prickle with dread.

"Listen, this is total speculation, more gut feeling from watching bad people do bad things, and I wasn't going to tell you until I had eyes on it…but your dad's phone is pinging off a cell tower near here, and when your girl left the hotel today, she grabbed an Uber north…"

Max didn't ask how AJ knew Emma was staying at the hotel. Or that she'd taken an Uber. AJ made it her business to know everything. Which explained the sudden burn of acid in his stomach.

AJ pulled her hood back up as she pushed open the door. "Let's just say that you might want to stick around for a few minutes. Someone tall, blonde and deceitful might be looking for a ride."

The door slammed before Max could fully digest the import of her words.

As he watched AJ head toward the park, she bumped into a familiar figure with a phone to his ear who was standing near a bank of fenced-in palm trees. The man shot her a dirty look before smoothing his suit jacket and striding toward the black town car—almost identical to the one Max sat in now—that slid up to the curb ahead of him. He watched, sick to his stomach, as his father got inside.

Moments later, just as AJ had predicted, a beautiful blonde appeared almost exactly where his father had been moments ago.

His muscles turned to steel as the full weight of her deception sank in, but Max forced himself to open the door, to get out of the car. As though she felt the animosity radiating off him, Emma looked up from her phone, stumbling on her heels when their eyes met.

His words were full of bite.

"Get in. Now."

CHAPTER TWENTY

HE KNEW.

The proof was in the rigid set of his broad shoulders, the depth of betrayal in his amber eyes.

And just like that, the cataclysmic collision course that had been spelled out in their crossed stars was set, about to play out beneath the warmth of the California sun and a cloudless blue sky.

There was relief in not having to outrun it anymore, a resigned sort of peace in not wondering when it would sneak up on her.

There was also a hurt so deep she could barely breathe through the pain, and she hadn't expected it to cut so deep.

But she hadn't expected to fall in love with him, either.

"I said get in." He ground the words from between his teeth.

She couldn't summon any ire at the command. In her sorrow, it struck her as Max being Max. And that's when she realized the missing him had already begun, even though he was standing right in front of her.

"No."

I can't. Please don't make me.

Being alone with him while he hated her was more than she could bear.

His jaw ticked with fury. Emma ignored the impulse to reach up and soften the knotted muscle. Instead, she took her cue from him and set her shoulders.

"I won't insult either of us by telling you I'm sorry for what I've done, because I'm not. Not all the way." She rubbed her right thumb against her mother's ring.

"I did what I had to. I needed the money, and I didn't know you yet, not like now, and the information didn't…never mind. No excuses. I did it, and I had my reasons. Just like you had your reasons for making me stay, right?"

His continued silence served as confirmation.

She nodded, dropped her gaze to the sidewalk beneath her pumps. When she looked up again, her smile was sad. "Only a fool would rehire the prime suspect in a security breach, and you're a lot of things, Max, but you're not a fool."

His jaw flexed. "I'm not doing this on the street."

"I'm not doing *this* at all," she said simply.

It's already done.

Emma wondered for a moment if the entire world had run out of air, or if it was just her lungs that the oxygen had abandoned.

There was pain in his eyes, in his voice, and he let her see all of it.

"I *trusted* you."

Her heart shattered into jagged shards that cut her chest with each breath.

"I know."

It had meant everything to have him share those broken pieces of himself with her. To share her sadness with him, too.

Being with Max had helped her find herself again. The Emma she was before her mother had gotten sick, the Emma she wanted to be going forward.

Even if she had to go forward without him.

Her gaze dropped to the hand that was strangling his tie.

The tie.

Her own hand flexed at the phantom sensation of his fingers entwined with hers.

He dropped it suddenly, snatching his hand back as though the silk had burned him. As though she had.

The ravaged look on his face tore at her guts. He tipped his head back. Closed his eyes.

She could see where he'd nicked himself shaving on the underside of his jaw, near his chin.

Then he smoothed the mangled silk with economical, precise movements. Restoring order. Setting things right.

She was losing him.

When he lowered his head, he was the picture of icily reserved detachment. His amber eyes were flat, controlled, staring through her as though they were complete strangers.

It was always going to end like this.

The reminder didn't keep her hands from shaking,

but she rallied as best she could, shoving her emotions back down to the pit of her stomach and locking them away.

"It's nothing personal, Max. Isn't that what you said?"

His nod was almost imperceptible. If she wasn't staring at him like he was her whole world, she might have missed it.

"Just business."

She'd fucked up so bad. She loved him so much.

"Just business," she repeated.

"I think this is understood," Max said, his voice devoid of any particular inflection, "but in case it wasn't clear, you're fired, effective immediately."

Everything inside her shattered.

"Perfectly clear."

Walk away. Just walk away.

Standing here wishing things were different was a waste of time, she reminded herself. And Max hated having his time wasted.

"Goodbye, Max."

Something flickered in his eyes. A beat slipped by, when he should have spoken, but he didn't. Hope pricked her heart. And then...

"Goodbye, Emma."

She needed to go. Her heels clicked against the sidewalk as she forced herself to move, to walk blindly forward, to get the fuck away from him.

Everything in her hurt.

When a cab pulled up to let someone out at the courthouse, she crawled in.

"Where to, ma'am?"

"Berkshire Suites, please. And then to the airport."

She wasn't sure when the tears had begun streaming down her face, but she hoped to God that Max hadn't seen them.

It had been a hell of a day.

All he wanted was to go home, pour himself a glass of Scotch, and then another, and forget he'd ever laid eyes on Emma Mathison.

But before that could happen, he needed Vivienne Grant to get the hell out of his office.

"She's in breach of contract. You can sue the shit out of her."

Max shot her a cutting look. "I want this over and done. Just run it as though she resigned. Make sure she gets paid out as per the original agreement."

"Minus the inconvenience bonus you tacked on?" Vivienne asked, looking up from her notes.

"Including the inconvenience bonus."

He didn't like the judgmental look she gave him.

"You're my lawyer, Vivienne. Not my executioner."

"You want to pay Emma big bucks to not do her job, that's your business. I just point out your legal options and do what I'm told," she countered, and the picture she'd just painted of herself as a docile, order-following lamb was so far from the reality of his ball-busting attorney that it brought a ghost of a smile to his lips, despite his sour mood.

"And that's why I pay *you* the big bucks," he reminded her.

She nodded in a gesture that he might have described

as distracted if she weren't looking at him with such intensity. Then her gaze dropped to his chest, and when he followed it, he found his hand was clenched around his fucking tie again.

The one Emma had used that night.

The night he'd given up control, given her control.

The night that would haunt him for the rest of his life.

Disgusted, he yanked the knot loose and pulled the strip of material from beneath his collar, balling it up and tossing it in the general vicinity of the waste basket beside his desk.

Vivienne raised her eyebrows at the atypical display. "What did that tie ever do to you?"

Besides fuck him in every way possible? Max thought darkly. He popped the top button, so his shirt would stop strangling him.

"Just make this all go away," he ordered, signing the documents in front of him before handing them to her.

She tucked them on top of her legal pad as she stood. "I'm sorry she's gone. I liked her," Vivienne said softly, but she'd already turned on her heel and left before Max could process the uncharacteristic evidence of his lawyer's humanity.

He leaned back in his chair.

The ghost of Emma was all over his office. The comfort of her cheek against his chest after his father's impromptu visit. The clash of their bodies when he'd shoved her up against the window and torn her skirt.

His desk.

Max swore under his breath and tossed the pen he'd used to sign Vivienne's documents on top of the speech notes Kaylee had left for him to review before the launch.

Emma had betrayed him with a man he despised, and he was sitting here like a lovesick cuck, remembering her hands on his body.

Get your head in the game, Whitfield.

She'd lied to him. The entire time she'd worked for him. The entire time they were fucking. Even last night, when things had been…different.

At least for him it had been.

His father's voice was in his brain.

You're soft. That's your problem. You care too much.

Well, now she was gone. For good.

Problem solved.

Max stood. He needed to move. He needed to go home. He needed that drink.

As he rounded the side of his desk, his gaze snagged on the limp carcass of his tie. The skinny end of the black and gray material was draped over the side of the waste basket, but the thick end lay unfurled across the carpeting like an abandoned snakeskin.

He grabbed it and shoved it in his pocket as he headed for the door.

CHAPTER TWENTY-ONE

"Welcome home, Mr. Whitfield."

Max nodded to the concierge but kept his pace through the lobby quick. He wasn't in the mood for small talk.

"Ms. Mathison left something for you, sir."

Her name echoed like a gunshot in his brain, stopping him. "Is she here?"

Gerald shook his head. "She left earlier this afternoon in a taxi. I'm afraid I haven't seen her since, nor did she inform me of her destination, though she had her suitcase with her. And if I may say so, sir, she seemed... upset."

The concierge looked at him expectantly.

"You said you have something for me?"

"Oh, yes. Of course, sir."

Max told himself he didn't care how she'd seemed as he waited for the man to round the reception desk and hand him a beat-up shoebox.

"Don't forget this." Gerald grabbed the manila envelope he'd tucked under his arm and set it on the lid. The way it was torn open struck Max as familiar, and

he realized it was the same envelope from the day before. In his office. The one Emma had been carrying
after she'd walked his father down to the lobby. Only
now it said his name in her elegant, slanted handwriting.

Max's fingers flexed against the cardboard as he
headed for the elevator, carefully holding the package
in front of him with both hands, keeping it straight and
still, like he was holding a bomb.

He stared at the ripped edge of the envelope as he
pushed the up button. Its contents had shifted slightly
when Gerald had handed it over, and the edge of a photo
peeked out, confirming his suspicions.

Oh, it was going to detonate all right.

When he arrived on the top floor, Max made a point
of keeping his eyes forward, heading straight to his
door, not giving into the absurd desire to go to her room
and confirm Gerald's report. To see for himself that she
was really gone.

Max walked into his suite, abandoning the package
on the coffee table as he passed it, not stopping until
he arrived at the bar cart so he could pour himself that
glass of Scotch.

He drained it in one go, topped it up and took this
round over to the sofa with him. Max sat on the middle
cushion, his legs spread wide. With a contemplative sip,
he stared at the envelope with his name on the front.

She was a consummate liar. He shouldn't give a
damn what she'd left for him. And even as he told himself that, he leaned forward, set his drink on the edge
of the glass table and grabbed the envelope.

Tipping the contents into his hand, he revealed a

stack of images printed on letter-sized paper. He flipped through the photos—candid shots of Emma and his father, a little grainy from the printer, but in focus, with a small time and date stamp in the bottom right corner of each. They were obviously taken with a zoom lens, by some PI his father had paid to document each meeting, no doubt.

"Leverage is the key to any good negotiation," he'd always said.

Bastard.

Reminding himself to breathe, he continued with the bittersweet torture. About half-way through the stack, the pain of seeing them together started to dull, and he found himself focusing solely on Emma, watching her betray him, again and again, in an assortment of outfits on a dozen different days.

She was beautiful. Even as she handed papers full of secrets to the man who wanted to ruin him. Even when he was trying to hate her for her treachery. Even when he hated himself for not being able to.

Max dropped the photos on the cushion beside him and leaned forward. Took a drink.

What the hell was wrong with him?

He rested his elbows on his thighs, pressing the glass to his cheek.

This was madness.

He took the last bracing gulp of his Scotch, and exchanged the empty glass for the shoebox, setting it in his lap.

Just like ripping off a Band-Aid, he told himself, and flicked open the lid.

Inside was a phone and a stack of papers.

He pressed the power button on the phone, and while it started up, he sorted through the rest.

Judging by the dates Emma had handwritten at the top—each of which corresponded to one of the date stamps on the pictures—they'd met quarterly for the last three years. But as he scanned through the photocopied reports on Whitfield Industries letterhead, detailing the progress of the project, his frown deepened.

Max had eaten, slept and breathed SecurePay for so long that it was easy for him to discern how incomplete the information was without comparing these documents to the originals. Large swaths of data were missing, and key dates had been changed, rendering them largely useless.

Emma had actually done a brilliant job of giving his father just enough real info to keep him from realizing how little he was getting. Luckily, Charles Whitfield was a proud Luddite, or Emma might never have gotten away with this.

Still, he thought uncharitably, nothing here proved blackmail. It was a bunch of shoddy reports about SecurePay, and some pictures of the two of them together. Hardly a smoking gun.

Idly, he grabbed the phone and scrolled through the texts. They reached back the full three years that he'd known her. Sparsely worded messages that consisted mostly of times, dates and locations, nothing to prove the identity of either sender, except for Emma's word. And Emma was gone.

Though he supposed the texts combined with the

dated surveillance photos and reports might line up in a way that proved his father was on the other end of the communication. If they could find his phone…

His thumb hovered over the screen as he got to the end of the messages.

The most recent text was dated this morning.

The morning after he'd carried her from the kitchen to the bedroom, and she'd touched and caressed his body with such tenderness that it had almost undone him.

The same morning he'd woken Sully at five to track down Croatian gingerbread, just to see her smile.

Thirty minutes after he'd left for work and realized he'd fallen in love with her.

Grand Park fountain @ noon.

That was it.

Four words and an @ symbol were the catalyst that had changed his world irreparably.

Max closed the text window with every intention of tossing the phone back in the box, but the sight of the voice recording app—the lone icon at the top of the home screen—stayed his hand.

Leaning back against the couch, he opened the program and hit Play.

The sounds of the park were tinny in the speaker— the muted shouts and laughter of people, the rush of the fountain as water slapped against the pavement—and then he heard his father's voice.

"Emma. I was pleased to get your message this morning."

Her laugh was bitter. "Well now. I've pleased Charles Whitfield. I can die happy." Though sarcasm dripped through the speaker, Max realized she'd just managed to confirm his father's identity on the recording.

"I was concerned after our time together yesterday that you might try to…*dissolve* our working relationship."

"I considered it, but you've made sure I'm trapped."

"It's good that you've finally realized that."

The joyous shrieks of children playing took over the audio for a moment before he could hear Emma's voice again.

"—this ridiculous plan to frame Max for insider trading will never work, don't you?"

"You underestimate me, my dear. I've been manipulating Max for his entire life. I'm quite adept at this point. Just look at you. Your mother's been dead for six months now, and I'm still holding her over your head."

Max's fists tightened at his father's jab, not the one at him, which was no more than he expected, but at Emma. Especially when she stayed quiet for a few beats after the verbal blow.

When she spoke again, her voice was low and dangerous. "I took your money and gave you information on SecurePay so that my mother would have the best care available, but don't you ever mention her to me again. You're not fit to speak of her."

His chest swelled with pride, not just for her return jab, but her ingenuity, too, as she established the parameters of the blackmail for the record.

But her next words felled him.

"Your son is twice the man you are! And tonight I'm going to tell him everything you've done. Everything

I've done. And I don't care what you do in return. So go ahead and unleash your debt collectors. I'll file for bankruptcy if I have to, but I'm not going to let you hurt him anymore."

"My God. You're in love with him, aren't you?"

His father's question beat in Max's chest, pummeling his ribs from the inside.

"How trite. Maybe I should have chosen Farnsworth as my inside man after all. At least he wouldn't have been such a handful.

"Here's something you obviously don't know about Max. He will never forgive you for your betrayal. You're so sure he'll let you pour your guts out to him? The second he realizes you've been in contact with me for the last three years, he'll stop listening. Cut you out of his life with the precision of a master surgeon. You think I ruined his relationship with his sister? With his best friend? I just waited. He did it himself."

Even sitting, the punch landed with enough force to make him stagger. Max's hand tightened on the phone until it cut into his palm.

"You might love him, but he is incapable of returning that particular emotion. He's just like me. And when push comes to shove, he'll put Whitfield Industries first. Just like I taught him."

"You're wrong! Max is nothing like you. He cared about John Beckett. And he still cares about Kaylee. About Aidan. He might have made some mistakes, but he's spent his entire life trying to make up for them, trying to do the right thing. You think you know him, but you don't. Not like I do. He's—"

Max paused the audio. He couldn't listen anymore. Shame ate at him, And the fact that she would still defend him, after everything he'd told her, after everything he'd done to her.

He'd blackmailed her. Doubted her. Lied to her.

He had no right to sit here and listen to her praise him now. Not when he'd done nothing but live down to his father's expectations of him. Not when he'd let her walk out of his life without putting up a fight.

Hell, he'd ordered her to leave him.

Max tossed the phone back in the shoebox, but when he started loading the rest of the documents, a Post-it stuck to the cardboard caught his eye.

Her pretty writing wrung his heart.

If you're reading this, then you got to the bottom of the box, and now you know everything. Well, everything except that I never meant to hurt you.

And Max? You're not like him. You're better than him.

Emma

He didn't believe in second chances. And in the most humbling moment of his life, he found that Emma had all but gift wrapped one for him.

He just had to accept it.

The realization settled into his bones, made him feel solid as he formulated his plan of attack.

Tonight, he was going to finish getting all the way drunk.

And tomorrow, he was going to make a phone call.

CHAPTER TWENTY-TWO

FOUR DAYS LATER, the results of that phone call were about to take effect, and Max was not looking forward to any of it.

"Where the hell have you been? I've been calling you all morning!"

He hadn't taken three steps into his office before his sister was on him, shoving speech notes in his hands and talking far too loudly.

"You look like shit. Jesus, Max. Are you hungover? That's just great. I would tell you how incredibly stupid that is, but it will have to wait until later, because right now you need to straighten your tie and get downstairs for the press conference. We're thirty minutes out, and we've got a thousand details to go over."

Well, here goes nothing.

"We're not launching."

His sister went still at the pronouncement. "You're joking, right?"

Max gave a curt shake of his head, prepping for the tirade Kaylee was about to unleash on him, judging by the flare of her nostrils and the clench of her jaw. Not that he blamed her. This was the one part of the plan that he'd been dreading above all else.

"And you're telling me this *now*? Half an hour before the packed auditorium of tech geeks and journalists are expecting you to blow their collective minds? You, the man who worships on the altar of 'it's all about timing,' are canceling a product launch at the last minute and—"

He lost track of her grievances in the buzz that was building in his head, drowning out the diatribe he knew he deserved. But she was wrong if she thought he hadn't planned out what was happening right now to the second. In fact, all he'd thought about for the last four days was *timing*…

That's what had been bothering him since the spyware had been discovered on Emma's computer.

This launch was everything, the focus of his business life for the last five years, and the idea that got him out of bed every morning for the last seven. He'd dedicated a large amount of resources to it, and if it flopped, it would be catastrophic.

But despite the reassurances he'd received from his cybersecurity team, Max couldn't get rid of the doubt that had attached itself to the base of his spine like a parasite.

There was an internal hack. On Emma's computer. Emma, who had already quit.

When his father wanted to manipulate him, he'd gone old-school—found a plant on the inside. Hacking wouldn't have even occurred to Charles Whitfield. And it was almost inconceivable that it was strictly by chance that Emma, his father's spy, would also end up the one targeted to be the fall guy for this hack.

Separately, it was a pain in the ass. But all those aspects converging just as they were preparing to launch struck him as too much of a coincidence.

An echo, AJ had said. *Like someone had walked the path before me, you know?*

Something was off. Something that, if it got out, could bury SecurePay for good. He should have noticed sooner, but he'd been too focused on proving himself. To his father. To Aidan. To the world.

The fact that all the decrypted code seemed to be worthless didn't soothe Max's unease. It just made him feel like he was being lulled into a false sense of security, so he'd continue with his plan to release SecurePay on schedule.

Something bad was coming if he went through with it. He knew it, despite the security reports. Despite AJ's intel. He felt it in his gut.

Emma was wrong. He *was* just like his father. He'd blackmailed her into staying at Whitfield Industries against her will and justified it to himself because it was for the good of the company. But if he pushed SecurePay through now, regardless of the breach, it wasn't just his ego on the line. It was his company's reputation. He'd covered up his father's sins for that very reason five years ago.

But Emma was right, too—he didn't have to be like Charles Whitfield. He could do better. He could do the right thing before it was too late.

"We're not launching," he repeated, breaking into his

sister's ongoing polemic when she paused for a breath. "We need to come clean about the security breach. I'm not putting SecurePay on the market until we figure out who's behind the hack."

Kaylee shook her head at the proclamation, not in protest, but in resignation. She had always been able to recognize when his mind was made up and nothing was going to sway him anymore. Even back when they were kids.

"This is going to be a PR nightmare, not to mention a financial one," Kaylee warned.

He knew it. God, did he know it.

"Yeah, well, get ready to earn your money."

She frowned. "It's not me I'm worried about. As it happens, I'm really good at my job, Max. You're the one who has to stand in the middle of the lion's den and throw the red meat."

Okay, he amended. Maybe *this* part of the plan was going to be worse.

Concealing his flinch, he shook his head. "Actually, I've got a meeting that I need to get to, so I'm going to need you to handle this."

He took in Kaylee's shell-shocked expression.

And in that moment, he wanted nothing more than to confide in his sister. Hug her. Something.

But he couldn't. Because if the purpose of his meeting leaked ahead of time, the last four days, the last five years, everything he'd risked on this project, would be for nothing. So he hid behind his usual brusque autocracy, hoping he hadn't already tipped her off with the out-of-character display.

"You're fully capable of making up a statement for the media and pretending I told you to say it. You've done it plenty of times before. And make sure you push home the fact that SecurePay isn't dead. It's just postponed until we get to the bottom of the hack."

Besides, he added silently. *By this afternoon, no one's going to be dwelling on the SecurePay postponement anyway.*

"You asshole!" The epithet ricocheted through the quiet of his office. He'd never seen Kaylee so worked up. "You expect me to believe that not only are you euthanizing your life's work on a whim, but you've managed to double-book yourself for the funeral, too?"

His voice was resigned. "If there was any other way, I swear to you I'd take it, Kale."

The childhood nickname felt rusty on his tongue. He'd stopped calling her that when he was twelve years old. When he'd cut her out, just like his father had wanted him to. Hearing it now brought color to her cheeks.

"Don't you dare call me that!" she hissed.

She grabbed the forgotten speech notes from his hand and looked him straight in the eye. "I quit."

Max frowned. "You don't mean that."

"Consider this my three-weeks' notice. Right now, I'm going to go out there and handle this for you, because that's my job. But I'm done giving everything to the family business, when most of the time, I don't even feel like part of the family.

"I have spent the last five years working my ass off for you, big brother. Trying to prove myself to you, and after all this time, you don't even have enough respect for me to tell me what the hell is going on?"

Max flinched at the assessment. "Kaylee…"

"Don't. I don't want to hear it. When I'm done kicking ass in the lions' den, I'll type up my resignation letter and leave it on your desk. Now, get out of my way."

And with that, his little sister turned and walked out the door, toward the press conference he'd just blown up on purpose.

Max considered going after her. He wanted to, even though he knew there was nothing he could do right now. Nothing he could say.

Besides, he'd watched enough flare-ups between her and his mother to know that when things got bad, Kaylee needed some time to cool off.

He'd call her tomorrow and set things right. When he could tell her everything.

Rounding his desk, Max opened the locked drawer and retrieved the phone from his safe. As he tucked it in his pocket his eyes lighted on the steel statue he kept on the edge of his desk. He reached out and traced the sharp edges of the flames that made up the horse's mane.

"I'm sorry, John. I'm going to make this up to you." The apology was no more than a whisper.

Then he set his jaw and walked out of his office. There would be time for self-recrimination later, but right now, he had somewhere to be.

CHAPTER TWENTY-THREE

MAX'S HEAD ACHED, but he couldn't be sure if it was the result of his overindulgence for the last four nights, the way his fight with Kaylee was still ringing in his ears, or the fact that Sully was pulling up to the cold stone fortress that was Max's childhood home.

He hated coming back here under any circumstances, but this visit was going to be particularly rough. With a curt knock on the door, Max braced himself for what lay ahead.

The dignified, balding man dressed smartly in a navy suit who opened the door was just one more ridiculous way his mother tried to prove that the Whitfields were both rich and dignified. The farce was almost too much to bear. Especially today.

"Where is my father, Newsome?"

"In his study."

Max stepped past him. "No need to escort me. I remember the way."

He barely looked at the posh interior, with its intricate pillars and its eighteen-foot ceilings. The familiar luxury was beneath his notice, as was the cream decor with blue accents favored by his mother that went through a multitude of tweaks each season. He'd long ago given up trying to keep abreast of his mother's penchant for redesign whenever the mood struck.

"Max? What a surprise."

As though he'd summoned her with his thoughts, his mother appeared at the top of the staircase in pearls and a Chanel suit, her plastic smile radiating tolerance tinged with reproach. He waited dutifully as she descended the steps.

"We weren't expecting you."

He accepted his mother's air kiss.

"But I suppose at least one of my children makes an effort."

Max had long ago accepted the fact that Charles and Sylvia Whitfield were flawed, power-hungry people who cared nothing for anyone beyond themselves. But for God's sake, Kaylee wasn't even here, and still his mother couldn't resist taking a swipe.

"I'd love to stay and chat, but I'm up to my neck in fabric swatches, and I have a million decisions to make before the interior designer arrives. Next time you're coming, be a dear and make an appointment with my assistant so that we can have a real conversation."

She didn't wait for a response before disappearing down the hall. Not that it mattered to Max. He turned and headed straight for his father's ornate mahogany office in the back of the house.

"You goddamn son-of-a-bitch."

The slur barely fazed his father, who was pouring himself an afternoon bourbon.

"Max. To what do I owe the pleasure?"

"Emma told me everything."

His father raised an imperious brow. "Well, well, well. I thought there was something between the two of you in the boardroom that day, but I didn't realize it was so...serious."

The fact that his father didn't even need to ask what he was talking about pushed Max to the limits of his patience, but he fought the urge to lash out, reminding himself again why he was here.

He schooled his features back into his customary bland expression. He would not give his father the satisfaction.

"Not that I blame you. She's a beautiful woman. Smart, too. But everyone has a chink in the armor. Unlike you, family is very important to her. She would have done anything to help her poor, dying mother. I snared her much more easily than expected. Luckily, her mother took quite a downturn not long after she started working for you, so it made her easy pickings."

His father took a sip of his liquor.

"Which was fortunate for me, because my next choice for informant was Gordon Farnsworth. The man loves to bet on the ponies. In fact, you should probably keep an eye on him. But he's not nearly as easy on the eyes as Emma, wouldn't you agree?"

"Don't you dare say her name," Max ordered, and his father looked taken aback by the venomous tone.

"Touchy subject, I see. Although if you already know the tale, I suppose I can understand your anger. It wouldn't do to have the CEO of Whitfield Industries fucking the woman who helped him commit insider trading for so many family friends, now would it?"

Max walked over to the bar and poured himself a twelve-year-old Scotch from his father's impressive collection. Hair of the dog. "So that's your game? Frame me for insider trading? Blackmail me into giving you whatever it is you're angling for, just like you've done to every person unfortunate enough to get in your way?"

The memories of what had happened to John Beckett rushed in, flooding his brain, and for the millionth time, Max wished he'd never mentioned the idea of SecurePay to his father back then, let alone John's tech brilliance.

And the worst part was, Charles hadn't had any intention of moving forward with SecurePay. He'd just bound John Beckett in legalese so that no one else could get their hands on the promising first steps he was making, or the patents he held.

Half the reason that Max had been so dogged in his quest to make SecurePay a success was to ensure John hadn't died in vain. That his legacy would live on. So he could show Aidan that his father's life had amounted to something. And once again, his father had found a way to ruin everything.

"That's one option. But I'd prefer if you just announced at the next board meeting that I'm coming out of retirement." Charles took a seat behind his ornately carved desk, some ostentatious remnant of the 1800s that he was inordinately proud of. "You and I can build Whitfield Industries together. Like we used to."

Max took a large swallow of good Scotch. "Go to hell."

"What are you going to do, son. *Report* me?" He sneered the words. "You didn't do it when that fool Beckett drank himself into a stupor and wrapped himself around a pole, because you were too weak. You could have outed me for blackmail then, but you didn't, because you cared more about Aidan's feelings than you did about vengeance against me."

Max nodded. "You're damn right I did. Because unlike me, Aidan worships his father. And I didn't want him to have to deal with the fallout of John's mistake, a mistake that would never have come to light if you hadn't sent out your low-life spies to pick apart his life just so you get enough leverage to use him like a puppet."

"People always think money is the goal, but it's not. Power is the goal, son. Without power, you have nothing. You never understood that, no matter how many times I tried to teach you that. It's how I know you're not cut out for business. You refuse to see how cutthroat it is. You're too soft."

"If that's how you feel, why do you want back in so badly?"

"SecurePay is so much more than I expected when you pitched it to me back in the day. The world has changed so much in my lifetime, and I realize now that you were right to keep an eye to the future. But as I told Emma when I recruited her, you still need me. You make unnecessary mistakes. In fact, you've made the most rudimentary error of all—dallying with the help is the road to ruin."

Max's hand clenched around his glass at the smear

on Emma, the way his father spoke of her like she was nothing more than his plaything. Like she hadn't played an integral part in getting SecurePay ready for market.

"How much? How much did you pay her to ruin her life? And gain leverage over me?"

"Over the last three years? Almost three hundred thousand dollars."

Max pulled out his phone and tapped through to his banking app so he could transfer the money. "There. Consider her debt paid. Your business with Emma Mathison is done. Don't so much as glance in her direction ever again. Do I make myself clear?"

Charles shook his head. "My God. I gave you more credit than that."

"Than what?"

"Than falling for her. I mean, she's beautiful. I'll give you that. But I always thought you were a master of separating business and pleasure. When you chose Whitfield Industries over avenging Beckett's death, over his son's friendship, I thought I'd raised a warrior. But now a pretty face has turned you into a lovesick fool. Don't you understand? I already have what I needed from her."

His father's smarmy chuckle slithered across Max's skin.

"I believe this is the part where you concede gracefully."

Max took a step forward and looked his father right in the eye. "I regret every day that I didn't take you down for what you did to John Beckett. And if the information you have on him wouldn't wreak havoc on

Aidan's life, I would do it right now. But I'm not bringing you back in to Whitfield Industries. Not ever. Because you made a mistake, too, in underestimating the lengths I'm willing to go to destroy you."

"A fine show of spine, son, but it's too late. If you don't welcome me back from retirement with open arms and a big smile for the camera, then I'm going straight to the Feds."

Max finished his drink and banged the glass onto the formidable, but ugly, desk. "Well, you're half right."

When Max walked out of his parents' mansion, it was to find the raiding party of FBI agents ready to finish what he'd begun. He stepped out of their way as they poured into his father's house through the door he'd left open.

Better late than never, Max thought, letting his thoughts drift to John Beckett. Thanks to Emma, he'd managed to avenge his tech mentor's death without having to reveal John's secret to Aidan. And just like that, the burden he'd been carrying for the last five years felt lighter.

He let the peace that came from doing the right thing wash over him as one of the agents stepped up to divest him of the wire they'd outfitted him with earlier.

"Mr. Whitfield? If you'll just wait, we'll have some questions for you when this is over."

"Send them through my attorney. I have somewhere else to be."

Walking past the bevy of nondescript vehicles to the end of the driveway where Sully was waiting for him, Max got into his town car.

"Back to the hotel?"

Max nodded. It was as good a destination as any, because he needed to find Emma, and he had absolutely no idea where to start looking.

Luckily, he knew someone who could help.

AJ's face filled the phone screen, but before he could open his mouth, she was already talking. "If you're calling to see if I got my thank-you money for helping to take down daddy dearest, then every single beautiful penny was accounted for and deposited, and I thank you for your prompt payment. It's a pleasure doing business with you."

"I need to find Emma."

To his surprise, she didn't admonish him for his dictatorial tone like she usually did whenever he skipped the social niceties. She just nodded.

"Since unlike you, I actually care about the environment, I forewent the charter and took the liberty of booking you a first-class ticket instead. I pushed everything to your phone—check-in information, car service, travel itinerary."

As if on cue, his other phone began buzzing frantically within the breast pocket of his suit jacket.

"Emma's staying at some gross, one-star hotel, so when you find her, definitely suggest going back to your place. I'm telling you, when she sees the suite I booked you, you are totally getting laid. It's that nice."

Max scowled at her, his mind running through the number of privacy breaches she would have had to commit to make all that happen, but she just shrugged.

"Ninja, remember?"

Oh, he remembered all right.

AJ made a production of glancing at her empty wrist, miming checking the time. "You'd better get a move on, too. You have just over two hours to pack and clear security, because honestly, I expected this call at least an hour ago. This girl's really thrown off your game."

"We'll talk about your tendency to overstep when I get back."

AJ flicked the warning aside. "Like you're going to remember to be annoyed with me by then. Your return tickets aren't for another ten days. Have fun. Send pictures. I don't want to see you in a suit until you're back on American soil. Oh! And don't forget your passport. Side note, I didn't know your middle name was—"

Max disconnected the call before he shoved the phone back into his jacket as Sully navigated the afternoon traffic that stood between him and his destination.

CHAPTER TWENTY-FOUR

RED ROOFS, GREEN TREES, azure water—Dubrovnik was a visual feast of colors. Emma strolled along the most beautiful pebble beach, the rocks warm and smooth beneath her feet, amidst the sounds of lapping water and happy people frolicking under the warm Croatian sun, willing herself not to succumb to the misery that dogged her every step.

Some trip of a lifetime this was turning out to be.

She sighed. Maybe a drink would help.

Angling herself away from the beach chairs and farther up the shore, she headed for the nearest beachfront bar.

"Um...*jeden* piña colada. *Mosim*."

The bartender smiled kindly, despite her pitiful attempt at Croatian.

"Make it two."

The sound of his voice hit her like a stun gun, freezing her in place, her synapses stuttering as her brain tried to make sense of what was happening.

Max.

Max was here.

He reached past her and set a few bills of colorful Croatian *kuna* beside her arm.

The barkeep's smile grew wider. "Right away, sir," he said in perfect English as he swept the money from the counter.

Emma had spent her first four days in Dubrovnik sobbing in her cramped, dingy room at the budget hotel, binging on self-pity and *medenjaci* cookies.

It would just figure that he would show up today, during her first foray into the world where she didn't feel like she was undergoing open heart surgery with no anesthetic, to rip open the wounds she'd worked so hard to stitch back up.

And it would just figure that her eyes prickled with overwhelming relief that he had.

Emma drew her first easy breath in five days.

When she turned around to confirm that she wasn't in the midst of a hallucination, he was much closer than she'd expected. Not crowding her so much as filling up space with his presence.

Her nipples tingled to attention at the sight of him, the familiarity of his nearness. Her teal bathing suit did nothing to hide her body's reaction.

Stupid bikini.

In her body's defense, Max was hard to resist when he was fully dressed in a suit. But Max in nothing but red boardshorts and Ray-Bans, his damp hair pushed back from his forehead? It took everything she had not to throw herself in his arms.

She turned back to the bar, rested her elbows on the scarred wood. "What are you doing here?"

"I'm on the lam, actually."

He mimicked her position against the counter.

"Well," she said lightly, forcing herself to match his conversational tone, "it sounds like you came to the right place. I understand there are no extradition laws here."

His mouth pulled up in a hint of a smile and her knees went weak. She took a deep, steadying breath. "So why are you running?"

"Because my board of directors is pissed that I pulled the plug on the SecurePay launch at the last minute."

The announcement caught her by surprise, and she turned to look at him. The ache in her chest returned, but this time it was in solidarity with him, and she felt better able to bear the hurt. He must be devastated.

"And because Kaylee is *definitely* pissed that I made her clean up the mess all by herself, so I could go have my father arrested for felony blackmail."

Oh, God. Emma sucked in a breath as he pushed his sunglasses up into his hair and met her eyes.

"And while this is pure speculation, I would imagine the FBI is *probably* pissed that I left the country while they were in the middle of raiding his house."

She didn't realize that she'd reached for him until her hand made contact with his forearm, an attempt to comfort him over the tumultuous events he'd tried to pass off in a joking tone.

"I'm so sorry, Max." Not for Charles. He deserved what he got. But he was Max's father, and that couldn't have been an easy choice, even after everything he'd done.

His gaze dropped to her fingers on his skin, and

when he looked up again, there was nothing light or jokey about him.

"I know who my father is. He's a manipulator. He plays people and makes money off it, and he doesn't give a damn that he's destroying people's lives in the process. And I can't tell you how sorry I am for what he did to you, using your mother as leverage like that."

Max dropped his head. "But none of that's really why I'm here." The confession was soft. "I'm actually looking for something."

"Oh?" Emma swallowed against the fizzy feeling under her skin, like her blood had been replaced with champagne. "Well, if it's *medenjaci* cookies, you might be too late. That's pretty much all I've eaten since I got here."

"Not cookies," he said, quelling her attempt to hit the release valve. "A second chance."

Her body quaked with the most sublime mixture of fear and optimism. "You're a long way from home for someone who doesn't believe in second chances."

"I'd say I'm exactly where I should be for a man who believes in love."

The words detonated around her like a bomb, and she couldn't breathe through the emotional shrapnel.

"You love me?" she asked shakily, hating the hope that twined through her heart. After everything she'd done, everything he'd done, she'd never let herself wish for this moment. And yet...

"Don't pretend you don't know there's something special between us." He pushed away from the bar.

Stood tall as he turned to face her. "You say you're all about taking chances, making memories. So prove it."

Emma gestured around her at the beach, at Dubrovnik in general. "I'm here, aren't I?"

"A pretty vacation isn't taking a chance. It's running away. Taking a risk when you don't have to deal with the consequences isn't taking a risk at all."

Max stepped closer, and she swore, despite the warmth of the beach-scented air, that she could feel his body heat, even though he wasn't touching her. She kept her eyes straight ahead, staring at the tanned column of his neck.

Ever so gently, he tucked his finger beneath her chin and lifted her face until their eyes met, and what she saw in those amber depths made her knees weak.

"Come back with me."

Something warm unfurled in her chest, replacing the guilt and sadness of the last few years with all the love she felt for this beautiful, complicated man who'd flown across an ocean to find her.

"Always so bossy," she chided, her dawning smile wobbling on her lips. "You can't just order me to leave. No extradition laws, remember?"

"Then I'm asking. I'm asking you to take a chance with me, Emma. To build memories with me. I love you, and I want you in my life."

Everything inside her broke open at the words.

"God, Max. I love you so much." She was already wrapping her arms around his neck, lifting onto her toes, as the words spilled from her lips a split-second before her mouth met his.

His arms closed around her with stunning force, pulling her against him like he never wanted to let go.

She didn't want him to.

It was heaven, being skin-to-skin with Max again, her breasts crushed against his unyielding chest as the sweet thrill of arousal loosened her limbs.

She'd missed this. Him.

She moaned in protest when he pulled away. He was breathing heavily as he leaned his forehead to hers.

"Emma?"

"Yeah?"

"We're about forty-five seconds away from me violating any number of public indecency laws."

She pressed tighter against the evidence of his claim, wringing a groan from him. His fingers dug into her hips.

"And since the last place I want to spend tonight is in a Croatian prison, we need to get out of here." He pressed a quick, hard kiss to her mouth. "Right now."

"What about our drinks?" She gestured at the fancy fluted glasses sitting on the bar, sweating with condensation, completely forgotten in the heady rush of lust. She wondered idly how long they'd been sitting there, even as he grabbed her by the hand and pulled her away from them.

"I hate piña coladas."

She practically had to run to keep up with his long strides. "I don't," she teased, even though she was as desperate to get him naked as he was to let her.

"Then I'll order you as many as you want when we get back to my room."

"How far is it? Because my hotel is just over there and—"

He stopped to face her so abruptly that she almost slammed into his beautiful chest. "I packed my ties, Emma. All of them."

The look in his eyes set her world on fire.

"Your room it is."

* * * * *

COMING SOON!

We really hope you enjoyed reading this book. If you're looking for more romance, be sure to head to the shops when new books are available on

Thursday
23rd August

LET'S TALK
Romance

For exclusive extracts, competitions and special offers, find us online:

f facebook.com/millsandboon

⧉ @millsandboonuk

𝕏 @millsandboon

Or get in touch on 0844 844 1351*

For all the latest titles coming soon, visit
millsandboon.co.uk/nextmonth